Jack of Hearts

Robin F. Gainey

Untreed
Reads

Jack of Hearts
By Robin F. Gainey

Copyright 2014 by Robin F. Gainey
Cover Design by Ginny Glass
Portrait of Shimoni on the cover is used by permission of the artist, Nancy Schutt.
Visit Nancy's artwork at www.nancyschutt.com.

ISBN-13: 978-1-61187-761-8

Also available in ebook format.

Published by Untreed Reads, LLC
506 Kansas Street, San Francisco, CA 94107
www.untreedreads.com

Printed in the United States of America.

Publisher's Note

This book is dedicated to my mother,

Ruth Baker Field

1907 — 1997

Mi manchi.

CONTENTS

"The gift which I am sending you is called a dog, and is in fact the most precious and valuable possession of mankind."

—Theodorus Gaza

Chapter One

T he week had been stormy in every way, but morning arrived with the optimism of dry windowpanes. Il Conte approached the Contessa as we were about to leave for our first walk of the day. A hopeful sign. There'd been little touching for a long time.

Not like the beginning. There once was hardly space for even a small dog to slip between them. Now, great chasms opened on the bed and the couch was never occupied by more than one.

The mood must have struck the Count as pleasant weather tends to fortify an impulse. As he placed a palm on her shoulder, his other hand swept the curve of her waist until it found a slender thigh. I sensed their quickened hearts, but for some reason the Contessa shrugged it off. Only a cool stare returned his favor. The Count's fingers, marooned there between trial and error, hesitated long enough to be brushed away as she passed through the open door.

The Contessa's voice was stern. "Shimoni, *vieni qui.*"

I followed at her heels, looking back at the Count as we boarded the elevator. He was pale with dejection: brows raised, and chin hanging as though he were a child who had lost his kite to the wind.

I hated to see him suffer, but couldn't blame the woman. Dog wrote the book on faithfulness. The Count had strayed. There was strange-dog all over his clothing. I dealt with the infringement of another canine as best I could. Exactly why the Count had wandered, I didn't know. What I did know: the fate of a simple shared chromosome seemed to make the Contessa unhappy with us both. And if she wasn't happy, no one was happy. Even though I loved the man, for this I, too, was irritated with Il Conte.

The elevator opened to a long passageway onto the street. Dirt swirled at my feet and *motorini* buzzed like summer flies through the busy *via*, nipping at my toes. Sterling tags danced and clattered at my collar as I stepped away from the frenzy of traffic to look up at our apartment. An old woman pushed her broom to the edge of a sixth-floor terrace as the shutters below banged open. A puff of soot fell like smoke past the Count as he leaned over a fourth-story sash, a swath of inky hair across one eye.

His voice boomed across the narrow street. *"Cara,* collect my shirts on your way back?"

"Do it yourself," the Contessa snapped. An aristocratic accent wrapped her words as nicely as putty-colored cashmere wrapped her shoulders. Gold bracelets on her wrist shuddered as she waved a finger at the Count.

My chest tightened. The woman's wrath grew like wisteria on a summer terrace, full and pervasive. Though she lacked the advantage of a keen nose, there was little doubt she knew what I knew.

He slammed the shutters closed and an angry echo spanked the air. Paradox to the Latin male, the Count was born a subtle man. Doors thought twice before banging behind him, and women searched for meaning in his voice.

No question lingered now.

I cupped my ears tight against my head to muffle the noise and trembled at the conflict like a cornered mouse. The hair on my flank quivered a nod to the stares from passersby. They doubtless thought me abused or, worse yet, a coward. I hated being judged on looks alone. I was, after all, of distinguished pedigree. But that blue blood ran cold in my veins.

The Contessa took my frequent display of shivers as a chill. She boosted the temperature of the apartment and made me wear a heavy coat to bed trying to cure them. Sweaty dreams and night-pants followed, adding physical discomfort to my tattered emotions. She had no way to know it was despair that made me quake.

I watched the shutters of my apartment swing back against the stone wall. Bits of weathered marble sill fell like hail to the street below. A flock of irritated pigeons, happily picking refuse from the gutter, took to the air. They crossed the sky in silence like an enormous pearl grey carpet and disappeared into the fog.

It was then I realized that it was in simple acts, whether pleasant or unkind, that points of view were turned. And in so turning, the flow of life was changed. Like the moon drew the tides to a different course, lives were altered until, one day, another shift corrected the stream.

I yearned for a way to put things right.

My nose bookmarked that place where the pigeons pierced the low clouds, their tempers boiling up into the daylight. I drew a long breath of rush-hour fragrance.

Mornings in Rome, sensuous and filled with sundry odors, are lost on the noselessness of man. Somewhere along the line of evolution, humans shirked scent for sight and, in my opinion, the finer details of living were lost. Blood and truffles were left to the skill of a good dog. The scent of Roman mornings was designed for dogs.

I pushed my snout into the damp air. The welcome aroma of fresh espresso and warm *cornetti* hung dog-low in the mist and beckoned. My ears perked to cathedral bells peeling across the city. Ten tolls. We were late to the *via* again.

My belly rumbled with hunger after a week of intermittent meals. The Contessa stood at my side on the steps to our apartment, in a thick wrap, oblivious to her absentmindedness. I shuddered at the chill. Once again, she had forgotten not only my breakfast, but my sweater. At least we were bound for the relief of the park. Not all routine had been abandoned. Yet, her distraction was taking its toll. Lacking the words to set her straight, I sneezed in disapproval.

I didn't need a temperamental woman to tell me my privileged life had changed. Intelligence was breed specific. A pedigree honed for acumen granted me the privilege of reason. Ears bred to detect the gentle movement of small creatures narrowed my focus. Yet, with my people now angry and silent, neither advantage served me well.

At first, I blamed myself. I knew human irritation sparked at the discovery of a chewed shoe or favorite undergarment in tatters. But I was no pup. Years had passed since I'd enjoyed a fine pair of Ferragamos. I closed my eyes, inhaling the intoxicating memory of fresh leather, but it was nothing more than fancy. I knew enough to keep my tongue contained. Even a cursory taste of buttery suede could ignite a costly binge. The thought made me drool as I searched my recollection for recent missteps. No ruined keepsakes. Never a soiled rug. Nothing.

These days, Good-dog was my middle name.

I waited for my Contessa to divulge the problem. As a rule, I was her confidant. Yet, over the past few weeks, the woman had been as tight lipped as a muzzled Terrier. No more secrets were shared. I was lonely in a way I never fathomed possible. Neither the comfort of Il Conte's hand in the middle of the night, nor the loving touch of the Contessa at daybreak, granted any relief from the obvious distance between us all. Still, I tried to see my bowl half-full.

At least I had a home.

I could imagine nothing worse than being homeless. Solitary, thin and rank, the curs roaming the park testified to that. So, I kept my tail down and my ears low, out of trouble, beyond the scope of blame. Days dragged on before I figured out the mistake was not my own.

The first clue crept to my mind with the Count's stealthy return after a long night out. The odor of emergency dog *biscotti* that the man kept in his jacket pocket just for me had evaporated—as had Il Conte every evening after dinner. Unless the man had taken to the delicacy of dried, crushed chicken entrails and liver parts, another dog enjoyed his favor. Judging by strong scent on his fingertips, it was a female—one of the taller varieties.

Self-esteem was never an issue for me, but the thought that my competition literally might look down upon me was galling. True, I was petite, but great things came in compact packages. Neither Caesar nor Napoleon stood above a crowd. My stature was a boon, not a drawback. Being a small dog was a badge of meticulous breeding. After all, dog was born of wolf. Centuries went into the perfection of downsizing.

I wore this honor with pride. Yet, alarmed the Count might prefer a larger dog, I feigned height every time the man was near, fluffing my fur to bolster my size, standing as erect as possible. Il Conte paid little attention.

Then came the final blow.

On the feather sofa the night before, just as I pushed my nose into a favorite spot between the man's sleeve and the warmth of his burly arm, a strange, misplaced aroma teased my nose. Roses, damp and sweet like the heavy fragrance of deep summer. It didn't take a guide dog to see what was going on. More than one bitch was stealing time with the Count.

Life, so far, had been lived in lucky spades. Now, I was at a loss to solve this turn of events. For the first time I felt more than hungry. Hollow.

No use, I thought. My dish lay barren again this morning, just as empty as my brain. Analysis was impossible under such diversion. With a shake of my head, I refocused on the street.

The Contessa dipped a shoe into the busy *via*. Anger in the woman's voice lately nagged me, suggesting I keep a distance, but her safety was my assignment. I ran beyond her into the rushing traffic, eyes alert. Cars and scooters screeched and honked. I stopped short, sitting down at a careful measure in the middle of the street, halfway between each curb. For one tenuous moment, the scene was a snapshot. All was quiet and still. Then the camera began to roll.

The Contessa's fine heels clicked across the rough cobblestones in the paused stream of vehicles. I lifted my snout, whiskers erect, giving a sidelong glance after the retreating figure, forcing my eyes away from the scowling gaze of angry drivers. She set one shoe on the opposite curb and I cast a hasty peek at the stunned faces in the windshields. As I fled to my Contessa's side, motors raced and voices cast vulgar epithets in my direction. I raised a leg to a signpost in answer. Crossing every street with the distinct aplomb of an urban dog, I was resolute in my charge as keeper of the Contessa and master of *la strada.* Yet, my life was chaos. All suffer and dread.

The Contessa moved without hesitation down the crowded street. I raced to meet her, cool wind rumpling my ears. The breath of winter was a relief, but my stomach was a knot. I passed the woman and leapt into the niche of a formal entry to chew a small, itchy patch above my tail. Pressing my back into the corner of the vestibule, I turned my attention to a low window.

A diminutive, frail dog cowered in the shadows behind the glass. Tall, serious doors, adorned by oversized hardware, stood alongside like sentries to the condemned. It was not a creature to which I normally attended. Aristocracy, after all, didn't mingle with unfamiliar riff-raff, even if it looked the tragic case. But little was the same since trouble arrived. Any frightened dog could use a friend. I cocked one ear and tilted my head in regard. The dog responded in kind. My heart crept to my throat. I felt as pitiful as this poor animal looked and was ashamed for ever considering angst a flaw. This fellow in particular, empty-jowled and scrawny, brought a void to my soul—like the first time the Contessa left me alone in the apartment. A howl threatened its way up my throat.

Instead, when I rose to salute the sad beast with a reassuring bark, a familiar echo returned. I laid my ears flat against my head in dismay.

This dog, I knew well.

Chapter Two

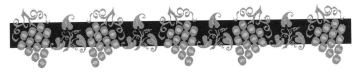

I studied myself in the window. My weight was off judging by the loose fit of my collar, but seeing it in the reflection, hanging sloppy about my neck, made me gasp. I drew a deep breath and sat down. Turning my head to profile, I studied a wisp of silken kerchief twined around a hand-carved leather collar given me by the Count. Woven there by my Contessa, the twining reminded me of her affection, and the man's regard. Its reflection in the window, like the photograph of a happier time, allowed me to begin to overlook the current hardship and my nerves settled. I checked the lie of my fur with a sideways glance.

Handsome still, if not fit.

Even looking the bit of a runt, it was important to present one's best. Too many times I'd left home with an ear cocked over my head, which elicited deflating chuckles along the way. I stepped back, allowing my entire figure to be displayed. Sporty tail, neat hair, expressive eyes and intelligent brow; I completed the aristocratic picture of my family.

I examined the high cranial area above my ears. Ample brain. Better to solve the problem. The Count favored someone else and things were not improving. Time was slipping away with every ounce of flesh. But where to start?

While blind faith was a comfort to those of modest wit, the intelligent dog's curse was logic. It refused the role of hapless pet. I turned to watch my Contessa, wondering to what length her inattention would go, and to what size I would shrink, when a pleasant sound pulled my ear. Water. *Un nasone*, a small, nose-shaped pipe, spilled perpetually into the street on the corner near via Ripetta. I listened as it poured onto the cobblestones. It recalled a vision: the small stream tumbling over smooth rocks at the bottom of a vineyard hill.

Chianti. My *villa* in the country.

Descending the stairs, I followed the splashing to its source. At the spout, I opened my mouth. The pure, icy flow washed over my tongue until my mouth was numb. I closed my eyes. In that creek, far away from the confusion of the city, there was order. Country life demanded it in the tending of the garden and the harvest of the vine. The Count and the Contessa loved to spend time in the vineyard. The happiest of times had once been there.

*

It was late summer and the grapes were full and heavy on the vines. With only a small leap, I plucked fruit easily from the lowest clusters. The Count and Contessa and I started early in the morning, picking the grapes along with the hired crew. By afternoon my nose was a lovely greenish purple and my belly was full. I stuck to the sweeter grapes: ones kissed by frost and wrinkled, tossed aside as fodder for the small dogs and wild pigs.

The Count and the Contessa worked shoulder to shoulder, often feeding each other a piece of fruit or kissing between the vines. They filled separate baskets on their own and when the crew had gone for the evening, the three of us retired to the winery. The clusters were stripped of grapes and the fruit tossed into an enormous wooden vat on short legs with narrow plank slats across the bottom. The Contessa washed my feet with soapy water, the Count and Contessa rolled up their pants and we'd all climb into the press. The Count and the Contessa giggled and danced. We squished the grapes with our feet until they were nothing but slurry and I was a pale, apple-green by the end of the night. Grape juice pooled in a broad, shallow vessel underneath. It was a lovely mess.

By the time it was filtered and aged, the Count called it *La Riserva*. It was the wine of celebration and only shared by the Count and the Contessa.

The Count said that the wine produced would be the best because the grapes were crushed by laughter.

"There is magic in it," said the Count. "Love's secret."

*

If laughter was the secret to love, we were all in trouble. The last vintage was crushed years ago and there had been little laughing for a long time. I licked my soaking paws.

The Count's voice descended around me like a cage. "Shimoni."

The scent of roses caught my nose and I growled, baring a row of upper teeth. If the Contessa didn't need the man's touch, neither did I.

The Count stared down like a Roman statue, bundle of shirts under one arm. *"E tu Brute?"*

He bent down to tug my ear and scratch the balding spot just beneath my collar, inviting assent, then slipped me the last bite of his *biscotti.*

This was the man I knew: of tender heart and delicious treats. Perhaps his infatuations were harmless, like those I discovered along the park. After all, the Contessa controlled the leash in both cases. There was no charge for a cursory bark and a sniff. I gave the man's wrist a thorough wash.

The man raised a single finger in the direction of the Contessa. *"Vai!* She's your charge." The Count cast a wistful look down the street. "Though, she makes it difficult to care." He disappeared into the cleaner's shop.

Warm air wafted into the street from inside the store, prompting the fine hairs on my muzzle to lay sleek and flat. It felt good to stand there a moment and warm myself, but the man was right: the Contessa was my duty. Rapt by her own distractions, she was easy prey for predatory scooters. I looked behind me once to confirm the Count's watchful eye was no longer keeping score, then made a beeline down the sidewalk.

9

His affection divided, at least the man still cared enough to scratch the chin of a small dog and worry after the Contessa. Clinging to that notion, I traced the woman's scent through the crowd. She was well ahead of me, shoulders set in purposeful obligation toward an invisible goal of the Pincian Hill.

The Contessa was a pleasure to watch, even though she wasted no time waiting for me to catch up. Her smooth, thick dark hair was the perfect frame to a patrician profile. Jaw set, brow knit by determination above fragile eyes, she was an irrevocable beauty. I raised an infatuated sigh and raced on. Before I could intervene, the woman edged one fine ankle onto the next street just as a *motorino* passed close enough to shave a bit of cashmere from her skirt. Without hesitation my Contessa moved in uncharacteristic reflex, nearly elbowing the rider from his cycle.

Brava. Danger warranted challenge, but I had never before seen the Contessa raise a hand to anyone. At least it showed that the woman was not oblivious to the risks of Roman streets. Not wanting to divert her focus, I refrained from issuing a cautionary bark. I took a lungful of air and held it until the woman found the safety of the curb beyond, and with that breath came an arresting stench. My nose wrinkled and my eyes watered. The scent was perfect.

I dropped my nostrils into the lusty odor. In the gutter beside me laid a large dead rat, belly bloated by a day or two of rot. I gave it an advisory sniff, and then stepped back. The rodent had taken on the warning of a three-day rule. Even a dog meant for hunting small game had limits. I considered giving the corpse a roll. The stink alone would be a credit. But the insinuating fragrance would prompt a bath. The day was young and already full of enough excitement. I glanced at the Contessa across the street as she smoothed her sweater and brushed a lock of hair from her brow. A few feathers of an unfortunate crow, no doubt picking at the animal's decay hours before, swirled like spirits above her head—a warning to those who dared to pass.

10

Many creatures lost their lives in the streets. Mindless traffic had no conscience. It only stopped for those who were bold enough to avoid eye contact. Eye to eye was as good as a dare: no need to stop for a pedestrian who sees the threat. Like a show of teeth to an angry dog, to a Roman it meant challenge. Only those who wandered aimlessly into the street were given yield. It was a tactic I perfected, and it served the safety of my Contessa well.

Without her, life would be intolerable.

The dog next door was sent to live with a young family after the loss of his mistress. Not long after, I ran across him in the park. The poor animal had been thrust into a litter of children who favored dressing him up like a doll. They pushed him about the city in a pram. The crushing embarrassment prompted a nervous condition. Incontinent at the slightest indication of excitement, the dog was relegated to a small room used for hanging wet laundry and collecting soiled clothes. I quaked at the thought and began to conjure a disturbing picture:

A lonely existence without the care of my Contessa; passed on by the preoccupied Count to an unknown relative or impoverished friend. Sharing a bed with a child not yet house trained, blamed for the error, relegated to the laundry, or worse, forever banished from the privilege conferred by wealth and status—thrust nose-long into the obscurity of a common dog.

Without question, a humiliating nervous condition would follow.

My head spun and my mouth watered as if I might be sick. I looked about for a small patch of grass to soothe my stomach, but the cobblestones grew thick and tight at my feet. A good shake of my fur and the vile image was gone.

I tried to slip the weighty thoughts to the back of my mind, making room for details. It was time for action. But action demanded direction. Until I understood the Count's transgressions, I was a dog without a compass. I raced across a break in the traffic to the safety of my Contessa's side. With head raised, I drew my ears back, ready to receive a gentle pat or soothing word. The

11

woman breezed by me without a sound. No matter. By now she was within the relative safety of a wide *piazza.*

There was nothing like a well-traveled square. I relaxed straight into canine nature: tail bristled and ears aware. To a creature of able nose and idle time, the allure of the gutter was undeniable, even under the pressing influence of the park. Instincts demanded a pause over the marvelous filth of the Roman streets.

With one eye on the Contessa, I hesitated over the squashed remnant of a roasted chestnut on the curb. Few things were held in higher estimation than the simple *marrone.* Sweet, rich, earthy: perfection straight from the hand of God. Stone cold, its odor still vivid, it must have slipped from a full paper cone the evening before. I excavated its soft flesh from a piece of charred shell and used my tongue to wipe the excess from my whiskers with a damp paw. The streets were ripe with all things fit for a dog.

Nights were always hectic in the city, *piazze* snug with young people even on an icy winter evening. One could bank on the mornings. Each day revealed a clean deck of odors. Puddles of sweet wine and yeasty beer, the bitter end of a spent cigarette, rancid gum, pebbly bits of *focaccia,* smoky marks of both dog and gypsy along the way; all mingled to produce a hearty stench that coated the fine hairs below my nose. To a dog, the brew defined Rome as The Eternal City: ubiquitous in all its glory.

Then, a familiar odor reset the dream.

Roses.

Suspended in the mist just above my head, it disturbed the cool air and the clarity of my thoughts. It buoyed my flagging spirit and begged me to follow. Across a crowded lane, I turned the corner into a tiny *piazzetta.* A gurgling fountain stood in the center. At its foot stood a perfect figure, like a holy vision in the haze: serenity amid chaos, empress of the square.

I froze.

She was a stunning bitch. All legs and tail, her dark fur fluttered in the breeze of scooters darting close by.

The scent of roses was not commonly found on a dog. This had to be the Count's accomplice. I searched the area around her for a woman likely to catch the eye of Il Conte, but the dog was alone. I hovered over her delicious scent. It warmed my lungs as the odor of a fresh, meaty shank warms the heart. But it was a bone still in the butcher's hand.

Union between the very tall and the very short quadruped simply wasn't plausible without the correct assignment of the sexes. Besides, sharing the same object of desire with the Count was tawdry. She was a mere degree of separation from the real mischief.

Still, one could dream. I rearranged the yearning into a more satisfying fantasy. A good length of leg on a female always caught my eye, but it was a cruel preference. Dog endures beating, famine, the desolation of homelessness. But our greatest pain is suffered in the unrequited yearning of impossible sexual conquest. God's joke on dogs dooms him to the limited selection of breeds of likewise fate. Facts often defeat dreams. That was the cold, hopeless reality. I shook off the trance.

The female had evaporated with the reverie. There was no evidence of the bitch. Only her perfume remained, faint now as it mingled with the vapors of passing cars and the aroma of warm *cappuccini* from a bar behind me. The curious blend curled into the safety of a mounting haze.

I scampered toward the *piazza*. I strained to catch a glimpse of the Contessa's elegant suede shoes through the crowd, going to ground for the woody scent of fine leather left on the stones. Nothing. Racing to the next corner, I examined the *via* stretched out before me. Twin churches stood a centuries-old vigil where two streets spilled from the bustling Piazza del Popolo, ancient gateway to Rome. Traffic flowed in a rush of noise and air. I ran, whiskers down, toward the headwaters.

Arrival into the square found the broad morning palette awash in dewy white. Fog had moved in quickly. It clung to my ears like cotton to a burr. Pedestrians crossed the *piazza*, visible only from the waist down, marching like fingers across a table. Bicycles squeaked about me in alarming proximity but I stood my cobbled ground, dropping my snout to the frigid stones. My nose was as reliable as radar, but it soon was seized by the cold. I stopped to gain a bearing.

It was I who was lost. Not she. The advantage of long limbs stood punctuated once again.

Ahead, from somewhere above the haze, a strange dog barked. The message was muted in the fog, like a voice through a thick scarf, but it offered a mark. The staccato rise at its end yielded a meaning: a woman down, in the *piazza*.

Panic rose in my chest. I turned to the direction of the call and spit a bark into the ether, the first thing to cross my mind: a description of the Contessa's shoes. *Puddle-brown chamois; a sensible heel, wide enough to bridge the cobblestones, yet an ideal height to accent the appealing curve of her perfect calf.*

No reply. I was panting. Visions of wild costumes and a child's pram swirled with phantom laughter in my head. Only the whine of a dueling siren from the end of the via del Corso overcame the lonesome song of the winter birds in the park beyond.

Though I was lost in a sea of people, I felt alone.

Chapter Three

I needed higher ground.

The Pincian Hill was close, but not close enough to offer a good view of the square. The fog closed around my throat like a white-gloved hand. Broad low steps wavered in the mist beyond, like a stairway to the heavens.

The church. I darted in that direction. Stairs rose to a chapel portico fronting tall, ornate wooden doors. At the top, I matched the crossing pedestrians head to head and enjoyed a grand view of the square.

The second oldest obelisk in the city stood sentry in the middle, a three-thousand-year-old beacon above the haze. I scanned the area. Madonna, in porcelain marble, lay prone to one side of the church entry. Fully polished and restored, she awaited return to her home inside.

I jumped into her lap. Standing next to the infant in her arms, I put my paws on the Madonna's smooth, round belly for a better view of the square.

A disheveled young woman and her bicycle appeared out of the fog as a police car passed in rushed indifference. She was trembling, but unhurt. Not the Contessa. I looked up in relief straight into the face of baby Jesus.

I bestowed a lick of thanks to its cool, alabaster cheek. *Grazie.*

My eyes scoured the circumference of the *piazza,* pausing at the edge of the Corso. On tiptoe, the Contessa searched the mist with her eyes. Position noted, I leaped into the square, tail wagging me in a beeline.

Her voice held no welcome. "Shimoni, *siamo in ritardo. Sbrigati!"*

Hurry, indeed. Not exactly the joyous meeting I'd imagined.

A morning bell tolled from the *campanile* in a corner of the *piazza* just as I reached the Contessa. I put my paws on her knee, coaxing her into making the usual fuss. She finally obliged, giving my head a tender tousle. I raised an ear in the direction of the ringing.

My bell, I thought, just as the woman was my Contessa.

Both were of unique sound, each making my heart beat at a more regular pace. Though the regal city wore a broad crown of a thousand bells, it was this solitary bell of slightly minor note that always brought me home. To a wee beast of splendid ear the distinction was simple to decipher. I wiggled my enthusiasm while the Contessa rubbed my spine. But the adoration these days was brief as usual.

She set off again, her strides short and quick. *"Andiamo."*

I accomplished a careless dash across the hectic Corso, its pace rising with the sun. My step quickened as I thought about all the females waiting in the park. Dodging a swarm of Vespas, I nearly caught a paw between the cobblestones before finding the hundred stairs leading to the Pincio.

The Contessa ascended each one with a certain bounce to her step. Perhaps she was leaving the lethargy of gloom behind, excited to breathe the pure air of the park green and move unfettered by the rush of traffic. Hopeful, I dashed ahead.

At the top, I traversed the sharp gravel to the soft, dewy grass. The daily search for a perfect spot to record my visit was on. Just as I settled into a certain angle most conducive to morning's relief, a choir of growls arose from the sparse winter foliage behind me. A chill parted the hair on my back. Though I tried to deny the hackles, they stood in answer. I froze, feigning an idle miniature of a Bernini statue. Instinct told me to turn and face the threat, but my feet refused to travel, laden by my one true fear: a mob of feral dogs.

I wanted to pant, but if I opened my mouth the dogs might mistake the show of teeth as a challenge. My only hope of protection was the presence of the Contessa. I hoped these Pincio cretins realized I was accompanied and had the sense to leave me alone. While a single dog is a creature of reason, a group of homeless mutts is problematic. Consensus is not a facile thing among a pack. Every dog wants to be the hero. Dogs fight amongst themselves on the way to war. Any war. The behavior of my littermates was a perfect example. I'd been on the ground floor beneath a tower of squabbling toes and tails too many times to count.

Though my youth was spent in confusion, the thought of my family soothed my nerves. I closed my eyes and tried to calm any fears by recalling the scent of my mother. The memory of her lay somewhere between the softness of a warm, furry side gently rising with her breath and the harshness of reprisal to a greedy litter for pulling too hard on her teats. On-demand feeding didn't suit her.

Her erratic behavior confused me then as my Contessa's did now. Both gave me the feeling that comes from eating something, the freshness of which is questionable. In time, my mother's temper turned to rage. As though the litter was something for which she hadn't bargained. Her patience dried up with the milk supply.

"*È troppo ,*" a voice said one day. "*Abbastanza.*"

The word hung in the air like an exit sign above a hidden door. Enough. Mother disappeared.

As in every tragedy, important lessons followed: life's greatest challenges often revolve around the angst of females, and dog's bliss depends on the humanity of man. My destiny lay somewhere in between. The Contessa's ability to rise above her own distress long enough to see my predicament was the only chance at safety.

Without moving, I looked her way. She stood at the edge of the Pincio, looking out over the landscape of the city, unaware of my peril. From the tenor of the growling, I measured the danger to be at least two meters away. The woman stood at ten times that distance.

I was clever and quick, and under normal circumstances I could outrun any dog. But, in my present state, all four limbs were undependable. I prayed in silence to the god of small dogs and gentle rescue. The brush rustled behind me just as the fortune of a single bark rang out from the wood beyond. In the time it took for the pack to be distracted, I raced to the Contessa's side. With a glance behind me, I found my friend Greta on the path near the trees across the park.

Merciful god.

Greta's fur shone golden even in the dull light of the foggy day. I gave a quick and thankful bark in return. My Contessa nodded and waved to Greta's woman as they rounded a stand of umbrella pine and approached along the broad pedestrian avenue bisecting the Pincio. Flanked with pines, palms and oak, it was the best place for the fashionable to stroll unfettered by dizzying city traffic. One could walk several kilometers to the Villa Borghese, the zoo, and the Val dei Cani where all the dogs met every morning, without the danger of a car or scooter. Long stretches of manicured lawn lay waiting for paws to dig. Birds filled the trees in every season begging to be hunted. Children played with balls that needed chasing. The Pincian Hill was paradise.

The two women met halfway on the path. Greta and I touched noses at the meeting.

Greta's woman was the first to speak. "Anything?" Her features were sharp, eyes sad and round like a spaniel's.

Divorce took its toll on her, infidelity at its root. And it was no wonder. Greta had explained it once as pure loss. No more vacations in the country. In fact, no country home at all. No maid, no groomer, no driver. No cook.

The word *cook* hovered above me like a hawk over trapped prey. No cook?

Few things compared to the possibility of losing the beloved woman who kept the country house filled with the scent of glorious food. And though the Contessa meant more to me than anything, *la cucina* had never been her calling. A life without the pleasure of a summer laden with fine fare was unthinkable. I was crestfallen.

"No nothing," Greta had said.

Possessions parted with their people. And Greta knew. Without the usual income for a proper holiday, she and her woman suffered the whole summer in the sweltering heat of Rome. Unheard of for anyone with means. Greta had grown thin, and her coat, though shiny, lay unkempt from lack of professional attention. The house on the beach was sold; the mountain place as well.

I touched my nose to hers. "The yacht?"

"Gone," she had said.

Like a hot sun simmering into the cool sea. The man took his toys with him.

"*Divorzio*. It starts with loss, ends with loss," Greta had said.

According to Greta, it all came to ruin. Both she and her woman had grown bitter in marking their loss as solely material.

I knew better.

I liked my things: a fine car, the *villa* in Chianti, trips to Capri—the cook. But happiness was the stuff of love, not the love of stuff. The Count and Contessa had all the trappings of both once upon a time. I looked up at Greta's woman. The greatest thing that she had lost was love. I sneezed to punctuate the point.

I sniffed the woman's shoes when she drew close to the Contessa. They were so worn, little leather scent remained. Yet, gypsy children, with little on their backs and less in their pockets, were happier.

Greta's woman repeated her question. "*Qualcosa?*"

The Contessa pulled a piece of folded paper from her coat along with a rumpled kerchief. "This."

My hunger suddenly deepened. I kept alert to anything edible falling from her pocket. Handing over the note, the Contessa touched the corner of one eye with the white linen. Greta strained as her woman pulled her up close by her collar.

I kept an eye on the woman as I performed a polite inspection of Greta's hindquarter. She was the darling of all the females I chased on the Pincio. And there were many, all shapes and sizes. I sniffed the inside of her thigh for any captivating scent. Though lacking a bit of luster in the wake of the financial ruin, her underpinning was as gloriously long as ever. Even superior to the bitch I'd seen in the *piazzetta* that morning. The way her stifles curved atop her back legs, like a lazy half-moon against her narrow waist, was unmatched.

Except, of course, by the Contessa.

I turned to admire the woman. My eyes traced the graceful bend of her legs from pale arching foot to perfect smooth knee beneath the skirt and beyond, as she took back the note, refolding it with care.

Greta's woman raised her voice. *"Lo sapevo!"*

"Now, I know it, too," said the Contessa. "All this time I thought he'd forgotten how to be romantic, when the truth of it is, he's forgotten *me*." Stooping to take me in her arms just before my eyes reached the lace of her undergarment, she raised me to her shoulder and laid her cheek against my jowl. "I should have figured it out sooner. He never could tell a lie. One corner of his mouth always gives him away. His smile hasn't been the only thing that's been crooked."

The note fluttered under my nose. Cedar: the scent of the Count—and roses. The aromas laid in wicked league upon the note, spelling out the stunning vision of the female in the piazza. My empty stomach turned. That explained the Contessa's deep distraction since she rooted through the clothing of the Count the week before. This was how she knew. I remembered the day she found it.

*

The Contessa spent all morning humming through her closet, changing from one outfit to another: chocolate-brown cashmere suit; striking pearl-grey and spring-yellow knit dress; basic black pantsuit with pearls. Today she was receiving a high award and wanted to look her best.

She was fond of special projects, anything that involved an animal. Known for her love of dogs, she was often asked to plan charity functions across the city for the benefit of Roman's canine citizens. The Contessa loved her work and was brilliant at planning events. She knew who to invite, where to seat them and how to make the event fun for all: include the dogs. Her parties were the most fun I ever had outside of Tuscany. She raised more money than anyone else, every time. And today she was being honored.

She raised a green linen suit to her chin, looked in the mirror, then at me and shook her head. "Too soon for linen."

She'd settled on the grey and yellow knit.

"Perhaps spring will arrive quicker if I dress the part." She patted my head.

We spent an hour in the bathroom trying various hairstyles, finally agreeing that the upsweep showed off her face best. She'd wear the simple gold coin earrings and one bracelet. No pearls.

"Always understate," she said as she looked at my reflection in the mirror. She looked at her watch.

We walked into the kitchen. The Count sat at the breakfast table. He looked up from his paper. He wore his finest woolen jacket, woven brown, grey and gold. Grey cashmere slacks and a crisp white shirt completed the picture of a very attractive man.

"Ready?" asked the Contessa.

"Yes, I must get going."

The Contessa wrinkled her brow. "Where?"

"I have a bank appointment."

The Contessa's voice grew sharp. "But what about the award?"

"What?"

The Contessa only stared.

"Oh," said the Count. He cleared his throat. "Well, I'm sorry, it can't be helped. The meeting has already been arranged. Others are depending on me to be there."

The Contessa was crestfallen. Her cheery mood turned to lead. The whole room turned gloomy.

"At least wish me luck, then," said the Contessa.

The Count rose from the table. "Luck, then." He gave a peck to the Contessa's cheek and headed for the door. "But you don't need me for that."

The door closed. The Contessa looked down at me and blinked away a tear. She drew a deep breath. "I'll not let him ruin the day."

She gathered her purse then looked for the keys to the apartment. On the desk near the door, in the kitchen, on the bedside table. They were nowhere to be found.

She looked at me. "He must have taken mine."

We walked into the closet and she began to go through the Count's clothes. Every jacket, coat and pair of pants was shaken for the sound of keys. Then she searched the pockets. As soon as she found a small note, the keys became unimportant.

She unfolded the scented paper with care. "*Ristorante* La Carbonara, one o'clock." The Contessa let her hand drop to her side and looked at me. "Today."

I sniffed the note in her hand just above where a small heart was drawn and a chain of x's and o's trailed to the edge of the paper.

We left the apartment door unlocked.

*

"Another woman," said Greta. Whiskers quivering, she allowed her lip to reveal a single gleaming tooth.

I yawned bewilderment. Licking the salt from the Contessa's cheek, I thrust my nose into the soft curls brushing her neck. They fell like silken threads against my snout, tickling the fine whiskers, sticking to my mouth. I knew that a noble dog's duty was to gild the human spirit. It was proving to be an onerous task. I sniffed the flowery perfume at the base of her neck. It was off, soured by something.

Fear.

I smelled it on myself. No rare perfume. Not handmade, but manmade: by the Count.

A chill took me. I turned my muzzle, shrinking from the cold wind. Drawing the fresh air deep into my lungs, I pushed the disturbing scent away. A pair of cheerful young pups tumbled across the grass nearby, ignorant of the world's concerns. I clenched my jowls, yearning for carefree days. Responsibility and dread weighed heavy. There was no happiness in fear.

The two women talked awhile longer, the Contessa holding me firm to her soft breast with one hand until Greta's lady leaned close in comfort.

"It may not be so serious," she said.

The Contessa set her jaw. "Lust is nothing more than fancy. Lunch is always serious. Besides, I made a point to pass the restaurant on my way to the award. They were sitting at a corner table nearly out of sight, his back to the room—but I saw her."

Her heart pounded under her sweater. She was steeped in anger.

"Just a passing flame…"

"She's stunning." The Contessa's cheeks burnished red with cold.

Greta's woman placed a hand on the Contessa's shoulder. "As are you."

The Contessa blew her nose into a tissue and looked at Greta's woman. Her words were cold. "She's young."

"She'll be too much work for him, you'll see."

The Contessa tucked the tissue in her sleeve. "Perhaps I should just be free of him."

I felt her heart skip two beats. She drew a short breath, as though the words had come uninvited.

"Nothing about it will be free," the woman scolded. "If you make a change, choose well. *Molto bene.*" She closed the top of her worn coat with one hand and pulled her gloves over bare, undecorated hands.

The Contessa straightened. Her soft features hardened as the sun broke through the fog for a moment to wash her face in bright light. "Change," she said, as though she had never before heard the word.

I felt her warm to the idea and her heart began to settle as she set me on the ground.

"Lucky," said Greta.

I looked down at her. "How?"

"You have the advantage."

I raised one ear.

"Don't you see? I never knew then what you know now," she said. She touched her nose to my ear. It was cold, leaving a bit of icy dew behind. Her eyes pooled. A soft, throaty noise rose up from her chest. She growled. "Use it."

The women bid their goodbyes. As they departed in opposite directions, Greta and I were pulled apart. I watched as a mangy tangle of mutts, caked in dirt from a week of rain, emerged from bushes across the lawn. They slithered as one along the short grass, winding their way in her direction, following Greta's beguiling scent through the verdant green like a garden snake.

Inbred mutts, I thought. Beneath concern of the noble.

I sniffed and turned away. Even though their threat had passed, I began to tremble. Mistaking it again for chill, the Contessa folded me into her coat. She stopped short of the stairs leading to the *piazza*, fumbling through her pockets. A glove emerged from one, and from the other, a photograph. She paused, holding it just below my head. Creased at the corners and faded by the light, it was worn at the edges by worry.

Mountainous rocks stood along the shore and a sea of butterfly-blue. The photo of Capri was unmistakable. A capsule of the Count and Contessa, arms entwined, clinging together like dust to a wet dog. Better days. I remembered them, too. The music of Elvis filled the air as the Count beat the Contessa at cards time and again or the Contessa teased that his dancing on the beach was ridiculous.

*

It had been a fine midsummer day. Gulls swept up with the wind currents against the Faraglioni rocks. We had taken a rickety boat and a radio to the other side of the island just before sunset and anchored. The Contessa slipped me into a tight-fitting life vest and we all fell into the salty water. The sea was so calm and the light so beautiful it looked like a perfect mirror to the caves at the edge of the water. We swam under the low ceiling and into the cavern. Emerald light beamed up through the sea and schools of tiny fish swam in concert just below my paws. I dipped my snout under the water, over and over again, trying to catch something for a snack. Each time I came up for air, I sneezed the sea from my nose and the Count and Contessa chuckled. The cavern reverberated with laughter until, after another foiled attempt at fishing, I came up to silence. The Count and the Contessa balanced in embrace at the inner edge of the grotto, immersed in a deep kiss.

The Count's voice was a whisper. "You are my charm."

Soon, swimsuits were on shore and the two were no longer laughing at my antics. Elvis sang from the boat bobbing outside the cave.

That was the first time I'd heard Elvis and I took his words to heart as easily as I took the golden notes into my ears. It was a magical time. "Good Luck Charm" was our prayer and that day Elvis became our patron saint.

*

I shook my head. Elvis sang no more.

25

The Contessa tugged at one of my ears and her voice shook. "Not so lucky now."

I nuzzled her hand in recognition of the cheerful memory. Happiness was a universal tonic. But there was no reaction. She held the picture for several minutes, as though sifting details of the years that fell between then and now, before tucking it away to find her other glove. Slipping them on, she looked out over the tiled Roman rooftops, then looked down to brush the tip of her finger across my nose.

"*Ho fatto fiasco,* Shimoni," she said. "Such a mess—and I fear it all began with me." She rubbed my shoulder with the back of her hand. "I don't care what I lose as long as I don't lose him. I just want to go back to the way things were. What road brings me home?"

Down the stairs, across the *piazza,* second right. As always.

But I wondered what fueled the woman's guilt. After all, I had seen no sudden change to prompt the man's indiscretion. Life was normal, proceeding on a predictable, even keel; a boat in calm seas. Perhaps that was the problem.

The Contessa ruffled my fur. "Did life get between us? Or was it ennui?"

Life in an apartment; the only entertainment, a bird in a tree on the other side of a closed window. Boredom and preoccupation. Both were able foes. I'd given up many a perfectly good toy to each, later slipping into regret when the object went missing out of neglect.

The Contessa pulled my snout to her nose. "No need to know where it started to see where it might end."

Even though she was angry with the Count, it was in the man she placed her hope. I laid my head upon her arm with a long sigh of inadequacy. I stared into the woman's eyes. At least she was talking to me again. But her depression was contagious. From my nose to the tip of my tail, I was leaden. We stood at the crown of the Pincian Hill as though we had reached a crossroad.

The wind turned up a swirl of fallen leaves. They twirled across the grass like a child's pinwheel. I watched them rise and fall in the fury of the breeze until a chill took the straggly hair on my chin. I turned to push my nose into the Contessa's coat. There beside me stood a gypsy beggar.

Dressed in black, her olive face was hidden in the shadow of a broad hat. The brim was still, even against the harsh wind. Though her palm was open, it wasn't empty.

She offered a fan of cards in one hand, clasping a thick, grey shawl around her shoulders with the other. *"Fortuna?"* she asked, waving the assortment of cards in the breeze.

Not your only game, I thought. I'd seen plenty of gypsies with their hands in someone else's pocket. I glanced at my Contessa's bag to make certain it was closed. Then I thrust my nose far toward the old woman. I squirmed to catch a scent and a clue to her intention.

The Contessa took care not to meet the woman's eyes. "No," she murmured.

"If you don't choose a card, the card chooses you." The woman revealed a tarnished grin, one gold tooth shining at the top. She pulled a single soldier from the fan with two bony fingers.

Her dress was disheveled. Her origin clearly lay outside the upscale neighborhood surrounding the park. I knew that placing her would be easy if I could sniff her wrinkled hand. I worked the air in front of the cards with my nose. No fragrance. Nothing. A breeze ruffled her loose shawl in my direction. I wiggled my nose in its wake. The odor should have read like a map, yet it was as pristine as fresh snow. It made no sense. I cocked an ear in question.

The gypsy regarded the card like an old friend, and then turned it outward. "The hanged man."

No hanged dog, at least, I thought.

The Contessa acted as though the old woman were invisible.

With a soft touch to my nose, the old woman spoke gently. *"Non literale,"* she said. "A card of change. *Transforma.*" Her eyes, large and black, sparkled beneath her hat in spite of the dull light.

I raised my head in question. The Contessa rearranged me in her arms, still not looking at the gypsy.

"Of the mind," the old woman continued, putting a crooked finger to her temple. She returned the card to the deck.

The Contessa straightened, pursing her lips in impatience as she did when waiting for me to deliver myself from the thick cover of shrubs lining the park. The beggar stood in silence then opened her hand.

"Per favore," said the woman, "a favor for the card?"

The wind blew a chilly breath across the *piazzale.* The Contessa used one hand to pull her coat close around her neck, frowning as she did when trying to find loose coins in the bottom of her purse, yet making no move to do so. I again tried to push my nose closer to the gypsy.

The old woman put a hand to my head in return for the effort. I licked her tasteless fingers. She stroked the space between my eyes until they drooped with pleasure. Then, without warning, she snapped so perfect a growl my way that I was sure she must have a dog hidden beneath her shawl. Her delivery of the insult was excellent. She spoke flawless dog. Her ability so surprised me that I responded in the way any dog would. I returned it.

"Stop." The Contessa recoiled. She turned one shoulder toward the woman as she pulled me away from the confrontation.

"Change your mind, the rest will follow," the gypsy called. She stepped in cadence to the words. *"Capisce?"*

Stone-faced, the old woman moved along the marble railing that fronted the precipice of the Pincio. She disappeared around the bend of the path. I raised my nose to the wind, still trying to divine her origin, but the encounter only reeked of the bizarre.

I sneezed twice and swiped a paw between my eyes where the gypsy had touched me. I sniffed my foot for a final hint. Only the sweet smell of the Pincio remained from strutting through its thick grass.

The Contessa stared again, for a long time, out over the domes and *campanile* of the city. I scanned the horizon, from the Monte Mario to the Janiculum: the dome of St. Peter's, the hump back of the Pantheon, San Carlo, San Andrea and beyond. I sniffed the air surrounding my Contessa. A thousand saviors lay before us yet hope seeped away, oozing away like blood from a wound. I wiggled to her face and licked her ear. She met this kindness with a partial grin and a touch of her nose to mine. At least I still made her smile. The Count's misguided affection was another issue. *There* was a mind to be changed.

The Contessa let me slip from her arms to the cool ground. Fluffing my coat with a brief shake, I sniffed the gravel for telltale trace of the beggar. The trail was cold.

"So, romance isn't dead, just deserted," the Contessa said. "Perhaps we can persuade the turncoat, no?" The woman regarded me with a single brow raised for emphasis.

I imagined Eve casting Adam a similar glance shortly before handing him the apple.

She cocked her head and pushed her tongue into her cheek. "*Transforma.*"

The Contessa started down the steps.

I led the way.

Chapter Four

B y the time we reached the *piazza*, the fog had lifted into sunlight. My usual composure returned. Knowing I had an ally in the Contessa buoyed my spirit. In collaboration, we could solve anything. Hunger struck me hard now. I led the way across the crowded square, weaving a tangled trail. I employed the elaborate detail often defined by canine intellect: a sniff here, a mark there, quick retraces for minutiae skipped in error. I kept just far enough away from the Contessa to cause her irritation. The method always quickened her pace. With breakfast overlooked, I was ravenous.

Through a jumbled army of feet and traffic down to via Angelo Brunetti, I arrived at the tall, broad wooden doors that fronted my apartment. Plopping down in front of the entry, I sat just beyond the shadow of the archway. The morning sun warmed my coat as I licked away a bit of motor oil from between my toes, waiting.

It was no longer the high threat of rush hour and the woman could take it from here on. My Contessa would chide the reckless behavior when she arrived. She was opposed to darting across anything. The Contessa moved down the street toward me. With her gaze directed to the pavement, she forged slowly through a short string of cars, forcing them to stop.

Just run, I thought.

Had she ever been brave enough to dare the chaotic traffic? Ever known the pleasant thrill of running with the cars racing along the Lungotevere skirting Rome's river? Had her ears been ruffled by the breeze of a Fiat passing close enough to fill her lungs with the sticky fumes of petrol? I thought not and was sorry. Bravery was necessary to life's excitement. And excitement was therapeutic. Any homeless dog who's every chased a rabbit knows that woes fade in the face of exhilaration. Worries about the Count might disappear if she dared to try something different.

The Contessa reached the door and shot me a disapproving look. *"Arriviamo sani e salvi.* No thanks to you."

Yet, she scooped me into her arms with a quick kiss and loving pat on the head.

Safe and sound, indeed. I licked her cheek.

A turn of a key opened the heavy outer doors. At the end of the smooth marble hall we entered a tiny elevator. The Contessa pulled the outer door shut and slid the double metal gates together from the inside. A little hesitation, a clang and a jerk, and the box rose. Big enough for only two people, it rattled up the hollow staircase, announcing every floor with a clatter as it passed the outer doors at each landing.

As we ascended, I licked the lipstick off my nose and swiped a paw over my head to smooth the hair. The greasy, tasteless gloss was not something I enjoyed, but it was a small price to pay for the ride. As we passed the third floor, she again pulled the photograph from her pocket.

"Perhaps it takes only one to change." She looked at it lovingly, a hum rising from her throat.

My belly, up against her chest, buzzed with every note. My heart kept rhythm with the melodic beat, "Love Me Tender." I closed my eyes and nestled my ear into her soft crux of her neck to better hear the throaty tone. A long time had passed since I'd heard the song, especially from her lips. It was the sound of hope. The Contessa must have a strategy.

Change. I felt her heart swell at the simple notion.

She looked me in the eye. "Shall we try for a miracle?"

I replied with a sure wag of the tail as the elevator set us free at our apartment. When she opened the door I wiggled to leap from her arms, racing in the direction of the kitchen, a picture firmly in my mind of the two embracing as they met.

Problem solved, crisis abated.

I stopped abruptly when I saw the Count. It was an odd image. The man was usually absent upon our return these days. Under the circumstances, his presence disrupted the smooth reunion of a dog to the breakfast bowl. I sat at the threshold, just behind the edge of the door.

Cappuccini? I wondered.

Il Conte used to brew them each morning, delivering a cup to the Contessa with a kiss before she stepped a slender foot from the bed. Any dog knows the importance of habit: same bush, same hour, same park, as it were. Ritual is a certain type of faith in the circumstances of our lives. But rituals once held by the couple had gone by the wayside long ago, cast off along with a welcome caress upon each return, and a final kiss at night. Perhaps, the Count employed a different approach since his rebuffing earlier that day.

A step in the right direction.

I leaned around the door and cranked my head upward. The man stood at the sink in an immaculate black suit, tall, sophisticated and chic. His eyes sloped in the direction of his ears, giving him the look of a man in constant search of absolution, which he had always used to great advantage with the Contessa.

Until now.

I listened for the familiar sound of frothing milk.

Nothing.

The morning sun sparkled on a small object in the Count's right hand. A tiny box from D'Angelo's pastry shop perched on the edge of the counter and he balanced a small treat between the fingers of his other hand. He fussed as though he were threading a needle, bringing his hands together carefully. I waited, unnoticed.

Thin curtains at the window above the sink swayed with a soft breeze that swept straight across the kitchen and into my nose. It delivered the same sweet, musty scent that fell with the crisp leaves of my beloved chestnut tree in the country every autumn.

Marrone.

A Mont Blanc nestled in the Count's hand. The Contessa called the bite-sized pastries little jewels. Made of whipped cream, meringue and smooth chestnut paste, they were exquisite in taste, and a rare luxury to any dog. My mouth watered. With any luck, every food group would soon be covered, from the cheese in the street, to the fat and sugar of the pastry. And it wasn't yet noon. I licked a wisp of saliva falling from the corner of my mouth and trembled. A Mont Blanc was a treat seldom available to a dog with acute concern for his figure, but a week of irregular meals countered its effect.

No harm in small treats to an underweight dog, I thought.

The Count gave a startled jump as the heavy door of the apartment slammed shut. He grabbed the small box from the counter and pushed it into his pocket as the perfect little pastry lost its balance, falling from his nervous fingers in the direction of the floor.

Without hesitation, I sprang to action. I skated on long toenails across the ceramic floor to intercept the delight as my tongue anticipated the first crunch of the treat that was about to be mine. The delicacy was in my mouth before it reached the floor, swallowed whole.

Bravo. I loved to show off. But, in my haste I never truly appreciated those happy accidents as I did when they splattered on the hard tile, needing to be methodically licked away. The greater the mess, the more the treat lingered on my tongue and clung to the whiskers.

This time the strike was quick and clean. The only real satisfaction lay in the knowledge that I beat the target to the tile. In fact, the jump was quite high. Both the landing and the swallow were painful. An uneasy lump wedged in my throat.

The Count glowered, raising his arm. *"Cretino."* He paused, lowered his hand to his mouth and pushed the small box deep into his pocket. Walking to the kitchen door, he swung it closed and turned. "Shimoni, your timing is *orribile.*"

I swallowed hard, took a deep breath and cowered. The man had never raised a hand to me before, even in jest. It was completely out of character. But nothing that day, so far, was normal. And as for timing: in my opinion it was perfect.

A noise from behind the door turned my attention to the hallway. A bottle was being pulled from the small wine refrigerator. The Contessa's footsteps grew louder as she approached the door.

The Count's face had taken on a deep shade of contemplation. Closing my eyes, I concentrated on another attempt to move the treat along. As I did, the man grabbed me in a very rude manner, turned me upside down and shook me hard just as the kitchen door swung open.

"One bottle left," said the Contessa as she looked up. "Why don't we—" She stood, goddess-like, in the doorway, Chianti in hand.

Even upside down I recognized the ornate crest on the label: a crescent moon and two stars. *La Riserva.* The magic wine.

"*Che cos'è?*" The Contessa's face was crimson with anger, her eyes harsh and cold. The pleasant smile and easy music on her lips were gone.

I never thought myself a whiner, like some of the overly elegant dogs that frequented the Pincio in the mornings, but the Count took me by surprise. The man had always treated me with the gentlest of hands. Now, a loud, effortless squeal escaped me, like the whine of a deflating balloon. Hanging there upside down, I imagined it came from somewhere else altogether. And as certain sounds do, it called a memory.

A motor trip to my country house, where I'd chased young wild pigs below the vineyard bordering a stream. They squealed the same high pitch now coming from a place so deep inside me I didn't know it existed. At once, I regretted frightening the piglets.

"What's wrong?" His hold unyielding, the Count fumbled for an adequate response as though his hand were caught in a jar of expensive winter truffles. "What's wrong is—"

"Out with it," said the Contessa.

"This creature has eaten my breakfast. He has no manners. He's completely uncivilized." Even angry, the man had the aristocratic good looks of a Roman: Apollo beneath a shock of ebony hair.

Stress reveals sober truths. Il Conte's words singed my ears. The man was no longer smitten with me; his warm hands and loving touches, nothing but a sham. All the midnight treats and ball tossing in the world didn't bury the facts.

My inverted position did not allow a good view of the situation. Even after a few missed meals, my figure did not permit me to bend far enough to nip at the fingers of my captor. Helpless, my only option was to dangle there, listen to the blood rushing to my head and the livid sounds echoing from the high vaulted ceiling to the bare floor below. The next move was the Contessa's.

"*Who's* the heathen? No man of manners treats anything as you do. You're absent compassion."

"*Compassione? Compassione.* Say you ever feel any mercy for me and I'll let him go," snapped the Count.

The Contessa gave the man a hard look that seemed to melt at the end into heartache. "*Pazzo,*" she chided.

Without question. Psycho.

"*Si,*" the Count returned, narrowing his eyes. "Ever wonder why?"

The Contessa delivered a stone-cold stare. "*Inadequato?*"

Even with my brain flooded, I knew a good answer when I heard one. What man didn't measure himself via sexual prowess? It was no wonder the Italian word for impotence described certain imperfection.

The Count turned in measured time to face the window and drew a long breath.

"Approaching your time of the month?"

Santa Maria. The wrong card to play. Every male knew the power of the phrase. No simpler words began so complicated and powerful a movement of luggage out the door, or woman to the march.

The Contessa's eyes became slits and she gnashed her teeth in the way of an animal before attack. I hung in the air, giving a weak shake of my one free hind leg, trying to think of a way to prompt the Count into releasing me.

The Count dropped me at the same time the Contessa let the magic wine slip from her fingers to the floor. When I hit the hard tile all I heard was the sound of shattered glass and for a moment I thought I had smashed into a thousand pieces, purple blood oozing from my veins. By the time I lay in the safety of her arms I was shaking so violently that I thought I might be sick. For a moment, I took fleeting pleasure in supposing I could lick the pastry from the cool tile after all, but as the Contessa settled us both into a puffy chair so did my stomach. All that remained was an uncomfortable mass sitting like a stone in my belly.

"*Poverino,*" she said.

She placed a soft hand on my warm back and stroked my heaving side. Her fingernails were the perfect length and their blunt shape gave a gentle tickle to my short, smooth underhair. My stomach rumbled. The excitement was so great that my breakfast was forgotten. Now, the thought of food held no appeal.

I gazed into the eyes of my Contessa with gratitude and she returned the gesture with a scratch of my head. But her expression was blank, like a dog beaten one too many times. The man walked from the kitchen to exit the front door. It closed with a bang and I jumped.

A mystery, I thought. The Count was not a stingy man. Treats were a rule of the house. While the value of the pastry was clear, to come unglued at the loss of a snack so small was ridiculous. It was just a small part of breakfast, after all. Had I not been the center of the fracas, my leg still aching from the pull, I could even see the humor in it: Man bested by beast. After all, Il Conte had been the one to proclaim that laughter was love's secret. Both the Count and the Contessa seemed to have lost their sense of humor. I nuzzled the palm of my Contessa's hand and she took the cue, using a soothing stroke along my back and tail. Her hands smelled of basil.

"Not so simple, change," the woman said. "He makes it difficult to care."

The words echoed those of the Count's that morning. It was clear to me that they both *wanted* to care more, at least. All was not lost—yet.

The Contessa rubbed a wine spot from my fur. She touched a thumb to her forefinger and examined the purple stain on her fingertip.

"What if that really was the last of the magic?" She looked out the bank of windows. It had started to rain.

The telltale fragrance of a melon on the counter, and the verbena soap the Contessa used for bathing, rose with the warmth of her body. The scent soothed my nerves. I was safe with someone I loved. My stomach would once again settle into hunger and something glorious would come for dinner, for that was the way of *basilico*. But the chaos was escalating.

Neither of my people made it easy for the other. As two dogs skirt each other in the park, estimating the give and take necessary to avoid a fight, soon the Count and the Contessa had to face each other, or walk away. I knew the only peace for any of us lay in reconciliation. Whatever fate they drew, drew me as well. It was up to me to take charge of the ship before we all drowned.

I curled into a tight ball on the Contessa's lap to think. Fearing the Count might return, pull me up and shake me by a flagrant leg, I pulled my paws far up under my belly and tucked them carefully away. My Contessa was silent. Only the slow beat of her heart, her delicate hand on my belly, granted me the comfort I needed to rest. But as I drifted into sleep, a final word from the woman turned my ear.

"*Abbastanza.*"

Chapter Five

I awakened to soft voices. I was alone on the couch. The Count sat at the salon table playing solitaire as was his habit in the late afternoon. The Contessa was in the next room, lost in the concentration of a phone call. Always engaged in something, her preoccupations had grown over the years. She lunched or shopped or attended meetings. I didn't mind and tagged along happily most of the time.

Il Conte played a final card and looked up at me. We regarded each other long and hard, the way dogs consider the merit of marking a rug in the presence of humans. Who would make the first move?

"I think Shimoni needs a walk," said the Count.

"I'll be just a moment."

The Count stood. "No, no. I'll take him."

Before the woman argued, the Count had a hat on his head and the leash he always used in hand. Safety was his sole concern. He understood well that his fate was bound to mine. When Il Conte was master, the only off-leash time came on the Pincio.

I was offended by the woman's lack of concern. After all, this was the man who tried to shake the dickens, and dessert, out of me just hours before. I owed it to her distracted mind, shook my head and laid it back upon my paws in denial. I had no desire to move just yet, but the Count insisted and I was obliged to follow him out the door.

We took the slippery marble stairs instead of the lift. I bounced from step to step at the man's heel. I kept a sharp eye on Il Conte lest he decide once again to attempt to dislodge the treat with a hefty shake. Winding around the box elevator to the entry below, Il Conte paused at the base of the steps to pull his pipe from his pocket. With it came a checkered kerchief that fell at my feet. I gave it a cursory sniff before the man retrieved it. The scent of roses and cologne trailed the linen square back into his pocket.

As soon as we were outside the building, I scanned the street for the man's canine accomplice. The rain had stopped. I lifted my nose to gather any hint that might announce her presence and wondered about the bitch's mistress. Long legs? A slender ankle? Only the damp air of dusk greeted me.

Even though the Count's words from that morning still nipped my ears, I was determined to remind him of the myriad pleasing features of a small dog. It was time to demonstrate my charm. I spied an empty bottle beneath a parked car, straining the leash to retrieve it. Crunching the plastic between my teeth, I invited the man to throw it for me. At first the Count was amused. He bent to smooth the tousled hair on my head.

Bravo. The Count just needed a little prodding. Soon he'd be back to normal.

But instead of reaching for the bottle, the man pulled a match from his pocket. He lit his pipe, drew a plastic bag from his pocket and watched me with great concern. It was as if he expected me to throw the toy myself. Indeed, the Count never regarded me so carefully in all my life. I dropped the bottle into the gutter. Each time I hesitated over an intriguing odor, the man took his pipe in hand, bent down through a ribbon of blue tobacco smoke and squinted in the dim light to examine any business in which I was engaged.

An audience was most disconcerting to a dog's concentration. Though I fancied myself many things, thespian was not among them.

The man moved down the street through a maze of people. The route was much longer than normal. Down the long via del Corso to the Piazza Venezia, past the stark white marble Il Vittoriano, up the sweeping Michelangelo steps to the Campidoglio, through the ruined Forum and beyond, it was clear the Count's mind was elsewhere. The air was frigid and far less appealing than during a summer walk. Warm weather allowed the fragrance of the day to linger into night. It gave a dog the pleasure of revisiting the day's events on the exhale of a frantic city in repose. Winter air was sterile and uninspiring.

The Count had forgotten to give me the comfort of my favorite sweater, knitted by the Contessa from regal blue wool. When sported, it encouraged a certain sense of entitlement. After all, I had not been born into nobility as the Count had, but had been added to it. A trapping, yes, the wrap spoke not only of my station but also of how important I was to my people. Without it, there was nothing to prevent me being viewed a common dog, nothing to indicate my prominence other than the fact that I was, of course, attractive by nature.

As darkness fell across the dingy streets, I padded along the uneven stones, my tail pulled down tight for warmth. The lump in my belly refused to budge. By the time we reached the Coliseum it was raining. Water puddled in the small crook between my ears, and dripped down into my eyes. We skirted the monument, walking back across the Foro over giant stone paving scattered like dice in some places; smooth and tight as a jigsaw in others. Lights illuminated the cavernous apertures of the Palatino along one side.

An ancient archway shielded two gypsy children from the downpour. They raised their palms to the rain as we passed and the Count reached into his pocket for a few coins. A box hid behind them, its contents squeaking in an odd, familiar way. I squeezed between the two youngsters for a closer look. As I peered over the side of the container I was met by a cold, slippery nose, then another, and another.

Puppies. Always ready to play and quick to idolize, they made me feel like a king. The smell of them was enough to cheer any heart. I wanted to have puppies of my own one day and lingered over that thought while the litter worked on licking the rain from my snout. They made me feel warm even in the downpour. Perhaps it was something I should start thinking about. What puppy doesn't add a little happiness and laughter to a family? And that was exactly what we needed. A tug of the leash brought me back into grim reality. At the moment, I had no prospects to employ in such a venture.

I figured we were set for home. My only focus was cozy warmth under the fluffy cover of my Contessa's bed. But home was not our destination. Down the broad gentle stairs, across a narrow street, past the turtle fountain in the ghetto, we entered a tiny bar through a double door. The room was blue with acrid smoke and soft light. The odor of damp woolen coats and whiskey hung heavy on the thick ether. I nestled up to the tarnished brass foot rail of the bar, hoping for a bowl of water. What came instead was a whiff of something that made my already upset stomach turn again.

Roses.

I strained the leash to get a look around the corner of the bar hoping to find the striking bitch I'd seen that morning. Pushing my snout as far as I could to the end, I cocked my head, allowing one eye to peek past the rail. There she lay, in regal sphinx-like pose before me. Her moist tongue blushed as she panted under the weight of a steamy room. Stunned, I stopped. The leash, tight around my neck, pulled at my throat like a choke chain. It begged a muffled gag that would be instantly mistaken for a growl. But there was no denying it, and it was met with grave contempt from the Cleopatra.

The Count jerked the leash. The queen disappeared behind the bar as I slid over the wet floor to the man's side. Sitting beside the Count was a tall, slender branch of a woman, dark and willowy as the long shadow of a cat before a low light. Her bronze skin laced the edges of a plush, soft pink sweater.

Her odor was so strong I gagged. It was as though I were in the maze of a rose garden in full bloom at the height of a Tuscan summer. I sneezed until my eyes stung and the back of my throat itched. The woman picked me up, lifting me to clearer air. The altitude granted me a good view of the long wooden bar. A tulip glass of *prosecco* bubbled and beside it, a heap of miniature Mont Blanc. I drew the sweet odor into my nostrils. The scent made my mouth water even as my belly ached. The sneezing ceased. Affliction abated, the woman tucked me under her arm. I licked my snout and examined my captor.

Her feline eyes were as dark as the Roman catacombs; the purse of her lips kissed the bottom of her small nose; her black hair was pulled straight back into a tail, giving her brow the exotic slant of a Siamese. But I needed no feline comparison to dislike the woman. The rosy odor betrayed her hand. She was the source of my Contessa's gloom. I needed less the confirmation granted in the man's fingers on her lean thigh. The picture was clear.

I growled softly and looked at the Count. The man cooed like a dove, running his fingers down the back of La Donna Rosa's neck. My stomach rumbled and I thought I might be sick.

Riffraff. I escalated the growl.

"*Abbastanza*," the Count chided. He took me from her arms and plopped me back on the floor, this time on the other side, away from La Donna Rosa's stench.

Enough, indeed. I knew the barren path of infidelity. I'd seen it in Greta's eyes. It all leads to loss, she'd said. Fear raised the hackles on my back. I tugged on the man's trouser cuff with my teeth.

Spellbound, the Count paid me no mind. The man was overtaken by a state known in canine circles as trance-asphyxiation. I understood his glazed expression. I'd seen it many times: a dumbfounded reaction to an overwhelming scent. A dog overcome by scent often runs in circles or, simply transfixed, stays glued to the offending odor like a mouse on sticky paper.

"You have something for me," La Donna Rosa said in harsh Roman dialect. "The one we saw in the window?" She sipped at the *prosecco* and popped a tiny pastry between her curled lips.

"*Ah, si,*" the Count faltered. The man shuffled through the pockets of his coat and pants. "I was hoping to surprise you, but—"

43

His voice trailed off as he dug into the cavities of his jacket and breast pocket. When his eyes met mine, the man raised an eyebrow as though he knew we shared a secret.

"You haven't lost it?" The woman leaned forward, dropping a bit of pastry to the floor.

I ignored it.

"Of course not," the Count laughed. "I know it is here—somewhere." He fretted through his things again.

La Donna Rosa placed her hand on his. *"Mi' amore,* you've forgotten it? How sweet. You're such a little boy. No matter, as long as it wasn't left around for someone to find." The woman paused to examine the Count's face. "I'll have it soon enough, and you as well. *No?"*

The woman reeked of lust, but not for Il Conte. Treats, I thought, and I wondered what she expected from the man.

The Count took her hand. *"Si, certo,"* he said. He looked down at me. "Patience, *cara.* As soon as I find the time is right."

The woman arched her back, dropping her head and shoulders like an alley cat poised to swat. "You're a fool. There's no right time to tell a wife you're leaving," she said. "You've waited long enough, and so have I. Now, you will do what you must. Or let me."

The Count straightened his posture and scowled. "I wouldn't like that," he said.

"I know what you like," she returned, scratching behind his neck. Il Conte dipped a shoulder in deference.

The Cleopatra poked her head around the end of the bar and curled the corner of her lip, allowing a single, pointed fang. Narrow eyes peered through a mass of frantic, wet curls. She glared at me, daring me to engage, but I was fully occupied by my whirling stomach and spinning head. The Count leaned his neck back into the cup of La Donna Rosa's hand. Then he sat up, took her hand in his and kissed it.

"Si sta facendo tardi," he said. "It's late. I must go."

Il Conte turned to serpent, I thought, complete with forked tongue and beaded tail. The man slithered out of the bar. I hunched behind him, tail at half-mast, mourning the story I'd pieced together.

The rain was falling harder. Streets glistened in water deep enough to hide the cobblestones. Even so, the Count took his time through the downpour. His attentiveness to my business never faltered as we slogged through the city. Just as the rain fell from the sky in sheets, we tucked into a covered loggia behind an open gate. A round, brutish stone face cast us a cold, horrifying stare from one end of the portico. The Count removed his dripping hat, leaned against the wall adjacent the angry visage, and stared at me.

"Ho fatto fiasco, Shimoni," the man confessed. "I've made such a mess."

Indeed. As big as the Colosseo, and twice the ruin. *Fiasco* seemed to be the word book-ending my day. I shook the water from my back and sat down on the dry stone.

The Count questioned the ugly stone face. "I can't have them both?"

Not without a pedigree, I thought. Polygamy was a dog's game. Besides, from the looks of La Donna Rosa, I doubted the Count loved her. Exotic, yes. But like admiring the fine bone of a Chihuahua, once the mouth opened there was only irritating yap. No breeding. I thought the Count many things, but none of them vulgar—until now. Again, Il Conte played the wrong card. But he wore no poker face. It was clear the man was miserable with the draw.

"I don't like myself much right now." The Count looked down at me. "I had rather be a dog, and bay the moon, than such a Roman."

A phrase passed from one Roman to another. The words from *Julius Caesar* were true. Yet, to somehow suggest that the ever-loyal canine was just one notch above the infidel was ridiculous. It was clear to me that Shakespeare had no dog. I mused at how the world might have been different: Dogs, Romans, Countrymen....

"*Miseria*," he said. "I never intended it go this far." He reached into his coat pocket, pulling out his money clip, a small card case and finally, a handkerchief. Wiping the rain from his face and neck, he regarded the top of the card case, then sat down on a short marble step next to the stone face. I jumped onto his soggy lap.

I sniffed the case in the man's hand, looking closely at the face on its front. The Contessa.

"But it is nice to think *someone* has time for me the way she used to." The Count turned to me. "Remember?"

A favorite memory rose to my mind, of a time before ritual became routine. A sunset walk in Chianti, the Count and Contessa, arm in arm, no hand free for the end of a leash. Always well ahead of them, I watched from the side of the road as they ambled up the hill to the *villa*, contentment paving their steps along the way. They would stop to kiss, Il Conte taking time to brush the hair from the Contessa's cheek, then pulling her to him with arms wrapped tight around her waist. He would whisper and she would laugh. We'd all race up to the house and into the bedroom, where the door would be closed just before I reached the threshold, every time.

Happiness is not an inward experience. It radiates like the sun. Those were much warmer days. It was true: the Contessa had gone from being busy with the Count to being busy with everything else.

But what bone doesn't become old-hat? It's chewed for a while, enjoyed, then tossed over for a new one. I looked up at the man.

Tossed over, I thought, just as the Count, bored and neglected, was tossing over the Contessa. I flapped my ears. Where did feelings begin to fade?

In the light of love we always look better to ourselves. Even a dog knows that if that light begins to weaken, so does confidence. Rain dripped from my snout. I dipped my head to let the water drain from my nose, and memory took me to a thunderstorm in the country years ago.

*

The weather was too foul for a sunset walk. In fact, the rain had denied any long walks for almost two weeks. The Count and Contessa curled onto the couch instead, beaming into a glorious blaze they'd built in the fireplace. They'd come up with a substitute for a contented stroll. As winter approached, afternoon treks were abandoned for the hearth. It was fine by me. The warmth of the fire on my back was heaven. I drifted in and out of sleep to bursts of laughter from the sofa. The Count was fond of poking a finger into the ribs of the Contessa.

"*Pasta,*" he would say.

She'd giggle.

It was something he'd do with regularity whether they were on the couch, on the bed or in an elevator. It was part of the fun. But, somewhere between fine high heels and sensible shoes, the laughter of poking fun became personal. Perhaps bored with the habit, she no longer gave a giggle at the tease but a snarl. And even in the clear weather of spring, the walks were abandoned over time. It was as though the couch had become too comfortable to leave. As a dog who is charmed by a warm fire thinks twice about the chase, complacency had overcome desire. Comfort is one thing, but a fire not tended soon goes out.

The fun ebbed away.

*

A few strands of silver hair at the Count's temples glistened in the streetlight. I supposed time had crept up on the man, its lens blurring the definition of his manhood. Something Il Conte saw clarified in the company of a younger woman, no doubt. Perhaps she giggled easily.

I licked Il Conte's chin. I knew what it was to feel unappreciated and, though disgusted, no dog likes to see pain. We'd shared too many good times for me to hold a grudge. A lot of pull toys over the dam, so to speak. I was willing to forget the ugliness of the morning under the dismal circumstances. After all, the Count *was* family.

The Count rubbed my head. "I didn't mean what I said in *la cucina* this morning, you know?"

I slipped my head over his hand and received an amiable scratch beneath the chin. At least the man's straying had nothing to do with a small dog, I thought.

But time was short, and the *missioni* complicated. La Donna Rosa was eager for an answer, and the Contessa's quiet word that morning was not lost in my sleepy haze: "Enough." It loomed before me as gatekeeper to oblivion, harbinger of loss. The same omen robbed me of my mother. I would not sit idly by to see its evil work on my Contessa.

"The only thing you lack to make you *more* civilized is speech," said the Count.

Speech. If I *could* talk, it was a situation easily cleared up over a *café corretto* and a homemade *gelato* from the corner bar. But I had no such gift.

Man was doomed to roam the earth without the benefit of canine insight. So far, the roaming part was being taken totally out of context. I yearned to find a way to clear up what was obviously a misunderstanding. Anything to avoid the disaster of *divorzio*.

"What road takes me home, boy?" The man pulled me to his chest. "If you talked, you'd tell me, *no*?"

Gathering the leash, he pulled me back into the rain. By the time we covered the long route back to my apartment, I was so wet and numb with cold it was as though I had become the rain itself. At the inner door, I paused to shake off the illusion, disturbing the lump in my belly and making a formidable pool of water in the doorway.

The place was dark and quiet. I supposed the Contessa to be already in bed and made my way through the darkness to the bedroom. At the threshold I stopped to note the stillness. No gentle breath, no rustle of crisp sheets. My heart raced as I ran into the room, landing in one long leap on top of the wide bed. It was perfectly made. Empty.

The hallway lights clicked on. I turned in time to see a large suitcase near the entry. The Contessa's hand was still on the light switch. The Count stood across from her, soggy hat in hand, silent. They stared at each other until the woman handed him the rose-scented note she'd found.

The man opened it part way before bowing his head. *"Cara,"* was all he said.

When the Contessa started to pass him he reached for her hand. For a moment, they stood in silent reflection as one stands at a sign-less fork in the road. I held my breath, praying for a smile of forgiveness to creep across either of their faces. Perhaps the Contessa was right. If only one person changed, miracles could happen.

I couldn't tell if the Count let the Contessa's hand slip from his, or if she pulled it away, but when it happened she moved to the door.

"Shimoni, *vieni qui,*" she called, turning to pass outside into the common hallway.

I ran past Il Conte, who stood in a puddle of stony silence, face contorted in a horror similar to the visage we'd seen in the portico. The man's sorrow tugged at my heart, but just as the Count had said that morning, the woman was my charge. So, I followed the Contessa's heel as the front door closed behind us.

Chapter Six

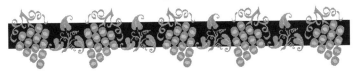

We spent the night at the most expensive hotel in Rome. But neither *Frette* sheets, the morning paper, *cappuccino*, nor *cornetti* for two made my belly feel better. The lump now lay firmly a bit aft of my stomach, which I was sure would never again be satisfied. Food held no appeal. Not even the warm, fresh croissant resting in a fancy blue china bowl by the cavernous marble bath.

Pacing the bedroom, I waited for my Contessa to dress and ready me for a morning walk. Still, I was conflicted, not at all excited at the prospect of greeting the other dogs on the Pincio. Gamboling with them was a worry.

I rallied enough enthusiasm to wipe my tongue across the cheek of my Contessa as she carried me down the grand lobby staircase. Amused by the doorman's jaunty monkey-cap, I managed a weak bark. The man tipped his hat when we passed, but the Contessa did not respond. A night without the Count had not improved her mood. My trembling managed to coax her into keeping me in her arms all the way up the street to the park. There, she placed me gently on the spongy grass just as the faint scent of sweet tobacco came swinging up the hill on the morning breeze.

I turned to see Il Conte peering from behind a street vendor's cart. He did not approach. It was strange behavior, but then, the man had taken a strange turn ever since I stole his treat. No doubt having two women in his life upset his bearings further. The man was going to have to make a choice. La Donna Rosa or La Contessa. Il Conte played enough cards to know when to fold a bad hand.

I wondered if the man had come to meet La Donna Rosa. Or perhaps he wanted to invite the Contessa back to our apartment. It was of little concern. My belly ached. As the Count fell behind a crowd of school children, I turned my cares inward. There was more important business.

I sniffed the inspiration of a fresh trace from an unfamiliar dog. I concentrated. Morning duties were certain to allay my discomfort. I set off across the park, my Contessa keeping careful watch a short distance behind. I lingered over all the stimulating scents that decorated the lawn and brush. When I crossed the Borghese garden and back again, with nothing to report but the success of other dogs, I began to consider my situation serious.

By the time we reached the edge of the Pincio, the Count still skulked in the distance. Unnoticed by the Contessa, he followed just far enough behind to blend into the crowd traversing the park. But I paid little attention. My pain was too great. Occasionally, when I lagged behind, the Contessa called to me in a soothing voice. *"Vieni, caro mio."*

Her loving tone gave me strength and I complied. But, at the top of the path home, before I even reached the comfort of the deep grass to one side, my belly ached in such a way that I was forced to lie prone on the sharp gravel for relief.

Far enough.

This sudden turn of events alarmed my Contessa, but I could go no further. She knelt beside me, laying a warm gloved hand on my side. I gave her a long sideways glance as she cooed to me in the encouraging voice that usually invited me into her lap. I couldn't face it. My eyelids drooped and flickered. I uttered a deep groan as she lifted me into her arms, tucking me beneath her coat. The last thing I remembered was the earthy scent of her perfume and the warmth of her body. A flood of agony carried me away to sleep.

*

When I awoke I was cold and confused and my belly burned. I raised my head to look through the bars of a small cage. One side of my face was numb from sleeping too long on it. My eyes felt sticky and my left lid altogether refused to open. One-eyed, I made out the blurry outline of a strange man in a white coat. The man held a small brown envelope, similar to the type of package that I liked to shred when slipped through the slot in the front door of my apartment. For a moment I thought I was home, awakening from a most unpleasant dream. I raised my nose, wiggled it a bit in the direction of the strange man, hoping for an indication to my milieu. The sterile atmosphere offered no answers.

Get up, I thought. Standing always gave a dog of small stature a better sense of the situation. Groggy, I was halfway to my feet when a sharp pain at my midsection demanded examination. I bent around to inspect my belly. It was bound by a thick white cloth and wide tape like a package of clean laundry. I had no memory of the wrapping. It was tight, and hot, and certainly not meant to promote discovery of any kind. Resigned to immobility, I commenced instead a visual inspection of the surroundings.

My lazy eye slowly came to life in the blaze of the overhead lights. A shiny table stood in the center of the stark white room. I squinted against the glow. Several large mirrors hung on the walls, intensifying the light in the windowless room and scattering among them a hundred men in white coats. Yet, I knew by scent that only one man stood before me, and that man was Il Dottore. I blinked the figure into singular focus. The veterinarian made a soothing sound, opened the cage and slipped his hand inside.

He brushed his warm palm across my head and down my neck, pausing to scratch in the exact place under the chin that gives a dog the most pleasure. I let my weary head rest heavy in the man's hand. A distant muddle of a familiar voice arose from outside the room, punctuated by the creak of a snug hinge. There stood my Contessa, a pair of louvered doors squeaking behind her. I could not contain my tail even though the wagging caused me pain.

"*Poverino*," she crooned. The sound was as comforting as the bell near home.

When she reached inside the cage, I automatically got to my feet despite the distress. Arriving in her arms I felt safe again. The pain no longer mattered. Nothing mattered but that I was with my Contessa.

The man in the white coat turned. *"Questo era la problema."* He passed the small package to the Contessa, placing it into her hand, and she opened its end to pour out its content.

Disbelief covered her face. Her brow wrinkled above widened eyes brimming with tears. They fell onto my head, dripping over my ears, stinging my eyes. I sniffed her soft sweater for the source of her anguish. Nothing but a pleasant smell laced the air, like lilacs in late spring.

Happiness. These tears were welcome.

"No more problems, *carino*," she said to me. "He's still mine."

Somewhere beyond the outer hall, a door slammed. Another squeak announced Il Conte. Dark suit in contrast to the white walls, the man stood tall against the doors.

He looked directly at the Contessa. "I've been to the hotel to find you. The doorman said you'd come here. *Che cos'è successo?"*

The veterinarian answered. "The little fellow had a rather large stone in the form of a diamond ring, *signore*. But I have removed it."

The Contessa addressed the Count in the same gentle tone usually reserved for me when she found me especially smart or charming. *"Mi' amore."* She slipped a ring onto her finger.

A change of heart, I thought. I was flushed as well, fine hairs rising on my snout. The Count reconsidered well. Gifts always help excuse bad behavior. All was right with the world: a dog and his two people reunited, happiness again the word of the day. And I: the agent bringing them together again. My tail wagged.

"My love," the Contessa said again. *"Che sorpresa!"*

The man became a chameleon, drawn and pale, fading so well into the light walls of the room, only his somber garment was left to mark the spot last seen.

A thin voice came from the direction of his suit. *"Si, una gran sorpresa."*

"*Grazie molto, caro.* I never dreamed."

The Contessa, busy admiring her hand, noticed neither the facial protest nor the pallor of the Count, but the change was not lost on me. Something wasn't right. I couldn't quite put my paw on it, but I smelled the man's apprehensive air from clear across the room. I turned my head to bring one ear closer to the couple. It had been so long since there'd been polite exchange between the Contessa and the Count, perhaps the man was stunned.

The Count regained his color and walked straight to us, wrapping his arms around us both. He kissed the Contessa on a cheek and gave a tousle to the wiry hair on my head with two clammy fingers.

"It's so fortunate you found it, *amore,*" the Count said.

My Contessa rested her bejeweled hand on the Count's arm. Light scattered across the ceiling above. I traced the dancing light to an enormous diamond, of lesser consequence than the pastry I'd eaten the morning before, but big enough to cause my indigestion, and the studied attention given me by the Count. My stomach turned at the connections I made in my head. The Mont Blanc had been filled with much more than whipped cream. I looked up into the umber eyes of the Contessa.

Bellisima. The woman was radiant.

"I thought I lost it before having the chance to make it a gift," the Count continued. "The rascal here must have found it and decided to make it a snack."

The Contessa rubbed her hand along the man's shoulder. "It's a lovely gift, but it's the thought I love more."

Il Conte gave a nervous chuckle identical to the one that had accompanied the search through his pockets for La Donna Rosa's ring the night before. The truth in it stung me like an irritated bee.

I was not the rascal. A growl shot my belly with pain, but I didn't care. No change of heart. I nipped at the Count's hand then drew up short. Relieved at the prospect of the woman's happiness, I would save my anger for another time.

There *was* good fortune in the finding of the ring. At best, it would be kept from another woman. At the very least, it restored the Contessa to a better temperament. Perhaps the love in her eyes would lure the man back, returning all to right: my life once again full of pampering. No more missed meals or cold walks to hellish bars in the middle of the night. Most of all: my people happy.

The Contessa's reflection in the mirror was clear, face bright, eyes hopeful. Before the Count lay the opportunity for a new start.

The Contessa wore an impish grin as she ran her hand up the Count's thigh. She poked a single decorated finger in his side and whispered, "Pasta."

The taunt itself was a truce. I examined the Count in the opposite glass, eager to catch a glimpse of redemption. Yet his face was a tortured mix of indifference and anguish—until his eyes met mine and the expression darkened to displeasure. Like those times I'd taken a toy not intended for me: a fine soft leather shoe or piece of silky clothing.

A toy not intended, I thought. The Count looked at the Contessa as though he had forgotten any fun had ever existed between them.

"It was all a mistake. Now you know," he said.

The man tightened his embrace to punctuate the point. Pain stabbed my side and I whimpered. The cry turned the woman's attention to the mirror, where she could see me clearly, and glimpse as well the Count's pained expression. A simple shift in the corner of his mouth, the small flash of a beaded eye and, in it, her mind was changed like the phase of the moon. Her smile faded, face tightening as it had when she first handed the rosy note to Greta's lady in the park. She pulled away from the Count's arms.

A gulf seemed to open up just below her heart.

Her eyes glistened, her voice a murmur. "*Si.* Now, I know."

Chapter Seven

W inter froze both time and my people's humor. Like a monk, I spent the hours in quiet recovery and contemplation. But there was no epiphany in the silence, only worry that life might never be the same.

I dreaded those few times the Contessa left me behind to attend functions that excluded dogs. Each time I feared she would never return, forsaking everything, including me, to be rid of the Count. I yearned for the advance of spring. Warmer days hastened the garden, and tending to greens was the Contessa's passion. Spring demanded we all go to the house in the country. Far away from La Donna Rosa.

Days passed, growing longer each week. Soon I awoke to sunlight instead of darkness. Winter receded. The invitation of an open window first prompted my Contessa to notice change. Barren trees in the courtyard below allowed a hopeful tinge of green. I stood on the pillows atop the bed and we greeted spring together. I demonstrated my improving health by jumping gingerly from a low chair. The Contessa approved. Finally fit for a long walk, she escorted me to the Pincio for my usual rounds.

"*Su, coraggio,*" she said.

Courage, indeed.

I was still bound up like an incomplete package: fresh rag around the belly, ridiculous cone about my neck. Far from a picture of Italian style. My friends at the park approached with care when I appeared in the gardens after the long absence. I didn't blame them. I had glimpsed myself in the Contessa's closet mirror.

Frightening, I thought. I understood their trepidation.

Dead-on I resembled a clown at *carnevale*. A broad collar obscured my body, paws peaking from underneath like mittens attached to the bottom of a child's coat. From a distance I could be mistaken for an obese dog of a wealthy shut-in, a pet bloated on rich cheese, confined to feather pillows. For the first time I was grateful for the mediocrity of canine eyesight. Perhaps most of my acquaintances would pass me by completely. No right-thinking dog dared approach. Certainly the attraction of any female was impossible in my present state.

No chasing today, perhaps never again. I imagined the rest of my life led in embarrassment, without company—in isolation.

The collar was too conical to allow a side view, but I expected I'd taken on a likeness to the fat-handled plunger resting neatly next to the commode. I hoped the collar masked my identity, but I'd had no bath since the incursion to my belly. My scent alone would betray me. It was a fear soon realized.

Raoul was the first to greet me. He was on the Pincio, without fail, early every day. Of boxy build, he had an odd limp of unknown origin that made him look a bit like a Fiat with a flat as he ambled along the path. I suspected Raoul's only ailment to be age. He was an older dog of important means. His master was in government. Elderly now, the old man's walks were limited to evenings. Mistress and master occupied a bench by the lake, and Raoul was permitted to roam. Daytime jaunts found a young page accompanying him to the park. This always precluded the usual romp, for the boy was unnecessarily nervous about letting Raoul off leash. He was convinced the old dog would bolt across the Pincio never to be seen again. So, Raoul and I were confined to the unsatisfactory pleasure of a pause and sniff. Even this simple evaluation was made difficult by the obtrusive cone meant to prevent any modification of the bandage. The old dog knew the meaning of the bandage.

I revered Raoul as a true bel esprit: supremely intellectual, in the way most who are related to government think they are. He handled the situation with discretion, making no direct reference to the costume. He chose rather to imply the appearance of a newly svelte figure since he'd last seen me. He was a consummate diplomat. Just like his people. Even I knew the fat collar made a Rafael angel look lean.

Raoul sniffed the linen, then sniffed me stem and stern. "Accident?"

"Discovery," I said.

I watched my Contessa. She strolled across the path to examine the new shoots of spring flowers pushing up through the dirt. I leaned into Raoul's floppy ear and recited the events leading to the bandage: the bad treat, the ring, the anguish and ill tempers—and La Donna Rosa. Raoul listened, watching a distant female skirt the freshly planted flowerbeds near the pond.

"Another woman," he said. "Ironic. One is usually enough to make a male feel lonesome."

I cocked my head. "The Count, lonely?"

I enjoyed Raoul's sage perspective on the fundamentals of human relationships. The old boy understood volumes about man and dog alike. I listened intently every time he commented on life, paying particular attention to any part regarding females. But, like this one, most concepts were too abstract to grasp. Raoul lifted his leg on a small tuft of long grass and looked in the direction of the pond. The female near the flowers gave a bark. Two more bitches joined her to root beneath the young plants.

"Monogamy can be a lonesome keeper," said Raoul, sniffing the air.

I watched the dogs skirt the park. "Dull."

Variety was life's reward, boredom its penalty. Yet brevity had its merit. I enjoyed my share of short trysts with a variety of females. There was little confusion in relationships of short term. It kept the contradictions of the feminine psyche at bay. It was democratic. It was orderly. The depth and duration implied by monogamy was fertile ground for chaos. Witness human relationships. The Contessa's reticence at the Count's association with another woman was proof.

"But devotion is a comfort, too," Raoul noted.

Perhaps, I thought, but anything depending upon the favor of one female is madness.

The collection of dogs from across the park headed our direction. We both stood tall and alert to welcome them. We all touched noses and danced circles around one another, twining legs and tails until one of the bitches threw an angry snap at me. The cluster moved off in unison to the other side of the pond. The Contessa paused in her admiration of the new flowers, her brow furrowed, her face displeased.

"Shimoni, *vieni qui*," she called.

Raoul gave his snout a long, slow lick as the group disappeared, and the young page moved Raoul down the path.

"Femininity," said Raoul behind him. "A fickle art."

I ran across the path to my Contessa. I pushed my snout into a stand of nearby roses, licking a few tender aphids from the tight buds as Raoul grew smaller in the distance. I sneezed a gnat from my nose, grimaced in pain, and sat down. At the edge of the rose bed, Greta came from behind a hedge. But not alone.

She shared the company of her lady with a self-important male dog of similar pedigree. He hovered close by, yet was visibly disinterested in her, attending to other things along the path instead: tufts of grass lush under the mark of a passing dog, crows crisscrossing the lawn, another bitch across the park. Anything but Greta.

She stood alluringly poised, unwilling to be bothered by the slight. Though rough around the edges, she remained tall and gracile enough to lead the usual procession of scruffy, stray males. They followed at a discreet distance, for her lady tended to carry a long walking stick or large umbrella. It was a cunning tactic. Though the curs of the Pincio may be poorly bred, they were clever about the impact of large objects on those attempting to mingle with landed gentry. None of them seemed concerned to be but a small part of a large crowd pursuing the same goal. Each schemed his rise to the top, hoping to be skimmed like cream into her fancy.

I was disappointed. The presence of another dog in Greta's life prohibited any discussion of indiscretion, no matter who the subject. Jealousy often had deaf ears. The very reference could be taken by the less confident as implication, invitation, or both. And the self-important were always less confident. Arrogance partnered insecurity.

Yet, a feminine point of view was key to understanding both sides. Greta could bring calm and order to my muddled mind. She'd suffered the experience of her woman. When she was close enough, I barked.

"Who's the chap?"

"The father of our future," said Greta. She looked up at her woman with soft eyes. "We sell a batch or two of puppies—buy a Cinquecento, and drive to the country for the summer. Isn't it a glorious idea?" She trotted ahead of her woman, pulling at the leash.

Her words lacked maternal tone. Had she no compassion? Or had the possibility that she might have some attachment to her offspring not yet crossed her mind? What was it about females that made them think they could ignore those who loved them? I watched a flock of ducks above head for the Pincian pond and skate a perfect landing into the glassy water.

When Greta was close enough to notice the bandage beyond the collar I sported, she paused to touch my nose in sympathetic gesture.

"*Poverino,*" she said, nuzzling the linen. "*Che cos'è successo?*"

"Il Conte," I said. "It's worse than we thought."

Greta shot a piercing glance across the path. Her inattentive male strained at the leash as the woman pulled them up close to greet the Contessa. Only then did he turn his attention to Greta. Nuzzling her jowl, he continued down her flank, rubbing his nose along her back until it rested just beneath her tail. The move left Greta unimpressed. She whirled around to meet him, teeth bared, a deep, prohibiting growl falling from her twisted snout. Greta's lady released both dogs and the male wandered off in the direction of another female across the way.

The woman kissed the Contessa's cheeks. She watched, eyes growing round like coins in the Trevi fountain, as the Contessa pulled a glove from one hand to reveal the huge diamond.

"*Mamma mia,*" the woman said, pulling at the fingers of the Contessa with one hand and clasping the other to her mouth. "Not for you? Are you sure?"

"*Certo,*" the Contessa said. "I saw his face. It was not that of a man bearing gifts."

Greta straightened and cocked her head to one side. She looked to the sky as though she were trying to focus on something beyond the clouds.

"Males," Greta snarled. "Always looking. And when they find it: trouble."

Greta shot me an irritated glance. She watched her male sniff the south end of a northbound bitch walking through the park.

I looked at Greta's male. "Just checking the nametag."

"Your Count is doing more than that," said Greta.

It was true, I thought. Il Conte was beyond superficial discovery. But what drew him to that no-man's land? Mannered and refined, the Contessa was a much more genteel mate than La Donna Rosa, whose exotic looks did little to disguise her brash behavior. I examined the Contessa's full lips and arched brows, dark eyes full of conviction.

"I don't get it," I said.

"Your Count does," replied Greta. "*Sesso.*"

Greta wasn't making sense. With humans, love equaled marriage, which, in turn, equaled sex—I'd seen it myself. Plenty of times I'd lost my balance on the blankets as a consequence of zealous affection between the Count and Contessa. Granted, some time had passed since the last ditch to the bedroom floor, but the potential was always there. I made a point to sleep in the center of the bed because of it, even though the issue seemed as dormant as the people sleeping next to me. Surely the Count could have his fun at home. After all, there were all those times behind closed doors. I thought hard about the last time I'd known of such antics.

In the beginning, the bedroom door stayed closed for hours. I spent the nights in the hallway, pushed up against the radiator for warmth, listening to low whispers and laughter. Love seemed a leisure then. But the trysts grew shorter over the years and the talk more concise. More like an appointment with the vet, I thought. Until one day, the door no longer closed at all. The two would crawl into bed without so much as a twine or kiss. Any bouncing was brief.

"Something's missing," I said. "He doesn't touch her much anymore."

"Does she touch him?" Greta sniffed my way. " Can't get it at home—then roam."

"All this, about sex?"

Greta cast her male a disapproving look as he vanished behind a hedge with yet another female. Greta knew the simple rule of canine partnership: the name of the game was procreation; the advancement of the species. Frivolous sex was not a preoccupation among dogs. I never thought to consider it a human behavior. The prospect made my head swim. Greta's insight was all well and good but it didn't define the core of the problem: the famine of affection at home. I shook myself, trying to clear my thoughts. Too much knowledge sometimes obscured the truth, like so many clouds blocking the sun. The Contessa's glove dropped to the gravel. I gave it a push with my nose as she retrieved it.

Greta's woman leaned forward. "He knows you know?"

"About the woman, yes." The Contessa slipped the glove back on her jeweled hand. "About the ring, I think no. Anyway, I have it now. He will have to spend his fortune on another if he intends to please her."

I measured the two women before me, one resolute and regal, the other pale and demure. Greta's lady once cut the same fine figure as the Contessa, but like Greta, she now suffered the casualty of indifference. I looked up at the Contessa, blinking her into focus. That she should share the same fate was inconceivable. I began to pant. Yet, neither the Count nor the Contessa seemed indifferent. If they were, they would simply go their separate ways. Inattention was the culprit, I thought, a certain lack of situational awareness. The only one paying attention was me, and I could see where it all began.

*

The Count and I had gone for a haircut. Bits of hair clippings fell like tiny feathers around the Count and I made a game of catching a single wisp on my tongue as he tilted back in the chair. When the barber was finished, he gave me a firm rub with a damp towel, fluffing my whiskers with a blast of hot air, and we were off.

The clean shaven, freshly clipped Count and I moved on to our next destination. Up the narrow stairs above a vegetable shop we stepped into a long, musty room with wooden floors and full-length mirrors. The Count tied me to a bar halfway up the mirror, music would play, and a woman appeared. This continued twice a week for two months. The Count tossed me a worried look from time to time as he moved across the floor. I'm sure he believed I thought him straying, but I knew better. I smelled no warmth between him and the dancer; heard no laughter. It was all business.

The Contessa loved to dance but the Count would have little of it.

"I have the feet of a nobleman," he said. "Both left."

The Contessa teased him ruthlessly whenever they danced. I suspected that last time they'd done so had been a decisive moment for the Count. At the country home of a friend, a handsome young man had cut in with the Contessa. They were such flawless partners, the small crowd stood still, watching. Afterward, the Contessa made no remark, but I could tell by the set of his jaw that the Count had paid attention. He decided to surprise the Contessa with his newfound feet. The clandestine lessons began.

The Count had put much optimism into his new abilities. He arrived home one night, eyes eager, poured two glasses of wine and turned on the music. But the Contessa had been on a mission of her own.

I had accompanied her that morning to a place that gave a special fluffing to her hair and eyelashes. The color was changed ever so slightly, and the lashes lengthened just enough to lure. She was stunning and eager to show the Count the new improvements.

When she entered the room that night he took her into his arms and the dance began. I sat on the sofa anticipating another night on the outside of a bedroom door. They both waited for validation. Yet, any dog could see they were both too wrapped up in themselves to notice the change before them. I slept on the bed that night.

*

Caring what someone thinks is no substitute for simply caring, I thought.

Greta gave my face a lick. The warm breath in my ear made the coarse hair along the peak of my back stand on end. Duty bound, her male responded to my instinctive but harmless reaction and we met nose to nose. I made the first move, turning to note the stranger's name, always displayed on the opposite end. The dog was completely unsympathetic. He lowered his head and set his jaw. Swinging around behind me, his posture of impolite familiarity betrayed him as more lupine than canine. I snapped a perfunctory warning.

At this, the Contessa lifted me into her arms to prevent a small dog from taking a sizeable challenge. I whined an objection as Greta and her beau fell in line together and trotted away. A legion of hopeful mutts brought up the distant rear and they all retreated behind a clump of early poppies.

I could have tackled the boorish male. Stature was no match for dazzling wit. Greta's male was a clear example of inbreeding: brains, the first to go. Assuming I ascribed anything other than casual friendship to Greta was folly. She was, after all, much too tall to ever consider any maneuver more serious than an affectionate touch of the nose. I sneezed in disbelief and swiped my nose across the petal-soft leather of the Contessa's expensive gloves. The threat of destitution weakened me more than the brief activity. I was glad to have the relief of a ride as we made our way home.

At via Ripetta, on the corner across from our apartment, we paused for a break in the traffic. A tall, well-dressed man approached in a waft of cloves and tobacco. He stood close to the Contessa, the arm of his leather jacket grazing the cashmere sleeve of the woman's sweater, as he gave me a dark-eyed wink.

The man raised his eyebrows and smiled. *"Ciao."*

"Buon giorno, Signore." The Contessa, as any Roman woman would do, looked straight into the eyes of her suitor, a gentle flush betraying her pleasure at the attention.

When the traffic cleared enough for passage, the stranger took the Contessa gently by the arm, guiding her to the safety of the opposite sidewalk.

"Grazie," said the Contessa.

I gazed up at the woman, raising one ear to her voice. It was strong and measured. She might as well have said, "I am worth a look, aren't I?"

The man tipped his hand to a dimple at the corner of his mouth and nodded. *"Grazie lei, bella."*

Blush in full bloom, the Contessa was in the middle of a shy smile when the Count turned the corner in front of her. He stopped short, dropping his head to look over the top of his sunglasses. Shoulders set, he stepped between the stranger and the Contessa. He took her arm where the man left off and started her up the street.

"*Chi e?*" the Count said.

The Contessa looked directly at the Count, her words soft-spoken and her eyes wide and dewy. "Someone who noticed me."

"I'm sure." The Count looked in the direction of the stranger, not at the Contessa.

"*Ma, caro,*" she said, "*niente—*" Sentence unfinished, she examined Il Conte as though he were as strange as the man who made her face color. A sly grin crept across her mouth as in discovery of something long forgotten.

Her word was audible to only me. "*Geloso.*"

Chapter Eight

Gliding through the front door of the apartment and into the kitchen, the Contessa set me onto the floor in front of my breakfast. I gave it a reticent sniff. It was fortified with a bitter dusting of medicine. I was bored with the sentence of bland food and daily medication. Weeks had passed without a decent meal. I was ready for a change.

The Count retreated to the den. The Contessa disappeared into the bedroom, closing the door behind her.

I discreetly blew a bit of the offensive powder off the top of my meal and ate. I tried to hold my breath, dulling the disagreeable flavor, but the medicinal taste lingered in my mouth like sour cheese. Though I was not yet fit for more than two or three outings a day, water was the only cure. I drank the bowl dry, licking even the drops I'd splashed across the adjacent floor. It would facilitate another trip outside before noon, but a rinse was crucial to the relief of my taste buds. The Contessa entered the kitchen with her coat on again, purse in hand. She refilled the water bowl and then headed for the front door. She called from the doorway. "*Ciao.* I have things to do. Shimoni's yours."

"*Allora,* but soon I must go out myself." The Count rumpled his paper and looked down at me with soft words. "I can be just as unavailable."

"He's had a good drink of water, so take him with you. But no strange food. He's still quite *delicato.*" The door closed behind her before the Count had time to quarrel.

Delicate, indeed. Nothing a good piece of beefsteak wouldn't fortify, I thought. Palate cleansed, I retired to the comfort of a low sofa to ponder my fate. My brain was a whirl of thoughts, all funneling down the same drain of destitution. I looked around the apartment, taking inventory of each fringe benefit in my privileged life.

From the center salon, I saw every adjacent room, a plush pillow just for me in each corner, coupled with the appropriate marks that make an apartment one's own. A bit of wooden wall detail chewed here near the breakfast bowl; the edge of an Aubusson gnawed there; tell-tale scratches worn on the more traveled path from the bedroom to *la cucina.* The picture grew dim under the droop of my eyelids. I was on the edge of sleep when the phone rang.

"*Si, cara,* soon," the man said. "But I'll have the dog with me, and two dogs will be too many."

Anytime we're together there are two dogs, I thought.

Il Conte placed the phone on its cradle and shook his head. He let his hand rest there a moment and looked at me. "What?"

I studied the photographs on the wall in the hallway. The gallery was a museum to the marriage. Glimpses of the couple's high points confirmed the fun they once shared. My favorite was in a large frame near the center.

*

An icy spring wind had been blowing a gale the day the photograph was taken. I was tucked into my favorite blue sweater. The three of us walked the long way from Piazza del Popolo across the river to the Vaticano. The Contessa squirreled me away into the bulk of her mink and we entered the cathedral. She had no idea what Il Conte was up to. It was all his idea: a photo of the family with the bronze of St. Peter. Since dogs were forbidden in the sanctuary, the documentation would be twice as amusing. Il Conte had a wicked sense of humor in the early days. Fortified by the Contessa's amusement, he made fun of everything and everything was fun.

He asked some hapless tourist to take the picture. Just as the camera clicked, the Count threw open the Contessa's coat and there we were, at the foot of St. Peter, Il Conte's hand on the saint's foot, begging permission to be granted into heaven. It was a keen joke. The Count suspected dogs need not apply to heaven for they live it out on earth. At the time I had to agree.

But the Contessa was not amused this time. She took her saints seriously. Smuggling a dog into the basilica was as far as she wanted to go. Photographic evidence of the blasphemy was another thing. She stormed out of the cathedral in a fury that matched the rising spring storm.

It was the first time I'd seen them argue. They didn't always agree but one could see the confidence they had in each other. Accepting a tease is nothing more than trust, no? Yet, he had made fun of her devotion and in doing so he seemed less dependable in her estimation after that.

She began to laugh less at his jokes. He began to joke less.

*

A simple act, I thought, and a view is changed.

The Count followed my gaze to the wall then walked in review down the line of memories. By the end of the exhibit, each frame held a single subject as though the Count and Contessa lived separate lives.

The Count pointed to the last picture of the Contessa. "You see? No space for me, even here."

He picked me up, ruffling the hair around my neck, making the tags on my collar jingle. "She only has arms for you, my friend, but she still has hold of my heart."

Raoul had said it. The Count was lonely in the worst way: in the company of love unrequited. I knew what it was like to be ignored. The Count might be absent in the photo but affection was the missing piece. It was as though it had been lost under the refuse of misunderstandings and mistakes. Life had taken on weight and the gain wasn't funny.

It was a difficult issue for me to understand. No dog takes himself seriously. If we did, let's face it, there would be no more rolling around in anything disgusting and we'd never tolerate wearing costumes. Begging? Forget it.

But I knew very well that there was a spark left between them. I needed only to kindle it. The issue was how.

The water in my belly suggested that it was time for a walk. I trotted to the apartment door. Perhaps a little relief helped the thought process. The suggestion of a wrinkled brow and restless glance aimed at the Count sent us on our way. The man was gentle with me as he fixed my leash. He even carried me down the winding stairs and into the street before setting me down onto the cobblestones. I gave the street a hasty review and proceeded to inspect a row of parked cars opposite my building. I looked for the appropriate tire, one with as many other marks as possible, for relief. Then I set about chronicling the odors, savoring each one, discerning them as critically as a wine master.

Fascinating.

The rubber read like a roster, names of passing dogs splashed across the treads like so many signatures on a page. I added to the entries, with careful attention to reserve a bit of shorthand for later. Partway down the right side of the street a familiar door stood open. The roaster. A pungent odor wafted out into the warming midday air.

Porchetta.

The succulent aroma of fattened pork roasting in the open wood oven seized my attention. My eyes grew heavy, deferring their focus to scent. I led the Count across the quiet side street and sat directly in the doorway of the roasters adjacent a butcher shop. As I lifted my nose in the direction of the glistening meat, my eyes met those of Guiliano, the butcher. An avuncular man, his red cheeks glowed from the heat of the open oven and sweat beaded his brow. He beamed a broad toothy smile at me.

"*Ciao, Shimoncello,*" he bellowed. "*Tutto bene?*"

Yes. Oh, yes. I wagged a greeting.

All was quite well. I loved Giuliano's lyrical pet name for me. It recalled images of Capri and the memory of the sweet, icy *limoncello* my Contessa favored in the summer. I liked my real name as well, though being of Swahili origin made the explanation difficult at times. It was the only word I heard from the Kenyan housekeeper my Contessa employed, the first day my eyes opened. The woman was tall, with shiny dark skin and a deep raspy voice. She laughed and pointed the first time she saw me.

"Shimoni," she exclaimed, stark eyes dancing.

Swahili meaning: down the hole.

Indeed, I was a dog who enjoyed a good root down a dark hole. Going to ground was especially fun when small, furry things were involved. But at the point of christening I had no idea what a hole was. Nevertheless, the name stuck and I was proud of its meaning. I became a master of holes. It was who and what I was. And, ending in a vowel, it easily passed as Italian.

Shimoni, Shimoncello. Either would do.

Nothing mattered. Not even the cone around my neck. After all, everything is fine when there is the possibility of *porchetta*. And the odds of reward increased as the butcher approached the revolving roast and the Count's attention turned to dialing a pay phone on a nearby pedestal. Before the Count interfered, Guiliano sliced a perfect sliver of pork to toss in my direction.

Without thinking, for the solution to anything that takes flight can only be lightning reflex, I sprang up to meet the offering. In midair my acute hearing discerned the piercing voice of La Donna Rosa on the other end of the phone.

"Ciao, bello."

At the same time the Count, determined to deny a forbidden food, thrust his free hand into the equation only to meet the able jaws of a hungry dog. Thus, a stream of foul language from Il Conte returned the woman's happy greeting. Tirade complete, the man's voice lowered into the dulcet tone of supplication as the woman on the phone blistered him for swearing so.

"No, no, mi' amore. It was Shimoni. I was cursing the dog. *Mi dispiace, mi scusa. Prego, cara mia, prego.*"

I gulped the stray piece of pork fallen from the Count's bitten fingers and licked my snout as the Count continued his apology.

Admirable. The man was an able beggar. Even a dog knew that the degree of groveling was always in direct proportion to the possibility of reward.

Can't pick a new partner, I thought, when there's already one in hand.

Guiliano roared behind us, a deep laugh at the crisis turned to calm. The Count hung up the phone. As we turned to walk toward the Tiber, the Count cast an evil eye in my direction.

"*Cretino. Gentaccia.*" Cretin. Filth. The Count sputtered a string of canine slurs as he sucked his injured fingers.

I trudged along under the epithets. I didn't blame the man, really. One of my teeth ached from hitting what could only have been bone in the Count's finger. But no blood was drawn. How bad could it be?

We trudged past the Piazza Augusto Imperatore and its weedy monument to that lonely ruler, along the via della Scrofa with its thread of sweet-smelling delicatessen and wine shops, to the cafes of Piazza Sant'Eustachio, near the open market of Campo di Fiore, and to the river beyond. Crossing over the river at the ancient Ponte Sisto, we moved along with a slew of grubby drifters lining the bridge.

As we skirted the chain rail on the other side, the Count accidentally scraped his fingers against the links. His voice boomed. "*Cinghiale miseria.*"

Boar misery. It was a crowning blow. There was nothing, nothing, lower than being likened to the kind of misery inflicted by a wild pig. Whether it be rutting up the garden or giving a nasty chase through the thicket, any connection with, or likeness to, a stinking, repulsive boar was the worst form of insult. I let my tail droop and my head fall until the cone round my neck grazed the cobbled street. It was as though the man blamed me for everything. I was very tired.

Exhausted, in fact. Certainly not ready for normal activities to resume. As the truculent Count pulled me along the buzzing Lungotevere, I lost all interest in covering any outstanding marks, enjoying any of Rome's heady scents, or seeing any familiar faces. Even the taste of *porchetta* faded into the blue fumes that followed the buses.

We walked deep into bohemian Trastevere, the elder neighborhood of Rome. With its narrow winding streets, small *trattoria* and artisan shops, it was as close to a village as one could get and still remain in the city. Not a place that kept the like of landed gentry. Just when I was sure things could be no worse, the Count came to a stop in front of a tall iron gate. Intricate and edged in luminescent paint, it was the kind of gate that indicated wealth and fine cheese. Contrary to its surroundings. Behind it twined a lovely courtyard of budding vines and winter pansies.

And cats.

The Count pressed a button mounted on the wall flanking the gate. A buzzer rang somewhere above us in the ornate apartment building that stood behind the gates. A soft voice followed from a space near the button.

La Donna Rosa.

Background music on the speaker matched that of the Puccini floating down from an open window. The gate clicked admission and we walked into the courtyard. The cats scattered, disappearing through metal grates in the marble.

I suspected the whole building was feline-infested.

We crossed the courtyard and climbed the broad steps to the second floor. The door was open a sliver, delivering the familiar fragrance of roses. It swung away to reveal La Donna Rosa, fully naked, arms outstretched into the music of a full-length opera, standing at the foot of an unmade bed. Her bronze skin shone against white sheets. Her breasts swayed like giant *gnocchi* making even me swoon. The Count was well past that stage. He dropped the leash without unhooking it from my collar, pushed the door closed and moved like a locomotive toward La Donna Rosa.

Turandot, Tosca…

In the blink of an eye, the man's clothes were on the floor.

Madame Butterfly.

The man and woman wound themselves together like a ball of angry cats, voices hissing and limbs darting without caution.

Addio, fiorita asil wafted down around my ears. Farewell, flowery refuge…

Addio a te. Farewell to you, too, I thought.

I gave a great yawn in embarrassment, but couldn't look away. It was as though I'd stumbled upon an infatuating scent that sickened me. Though pleasant on a primal level, it turned my stomach.

And then it was over.

Even though it had been a while, I had seen my Contessa and the Count tumble the bed before. In the end, the air was happy and warm with emotion; they'd talk and giggle, always in each other's arms. I waited to be called, as I was always called at home, but the invitation never came.

The man rolled to the side of the bed, well away from La Donna Rosa. He exhaled a long, languid breath. *"Mamma mia."*

I sniffed the air. It was cool and empty as a shallow grave.

"Si, caro." The woman crawled to him and opened her mouth as if to eat him. She clenched his chin between her teeth, and growled. "I'm yours."

I barked at the threat.

"Silenzio," chided the Count.

The woman turned to look at me. She laughed a high, stinging pitch. *"Scherzo.* He looks like the Joker in a deck of cards."

The Count glanced between the two, then raised an eyebrow. "The cone is only temporary, to keep him from chewing his bandage. He's still *delicato*."

I narrowed my eyes in disgust. My condition was obvious to anyone with half a brain. The woman was *so* common. How rude. Not noble in the least. It was never polite to point out a disability.

"I thought you liked dogs," said the Count.

"I like *big* dogs. If I wanted something small, I'd get a cat." La Donna Rosa spit a burst of air from her lips. "Take him away," she said, "unless—you *need* an audience."

The Count worked the side of his lip with his teeth, looking at La Donna Rosa from the corner of his eye. "I can't just leave him outside to roam."

"Then tie him to the fountain below," she said, raising her nose in dismissal. "*I* don't need another pair of eyes."

With that the Count pulled on his pants and undershirt. He escorted me downstairs and attached the end of the leash to a ring at the base of the fountain in the middle of the courtyard.

"Sorry, *ragazzo*," said the Count. "I'm not much for company today. You'll be better off down here." He scratched me beneath the chin before disappearing up the creamy marble stairs toward the sultry music still hanging in the air.

Disgusting. The man left me tied, unattended in an unfamiliar courtyard, without water to boot. True, I was proximate to a fountain, and its trickling stream fell into a pleasant gurgle, but its relief was well out of reach to a dog of short stature.

Perhaps sleep would cleanse the sickening vision. It was perfect napping weather as far as I was concerned—except for Puccini in the background. The high notes hurt my ears and the base tones annoyed the sensibilities. Now it would forever remind me of this moment. I much preferred the rhythm of Elvis. "Hound Dog," to be exact.

That's culture. Upbeat and uncontained. I yearned for the civility of happier times set to the music of *Santo* Elvis.

Life was lively swing, not measured scale. Thank goodness my Contessa enjoyed the same or existence would be misery indeed. I curled into as inconsequential a mass as the cone collar allowed and fell into sleep as soprano notes sailed high above me.

Chapter Nine

I batted the sleep away with a paw to one eye. My heart drummed in my ears. All but one vivid portion of a dream retreated as I opened my eyes: an indelicate inspection of my ear by some extraordinary beast.

I shook my head twice and raised a foot to swipe relief, as well. There, from the corner of my eye, they appeared. Three large figures peered down from the fountain's edge, ears pinned, spines arched. A clump of cats, gross in every sense of the word: fat, ugly and, as the first offensive unkempt scent drifted past my snout, filthy.

Something rotten. I sneezed once to punctuate the opinion.

One of the creatures growled.

Roman cats were odious. Good for nothing but the favors from troops of *gattare* who acted as benefic patrons: leagues of elderly women caring for strays as their civic service. My old friend Raoul believed Rome's feral cats outnumbered its citizens. They certainly outnumbered its dogs. An intolerable inequity. Neither a soother of man's soul nor redeemer of man's grace, a cat was life's perpetual guest.

Takers, not givers.

Felines plunged from favor with Egypt's fall and dogs rose with Rome, as the she-wolf raised Romulus and Remus. No cat ever sat beneath the table of a fine restaurant on the via Veneto, nor inside a fancy via Condotti store. Man's reverence of dog confirmed canine superiority. After all, would dog be held so close a confederate if he were daffish?

No. The truth was always simple.

A second cat joined the chorus of low growling. I straightened my back and scanned the lineup of infidels. Though most cats described themselves as cerebral, I found them reactive rather than thoughtful. Cramped by contempt, their minds had little room left for logic. Otherwise, they would have lifted themselves out of squalor long ago. I sniffed. Superfluous, like gypsies, fleas—and La Donna Rosa: nonessential and inconvenient.

As soon as I made eye contact with the largest of the three marauders, it joined the chorus in harmonious warning. The sound reverberated around the inside of the cone about my head, tingling the fine hair in my ears like the buzz of a bee at the center of an open bloom.

I used restraint when it came to barking. My Contessa chided me as a pup for disturbing the peace, such as it was, of the Roman streets. I learned instead to express opinion using various body language. A raised profile, a sideways glance, an ear pinned, lip curled to bare a tooth: that was the way of a noble dog. Yet, it occurred to me that the creature in my dream might very well have been one of the three impudent felines poking their business into my ear. A daring advance given the proximity of my collar.

Invasion. The only rebuttal: indignant, pervasive barking.

To my misfortune, the small-minded cats took the display to be a comment on their general character rather than the warning for which it was meant. In truth, it was a bit of both. In one coordinated leap, all three attacked, clawing and biting their revenge across my already injured form. The clatter was deafening.

My first reaction was to fight. For an instant I was at the top of the oscillating heap, but the cone about my neck proved a hindrance. The cats used it as a shield, throwing claws and swipes in safety. I tried to leave the cone behind in a dizzying display of circular maneuvers, but I was outnumbered, outweighed, and cats had no principles when it came to a fight. I turned to run; an effective retreat only as long as the length of my leash, which was still attached to the base of the fountain.

Against the severe walls of the Roman architecture, the effect of the sharp bark and squeal of a dog in distress was immediate. The space shuddered like the bells of St. Peter's on Easter day. Before long, windows flew open, revealing faces of angry and anxious people alike; all witness to the assault in the courtyard below.

The cats were relentless. They had resolved to etch their frustration with countless generations of arrogant mutts on the hide of one hapless canine. Just when I was certain to be remembered as Santo Shimoni, martyr for all cat-hating dogs, the Count appeared. The man descended the stairs shirtless, pants zipped yet belt undone. A towel flapped around his neck as he banged a large saucepan along the banister. He dipped the pan into the fountain and doused us all with water. The feline thugs dispersed.

I huddled, a wet mass on the cold, hard stone at the base of the fountain. I looked up at the Count, so happy to see him my lip curled with pleasure.

The man stooped to rub a hand over my eyes, pausing at a deep scratch on my nose. "You're a Joker, all right."

A call came from above. *"Che succede?"*

La Donna Rosa appeared, shoulders bare behind an open window. She leaned out just far enough to reveal the deep cleavage of her breasts as they pushed up against the sill.

What happened, indeed.

There was no question in any of the minds behind the interested faces now turned. Soon it would be the talk of the town. Rome was a small place. The fine family linens were airing and they were smutty to be sure. Squeezed between dishonor at the paws of feline thugs and the Count's disgrace, I began to hiccup.

As often happens when circumstances become intolerable, asylum is found in instinct. I regarded the Count, who now sat on the steps of the fountain. The man presented a certain angle to his leg, reminding me the value of a good hump in abating loneliness. With guarded optimism, I moved to mount the man's knee and began to concentrate.

"Esattamente, Shimoni," the Count said. "Get it where you can."

Il Conte gave me a pat, shook off the misguided affection before it granted any solace, and untied the leash.

We ascended the stairs, towel around the Count's shoulders, saucepan dripping a trail of water behind him. My bandage, in tatters, now rode loosely about me, rubbing my back legs raw at each thigh. I sneezed the blood from my nose. It flew in droplets, lining the inside of my collar like a work of modern art.

La Donna Rosa stood at the door of the apartment, shirt clasped to her bare breast. "Ah, his bandages have been chewed *for* him," she sneered.

"*Gatti*," said the Count.

"What kind of dog takes a beating from a cat?"

I took a few steps into the room. *That's cats,* I wanted to say. Plural. The woman apparently had only one skill. Listening wasn't it. No one compared *me* in disfavor to a feline. I eyed the suede furniture. A few steps more and I began to raise my leg on the corner of the sofa. It was a move not used in years.

The Count yelled, "Shimoni!"

Before the affront was complete, the man jerked me away. I slid across the slippery floor to his side and sat down. I glowered at La Donna Rosa, who returned the expression. Disgusted, I broke off the stare and examined the room in a way my first riveting visit had not permitted.

The flat was simple and clean, but stark. Neither carpet, nor photographs, only a single white sofa, a broad, low metal table with a tall vase and single rose, and a bed of tangled covers in the glimpse of a room beyond. I sniffed the air through my bloody nose. Beyond a few stray hairs strewn across the wooden floor, there was no trace of the dog that accompanied her to the bar that night.

"He's ruined. I'll fetch more wrappings and change the bandage," said the Count. "He needs to be cleaned up, or there will be hell to pay."

I lay down on the bare floor, contemplating the excuses to be paid out in order to explain my injuries to the Contessa. Blood oozed from a front paw that had been caught between a pair of fangs. I considered licking it clean before the impact it might have on the Contessa dawned on me. The injury ensured a host of uncomfortable questions for Il Conte.

Tied to a fountain? Attacked by cats? The why and the how of it all would make for good listening.

I sat up and placed weight on the ailing foot. Blood dripped onto the floor. It was time for reckoning.

The man pushed the shirt into his pants and found both shoes. He smoothed the black hair from his brow with a couple swipes of a hand.

He gave a short tug to my tail. "I'll be back."

"*Presto*," whined La Donna Rosa. "I'm not a dog-sitter."

She exchanged another cool glance with me as the man closed the door behind him. Her grudge was as glaring as her stare.

"*Idioto*. Can't defend yourself from a little competition?" She buttoned up her shirtfront and pulled the wisp of a skirt over her narrow hips.

I held my ground.

"You are as stupid as she," said La Donna Rosa.

There's wisdom in cheating? Stealing another woman's husband indicated craft, not intelligence.

"She has everything," she said, fingering a small diamond drop at her neck, "but not her man."

I sat down. Neither do you, I thought. The tie between them was want, not care. Even a small dog knew the difference.

La Donna Rosa pulled a lipstick across her mouth and fluffed her hair in front of a large mirror on the wall. She examined her reflection, then wiped the corners of her mouth as one might do following a feast. Our eyes met again in the mirror. "I won't be young forever," she said. "With age, the only things a smart woman needs are better shoes and bigger jewelry. I'm working on the latter, first."

Her voice purred. "I'll have it, even if I have to get it myself. Once it's mine, she can have him back." The woman turned to me, bending closer to my face. "If you weren't so greedy, it would be on my finger now."

Justice awaits every thief, I thought. La Donna Rosa had no interest in Il Conte, only in the trappings. I remembered the words of the Contessa: "It's the thought of it I love more." After all, real love has no proof, nor needs any.

I snarled in defense of my Contessa. La Donna Rosa shrieked in return. Grabbing a large book from a corner table, she heaved it my way. It fell smack beside me on the floor. I yelped and scrambled for cover behind the couch. Trapped. I peeked around the sofa. La Donna Rosa puffed a spray of rose water at her neck. Her dark eyes radiant, she glowed under the flush of anger. More blood trickled over my jowl. It dropped with a plop onto the cone collar. I resisted the urge to lick it clean, making every effort to appear in tatters for the Contessa, but perhaps there was little reason to try.

The Contessa and I had spent a whole night in a hotel, yet the Count was not swayed. He was dazzled. La Donna Rosa still held her spot as chief ally. I watched her bare feet, red nails, pad across the floor. The man would follow them right out of the picture. Soon he'd be packing the warm wool rugs, the comfy oriental divan, perhaps even my favorite feather cushion. I saw it all: the Contessa falling from favor to depression; I, living the unstable life of a refugee, dodging the effects of the woman's ire and neglect. And the Count, picked clean, left alone. I licked the drool from my snout. No winners. We all stood at a crossroad.

The tip of my feet peeked from beneath the cone. My well-manicured toenails quivered. The fortunate life was over. Hopeless, I laid my head across my paws to await the man's return. But the squeak of the door called my attention. I inched over the cold floor to the edge of the sofa. Leaning into the leather, I tilted my collar to one side to peek an eye out around the furniture. There, in the entryway, stood the Cleopatra.

And the gypsy woman from the park.

Chapter Ten

I set my sight on the open door, closed my eyes, and ran. Cleopatra met me head on at the threshold. Her scent was captivating. Like the temptation of warm bread. I gave her belly a cursory sniff, hesitating while reason argued for a swift departure. There was no cause to linger. The bitch had grown no shorter since last seen.

She sputtered a long, deep growl as I nosed her brisket. I scooted between her legs as she reached down to nip my tail, and the spell was broken. I shook her off before she took firm hold. At the top of the stairs I looked back. A bit of my fur trailed from the corner of her shiny black mouth, and there beside her stood Greta's woman, leash in hand, wide-eyed, mouth agape. She stared as though I were a wild animal escaped from the zoo.

The gypsy was gone.

My impulse was to ferret out the gypsy, discover her connection to La Donna Rosa, but the desire to give ground to the situation trumped the instinct. Discovery had to wait.

Greta's woman called out. "Shimoni."

It was more a cry of surprise than a plea. It didn't slow me. Even under the pain of my wounded paw. I descended the long stairs in exactly three leaps—a record for the distance. I crossed the courtyard to the iron gate. Barrier to freedom, it stood locked. I put my paws on the bottom rail and pushed my nose through the long bars. They were too narrow to offer freedom, and too robust to allow chewing. From behind came a cold nose. I jumped with a start. Greta. She raised an eyebrow and sniffed the raw tip of my tail.

"So, you've met," she said. Greta tossed a cool glance in the direction of the Cleopatra, who strained at the leash, now in the possession of La Donna Rosa. Her own leash trailed behind her, clicking against the marble tiles as she met me.

I watched her woman descend the stairs. At the halfway mark, a bell chimed and the gate buzzed a welcome. With that the Count opened the prison door. I darted through his legs. Greta followed. Dodging cars and people, we ran across the Ponte Sisto. Motorini flew like bees across the busy streets and the aroma of *pizza* and *panini* beckoned as we fled. But there was no time for delay. Our tongues whipped in the wind as we raced straight down the long via Giulia to where it met the river again before turning up via Ripetta towards home.

The doors of my apartment were closed tight. We sat down to collect ourselves, panting great spools of saliva as we waited.

"You're a mess," said Greta. She leaned over to sniff my trailing bandages.

"I hope so," I said.

"Why?"

"The fur will really fly when my Contessa sees me. The Count will have to shape up." I scraped my sore nose across the sidewalk to freshen the wound.

"Or be out of the picture in no time," Greta replied. "Are you crazy? The last thing you want is to push him out of the house with his bags packed." She walked to my side and licked the blood from my face. "Remember, *the man took his toys with him.*"

I shook my head to clear a drop of blood from my chin. I wondered if Greta ever had a single thought that originated outside a bank account. Yet, in a way she was right. With them separated there would be less chance of getting them back together. I let her clean me up, leaning into her shoulder as she worked on my paw. The faint hint of roses clung to the hair about her neck.

The Cleopatra.

"Why were you there?"

"I live there," Greta said. "The bitch and I walk together twice a week, when her woman entertains a friend. And you?"

"That's no friend. That's Il Conte."

"So, *that's* your competition," she said. She shook her fur and licked the blood from her snout.

"Does your woman know?"

"I've never even smelled him before today, except on your Contessa's clothes. We've never seen him." Greta's nose twitched as a late afternoon breeze carried the scent of roasting pork from the corner roaster.

I looked up at Greta. "Well, we've *all* seen him now."

"Just another in a long line," Greta said. "That woman has a new one every season or so. She keeps them until they give her something expensive, then moves on. Wait it out. Won't last." Greta looked up the street in the direction of the butcher.

"Long enough for the marriage to fail. Then what?"

Greta looked to the exact spot where the pork was turning on its spit. Her tone was irritated. "Divide things up and join the club," she said. She turned and looked me up and down. Her lip curled on one side, as though she found the whole thing amusing.

"Fine, for you," I said. "You're already a member." I sniffed. Her sardonic wit was unbecoming.

A flea-bitten stray crossed the street ahead of us, foraging the stones for scraps, swiping at a loose ear with a hind paw. I scratched at the tall doors.

"Bad things happen to good dogs," Greta said.

"Not if I can help it." I looked at the shutters above and barked.

"Then you'd better get out of Rome—away from that witch. Right now you're living in a house of cards."

Witch, I thought. The gypsy woman. I stopped barking. "Who was that old woman at the door?"

"What woman?" Greta scratched an ear and sat down.

87

"The gypsy hag. She was there with the Cleopatra when you all appeared."

"Didn't see her," Greta said.

"She's been dogging me," I said. "Every time I get that bottomless feeling in the pit of my belly, there she is."

"You mean every time you see her you get that feeling," said Greta.

I tried to make sense of the difference.

A screech rose at the end of the street. We turned in time to see the Count run straight into a passing car. Buffeted by the side of the vehicle, the man was knocked back onto the curb, where he sat regaining his composure. A woman leapt from the driver's seat of the car, now pulled over to one side. A crowd gathered.

My heart raced. I took a few steps in the direction of the accident, then stopped. I raised my nose. Fumes, *porchetta*, tobacco smoke and *espresso* from the bar next door—but no harm.

"He's all right."

Greta stared wide-eyed at the gathering in the street end. "There's an interesting idea," she said.

"What?"

"You're all they have. No heirs, no division. Death," she said. She looked in the direction of the Count. "Small cost if you ask me." She licked a paw.

"*Pazza.*" I took a step back and sat down.

"Not so crazy an idea," said Greta. "The cheating stops. That would have to make your Contessa happy, no?" Raising her brow, she sucked the air through her teeth. "Otherwise, a house divided."

"I don't think that's what the phrase means," I said.

The Count appeared from behind the car. He brushed his clothes with both hands, smoothed his hair, then waved the driver off, shaking his head. Reaching the corner of the street, we caught his gaze.

Greta looked at me. "You have a better idea?"

I groaned. My neck hurt from the weight of the cone. Though light, it was as though every thought I'd ever had was scooped up and cosseted by the collar. The metallic smell of blood, dried on the inside of the plastic, made me sick.

"I prefer a more humane solution, that's all," I said. "I actually like the man. Besides, the Contessa was happiest when he paid all his attention to her, and that wasn't so long ago."

Greta's dark suggestion surprised me. She was unusually vengeful these days. Bitterness was corrupting her. She still hadn't moved past the uncoupling of her people. For her, the past was everything.

"Let me know how that works out for you," Greta said. She gave a slow, skeptical lick to her nose.

The Count reached us and attached a leash to Greta's collar. "So, the Joker has a partner. I guess there are two in every deck, no?" He opened the entry doors.

I bounded ahead, up the long stairs, leaving the man and Greta to await the lift. I limped as fast as I could up the steps. At the door to my apartment, I heard the voice of my Contessa. She spoke in low, measured tones, to no answer.

The phone.

"*Si, sicura,*" she said. "I'm sure they are together. I will go out now to look. When I find Greta I will call you."

Greta's woman.

"You're quite right," said the Contessa. "There's no reason to delay."

Delay what? Divorce? Desertion? I put an ear to the door. The elevator clattered behind me as it crawled from floor to floor. I slid my head to the crack under the door and pressed my head against it to improve my hearing.

"Oh, I have a plan all right. Thanks for your call. *Ciao.*"

The phone clicked.

The Contessa gave a sly chuckle on the other side of the door. "Do I ever have a plan."

Elevator doors slid open at the end of the hall. I looked over my tail to the Count beyond. Greta's toenails slid across the smooth floor as she strained at her leash. She barked once, inviting the apartment door to open.

There was no time to present myself in a tidy fashion, so I sat down, prepared to take the brunt of her wrath. I would be seen in all my disheveled glory.

Perhaps not a bad thing, I thought. Messiness always raised her ire. A woman scorned could bend the will of God. Just ask Caesar. And the Count's will needed immediate bending. Of course, groveling was a logical first step. I cowered, hoping to give the Count an idea.

But Il Conte just stood there, suit torn and dirty from his fall, eyes on me, as though waiting pronouncement of death.

No apology, no tender touch.

The man's refusal to concede made me angry. Il Conte wasn't even trying. Maybe Greta was right. I returned the man's stare, beginning to think the unthinkable. Perhaps there *was* only one solution. The Count would have to be dispatched.

The apartment door opened. The Contessa scanned the scene, from the top of the Count's head to my tattered bandages. Greta yelped. I turned to the Contessa, expecting to see a look to kill.

The woman only smiled.

Chapter Eleven

At the rustle of clothes, I lifted an eyelid to the Contessa. She stood in the closet, pulling things from a shelf and folding them into a suitcase. I raised my head. The long windows in the bedroom were open wide. Jumping from the bed, I was careful not to land too hard. My belly was yet a bit tender if I moved a certain way. I put my paws on the sill to examine the city. Over the rooftops I saw clear to St. Peter's. A pale slice of moon waxed low in the morning blue, like a lazy, half-open eye. Cherry trees in heavy flower stood near the Vatican. Spring was in full bloom.

"*La campagna*, Shimoni," the Contessa said. "We're getting him out of town." Her voice did not carry the harmony of anticipation. She went about her packing, stoic and silent.

Yet, it was a heady pronouncement. It seemed reasonable to me. The Contessa had met the Count in Chianti. Perhaps it would be there he would come back to her. I'd heard the story many times. It was a good one. Both were fond of telling it but neither had told it lately. Perhaps, if they recounted their story more often, things would end well, I thought. After all, love stories always had a happy ending.

*

She was a shop girl in Siena. The jewelry store belonged to her father. The Count was a customer. He bought charms and bracelets for an array of women he fancied. Nothing too expensive, nothing overstated—and he never came in unless the young shop girl was there. Soon, he and the shop girl were lunching after his purchases. A *cappuccino* here, a glass of wine there.

Since Siena was a small town, she frequently saw the baubles the Count bought displayed on a number of dazzling women. She didn't think she had a chance with the Count. Her beauty was not

91

fierce but soft. But they continued to spend time together and she fell miserably in love and dreamed only of him. Long after they became friends he confided in her one day at lunch that he planned to marry. He wanted her to help him choose a ring. She was crestfallen yet gracious in accepting the task.

She and the Count spent the late afternoon pouring over diamonds at her father's store until, just at sunset, the Count made a decision. He pulled a single perfect square-cut gem from the case—not too expensive, not too overstated—and placed it on the shop girl's finger.

*

Yes, I thought, Chianti will win him back.

A waft of fresh earth rose from the terrace below. I filled my lungs with hope, leaning out the window for a better view. A woman worked her hands through the soil of a window box. Potted geraniums stood by, ready for a new home. Their bitter smell clarified a single thought.

Digging. Spring's delight.

With ample blossom on the *Platani* along the Tiber came the first moon of spring. The time for overseeing vines, crafting spring cheeses from the ewes of newly weaned lambs, cutting sweet hyacinth and preparing the garden was at hand. Rome was to be abandoned for the country, far away from La Donna Rosa. The wild *campagna* harbored a host of opportunities to end a man's life. The motive was ripe.

I slipped carefully across the room to a full-length closet mirror. My Contessa had removed the awful cone and cut away my tattered bandages the night before. I performed a cursory inspection of the insult to my undercoat. It was pale and bald; if the hair never grew in again, a genuine embarrassment, indeed. Dirt exhumed would cling to the naked spot and be difficult to shake, but it was of little concern. The arrival of spring conferred the optimism winter lacked. I was back to normal, save a twinge now and then about my belly. Things were looking up.

A clatter of keys echoed from the hallway. I followed their promise. Moments later, the Count, the Contessa and I were in the shiny grey car with soft, shoe-leather seats, bumping along the broad, hectic street flanking the river. I put a back paw on the armrest of the passenger door for a boost.

Against the southern current. North, the direction of Siena.

The landscape raced by with dizzying speed as the Count maneuvered along the ancient, narrow via Cassia. Soon the traffic thinned. The road was open but winding, and the man approached each corner as though denying what lay beyond.

I thought it reckless. We needn't *all* die.

We were at Il Conte's mercy on every outing to the country, for the Contessa didn't drive. He glared from behind the steering wheel with the vengeance of a condemned man. The queen was leaving the city and the man was obliged to follow. The Contessa sat in the seat beside him, serene in her victory.

A country voyage was the right prescription. Perhaps the whole sordid affair lay behind us. Surely the Count's distance from temptation, the progress of spring and its happy roll into a lazy summer, would remedy the situation. The Tuscan sun would change their luck.

"Better to stay in Rome, I think," said the Count. "I read in the morning paper about this very road. More people die on it than any other in Italy."

"It's not the road. It's the way it's driven," said the Contessa.

I had to agree with that. I dug my toenails into the upholstery.

The Contessa leaned into the back of her seat and sighed. "I'd rather hear a story with a happy ending," she said, looking out the window.

"It's just a simple fact." The Count gave her a crosswise glance. "Besides, I don't like fairy tales."

"That's a bit like saying you don't dream, isn't it?" She chewed the tip of her thumbnail.

"I prefer reality, that's all."

The Contessa looked hard at the Count. "It was dreaming that got us this far, don't you think?"

True, I thought. She always said she'd dreamed the Count into her life. Life was nothing if not dreaming possibilities. It was time the man started to dream a few of his own.

The Count kept his eyes on the road and frowned.

There'd be no sweet stories that day.

I yearned for the windows to be lowered. The emotions circulating about the car were stifling. Anguish and hope were an odd couple. I wanted to feel the brace of spring in its entire wild aroma—*rosmarino*, artichokes, pork on the hoof—but the Contessa's freshly coiffed hair kept the windows raised. I pushed my nose against the window to steady myself. The car negotiated the serpentine road, valley to crest, and down again, past flocks of sheep grazing across lush broad meadows. We wound through tunnels of dark untamed oak and beech woods and into the bright open fields again. The contrasting light kept perfect time to the music emanating from rear speakers as Elvis sang "Mean Woman Blues."

I turned and balanced my paws on the back of the Contessa's seat. Il Conte cast me a sideways glance and slight smirk. The words of the song danced inside the car.

I gotta woman as mean as can be—

I nuzzled the woman's neck.

She makes love…without a smile—ooh, hot dog, that drives me wild—

The woman looked at the Count from the corner of her eye and tapped her foot on the floor of the car to the rhythm of the music. It was a familiar beat and, though I hadn't heard it in years, it brought me right back to the first time I heard it.

94

*

A tiny garden restaurant at the top of the Spanish Steps; beautiful plates of food coming one after another. Ripe cheeses, shrimp raviolis and bitter greens. The tinkling of glasses filled with effervescent liquid. Always someone in the restaurant we knew. I loved celebrations. Birthdays, Christmas; any holiday was a perfect day. But on an anniversary, love was contagious and always flowed like champagne.

I don't know which year was being celebrated, but it was the first one I had attended. I was still a pup and couldn't be left alone so the Contessa tucked me into an oversized purse and off we went. The waiters met every request. When the last table of guests departed so did the waiters and we were all alone in the restaurant, Elvis on the stereo. "Love Me Tender," "It's Now or Never," even "Good Luck Charm." The Count and Contessa drank champagne into the night.

Just as "Mean Woman Blues" started to play, it began to rain, first a few large drops here and there and then, a downpour. I sat in the purse under the cover of the table, content to be dry, but the two didn't seem to mind. They huddled under a terracotta overhang as the beating rain kept rhythm on the smooth terrazzo floor, laughing and twirling until daylight turned the sky a pearly grey.

*

Il Conte narrowed his eyes as though the same picture had come to mind. He let his eyes shy from the road long enough to follow the taut curve of the Contessa's calf from the crook of her knee to the caress of her shoe. Then...

She's almost as mean as me.

The Count hit a button on the radio and there was silence.

It made no difference. I was dizzy with the beauty and potential of springtime. Chianti. There did not exist a better place. It was wild and tame at the same instant; the perfect dance between the familiar and the strange, reason and adventure. I could hardly wait to begin a dance of my own. I yawned in anticipation and gazed out the window.

The fragile green of spring anointed everything in sight. Thousands of adolescent leaf buds laced the corduroy of grapevines across the hills. Streaked with tall, brilliant mustard and silvery olive trees, broad fields blended into brilliant swaths of forsythia. I longed for the first bitter taste of tender shoots that tinged the dark Tuscan soil; chives and garlic tops in the garden. The corner of my mouth watered where I sat with my snout pressed up against the window, and I licked it as it ran down the cool glass.

We turned onto a long, circuitous driveway bordered by rows of soldier-straight, black cypress. The trees threw shadow bands that fell like serpent skin against the late afternoon light. The car rolled along the edge of the hillside, up to the lovely ivy-bitten stone of our *villa*. It stood a whisper's reach from the exquisite bell of the *Duomo* in Siena to the south. When the car stopped, my Contessa opened the door. She carefully lifted me to her chin for a quick kiss, then set me on the gravel drive.

I inhaled a long breath with eyes closed and nose lifted. Just to smell the fine, clean air, the faint hint of damp rosemary, to detect the tease of blooms on the desultory vines of the old wisteria that clung to the portico, was healing to my spirit. The Contessa portaged me across the drive to the great arched door beneath the vine-clad *loggia*.

As we arrived it swung open to reveal a chubby, red-cheeked woman.

The woman bellowed my name from across the driveway. "Shimoni."

Grazia, the keeper of the house and all delicious things, scooped me into her arms. She was round and soft like a sheepdog and drew me so deep into the cushion of her chest that all I heard was her muffled voice. She was hopelessly doggish. That is to say: she knew the manner and sensibilities of dogs, understood their needs and inhibitions, and shared the same carefree joy in the living of her life.

I extended my tongue to sample the satisfying taste of garlic always oozing from her skin. It promised the certainty of finer things to come.

"*Ti ringrazie,*" she said.

After a loud kiss behind my ear, she carried me into the house to fawn over my condition properly. Setting me gently on the smooth wood floor, she bent down to give me a gentle rub under my belly. As she did the locket around her neck opened to reveal a tiny black-and-white portrait of an old woman. I rolled gingerly on my side to offer up the tragedy to full view for Grazia and eyed the picture. Something about it was very familiar, yet I couldn't put my paw on it. The woman in the photograph had eyes as big and black as those of the Roman gypsy who taunted me. A shiver ran through me at the thought.

Grazia's voice was warm and languid. "*Poveretto carino.*"

The *r*'s rolled off her tongue in a pleasantly sensational way that calmed me.

Poor little dear, indeed, I thought. How true.

All, or at least as much as I hoped for, was coming right. A suitable fuss was being made. Soon, I was certain, warm, creamy *polenta* would rest in my dish. It was the signature of Grazia's affection but first, the long car ride had left me with the feeling that I needed a bit of a stretch and piddle. Looking past Grazia down the long hallway to the kitchen, I formed a strategy. Exit through the kitchen provided a quick check of available snacks. That accomplished, I would quit the house to examine the broad lawn stretching to the vineyard. I got to my feet, careful not to show too much vitality.

Slow moves.

I made a gradual motion across the salon in the direction of the kitchen. My nails tapped the wide planking and the hollow noise echoed off beams that framed the high ceiling. I maneuvered past massive dark furniture to my favorite room. The kitchen was awash with afternoon light. I followed a sunbeam from the old marble floor to where it fell from the glass patio doors. It was then, between feign and forage, I first saw her.

Squisita. Exquisite.

Behind the *terrazzo* doors an aquiline nose kissed the pane. Bright eyes, like black grapes in harvest, gleamed through brilliant white fur. She was the loveliest female I had ever seen. This was La Cagna Squisita. I was afraid to move a hair. The image might be only a phantom. Any sudden motion might startle the ghost away.

But, as always, emotions betrayed me. My tail began to tremble. As soon as it did, the creature on the other side of the glass wiggled. The enthusiasm of her tail wagging made her seem larger than she was. And she was a good deal larger than I.

But not impossibly so.

Her form was slender, her delicate long legs perfectly balanced. The jewels on her regal collar danced the midday sun into my eyes. I knew then that life was about to become very, very complicated. Before I had time to offer a polite response to the fervor, my Contessa lifted me off the floor.

"*Aspetti,*" she murmured. Wait.

Grazia entered the room. She placed her hand on the doorknob.

I began to quake as Grazia prepared to let the female into the kitchen. I wanted nothing more than to meet this creature nose to nose. I struggled against the Contessa's hold. Restriction from the intimate details of a proper introduction was unreasonable. The woman didn't understand the ramifications. First impressions were important. She turned to leave the room with me in hand. I barked an objection. No matter how the turn of events progressed, this female would always remember me being bound by the arms of my Contessa, steered like a child out the room.

It was the exit of a fool.

At the top of the stairs I heard the *terrazzo* doors open to a waltz of toenails across the tile floor of the *cucina*. I wiggled uncontrollably. I hoped to slip the grasp of the Contessa, but she had a firm grip and determined eye. Only when the door to the bedroom was sealed did I enjoy the freedom of the floor. I set my nose to work for clues and scrutinized the rug, skimming the entire area with dogged determination.

Nothing.

No scent of La Squisita anywhere in the room. I held my breath, bracing for the belly pain of a high jump onto the window seat next to the Contessa. Scanning the yard, I caught the last glimpse of Grazia as she led the female into her small apartment behind the main house. I leaned my jowl against the sill of the window and whined. The woman emerged alone and walked to the *villa*. When the *terrazzo* doors slammed below, I jumped to the floor. I sat down adjacent to the bedroom door tossing a polite bark and a plaintive look at the Contessa.

"Hai bisogna di una passaggiata?" she asked.

A turn around the yard, indeed, I thought. It had been preempted long enough. Suddenly, my passion to reach the yard became vital as I calculated the hours passed since my last relief. Time was of the essence. I shifted my weight from paw to paw, anticipating a hasty descent to the comfort of the grass.

Andiamo.

Springtime at the *villa* had always been unrestricted. The peril of stray bullets from autumn hunters was months away. No other threat warranted constraint. I enjoyed freedom of the yard and wood. I was eager to lead the way over every path I'd ever crossed, and mark just as many. Standing at the door, I trembled. The Contessa rubbed her hand along my back. She gave an affectionate tug to my tail. Then she did something she had not done before on any spring visit to the country. She fixed a leash to my collar. We descended the stairs together.

Chapter Twelve

P risoner in my own *villa*. The confusion of the city dogged me still. Nothing was normal.

The Contessa and I reached the bottom of the steps. Light at the end of the hallway to the kitchen beckoned. Relief of open ground lay beyond—even if it was at the end of a long leash. In the hall, Grazia was busy straightening a row of photographs hanging along the wall. The Contessa stopped to regard a large portrait of her and the Count. I looked up to inquire about the delay. In the photo, broad smiles shone under the warm light of large candelabra flanking them. Their wedding.

"Handsome couple, *Signora*," Grazia said.

The Contessa's eyes glistened. "A happy day."

The Count emerged from the salon, newspaper in hand. "It rained." He cast the words behind him without emotion as he passed by and disappeared into the kitchen.

The two women frowned.

How romantic, I thought. What an ass.

The Contessa looked across the salon to the large, comfortable sofa as though she wanted to fall into it forever. Her voice was soft and low. "Rain's not always so bad."

My ears drooped. It might be spring, but reconciliation was a late bloomer. I wondered why it seemed that good times only got better and bad times just got worse. I eyed the staircase. If I could trip the Count at a high step, his neck just might break.

I shook the thoughts from my head. Grief was grief, whether it was death or divorce. Both were separation. Neither would deliver the Contessa to happiness, but I simply couldn't see another way.

"Never mind," Grazia said, putting a hand on the Contessa's shoulder. "Men are not made of memory, but desire." She waddled up the stairs in the direction of suitcases in need of unpacking. "The way to a man's heart is not through his brain, after all."

The Contessa stiffened. I felt her anger rise. Another whiff of fear shuddered my nose. My belly was tight under the influence of a full bladder. I plead a soft whimper.

The Contessa glanced at me, then resumed her voyage to the garden. Through the *cucina,* past the Count, who stood at the sink peeling an orange, and out the *terrazzo* doors—freedom. Upon arrival to the garden, I led my Contessa to the roses where I accomplished a lengthy relief. I hoped the symbolism was not lost on her.

"Shimoni, *no,*" she chided.

Yanking on my leash, she pulled me away from the flowers. She scanned the vineyard, posture squared in a way that revealed her irritation. Her mood was usually buoyed by a visit to the country. Confused, I moved away from her heel. I had my own concerns.

The lawn and bush were filled with female fragrance. The sanguine scent of La Squisita made my heart race and concentration wander. I struggled to maintain focus. I reflected upon the time that passed between visits as I skirted the perimeter of the yard, Contessa in tow.

We went to see the mountains last Christmas, not to the *villa.* The last time I was in the country, the report of gunfire heralded the hunting season. The time of year I preferred least. The Contessa only allowed me to travel the yard and vineyards at midday. Then only at the end of a leash. She kept me locked inside the house at the most preferred times: dewy morning when the worms still wiggled through wet grass, and the cool of late dusk just when the toads made an evening leap across the *terrazzo.* I was always happy to leave the irritation of the baying hounds and buzzing bullets behind for autumn in the city. Ripe, chewy chestnuts, the relief of cool weather—freedom on the Pincio. I sniffed the air. It was deep spring. If Grazia had taken a puppy just after our departure last fall, it might be a similar size to La Squisita now.

Young, yes, I concluded. But youth conferred no aversion to romance. La Donna Rosa was young. Yet, she enjoyed the thrill of adoration. Even at the bidding of a scoundrel. I eyed the Count standing at the kitchen door, orange segment peeking from the corner of his mouth. I looked up at my Contessa. We stood at the edge of the terrace.

She held my leash in one slender hand; the other smoothed the silvering hair at her temples. The Contessa was striking, standing in the blushing light of the setting sun.

Always well turned out; a wedge of scarf around her delicate shoulders; the subtle touch of golden jewelry. I was proud to be cared for by a woman of such beauty. I had never seen another creature compare to the Contessa.

Until today.

There were plenty of females in the gardens of Rome. All held a particular attraction. Obedient to the wanderlust heart of a Roman dog, I had sampled my share of female fragrance, never settling on a true preference. No other captured my attention as had La Squisita. The set of her tail atop her bouncy quarter, the turn of her dainty nose, her polite restraint at the door until my own tail gave away my intent. This, indeed, was a noble dog. She was intoxicating.

I might never regard another female again, save Squisita. I imagined myself confined to a simple sideways glance now and then at a passing temptation, as any male often did without feminine reproach. It was the way in which the Count should attend the Contessa. The man was not a common dog, merely misguided. He was, after all, a noble. The noble should act as such, I thought. In the distance, I heard a whistle.

Umberto, Grazia's husband, rounded the nut trees adjacent to a backyard apartment. As always, the man carried a long spade and wore a bright shirt, the former to lean upon whenever the midday sun began to take its toll, the latter to thwart the birds. As was his habit, he carried a large bouquet of spring flowers to give the Contessa upon her arrival.

The Contessa always acted surprised at receiving them, her face coloring at the attention. The Count always raised a brow and peeked over his glasses at the man whose job it was to tend the garden and anything else that needed fixing. It all seemed benign enough to me. After all, it was supposed to be everyone's job to keep the Contessa happy. The flowers, the making of morning *cappucinni,* were merely items on Umberto's to-do list.

He spent most of the time outside. The Tuscan heat tanned his face brown and smooth like the fine leather of an Italian shoe. He was tall, with the good looks of a Rottweiler—rugged and crude—exciting in an unpredictable way. He had a devilish grin and sparkle in his eye, but the benevolent mood changed over the years. Hands that once comforted small dogs were now reserved to tending the garden. A loving touch was rare. But I remembered a time when treats came unfettered. I would bide my time. Perhaps the man would return to his days of plenty. Umberto approached the apartment.

I arranged myself for the pleasure of a proper introduction. Poised and aloof, I sat on the lawn at the bitter end of my leash, gaze directed at the apartment. The door opened. La Squisita bounded onto the grass. She took one look up the slope to the *villa* and made haste in charging me.

I was so surprised at her hostile greeting, I hardly felt the pain from my half-healed stitches. She tumbled me backward into the rose bushes, pinning me neatly against the low stone wall. I struggled back a squeal. Any cry would again make me look foolish. Most of my female encounters were abbreviated. A touch of the nose, a gentle suggestion, then—a fleeting good-bye. Being unaccustomed to the protracted company of female dogs, I was as yet unfamiliar with the role of an idiot.

The Contessa stamped her high-heeled foot on the flagstone terrace. She shrieked at La Squisita with such vigor that I began to shake. The intruder's retreat should have been imminent, but she held her ground. The look in her eye admonished I had better do the same. I froze, deferring to the more aristocratic position of polite request.

I looked away in deference, expecting concession, but Squisita remained motionless above me. The feminine mind did not always conform to expectation.

When Umberto reached the scene of the misunderstanding, he firmly took the female by her fancy collar. She coughed and gagged as he hauled her away.

"Mi dispiace, Signora," he stammered.

Sorry, indeed. After all, whose *villa* was this anyway? I righted myself onto the cool *terrazzo*, dumbfounded, dreams dissolving.

Umberto withdrew La Squisita to the apartment. The Contessa offered a small, fragile dog the safety of her arms.

No grazie, I decided. Thank you, no.

I would walk into my house on my own, preserving dignity and politely leaving La Squisita to contemplate the consequences of her actions. For I was a noble dog. The female was a lunatic. An obvious mix of pedigree.

Pazza, I thought, quite crazy. No? After all, it was my *villa.*

I employed the swagger of a roving king: the walk of superior implication I reserved for the cretins of the Pincio. Crossing the terrace, I paused nonchalantly at the rosemary hedge that skirted a juvenile crowd of geraniums at the *cucina* door. I relieved myself in full view of *la pazza* before she disappeared into her quarters. The Contessa swung the door open. Its loud squeak announced my entry. With a fleeting look behind, to nowhere in particular, I made a smooth, unconcerned transition into the house.

She was common after all. One could never judge a dog by its collar. Manners must be bred.

I watched Grazia from the corner of my eye. She was busy with a large bowl in the middle of the sink. I wondered how a woman as irrepressibly jolly as Grazia harbored such a contentious creature. How Umberto, with his kind eyes and large, hard-working hands always smelling of fresh, damp earth from the garden, raised such an ignoble individual. I lingered over the water bowl, recharging for an after-dinner turn around the lawn. Then I collapsed into the pillow that rested under the table just for me. I laid my head on my paws, scanning the cozy room.

A charming open fire burned by my side. Open cupboards filled with stacks of china and silver lined the room. A stout wooden table stood above me, its top riddled with cracks that allowed the sun to fall through in streamers across my eyes. I sneezed at the light. Grazia turned away from the sink, bent to smooth my fur and returned to her work. I heard the soft plump sound of dry polenta as Grazia slid it into a pot of boiling water on the stove.

Dinner. I would stay awake at least that long. An examination of the remaining kitchen kept me conscious. A fat bird passed by the window and I watched its shadow cross the floor and vanish into the corner of the room. There, a long black rifle rested near the *terrazzo* doors. It stood ready for the appearance of flocks heading north. When Grazia was not cooking or cleaning, she loved to shoot birds.

Incongruous, I thought. Crack shot inside a gentle soul. But I always enjoyed the fruit of her skill. The roasting of poultry was something I looked forward to, no matter the season.

Small birds were plentiful from spring through fall. Soon there would be more to my *polenta* than cornmeal. I watched Grazia, tan face wrinkled like a walnut, fussing over dinner until I could no longer keep my eyes from closing. The very definition of dog-tired: done in, used up, worn out and shattered, I was spent by the vicious turns of the day.

Dead-end into the defeat of an impolite introduction, I heaved a deep sigh into the relief of my cushion. Dinner could wait. I slipped into the repair of sleep: restitution for a damaged dream.

Chapter Thirteen

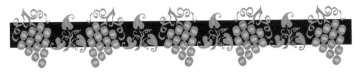

I spent the evening confined to the *villa*. Anxious and bored, I was reduced to hunting for anything to keep my mind from La Squisita. From a basket of dirty clothes I found a lovely article of silken ladies undergarment; a single, filthy garden glove from under the *cucina* bench, well worn and ripe for alteration; and even a delightful-smelling rusty scouring pad from behind the trash pail, complete with tasty bits from dingy kettles.

No matter the project, my Contessa intervened. She put a stop to every serious chewing attempt. In resignation, I returned to the satisfaction of sleep. I passed the remaining day on the comfort of my soft chamois bed in the warm kitchen until the Count's voice woke me.

Darkness covered most of the kitchen. A gentle light from the hall lamp fell through the bottom of the door to the *cucina*. The man's tone was soft and low. A tenor reserved for La Donna Rosa.

"*Si, cara,*" he said. "Yes, yes. I miss you, too." His tone was unconvincing. The floor creaked as he shifted his weight from side to side. He raised his voice. "*No, no.* I told you. You mustn't come here." A long cord swept the floor as he moved the phone from one ear to the other and spoke softly. "I have a plan," he said. "*Pazienza.* You will have the ring."

I heard a loud click from the phone even from the kitchen. La Donna Rosa hung up mid-sentence. I scanned the kitchen for company. Grazia had disappeared. The clean scent of washed dishes filled the air.

Alone.

I stood. Moving quietly to the door, I listened for the Count. The Contessa must be well upstairs for such a conversation to take place. She was irritable since reaching the *villa*. No doubt she knew more than she let on about our last afternoon in the city. My shoulder ached from La Squisita's tumble. I wondered if the Contessa ever growled with displeasure at the Count or rolled him in unexpected anger.

Surprise attacks, I thought. One mean dog inspired another. The behavior caused many an eye to wander. But it didn't excuse the action. Separation between the Count and his courtesan did not appear to be working. I regarded a ladder propped outside the window. Perhaps I'd lie in wait for the Count to reach the top rung one day and knock it from beneath him. With a swing of the door the man entered the kitchen.

He rested his hands against the stone counter. *"Miseria."*

It was then I realized that male behavior depended on the mood of the nearest female. Squisita's rude conduct certainly had made me think twice. I gave a quiet bark.

The Count turned to look at me. "What creature but a woman grants pain and delight in equal measure?"

He broke a piece of *pecorino* cheese from a wedge that lay covered on the sideboard and tossed it my way. A large bowl piled with fresh *fava* beans sat on the side of the sink. Lifting the bowl, the man placed the cheese on top. He moved to the patio doors. I yawned, stretched and followed the Count into the night. We walked to the edge of the lawn. It was dark, but not enough to hide the notion of long rows of vines, like seats in a darkened theatre. A nightingale performed somewhere on the mountain. The stream clapped along the stones below the vineyard.

I skirted the perimeter, tagging each clay container of shrubs and flowers. Umberto had moved them a few feet clockwise. I was grateful for my keen nose, for my eyesight was unpredictable in the singular palette of darkness. I wished Umberto would settle on one arrangement and stick to fixing the garden. It was disconcerting. As anyone remotely doggish understands, a dog depends on the constant fixture of the landscape to guide him, as a sailor does the stars.

We reached the edge of the grass. The Count set the bowl on the stone wall. Together, we marked the diminutive lavender that bordered the grass.

I would miss these times. The Count was not a bad man, merely misguided. I hated to think of scheming his ruin, but if one person had to be thrown overboard to save the ship, so be it. A shame, though. In a strange, primal way, I felt I understood the man.

The Count eyed me as though he knew what I was thinking. We regarded each other, standing side by side under a sliver of spring moon. The stars twinkled a salute and something passed between us, faint but certain, like the air moved by the wing of a dove: a sense of common destiny. Deuces in the moonlight, scorned by Venus, we surveyed the situation. Our shadows crossed the lawn in the pale moonlight. The silhouette resembled one large, unfamiliar creature in repose: one being of two minds and similar disposition.

Simpatico, I thought.

I knew then that I could never harm the man. Lives were repaired through reconciliation, not wreckage. There would have to be another way.

We walked down to the edge of the grapevines that stood in tidy rows and reached across the gentle slope toward the creek flats below. I strained to see through the darkness without success, impatient to glimpse movement at the water's edge. The stream drew all things wild from the wood. The bank of the creek was an ample area for both man and dog to respond to the activity of such creatures. I gave a scratch to one of my ears, pausing once to snap at a moth that flirted with my nose.

Il Conte rested his arms on the stone wall skirting the lawn. Under the waning moon, bats dove and turned in pursuit of the year's first crop—insects.

Time to plant. Umberto always sowed seeds on the waning moon. Tomorrow would be a full and busy day. I was the man's best help in the garden. Umberto learned that he only needed to point out the placing he desired for each seed. An expert at holes, I accomplished the rest.

I considered that it might be time for bed, but music spilled from the apartment Umberto and Grazia shared. Curtains swayed through the open window. The slice of moon washed each pane with glassy light. I was surprised by their common affection for Elvis. The perfect choice of music for the night. Sleep could wait. It was the cusp of spring, the season of promise.

Grazia passed by the window and stopped. From my place on the rise above her apartment, I saw she was alone. Squisita must be sleeping. Yet the light was still on. There was always the chance she might take one last turn around the yard. My heart leapt at the possibility. Like sparking with a Doberman, the thought was just dangerous enough to be exciting. I looked from the yard to the winery. No sign of Umberto. His truck was gone.

A game in town.

Umberto used to play cards with the Count. I sat under the table watching as he passed cards from his pocket to his hand, unnoticed by the Count. Umberto always won. Il Conte gave up the contest, unwilling to play with a cheat. Umberto spent much time out of an evening ever since.

When I turned back to the window, Grazia had disappeared. The Count and I sat on the grass. "Unchained Melody" filled the air. The man shelled the *fave* and I stood ready to receive. A window squeaked open from the second story of the *villa*. At the sound, we both turned. Light flooded the bedroom, and highlighted on sheer pale drapes that billowed in the cool evening breeze was the silhouette of the Contessa. Il Conte froze at the vision. He watched her like a hunting dog fixed on small prey.

"Non cede proprio niente." He looked at me as I stood eager to accept a fresh bean. "She never gives in."

You get what you give, I thought.

The man stared at the soft image on the gossamer curtains. His chin tipped in the direction of the window and his eyes narrowed. *"Guardi la."*

The woman pulled her sweater over her head to reveal a perfect figure. Soft breasts above a scant midlife belly, model to Raphael. The Count's eyes flashed in the moonlight, his expression, awestruck. Like finding a golden coin in the sand.

"Mamna mia," said the man softly. *"Sono un idiota."* He shook his head.

Si, I thought. You *are* an idiot.

I wondered why he didn't just write her a note like he used to do. It was a common, sweet form of communication they once both used to remind each other of their love. And I, the messenger.

*

The Contessa had started it. She pulled a calling card from the bureau, took her favorite gold pen in hand and copied the words she'd read in some book or magazine. She taught me to carry the single small note to the Count. For every one I delivered, he pulled a treat from his pocket and read the card aloud.

There was Shakespeare. "They do not love who do not show their love."

And Leunig. "Love one another and you will be happy. It's as simple and as difficult as that."

And Yeats. "I have spread my dreams beneath your feet; tread softly because you tread on my dreams."

Brief reminders of the commitment they shared, I thought them all brilliant. It was clear that some humans had a knack for translating a few simple tenets of dog-logic into poetry.

The Count would speak every word he wrote on the back of each note.

For one, "I will show you every day."

Another, *"Simplice."*

111

And again, "It is I, the dreamer."

I returned each to the Contessa.

Another card, another cookie.

She saved all the notes in a thick book with plastic pages. We used to look at them often.

*

I hadn't seen those little notes for some time.

The man watched the Contessa slip the stockings from her legs, then disappear behind the wall. He looked down at me and finally threw a *fava* my way.

"No use to try anymore," he said. "I'm better to get it in Rome."

I gave the bean one gratuitous chomp and swallowed. I looked up again at the bedroom. The window was dark.

So—Il Conte admitted it. Sex. Greta was right. I bowed my head, laid my ears back and whined.

"Shhh," said the man. "What do you know about it? Dogs have their pleasure when they want."

I sneezed in disbelief. Had the Count met La Squisita?

"Somebody has to want to do it," he said. "What would happen to the world?"

Amen. I looked in the direction of Grazia's apartment, fantasy temporarily clouding my thoughts. The window was dark, the music stopped. No clandestine meeting tonight.

I walked closer to the man and watched his hands concentrate on the broad *fave* pods. The Count split them open to reveal the pale, fat kidney-shaped nuggets, carefully pushing the small bitter nub from each bean. Small bits of the salty, sharp cheese followed each bean as he ate them. Once in a while he tossed a bean, then a little cheese, in my direction. We enjoyed a game of catch until the fodder was gone. I licked my snout clean.

The man picked up the empty bowl and walked around the side of the *villa* to the car. I followed. The car was glossy, its daytime dark grey coat turned to luminescent pearl under the moonlight. I sniffed the front tire. It was dry, the odor of the rubber like distant smoke on an autumn day. Dew had not yet fallen.

Il Conte slid a hand over the sleek hood with affection, then examined his palm.

"Bene," he said.

I loved the car, as well. It was low and lean and fast and made my stomach feel light inside when it dashed around the Tuscan curves. The Count washed it every time we came to the country and used the water spray to cool me in the heat of summer. Umberto could have done the task, but Il Conte was particular about who touched his car.

The Count put the bowl on the ground, walked to the trunk and opened it, pulling a large piece of cloth from inside. He draped the vehicle as he would a woman with a fine fur. Mission complete, he retrieved the bowl and we walked back around the house. At the edge of the lawn the man hesitated, looking up to regard the Contessa's window once more.

Spark, I thought. The engine still turned. It was clear in the man's captivation at the window, and the woman's warmth toward the photo in the hall. It may be war, but the battle was not indifference. Somewhere beneath misunderstanding there was a glimmer of hope. The puzzle was how to kindle it into flame.

"Change your mind," the gypsy woman had said.

She was right. Now that I knew the real object of the Count's desire, it was time for a different strategy.

The task was at hand, but the night tempted. An owl swooped overhead, a gentle rush of air from its wings giving way to a host of odors. Whiffs of new onion tops and tiny bitter green tomatoes wafted up from the garden. They mingled with a lovely putrid smell of compost from behind the winery. The first cuttings of fresh grass lay across the lawn as mulch. I bent my head to smell their sweetness, inhaling deeply to best appreciate the ripening body of the season. With a full lung came a certain scent. I froze.

La Squisita was not a cretin, nor impolite, nor even *pazza*.

Not crazy, I reasoned.

In heat.

Moths whirred around us as bats gave chase and *zanzare*, mosquitoes, whined a rival to cricket song in the vineyard below the garden. The cool night air shuddered in promise and delight. Hair stood up on the back of my neck. Revelation was thrilling even in the absence of resolve.

The man pushed his hair back with one hand and moved to the patio doors. I gave a final mark to the lawn and retreated to my castle a little wiser for the walk. At the dinner bowl, I paused to sniff my food. The polenta, now cool and firm, was perfect. It was topped with a thoughtful bit of fresh ricotta cheese made from the first milk of ewes following the spring lambs. As I chewed I thought about strategy for the coming morning.

Spring. A new world and fresh starts. *Domani*, a new day.

Chapter Fourteen

As a rule, I was not the first to leave bed in the morning. The art of the small dog lies in the enjoyment of life's pleasures. Few things matched the appeal of good food and long sleep. But when the smell of fresh *cornetti* wafted up from the kitchen below in a perfect question mark, I answered.

The Contessa stood in front of the dresser wearing loose pants and a crisp shirt, sleeves rolled to her elbows. A checkered scarf protected her neck. She pulled the rings from her fingers, a shiny watch from one wrist, and a heavy bracelet from the other. They clinked into a small dish on the low bureau next to the window seat. She opened the window wide to let in the morning air and turned for the stairs. Time to dig.

The large diamond sparkled on the dresser. Light danced through the jewel and jumped from the dish across the ceiling to the closet where the Count emerged. The man scratched his head and yawned until the glimmering light caught his eye. He stood still, staring at the ring.

The open window invited sound from the garden below. I leapt to the window seat. The Contessa joined Umberto and the two chatted and laughed as they worked a hedgerow in the vegetable garden below. The Count narrowed his eyes and frowned. He put a hand to his mouth and chewed the tip of a thumb. With one eyebrow raised, he straightened. He gave me a long look.

"It's a big garden," he said, rubbing his chin, "they should spread out."

Ridiculous. No reason to be jealous of Umberto. The man would never stray from Grazia.

The Count turned back to the window, leaning on a hand on the bureau. His fingers touched the jewelry dish. Then in a flash of light that caught me directly in the eye, the ring was in the man's jacket. I sneezed.

The man turned to face me. "Another can't be bought." He hesitated, examining me as though suspecting my undercoat were covered in fleas. "But stolen?" He raised a corner of his mouth. "*Sì.*"

The only suspect, you, I thought. I glared at the Count. Who else might stoop to such a crime? The man was such an idiot. And just when I thought there was a glimmer of hope. That gleam wasn't coming from the ring.

Eyes fixed on me, the man placed a hand on the bureau behind him and slid it along the polished top in slow deliberation until the dish tumbled over the side to the carpet below. The jewelry scattered, a bit of it clattering down a small vent behind the dresser.

"And you, *Signore,* with a lengthy record," the Count pronounced. "Sorry, *ragazzo,* in the interest of resolution, the Joker takes the fall."

I gasped, bolting away from the scene of the crime, down the stairs. Visions of a stark surgical office and the broad cone collar rushed to my head. Only a fool took on trouble twice. I raced into the kitchen and slid into the patio doors with a thud. They were closed tight. Beyond, Umberto and the Contessa bent side by side in the garden. The woman was already up to her elbows in dirt. I sat down and whined.

Deep into a busy morning, Grazia stood at the sink rinsing rags after cleaning the *villa* windows.

"*Che succede?*" she asked. "You want to join the *Signora*?" She glanced out the window to the garden. "She digs with a vengeance today."

I looked to the garden. Fresh earth flew through the air in all directions.

Like a gravedigger, I thought.

"I know why," said Grazia. She looked down at me. "Do you?"

Do I.

"I do the laundry," she said. "I clean the pockets."

I cocked my head. Grazia twisted the corner of her mouth like a cat eyeing a bird. The woman knew of La Donna Rosa.

"Notes from someone I've never met. Receipts for things I never see. He should be shot," she sniffed, "a fine lady like that." Grazia stooped to scratch my head. "Don't worry, it's our secret. I won't embarrass her. But she's not alone." Doused in sunlight, Grazia stood plump like a large, soft doll: the perfect figure of sedentary domestic life. She put the last cloth into a pail on the floor next to her and wiped her hands dry on her apron. "You men," she said to me. "Don't you know that having is never so great a pleasure as wanting?"

The winemaker passed by the window, leaving the winery after a cursory check of newly bottled wine. He looked like Grazia's twin: medium build and rotund, with a warm smile and gentle way. Raising an arm her direction, he wrinkled his brow like a basset hound and winked. Grazia waved, beaming a generous smile. She retrieved a small piece of Venetian glass from the window over the sink and carefully held it with care up to the light as the man disappeared into his car.

"Bello," she declared.

In the shape of half a heart, the glass was an oddity. I wondered if it was broken. I suspected from the loving way it was handled, it came from someone dear.

Umberto must have the other half, I thought.

Grazia washed it under a ribbon of steamy water from the faucet. I whined again.

"Aspetta," she said.

Wait, indeed. No time to lose. If she'd ever had a knife taken to her belly, she'd feel the same. I heard the Count's footsteps on the stairs and trembled.

Grazia's tone pleasant and warm. "Poverino."

The urgency of my mission melted. No need to be rude, I thought. I would give her a lick before retreating to the safety of the open air. On the way to her side, I walked past my breakfast bowl at the base of the *terrazzo* doors, just under a row of coats that hung on the wall above. Next to the bowl was a fine linen handkerchief. Exquisite lace bordered the edges and a thin satin ribbon wove its way around the border. I nosed it gently expecting either sweet perfume or sour body odor to give its owner away. Nothing. Strange, I thought. Even things freshly washed had a scent. This item was as odorless as ice. I took it partially into my mouth for a more thorough check, but as I did, the small ribbon found its way into my throat and I gagged. Grazia turned and shrieked.

"Shimoni, out!" she said.

I opened my mouth and the kerchief fell to the floor.

"How did you find this?"

I looked at the coats hanging above him.

"Must have fallen from my pocket," said Grazia, as she pushed it back into her jacket.

I sniffed the bottom of the coat. A gentle blend of laundry soap and garlic laced the edge. The kerchief should have had even this slight scent. Strange, indeed. I took on last long breath of the sweet odor of Grazia's coat before the smell of ham beckoned from my bowl nearby. I bestowed a felicitous salutation with a brush of my tongue to Grazia's unshorn ankle when I was finished.

"*Buon giorno, carino,*" she responded. "That's better."

The front door opened and closed. The Count was out of the house. Crisis passed, I walked into the warm sunshine streaming through the window. Raising my nose, I sniffed for any clue to La Squisita.

Nothing.

Grazia was deep into the baking of bread, dough sticking to her fingers. I walked back across the room to put my paws on the window. My toenails ticked at the glass. Grazia met the hint with a swing of the patio doors and a puff of powdery flour.

Onto the patio and into the grass, I hesitated at the clay pots surrounding the lawn. I was systematic in marking the pots as I passed them. Careful to maintain my nose aloft between each stop, I searched for any subtle hint of female. A round of the yard was made, past the immense chestnut tree that stood guard to one side, and back to the patio.

The lingering scent of overripe melon and tobacco weighed heavy in the air. Grazia delivered warm, flaky *cornetti* to a table on the sunny terrace. Il Conte walked from the front of the house to sit for breakfast. A pipe dangled from his mouth between sips of *cappuccino.* He played an early game of solitaire, slapping the cards on the table quickly as he drew through the deck. The bright morning light was warm. The man wiped a linen napkin over his forehead and removed his jacket to the back of a neighboring chair.

I fixed my gaze on the landscape beyond the lawn. The details of the garden were clear; the land beyond a mottled blur. I glimpsed a white figure at ground level hidden in the garden vegetation. Ignoring the unreliability of my vision, I raced through the grass in the direction of the vision. It could only be one thing.

La Squisita.

I covered the distance from the patio to the garden before anyone noticed. Only the telltale sound of a growl I attempted to muffle, and the clatter of long, citified toenails on the flagstone terrace, lingered in my place. The struggling springtime flora of the vegetable patch, bound by stakes and strings, shielded each stand from the other. Mazelike, it foiled my attempt at a smooth arrival.

A fresh start, I thought. I crisscrossed the paths between the rows, nose scouring the tilled soil. Then, between the sugar peas and baby long beans, I glimpsed the chaste white peeking through the fragile trellis. I stood halfway from either end of the garden. There was only one thing to do in order to catch her before she fled my advance. I broke straight through the flimsy fencing.

Tomorrow arrived, I thought. Without hesitation I presented myself to Umberto, who was dressed in a bright, freshly bleached white shirt. Like a warrior, I stood head to head with the gardener.

The man, straddled on all fours, ceased his weeding at the base of a long row of string beans. I froze into the resolute statue of a Roman legionnaire, clad in lattice armor, wreath of curly sugar pea tendrils round my head, an unceremonious long bean up my nose.

"*Santa Maria,*" Umberto shouted. The man immediately found his spade.

I sneezed the bean from my nostril and turned to run. Umberto cursed in a manner so disturbing that I was inspired to head for the nearest exit of the gate. The armor I wore was still attached by several wires to the remaining trellis. As I ran, the train behind me became heavier as it accumulated into the total ruin of the entire row of new growth. By the time I reached the gate, Umberto had firmly planted his oversized foot upon the long parade. This halted the procession with enough force that I broke through the mess, hacking and choking as the traces pulled at my throat. Up the slope of the lawn I found the safety of Grazia's arms.

I tried to compose myself: an indifferent sideways glance, slow lick of my chops, profile raised in nonchalance. I was as serene as possible, though my heart was ready to burst.

A lightning retreat, I thought.

I hoped Umberto had insufficient time to recognize me underneath the vines and fence work. Swallowing hard, I averted my eyes from Umberto's piercing stare. Perhaps the man might believe some other fiend laid waste to his hard work. After all, there was a horde of wild things in the wood that found its way to the garden from time to time. But the determined stride of the man's walk and the twisted scowl on his face as he approached the terrace verified the worst. Disaster was about to fall on the small, well-intentioned shoulders of a certain small dog. The vicious transformation in Umberto's normally steady countenance set me to shake like I never had before.

Grazia released me to the flagstone terrace and I took cover behind one of the massive clay pots. She retreated to the kitchen.

Coward, I thought, as I watched her disappear into the *villa*. I swept my ears back, skulked in the shadow of the urn, and watched the frenzy from a corner of the patio.

As Umberto set one foot onto the *terrazzo*, Grazia emerged from the kitchen waving a large wooden spoon with one hand, a shiny lid with the other. There was a delightful pitch to her reproach. I pricked my ears and pushed my nose beyond the safety of the terra cotta.

"Attento!" She intercepted Umberto at the edge of the grass, admonishing him for chasing such a diminutive dog—an invalid as well.

It was true. Now that she mentioned it, I was feeling a bit worse for the wear. Of course, I was not yet recovered from the ordeal of my surgery. I could afford no further trauma. Besides, it was a simple misunderstanding and, with a small dog on the premises, one should really make sure there was ample room under the trellis for easy access in the garden. Grazia's swift attention to my grief confirmed her status as faithful patron.

Santa Grazia, I thought, shield and weapon in hand. True liberator of all dogs under false indictment and castigation.

Umberto shrank from the threatening utensils. He retreated to repair the trellis.

The Contessa landed on the terrace in a suit of dirt, fresh from the garden.

"Dov'e Shimoni?" Her eyes scanned the yard, then rested on Il Conte. "What did you do?"

"Mi? Niente." He slapped a card onto his game then searched the display for possibilities. "I'm done here," he said.

"You may be done," said the Contessa, "but I'll finish it." She pulled the top card in his hand and placed it in the pattern on the table.

The man looked startled. "I missed that."

"I'm shocked," said the woman wryly. "Only one thing gets *your* attention."

I peeked out from behind the cover. The Contessa saw me right away. She beckoned to me and I followed. My heart swelled as the Contessa lifted me into her arms. She smoothed the evidence of the mishap from my hair and set me carefully on the terrace next to her.

Grazia tidied the patio table. The Count picked up his jacket, which had fallen to the patio in the frenzy, ceded a raised brow in my direction, and headed for the kitchen door. I followed. As long as the man was home, there was a chance at retrieving the pilfered gem. The coat hung low on his arm. I nipped at a corner until I had firm hold, then planted all four paws. The jacket slid to the ground.

"Shimoni," said the man. *"Cosa ti fai?"*

A smart man would guess what I was doing. Quick to use my nose, I rifled through the jacket. Empty. Empty. At the last pocket, the Count managed to snatch the coat away.

He slipped it on, scowling at me. "You think you're so clever." He patted his pocket and the keys rattled. "I have my reasons for this."

Il Conte lifted his briefcase from the kitchen table. The *terrazzo* doors opened.

In stepped the Contessa. *"Dove vai?"*

"To the city. Something's come up."

The Contessa's voice was incredulous. "We just arrived."

"I have an early meeting tomorrow."

"I'll bet," the woman said under her breath.

The Count turned. *"Come?"*

What, indeed, I thought.

"Do as you please," said the Contessa. She turned back to the garden, slamming the glass doors hard. The windows shook and rattled behind her. Grazia's shotgun, resting in the corner of the kitchen, slid to the floor with a crack and fired.

The Count ducked. Pots rang out as they swung like church bells above the stove and buckshot rained from the ceiling. I raced across the kitchen and down the hall as though it was I who was blasted from the barrel.

The man bellowed. *"Scatenata."*

Unleashed, I thought. The entire household. A crowd ran through the patio doors at the sound of gunfire. All talked at once in a flurry of alarm and inquisition.

I met the Count at the front entrance. The man opened the door and it banged hard behind him. The photographs in the hallway swung against the wall. The Contessa watched from the *cucina*, then turned to exit through the patio doors. I put my paws upon the windowsill looking out to the portico. The man removed the car cover, folded it into the trunk, and the shiny grey car rolled down the driveway skirting the steep hill.

The ring was gone.

I sniffed the window. Spotless under the morning hand of Grazia, it smelled of cleaning solution. My nose trembled.

Ether, I thought. Cologne of the infirm. My belly began to ache. I was doomed.

Any hope to reclaim the diamond faded as the car disappeared. I leaned my shoulder against the sill and stared hard at that spot where the car vanished, long after it dissolved in the direction of Rome.

Chapter Fifteen

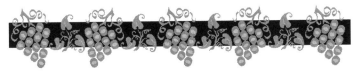

G razia cradled the shotgun in the crook of her arm. She lifted it to her sight, checking for damage to the barrel, then leaned it into the safety of the kitchen corner.

She scowled at me. "Haven't you caused enough problems for today?"

I tucked my tail at her accusatory tone. It wasn't my fault the world had gone to hell. I looked out the window to the garden. Umberto was the culprit.

As Grazia crossed the floor to the sink she paused, bending to retrieve the bullet from underfoot. "A waste of ammunition," she chided. "If you're going to aim, aim to kill."

My pleasure, I thought. I moved to the comfort of my pillow.

Grazia returned to the next item of the day: finishing her bread. She kneaded dough on a thick board set atop the counter. Small puffs of flour rose and fell with the rhythm of her breath. She gazed out the window above the sink in the direction of the garden. Umberto was digging long furrows in the dark soil, planting spring seeds.

I enjoyed the bounty of the garden: crunchy peas and beans, soft squash and sweet tomatoes. My belly rumbled, though it was still full of *polenta*. I returned to my empty bowl, pushing my nose through a few remaining crumbs. My Contessa entered the *cucina*. She washed her hands and took a seat at the long kitchen table across from Grazia. Stroking my head she watched the busy woman pull and fold the dough.

Grazia broke the silence. "Another woman."

My breath stuttered. I was awed by the admission. Sharing her suspicions with me was one thing. I never dreamed the woman would confront the Contessa.

She straightened with a start. Her face flushed. *"Come?"*

"Umberto," Grazia said.

The Contessa settled back in her chair. She looked out the window to the garden. Her cheeks paled into neutral. "Umberto?"

"He thinks I know nothing. About any of them. But I know it all."

I was shocked. I'd seen no cross words between Grazia and Umberto. If disagreement alone bred faithlessness, I couldn't fathom why this man strayed. Yet, it explained the myriad scents covering his trousers after each late-night trip to town. I had chalked it up to riding the crowded Siena buses that skirted the town. Umberto was riding something else, indeed.

"And you permit it?" asked the Contessa.

Grazia looked at the Contessa. "It permits me, *Signora*. The knowledge releases my obligation." She raised her eyebrows for punctuation and wiped her hands, dusty with flour, against her apron. "At first it mattered. After all, what Latin man doesn't take a mistress from time to time? As long as he only had them for sex, I could bear it. Then came lunch."

"Odd, how something as simple as sharing a thought means so much more than sharing a bed," said the Contessa.

"We've shared neither for years. It's a thing I don't miss. Now it's a rule of the house." Grazia moved the spongy dough to a wooden bowl.

"After a while it's more routine than romance anyway," said the Contessa. She twisted the corner of her mouth, resignation in her voice. "I guess it loses its allure."

"Love is always easy in the beginning. Then the newness wears away, and the work begins. Umberto is lazy. The only allure he knows is in the novelty. Sex may lose its sparkle, but not its merit," said Grazia.

The Contessa tipped her chin in question. Her affectionate hand pulled away. I put my front paws on her lap.

"*Sesso, Signora,* does not define love," Grazia continued, "but commemorates it. If there is love, sex reminds us." The woman wiped loose flour from the counter as she spoke. "It cleans a lens clouded by the grit of every day: dirty socks on the floor, broken doors that go unfixed, anniversaries unnoticed. In that clarity we see again what we love. If love is absent, only emptiness reflects."

"You don't want him back?"

"Only a fool fights for a rotten apple." Grazia turned to face the Contessa. "But if the prize is worth it, one takes poison."

The Contessa looked through the glass doors, eyes round and dark as a new moon, as if trying to see something in the wild wood beyond the stream. "Do you ever find it hopeless?"

"I find it fair. Men want women who want *them*. Why should I keep him from it?" Grazia pushed a thumb into the dough and examined the return of the rise. "I've only been hopeless once." She moistened a towel under the open faucet, wringing it to damp. "When I was a girl my mother's aunt lived with us," she said. "An old woman from the east, her name was Speranza. She talked to herself, cast odd spells. But she was very wise—if you'd listen." Grazia stopped to gaze out the window and smiled. A blush came to her cheeks.

"I had a hopeless crush on a handsome boy in my class. He paid me no mind at all. But I followed him like a puppy. *Miseria*. One day my great-aunt walked the mile to meet me at school. She saw me, ragamuffin, tagging along after the indifferent boy. Not one word passed her lips until we reached home. Then she put her arm around my shoulders and said, 'If you chase it, it runs—if you run, it chases you.' I never followed the boy again. Soon after, he followed *me*." She turned the tap to a stream of hot water and rinsed her hand.

"What happened?" asked the Contessa.

Grazia shook her head and laughed. "I married him." She let a long breath slip from her mouth, her face troubled. "Under that vow, I will not be the first to leave." She opened the window to the steam rising over the sink. "These days, I prefer to stand still; he prefers to chase." Her eyes met Umberto's as he passed by the window, whistling, hoe in hand, headed for the garden. "And he is as willing to cheat as he is to work."

Grazia's voice carried neither distress nor contempt. Only a hint of sadness tinged its edge. She moved the dough to the stovetop and covered it with a damp cloth. The Contessa slipped me from her lap and walked to the patio doors. Umberto moved from the garden to shepherd La Squisita from shrub to shrub around the yard. I glanced at the duo, but it was hard to pull my eyes away from those of my Contessa. She watched the man carefully. The air was thick with the excitement of innovation turning her mind.

"*Mi dispiace,*" said the Contessa.

I pushed my nose against the window to watch Squisita dig beneath a bush in search of something hidden. I inhaled deeply in hope of catching her perfume. In so doing, suction fixed my nostrils to the glass prompting a sneeze announcing the surveillance. The female strained at her leash in my direction.

"No need to be sorry, *Signora,* there is plenty to occupy me," Grazia said. "One day he'll dig a hole too deep, and he'll be gone." Her eyes gleamed. She traded her apron for an overcoat. "I'll take the truck to church."

"*Si,*" the Contessa responded with an eye to the yard. "*Va bene.* Should I start the bread?"

"I'll be home before it's time to bake."

Fresh bread. Grazia's masterpiece.

"No need to rush. Let me start. It's been a while since I've baked."

She opened the door for Grazia and closed it behind her as she said, *"Ciao."*

My tail went limp. The prospect of *pane alla Contessa* did not hold the same appeal. Her delicate hands were not made for kneading. She leaned into a small mirror adjacent to the door. I sensed that the making of bread was last on her list. Smoothing her hair, she daubed the corner of her mouth and licked her lips.

She attached my collar to a leash and we emerged into the yard. La Squisita stood stock still, tail flagged, pale and perfect as a Vatican statue. The woman allowed me only the subtlest introduction at the end of a taut line. Our noses met. Sweet, warm breath feigned a tenuous caress. But the scent of heat had disappeared. It must have been leftover from her bound around the yard the days before. I moaned under my breath. The opportunity for an instant connection, so to speak, was over—for now. Courtship was to be longer.

At once, we bounced at the end of our tethers. All misunderstandings seemed to fall away under protection of the restraining order issued by a leash. I noted the value of common restraint to any good relationship as the four of us walked politely across the lawn. Squisita was strangely quiet, as always.

Shy. I found it intriguing and frustrating at the same time. I yearned to hear her voice.

"I guess they have decided to get to know one another better," remarked the Contessa.

"Never too late," replied Umberto. He tilted his head.

I barked twice, trying to coax Squisita into doing the same, but she was silent, only giving a bounce or two in reply.

"A dog like that usually has a healthy bark," said the Contessa. "She's so quiet."

"She'd ruin the hunting from here to *Firenze* if she had a voice," said Umberto. "The vet took it while she was still a pup. That was our deal if I couldn't have the hound I wanted. Grazia got the dog she preferred if I could depend on its silence."

The Contessa managed a painful smile at the information. I stopped to chew the small buds on the wood rose as I examined Umberto's face, sniffing the air for intent. It was a cruel thing to silence a dog. Barking was seldom without good cause. I gave Squisita an understanding nudge as we continued on through the vineyard gate, down the rows of expanding grapes, and headed for the banks of the creek.

She wasn't shy, I thought. She was mute.

Sunday afternoon. The area was absent normal staff that nurtured the grapes and blended the wine. I took advantage of the chance to mark the progression of the journey without reprisal. Squisita might still suffer under the impression that this place belonged to her. I marked everything.

The couple lingered as well. At considered positions, they fondled the tender vines, caressing tiny clusters of grapes that lay hidden underneath the new growth.

"Under the new leaf," said the Contessa, "*sorpresa.*" She turned her thumb under the bottom of the leaves to reveal a budding cluster. With a coy grin, she let her hand touch the man's as if to tease.

Umberto examined the woman's face as he would a garden tomato, testing its ripeness, considering the optimum time to pluck it from the vine. "A very *pleasant* surprise."

Down, boy, I thought. I was willing to excuse the impropriety of the episode to a point. The day had taken a happy turn. Yet, the morning frenzy in the garden, along with the new information granted by Grazia, caused me to rethink my estimation of Umberto. I raised a leg to the trellis stake adjacent Umberto's feet.

"Rascal," chuckled the man. He shook one leg in jest, then leaned down to pat my head. An easy, crooked smile that made one cheek bulge crossed Umberto's handsome face. It gave him an uneven appearance, slightly off kilter, a nod to his character. I cast him a sideways glance. The man was unstable.

Yet, it was good to see the Contessa share a pleasure with a man so obviously devoted to anything leafy, something she treasured. She was smiling again. Things were improving.

When we reached the flats, Squisita and I demonstrated our amicability enough to be set free. Memories of false starts and confused possession were left behind. We leapt and twirled in the lengthening grass along the stream. I delighted in the play. The body language Squisita used to convey herself—a sideways glance here, a wiggle of her rear end there—was charming. I understood her meaning and the challenge captivated me. Relieved to find the balance of a pleasant personality to Squisita's darker side, I relaxed.

We ran the length of the stream to the fence designating the border of the vineyard. There the creek widened, its water thinning enough for us to splash across to the other side. We loped along the opposite bank. At the edge of the dense wood, we stopped to shake the moisture from our bellies. Squisita struck a quiet pose and turned an alert ear to the wood. A soft rustling from the thicket. I knew the noise. Small animals rooting in the loose dirt of the underbrush.

Piglets.

It was an opportunity for entertainment, but I also knew from experience that young pigs were generally in the company of wild, unpleasant sows. Every summer the angry creatures vexed me. The battle was long and stubborn.

Not the time, I thought. Large pigs were a greater problem to a dog of middle age and recovering health than to a tall, spry dog of foolish youth. I barked a caution to Squisita. She bolted through the brush.

Male vanity, and my position as a noble, compelled me to follow her into the forest. And, I admit, a brave heart propelled me toward the snapping undergrowth indicating Squisita's path. But my level head hoped she would either meet a litter of unattended piglets or come to her senses before she reached the sow.

I closed my eyes as I wiggled through a sticky mass of thorny underbrush and thick vines. In the momentary darkness a breeze nudged my flank suggesting the close and rapid passage of a large creature in the opposite direction. By the time I opened my eyes, all that remained was a pleasant odor in the wake of La Squisita, and the repulsive features of a stubbly sow. Her nature was decidedly disagreeable. She barreled through the thicket in my direction.

A mother's fury, I thought. Best avoided. I wondered if Greta would adopt the same attitude about her puppies. Such behavior would dampen their morning romps across the Pincio.

Fancy footwork prevailed as I sped past the pig just far enough to cause her to turn. I then doubled back to pass her once again before her bulky form allowed her to turn in the dense scrub. Toward the edge of the wood I raced. She grunted her displeasure in the distance. I splashed the stream to the safety of the opposite bank, a short distance from Squisita.

La Squisita, calm and poised, sat on the sand as if nothing frightful whatsoever had occurred. In fact, the elevation of her profile suggested a certain inquiry into, if not an irritation with, the tardiness of my return. Next to her, the oddest image of all: Umberto locked in shared embrace with the Contessa. The clinch suggested much more than a mutual admiration for horticulture, the music of Elvis or the recent bravery of a certain small dog. I circled the couple twice, sniffing Umberto's shoes and pants.

There was little air of warmth about them. And the woman's feelings read cool as well. The ether was as bursting with hollow intent as it was in the apartment of La Donna Rosa. Yet, there was no denying the picture. I sneezed a bit of brush from my nose. Cheerless, I looked up at the man.

Persona non grata. A commoner, as well. The hot sun beat down upon me. From the oven to the flame, I thought.

Squisita sat unmoved by the vision; unaware of the implication or impact the moment might have on our lives. My stomach tightened.

The end. Not only would the Count leave, but most likely, Grazia, as well. Nothing was certain. I might even find myself without the Contessa. My kingdom may be defined but it would be without a queen.

"No cook," Greta had said.

Using a back paw to scratch a bit of dirt from my ear, I regarded the couple before me. Both in work clothes, they were grimy, yet the elegance of the Contessa shone through. Umberto, however, was coarse from his rough shirt to his scrappy hands.

A repulsive combination. Like fine olive oil and water from the tap. My emotions were mixed, jumbled like a week's worth of leftovers, difficult to distinguish and slightly sour. I sat down. All I wanted to do was define a simple scheme to bring my people back together. But the first order of business was covering up the stolen ring. One indiscretion was all I could handle at a time.

Squisita walked to my side and licked my jowl. My ears drooped. I relaxed. Doggish optimism was contagious. Squisita gave my face a final lick.

Hope, I thought. I looked up at the couple as they walked toward the *villa*. At least the Contessa seemed content. I glanced at Squisita. The object of my desire finally had come around. Even the worst of days could have a happy ending. I gave Squisita an affectionate nudge.

Having was *much* better than wanting, I thought. Grazia was misinformed.

Chapter Sixteen

At Umberto's apartment, the couple hesitated. Hand in hand, they were silent. They exchanged a long look: no warmth, nor adoration, but promise. A stilted pact. Then they slipped their grasp and parted.

I followed the Contessa up the slope of the lawn to the *terrazzo*. I stood on the flagstone patio and stared. Her face was flushed. She paused at the patio table, gathering the cards left behind by Il Conte. Tapping the deck on the glass top once, our eyes met.

"Che cos'è?"

I licked my snout slowly. What, indeed.

"Don't look at me that way." The woman pulled her gaze to the vineyard below.

The accusatory tone of her voice made me uneasy. I looked around to see if there might be something amiss, but I knew in my heart that her accusation was rhetorical.

Guilt.

"That day on the corner in the city," she said, "you saw the Count's jealousy." A cloud of crows flew overhead, dappling the Contessa's pale skin in shadow as she watched them pass. "It just might work." She giggled. "He *is* handsome enough—and attentive. And Grazia has written him off. It will make no difference to her. In fact she might enjoy him being used for a change, instead of the other way around. It's clear he can be easily led. Umberto, the fix-it man."

More like in a fix, I thought.

At least it was an idea. Better than anything that had crossed *my* mind. Perhaps this was just what the doctor ordered. The crows swirled in the air, sputtering, one after the other, onto the garden fence. I raised a front paw in the initiation of a chase. When the woman walked toward me, I paused.

"Well—" she said, "two can play."

It was the tone she used when trying to get me from underneath the bed for medicine. Unconvincing then; unconvincing now. Yet, I would go along. There was no alternative. She shuffled the cards between her hands. I listened as they rustled through her thumbs.

Umberto emerged from the apartment and headed for the garden.

Solitaire. The only safe game when you're playing with a cheater. Perhaps there was still time to avoid blame, if I could only think of something. I examined the Contessa's bare hand holding the cards, then bent round to sniff my belly, imagining the incision reopened. Of course, it would all be for naught. There was no ring in my belly this time. Censure would be mine for depositing it at some secret place around the yard.

Disconsolate, I dropped my snout and looked at my feet. They were filthy from the creek side. My gloom was sure to be protracted with a ban from the house.

The Contessa put the card deck on the table and walked to a broom standing against the *villa*. She swept the grass cuttings from the edge of the patio as I moved to protection underneath the table. Concentrating on cleanliness, for it was easy admission back into the *villa*, I licked the mud from my feet. Grit crunched between my teeth. I swiped my tongue over them to clean away the residue and examined the ground. Crumbs from the Count's breakfast lay spread about. I pushed my nose through the fallen bits of flaky pastry. Following their trail in a circle around the man's chair, I licked a dark path over the pale, flat stones. The pieces were still crispy. I closed my eyes and let the flakes dissolve on my tongue.

What's fare is fair, I thought. In all cases, food was the answer. It always had a way of solving problems, or at least lending a pleasant delay to their solution. I gave a final lick and opened my eyes.

There, at the base of one of the claw-footed chairs—a glimmer of hope: the ring.

When the Count's jacket had dropped on the patio earlier, the ring must have rolled from the pocket. It lay before me sparkling in the midday sun; treasure amid the scraps. The gem rested on the dark stone like a star in the night sky.

As perfect as man is flawed, I thought. I blinked to clear my vision.

Glancing at the Contessa, I moved with care. If the woman saw the ring in my mouth, I was finished. Nipping it between my teeth, it grazed the *terrazzo* as I lifted it from the ground. The scraping noise buzzed my ears. I stopped, nibbling the ring further into my mouth. Eyes on the woman, I glanced at the bedroom window above. It was wide to the fresh air. My gaze slipped to the *cucina* door. Open.

Stealth. If the Contessa followed me into the house, she would head straight for the room to change. I sucked the stone onto my tongue and turned it over and over. It was cool and smooth; harder than ice. My nerves began to rise and, with them, saliva pooled in the bottom of my mouth. What I needed was a distraction. A bark toward the vineyard would do it, but was impossible with my mouth occupied. There would be no return trip for the gem to my belly. I pushed the ring into my jowl and swallowed with care. I cast my Contessa a crosswise glance and moved a paw in the direction of the *villa*.

The woman ceased her sweeping. Her attention turned to the murder of crows sitting in the vineyard.

Perfect.

They cackled and cawed a boast, warning their intention to raid the newly seeded garden. The uproar brought Umberto into the yard. As the woman watched him wave off the birds, I slipped through the kitchen door.

I trotted down the hall and skipped every other stair to the bedroom. Jewelry still lay strewn across the floor. The Contessa had not returned to the room since breakfast. I pushed her watch with my nose. There was no way to collect the mess. So I walked into the middle and dropped the ring. The flutter of wings brought my attention to the open window.

A crow stood on the sill, turning his head from side to side, eyeing the sparkling floor. It was a bold move. The local crows knew my wrath, but the lure of shiny things is overwhelming to the raven. Even a dog knows this. The shiny tag on my collar was eyed more than once by bandit crows.

The bird swooped from the window to the floor. One glide and the ring was in its beak. Before I turned to snap, the Contessa surprised us both. The bird fled without measuring its exit. So shocked was it by the woman, it missed the window altogether. Slapping the plaster wall with a thud, it slid to the floor in a mix of under-feathers and dust.

The ring dropped from its grasp, bounced twice, then skidded across the bare floor at the edge of the room. With a rattle and a clang, it disappeared down a vent.

The woman shrieked. I charged the crow. The bird eyed the open window with caution and fled. Up and over the window seat, side curtains billowing in the commotion, I had one leg out the window before the Contessa pulled me to safety.

How much had she seen?

"Che cos'è successo?" she asked. "My brave little boy. *Molto coraggioso."*

Si, è vero, I thought. *I* was the enforcer.

"Ladri," said the woman. "Nothing but grifters." She placed me on the floor and stooped to gather the fallen jewelry.

Exonerated by a thieving crow, I thought. I shook off the idea. There would be no appointment with the vet. And even though the ring was being held hostage by a heating vent, at least it was out of the reach of Il Conte. The Contessa knelt at the opening in the floor. I joined her. She lifted an ornate iron grate off the orifice. We both peered down the dark vent. It looked bottomless and empty. The ring was gone.

"*Miseria.*" The woman shook her head and looked at me. "Well, at least we know where it is."

The accident was a perfect strategy. I only wished it had been my idea.

A car door slammed below. I hopped up to the window seat. As Grazia walked to the house, Umberto climbed into the truck and rolled down the driveway.

The Contessa watched the truck disappear. "It will have to wait."

The phone rang and the woman answered. I heard the Count's voice on the other end of the line. It was measured in its speech, but the tone was frantic.

"*Si, si,*" said the Contessa, "of course. Everything's fine here. Why do you ask?"

The ring. Il Conte was missing it by now. My ears perked at the news. I imagined the man fuming, face red, eyes bulging as he searched his pocket for the ring and came away with only keys.

My Contessa hung up the phone and looked at me. "He'd be furious if he knew I'd lost it. You don't tell him, and I won't." She pulled the window shut. "Besides, if he saw it first, he'd never let me know. I won't have it back on the hand of another woman. Umberto will have to fix that, too."

At the mercy of madmen. Between Ahab and the whale. I shook my head. The best plan was a simple plan. One focus, one result. At least the ring was out of the picture for a while.

I concentrated on the details of the day while a rumbling rose from my belly. The Contessa disappeared into the bathroom and a sea of noise rose up from the shower. I stretched, giving the vent a final sniff, then retreated to the kitchen and the sanity often found in a bowl of fresh polenta.

Chapter Seventeen

D usk reached the *villa* just as Grazia finished baking the bread. She divided the dough that, overlooked by the Contessa, had overflowed its bowl. It stuck fast to the cover of a dried-out cloth. Grazia scraped the linen with a dull knife and rolled the remnants of dough into little balls for me and Squisita to nibble.

The dinner dishes were washed, the kitchen cleaned, but still Umberto hadn't come. The smell of hot *pane* permeated the house, casting a comforting calm over the day's insanity. The Contessa mentioned nothing of the ring to Grazia.

Smart move. The fewer told, the better. The ring was safe as long as the truth was kept from Il Conte.

The Contessa remained quiet the rest of the day, keeping to herself in the *villa's* front salon, reading through old books and new magazines. As soon as the sun slid behind the low western hills, and I'd taken my last excursion into the yard, I begged the woman to retire. I was exhausted. Excess knowledge takes a toll on the psyche of any dog. All I wanted was to sleep until the sun rose again. Morning always clarified a situation.

The Contessa needed no excuse. With one short whine and a lick she was convinced. When we entered our bedroom, the woman turned on her music. She pushed the window open. At the heating vent, we both paused, giving the dark shaft a long, wistful look.

"Domani," said the woman. "Umberto will fetch it tomorrow."

Bad idea. A visit to the bedroom was an invitation to more trickery. Besides, the missing ring granted time for finding a solution to the dire straits.

Low booms sprang from the heating vent next to the outside wall, followed by a gentle push of warm air out the grate and the Contessa jumped at the noise.

"An old house," she said, "creaks more every year. The only solution is to knock it down and start again, but that's like digging up the plant because one tomato's bad." She put her hand on the wall in a gentle caress of the *villa*. "There are still good tomatoes on the vine, *no*?"

I jumped onto the bed, settling into one of the fluffy pillows. The woman changed into a silky gown, then pulled a large, thick book from a low shelf and crawled under the feather covers beside me. Turning the glossy pages of the photo album with care, she reviewed them front to back and back to front again. Now and again she chuckled or sighed, until the evening turned to chill.

I curled into my customary spot for the night: a shallow depression in the warm crook behind my Contessa's knee. She laid a soothing hand across my flank. Her touch was relaxing. Yet, so much had happened it was difficult to fall asleep. My eyes fluttered with a montage of snapshots from the day.

A breath of musty air puffed past my nose. I raised my head above the thick book to get a better sense of the odor. A broad page from the album turned and, like old leaves beneath a porch, the scent of memories from seasons past beckoned. I stood up, moving closer for a better view.

The Contessa fingered each page with a gentle touch across the surface, as though it might crumble. There were dozens of old pictures—and the note cards.

The Contessa smiled. "Ovidius," she said. "Love is no assignment for cowards." She looked at me. "True, yes?"

I returned the gaze, then watched as she moved her hand across the page to another card. "Ogden Nash," she said. "*Americano*, Shimoni. *Poeto*."

I looked at the card. The writing was small because the words were many. The Contessa pulled her glasses from the bed-stand and pushed them onto her nose.

English was not a second language for me. But the way they sounded on her lips was beautiful and I gleaned by the tone of her voice that they tickled her in some way.

"To keep your marriage brimming, With love in the wedding up, Whenever you're wrong admit it; Whenever you're right shut up." Her body shook with laughter. Perhaps some progress was being made. The memories made her happy.

She wiped the teary laughter from her eyes and settled into a chuckle. I watched as the page was turned. She read a few more of the notes, smiling as if she remembered each time she'd written them. Then her face changed. The smile faded into contemplation. She used one finger to trace a single short sentence on another small card in the middle of the page.

The Contessa's chin quivered and a small tear rolled down her cheek. She swallowed hard before the words, "True love stories have no ending."

I nuzzled her hand, licking the warm space between her fingers. Adjacent my nose lay an assortment of photographs. Me, my Contessa and the Count; trips to the mountains and the beach; holidays, birthdays and Christmas. The image of them was warming. I looked up at the Contessa. Her dark eyes shone pale in the reflection of the pictures. She laid her hand across a photo of the couple. They held each other so close, no light fell between them, faces bright with optimism.

"Not so long ago," she said, "but many miles in between. Who took the first step away?" The woman put her hand on my back and scratched at the base of my tail. "But we both hurt. It's difficult to change for someone who's wounded you, no?"

I put my paws on the woman's chest and licked her chin. It was salty and soft, and I tasted something intangible.

Regret. Like leaving a favorite toy behind on a train that pulled from the station. I turned back to the album. For a moment the photos provided comfort, but the feeling was hollow. Something was missing.

Squisita.

Though I hadn't known her long, in all her silence, she seemed to center me. For once, I had to divine how someone else must feel, for she couldn't tell me. I had to really care. And that meant everything. For me, time began that day at the *terrazzo* doors, when I'd seen her first. The recollection still took my breath away. Any happiness before was halfhearted in her absence; incomplete.

The click of toenails came from the terrazzo below. I raised my head and lifted my ears. La Squisita and Grazia, headed for the apartment. *Buona notte.* I drew a long breath. She was my bright spot; without her, things were lost. I yawned and circled again a time or two before resettling. Digging up memories was hard work.

Umberto's truck rumbled to the back of the house. I looked toward the window as the Contessa flung back the covers. She crossed the room to the side of the curtains, peering through the gauze as the car door slammed. The entrance to the apartment banged closed from across the yard. The woman delivered the photo album to its shelf, and restarted the music before returning to bed. The wavering voice of Elvis wafted across the room. "Are You Lonesome Tonight?"

Yes.

The man's voice was almost as good as a pair of warm arms. The Contessa lay on her back and stared at the ceiling. I moved to the head of the covers and burrowed beneath the blankets. I braced myself against the warmth of the woman's belly and slipped between the cleavage of her warm, soft breasts. The air under the sheets was close and balmy. Like the breath of La Squisita. Her odor still clung to my fur. Imagining us, nested together, shooed the loneliness away. The Contessa snored softly. I closed my eyes to the darkness and drifted into sleep.

*

Rain pummeled the window pane. The Contessa and I awakened at the same time. I leaped from the bed to the seat beneath the window. Disorganized showers scattered across the narrow valley. Heavy blossoms on the chestnut tree drooped at the threat. Dressed in bright slickers, a few people in the vine rows weeded around the base of each vine. They sang to pass the time, binding languorous shoots that scrambled along the trellises in all directions.

"*Buon giorno,*" saluted Grazia. She delivered the luxury of a late breakfast to the Contessa on a bed tray and a small piece of boar sausage into my mouth. "*Tutto bene?*"

Yes, I thought, things are quite well when the morning begins with sausage.

"I didn't sleep so well," said the Contessa. "I think I'll just have a bite, then rest a little more."

"*Certo, Signora,*" said Grazia.

I jumped to the floor and padded down the stairs ahead of Grazia as she returned to the kitchen. My bowl cradled a feathery heap of scrambled egg whites crowned with the remains of a perfect small piece of pig sausage. I wasted no time licking the bowl clean. Underneath it all was the small knuckle bone of a young calf. A simple gift commemorating the new day. I gave Grazia an affectionate glance and lifted it gently from the bowl. At the *terrazzo* doors, I asked politely for access to the yard. A short whine through a full mouth. Grazia obliged with a satisfying scratch behind my ear. The door opened.

The shower had passed, but the clouds were still low and dark. The smell of the day was fresh and glorious, like a clean bowl of clear water. I trotted out into the wet grass, tagging the oil jars as I went. Umberto had again moved them around, this time to the left a few feet.

Like his women, I thought, rotated frequently.

Round indentations lay in the dirt where the pots last rested. The damp earth wiggled with worms disturbed by the relocation. I nuzzled one of the writhing creatures with my wet nose. It was slightly sticky, with the odor of *funghi*: disgusting and delectable at

145

the same moment. Few things matched the mushroom. Except the worm. As I considered the value of a snack so soon after breakfast, I nosed the earth for a soft spot to begin a new hole.

There was treasure buried all over the yard like money in the bank. I relaxed in the knowledge that no matter what happened, I would eat. I pulled my paws through the dirt, a little on one side, then the other. Soon the excavation was even and deep. A masterpiece. I set the bone inside and sat down to regard my work.

Perfect.

The cache was often of less importance than the beauty of the hole itself. And that, of course, depended on the art of its creation. It was not, after all, how big the hole was or what it held, but the engineering involved.

Umberto emerged from the winery below, basket of freshly cut baby vegetables in hand. He disappeared behind the building. I supposed Squisita might be close behind. I pushed loose dirt back into the hole and loped down the hill. Rounding the winery, I arrived just in time to see Squisita peering out of the back window of Umberto's truck. The engine turned and the vehicle crunched along the gravel path toward the main road below the *villa*. I stood in the middle of the driveway after the truck disappeared. I sniffed bits of raw produce in the well of a muddy tire rut, trying to recall the various outings he took.

The market, I concluded. Melancholy at the prospect of a lonely, tedious morning, I turned to make my way back up the hill to my *villa*.

Halfway to the top, a crack of thunder split the air. The broad open doors of the winery stood wide. I ran to shelter and, under cover, watched the rain fall in transparent sheets across the valley.

I looked around. The interior of the building had seldom been explored. The winemaker discouraged the assistance of dogs in the making of wine. Now, alone among tall rows of shiny tanks, I made my own additions to the blend. I raised a defiant leg at the foot of one tank. Steam rose from the mark. Like fermented grapes on the compost pile, the musty, drunken smell of the place was intoxicating.

My gaze settled on a ladder propped against a high loft full of bird sounds.

Stairs beneath it offered an earthy aroma, reminding me of worms on the lawn. The appealing scent beckoned exploration. I followed the stairs leading to a damp room filled with stacks of large wooden barrels. I gave a hearty sniff to those resting on the ground. Letting my tongue pause at dark stains that bled here and there at the seams of the wood, I noted the scent of acorns and berries. But there were no acorns in the crannies between the barrels, nor berries a dog might enjoy.

I bounded up the stairs to rest at the base of the ladder that met the loft.

I caught the flicker of a beating wing passing like a shadow across the upper wall. Mesmerized, I watched swallows dart in and out of a second story door that opened from the loft to the sky above the garden. The birds swam across the sky like schools of fish. Diving, pausing and plunging, they painted their way across the canvas of storm clouds.

The rain beat the roof in time to the movement of the flock. Then, all at once, the sky opened and water fell in sheets. Noise filled the winery like applause. The birds retreated from the arena of the heavens to the dry loft in a sudden rush. The winery vibrated with the chaos of their song amid the storm.

Seized by the instinct that drives a dog favoring the hunt, I yearned to reach the loft. Without a care to danger, I began to climb the ladder. As I ascended, the scent of ripe pork caught me.

Prosciutti. I'd seen Grazia climbing the ladder with such a prize, hanging it to dry under the eaves. I concentrated on the climb in earnest. Several rungs up, a rude hand grabbed the scruff of my neck. The winemaker.

The man gingerly removed me from my purpose, tossing me headlong into the insult of inclement weather. I stood in the cool rain and looked behind me to the open door. The man smiled.

The hams, I thought. The man was protecting the *prosciutti*. Everything in the winery fell under the jurisdiction of the winemaker. I sneezed a raindrop from my nose. The defense of edibles was a serious matter. I tossed the man a forgiving look and headed for the *villa*.

Rain still poured from above. The people in the vineyard raced for the cover of their cars. They headed for home, the comfort of dry clothes, and the long midday meal.

Lunch. My belly grumbled at the thought. I looked back to the winery.

The winemaker climbed the ladder with a bottle of unlabeled wine in one hand. Perhaps the man intended to take lunch with a bit of ham. It was his prerogative, after all, and his obligation. The sampling of the wine was his job, no doubt of the *prosciutti* as well. I shook the rain from my back and decided to revisit my breakfast bowl.

As I reached the patio, Grazia emerged from the *cucina* under the protection of a broad, black umbrella. She waddled past me, across the lawn, down the slope toward the winery as though I were invisible. I caught up to her as she entered the building. I stood just inside the broad doors, out of the driving rain. Grazia stopped at the foot of the ladder, tilted her head back as she always did in laughter, and looked up to the loft.

"*Ciao, caro,*" she called.

I followed her gaze. My eyes met those of the winemaker at the edge of the loft.

The winemaker called out. "*Ciao, bella. Vieni qui.*"

The woman chuckled roundly, broad girth quaking as she began her ascent. Upon reaching the top, she spilled over into the loft like a scoop of *gelato* from a child's cone, disappearing beyond its edge in a pool of laughter. With a whoosh, the swarm of swallows exited the loft.

Uccellini.

Grazia was expert at cooking these wild young birds, bathing them in oil and toasting them on the open spit above the fire in the corner of the *cucina*. Delicate bones, I thought, brittle between the teeth. Salty and crisp like thin fried potatoes, and marrow sweet. I whined. There was no reason to leave me behind. I was always helpful in hunting.

Besides, I wanted to see the forbidden place, to chase the birds, to sniff the hams. Straw spilled over the side of the loft. It wafted through the air like so many feathers, settling here and there on the ground below. Grazia and the winemaker scuffled and puffed above me. I braced myself.

Gunfire, I thought. It always capped the hunt. Grazia was a crack shot at bagging anything that flew. She never had to shoot twice, and always aimed to hit the heart.

"No creature should suffer the lengthy demise of a poor aim," she'd once said.

Birds fell like fists against the ground when Grazia joined a hunt. She'd taught me to retrieve them gently, for bruises left tough spots on roasted flesh.

But no shots came. Only persistent panting. The noise fed my imagination. Thoughts swirled in my head as I slavered and complained.

Shoot, I thought. Few birds scare to death.

I had tried that once. A flock of geese, an open field; I was certain a surprise attack would stop at least one beating heart. I skulked through the tall dry grass until just upon them—then surprise. I took aim and ran, only to be confronted by a giant gander, wings spread, bill open. The creature must have had ten pounds on me. I cut off the charge, banking a tight turn, but not soon enough. The goose nipped clean all the hair from the end of my tail. No casualties. No fright. Save my own. It took a whole afternoon to recover under the *cucina* table, back to the comfort of an autumn fire. No, birds do not scare to the table. But small ones, I could corner. I was as swift as any winged creature, whose only advantage, in my opinion, was flight. I outwitted most birds foolish enough to tease me. Grazia and the winemaker needed my help. I barked repeatedly and began to climb.

Halfway up, a back paw slipped, slicing a splintery step across my thigh. The ladder gripped me in a most indelicate position, wide rung resting precariously at an unfortunate spot between my back legs. I yelped.

With that, the face of the winemaker appeared over the lip of the loft. I froze. The man rested his chin at the top rung and cracked a smile. I watched in disbelief as he pushed the ladder back with his hands. He rocked it into a vertical position, then back again.

Stupid. The man was not bright in things beyond the vine. The fact that dogs lack the inherent ability to cling escaped him. But neither did he understand the truth about dogs: we were cleverer than humans. We depend on our wit, and God's infatuation, in order to survive.

I held my breath, counting on Providence as the ladder tilted. The slippery rungs lay firmly wedged into the crooks of my legs. I hung like a ham on a hook, riding the rails out into the air and back again. I eyed the straw-strewn concrete floor below, just as Grazia appeared to playfully chide the man.

"*Caro,*" she said, "*attenzione.* He doesn't have wings."

Wings, indeed. If I had wings I'd be as safe as the uncaptured birds in the loft.

"I'm only playing with him," chuckled the man. He slowly tipped the ladder back against the loft, but it was of no use. I could neither go up nor down.

"I will have to rescue him," said the winemaker. The man swung his legs over the lip of the loft and in doing so, lost hold of the ladder. He made a hasty grab, saving it to deliver us back to earth, but its capture came with a jolt.

A thump and a cry, and I struck the pavement.

"*Santa Maria,*" Grazia cried.

Then, seeing that I was intact, she laughed.

Grazia was usually mindful of the predicaments of small dogs, but now she was flushed and unconcerned. It was as if the whole affair was for her amusement. The man joined her cackling. They wrapped their arms about one another and nuzzled each other warmly. I sat on the cold floor below; pride bruised, hope dashed, but unhurt.

A solitary bird flew from the loft to the safety of the open air. I shook the straw from my fur and stared at Grazia. I supposed the woman too consumed by the capture of small birds to notice my situation. Focus was necessary to successful pursuit. But when the couple climbed down out of the loft with nothing to show for their work, I was astonished.

Incompetent, I thought. Had they invited me to the hunt, a slew of *uccellini* would be cooking on the grill that night. I trotted up to Grazia, sniffed her hands and the pockets of her apron for a hint of small bird or *prosciutti*. Nothing save the sweet smell of straw, the winemaker's cologne—and suddenly little doubt in my mind at what just occurred in the loft above.

The rules of the house had changed.

Disgusting. I felt ill. Like when I tried to focus on things that passed by the car too quickly.

Yet, the air about Grazia was warm like the *cucina* fire. Contentment radiated from her pores like sweat from a day under the hot sun. Still, I was appalled. A good meal was forfeit for the sake of impropriety. I indicated my irritation by turning my back on the offer of Grazia's arms. I walked unflinchingly into the thundering storm, in the direction of my house.

Pandemonium.

Rain dripped from my belly. All I wanted was the comfort of shelter in the warmth of the *cucina*. I would curl upon my pillow and await the return of La Squisita. Her antics were staid compared to the bedlam these humans created.

I closed my eyes to the wind and let my instincts guide me to the *villa*. My nose was first to arrive at the wet *terrazzo* doors. Closed tight. Admittance denied; I retreated to the patio, taking cover under the wide table.

The rain splashed up as it hit the *terrazzo* hard. It turned to spray, gusting under the table in the wind. Turning my back to the weather, I watched rain drip from the full blooming lilacs near the *villa*. I narrowed my eyes to the water streaming from my brow and sat heavy under the weight of my soggy fur and flagging spirit. As the gale whipped my ears I did my best to picture the marshal of summer and its improving days.

Chapter Eighteen

I was deep in thought when the *terrazzo* doors squeaked open. The Contessa stood in the doorway, dressed, cappuccino in hand. *"Che succede?* What are you doing out there?"

There was no time to waste. I darted for the kitchen, crossing the threshold just as Grazia walked back up the slope from the winery. When she entered the kitchen, I gave my body a vigorous shake, dousing her with secondhand rain.

"Shimoni! What's the matter with you?"

"He's been huddled in the storm, under the table," said the Contessa. "I just let him in."

Grazia cast a cool glance my way. "Sulking? Don't worry. The world will not end. *Capisci?"*

Too late. I understood. She had a secret. Who didn't in this house? Still, I was aghast. It seemed as though the only creature left on earth of any dependability was dog itself. The rest were a fickle lot, indeed. The whole world was a jumble: La Donna Rosa and the Count, the Contessa and Umberto, Grazia and the winemaker. They were all *pazzi.* La Squisita and I would no doubt end up crazy, as well.

Grazia glowed from head to toe. She wore a gentle smile on her full lips as she adjusted her undergarments with a soft, discreet hand to her blouse. "Lunch?"

"Not for me, thanks," said the Contessa. "Where's Umberto?"

"At market, I think."

The Contessa opened the patio door. She walked onto the wet flagstone. I followed as far as the door. I had no wish to return to the outdoors just yet. The rain stopped and thin rays of sunlight teased through the clouds. The ground steamed under the spotty light. The woman stood facing the *villa*. She examined the wall, putting a hand to her chin and wrinkling her brow.

Grazia stood at the door. "Something wrong, *Signora*?"

"No, no." The Contessa paused. "I was just thinking. A fireplace in the bedroom is a nice idea. I found this picture in an old magazine. *Un bello camino, no?* Probably have to tear into the outside wall, though, for footing"

Grazia joined the Contessa on the patio. "*Si, si*. A big mess." Grazia chuckled. "That will keep Umberto out of trouble for a while."

Both women laughed. The Contessa let her eyes follow Grazia as she returned to the kitchen. Her laughter faded into thought. She returned a serious gaze to the *villa* wall. The rumble of Umberto's truck pulled her down the hill to greet him. La Squisita's jump from the cab was enough to lure me from safety in the kitchen.

"I have a problem," the Contessa said when she met Umberto.

The man leered in her direction. "I know." He snapped the gum in his mouth as he pulled several empty burlap bags from the truck bed.

Squisita and I bounced around the front of the vehicle, exchanging fleas and other intimate details.

The Contessa sounded annoyed. "Besides that."

I stopped bouncing to better hear the conversation, but Squisita would not be still. She continued to dart and weave in an effort to entice me into joining the frivolity. I snapped a warning. Squisita shied in surprise. She apologized by way of a thorough snout wash with her soft, warm tongue. It was an able distraction, but I kept one ear well tuned.

Umberto stopped what he was doing to face her. "*Mi dica.*"

"I've lost a piece of jewelry down the heating vent," she said.

"No easy find, *Signora*."

"*Perché no?*"

"The *villa* is very old." Umberto rubbed his forehead. "The vents were not always vents. They do not stand free, but in the middle of solid wall. One cannot simply walk through the cellar to find one, Contessa, and open it at the bottom."

Of course, I thought. The woman knew this. She cursed the sounds that came from the heater. She was well aware the vents were impossible to change through the solid wall without great effort. Why ask?

La Squisita continued her work, moving to the top of my head. The eyes were the first to succumb, half-closed, then three-quarters. Finally, blind to the couple before me, and deafened to the conversation by the smacking in my ears, I was powerless to think under the spell of Squisita. Words came, but their meaning was lost.

"If the Count finds out I have been so careless, he'll be very angry." The Contessa lowered her chin. She looked up at the man through her dark eyelashes.

Blah, blah, blah, blah, blah.

"It will be a great amount of work," said Umberto, "and mess. There is no way to keep it from Il Conte."

Blah, blah, blah.

The Contessa nodded. "Hmm. What about a remodel?"

The man tilted his head toward the *villa*. "To do what?"

"A fireplace, perhaps?" she suggested, pointing to the house. "On that outside wall. The footing has to go into the ground. That allows you to get to the base of the vent with a good excuse. I'll tell the Count the ring is out being sized. It will buy the time to have you retrieve it—if you're quick."

Blah, blah.

The woman had moved to the *terrazzo*, Umberto in tow, pointing and pacing, by the time the spell was broken. La Squisita sat close by under a sunbeam, grooming her white hair, point complete, my irritation dissolved. I ran up to the patio.

"You'll have to move into the guest room," said Umberto, "and it won't be as quiet as your quarters. Your privacy will suffer." The man gave her a lecherous grin.

Why move? I thought. The guest bed was half the size and suffered the fate of a lean, hard mattress. Residence in the spare room was only a last resort. The couch was a better offer.

"The kitchen is below the guest room," said the Contessa, "but I don't think it will be too noisy."

Umberto tossed her a sly smile. "It is *your* sounds that may be overheard."

The Contessa stared as though trying to picture the last time any clandestine sounds had come from the bedroom. She looked down at me with a slow bat of her eyelashes. The corner of her mouth quivered. "Oh, well. What does it matter, anyway?"

"Only that I will have to take my *caffetto* in the kitchen and keep an ear tuned to the ceiling from now on." Umberto wore a wicked smile. "I like those sounds."

The Contessa drew a long breath and lifted an eyebrow. "You might have quite a wait for that and this can't take too long."

Time was a relative thing in Rome. In the countryside it was an honored practice. In Italy, nothing moved swiftly but the back of a hand to a woman's ass.

Sweat dripped from Umberto's brow under the breaking sunlight of the afternoon. "It will be well into *autunno*."

The Contessa straightened. "It'll be summer's end."

He wrinkled his brow as though unconvinced, twisting his lips at the proposition. "A great amount of work to put things right," Umberto mumbled.

"*Sempre*," said the Contessa. She followed Squisita and me into the kitchen. "It always is."

Chapter Nineteen

T he remodel was well underway when the Count returned from Rome. He'd only been away a week, but the weather had been warm and the lilac blooms had turned to brown. Umberto had been kept busy and the Contessa had kept to herself.

The Count's brow furrowed in consternation as he examined the bedroom. *"Un camino?"*

"Si, a fireplace." The Contessa walked to the door, answering him at the exit. "I need *something* to keep me warm."

The Count fell silent. I sniffed the man's slacks. La Donna Rosa. I examined the jacket over the bedroom chair. Hair from the Cleopatra on its edge. Il Conte watched me nose the fabric.

His tone was chilling. "The Joker." He reached down to push me off the scent. Walking to the dresser, the man tapped a finger on the jewelry dish. "She's missed the ring?"

The man looked around the room. Everything was packed up or moved.

Ring? I tipped my head, innocent façade in place.

The man drew a long breath, holding it for minute before exhaling. He loosened his tie and walked to the gap in the outside wall. Plastic sheltered the room. The sheet rattled in the breeze. The vent was a wide gaping hole leading straight to the basement. Dust sprinkled the floors. The Count's eyes rolled from side to side as though he heard voices from the walls.

"It's here, somewhere," he said, looking down at me. "The Contessa's making me suffer, and so are you. I promised that ring to someone else and it's a vow she won't let me break. If you hadn't eaten it in the first place, it would be on her hand and I'd be rid of her."

So that was it: the truth. La Donna Rosa had said as much. It was good to hear the words from the Count, as well. Why had it taken him so long to admit it? *This* crime had a noble purpose. I wiggled approval, yet I was bemused by the Count's naïveté. The *fiasco* was far beyond being solved by a single act. Little did he know just how complicated things really were. I headed for the door. At least the man was on the right track. The ring was a fair trade to bring order to the house.

"If I can't find it she'll come here to find it herself. Is that what you want?"

I stopped. Of course not, I thought. That would ruin everything. We didn't need another iron in the fire. The blaze was hot enough.

"Anyway, that is something I won't allow, no matter the cost. The Contessa might forgive the indiscretion but not my choice of accomplice."

I couldn't argue with that. I hopped down the stairs and made my way to the kitchen. As always, food was the answer: egg whites and golden polenta, a handful of chopped *prosciutto* gracing the top.

The sound of the Count's heavy steps filled the hallway. I stopped chewing to listen as the Contessa passed through the kitchen. The two people paused as they met. Then came the question.

"In the garden again?" asked the Count.

"Not today."

"You must wear your ring, then, *cara*, It shows you off so well."

I tossed my head, flipping the flap of one ear over my brow to hear better. The Count stopped breathing, waiting for the answer to come. How lost *was* the ring?

"It's too loose," she replied. "Sizing it will keep it on my finger. I took it into town."

Il Conte exhaled long and loud. "You should have given it to me, to do it for you in Rome."

"It can be done as easily in Siena," said the Contessa. "My father's shop may be closed now, but there are others. Better to keep it close by, don't you think?" The woman's steps began again as she ascended the stairs and called behind her, "We wouldn't want it to go missing, would we?"

I imagined the smirk on her face; the crestfallen look of the Count. I began to chew again. The banter reminded me of the dance of the dogs every morning on the Pincio. Dodge and weave, duck and jump. Nothing but a game.

I swallowed hard.

It was my perfect life they were betting. And it had been perfect from the time I opened my eyes.

*

It was late spring. I didn't know it then, but my nose caught the scent of every blossom and bloom as it opened in Rome. Cherries, chestnuts and laurel, the air was sweet perfume as it wafted into the kitchen of the apartment. I still sported the bow that I had arrived in. I was the Contessa's birthday gift.

The Count had found my litter through a friend. He came to visit, intent on choosing a female. He picked up each of us, though, just to measure one against the other: the lie of our fur, the number of spots, which one of us had the most aristocratic look. But, as any dog knows, personality trumps profile every time. The minute he touched me, I growled to demonstrate my brave character.

"*Corraggio,*" he said as he picked me up. "A noble trait."

The scent of his hands was cedar and tobacco, not unlike the woods I was bred to hunt. Instinct took over. I knew the instant I smelled him he was mine.

The Count tucked me into fluffy blanket and off we went, onto the streets of Rome. More scents, more sounds. I couldn't wait for my eyes to open so I could see it all. Life was going to be fun.

When we reached the apartment, the Count tied something crinkly around my neck and placed me into a comfortable nest of sorts. It was very small. I could touch each side of the container with my nose. But the cushion was soft and warm. The trip from across the city had been exhausting. After an adequate pull on the nipple of a bottle, I fell right to sleep.

"Oh, my."

I awakened to a woman's soft voice, breath scented with green apples as she kissed my head. La Contessa.

"The most precious gift," she said. "How did you think of it?"

The Count's voice was soft. "Puppies are love."

I heard them kiss.

"I give mine to you," said the Count.

Serenity beyond compare descended in the household that summer. There were treats and toys and outings; things to chew and things to chase. It seemed the Count and the Contessa were always surprising each other. Gifts appeared nearly every day.

But a simple dog had been the most precious.

*

Summer now blazed an angry peace. The project lurched forward. Many days, the work was postponed for toil in the garden, because growth and harvest wait for nothing. I dug great holes around the perimeter of the garden and Umberto filled them with stubby, young dahlias that would grow into giants along the fence come fall. As long as the Count remained at the *villa*, Umberto assigned himself to Grazia's side, and the winemaker sulked. Il Conte and the Contessa skirted each other like territorial dogs. Long mornings were spent in silence over *cappucini* and the daily paper. Afternoons were passed in the company of others. The Count made only one brief trip to Rome, but I overheard many conciliatory calls to La Donna Rosa made in secret.

By August, the hole in the *villa* wall had been taken from the second-story bedroom clear down to ground level in order to lay the foundation for a fireplace and chimney. The heating vent lay wide open to the patio on one side. Umberto took a long flashlight, lay down on the *terrazzo* and slid his upper body into the chute. I stood by, nose down. Small creatures often ran from newly disturbed places. But none appeared. Only the reverberations of Umberto's soft cursing escaped the opening.

"*Santa Maria,*" said the man as he emerged. He dusted off the grit from the vent in a great puff.

I sneezed as it filled my lungs. No ring.

"*Niente,*" Umberto confirmed under his breath.

The Count passed by, lingering at the gap beside Umberto, sucking on his pipe.

"A project," he said, shaking his head. He watched the Contessa pick small tomatoes from a bushy vine in the garden. "She has a way of stirring things up, doesn't she?" The corner of his mouth raised a smile.

Umberto kept his eyes down, removed his hat and scratched his head. "*Si, Signore.* She knows what she wants."

The Count regarded Umberto as he would a hippopotamus: ridiculous, but still a hazard. "Does anyone know what that is? Or how much it will cost?"

A rhetorical question, I thought. The very definition of a woman.

Grazia emerged from the *cucina* with a bucket and sponge. She placed them next to Umberto. Without a word, she returned to the kitchen.

"Smart men only guess," said Umberto, "—and pray."

"Quite a mess," said the Count.

Umberto looked up. "It's just started."

Il Conte grunted a nod and moved on. Umberto took up the pail and sponge and headed for a long trestle table under the big chestnut as a whistle rose from the vineyard below. I scanned the perimeter of the vineyard. Squisita appeared at the end of one row. I ran to join her. Songs and laughter radiated from under straw hats bobbing along rows of frantic vines. The vineyard crew was in full force. Foliage was pruned to admit the perfect amount of light, ripening the young grapes to their best advantage. We paced the area, alert to any scraps of cheese or bread left behind from a morning snack. Much land was covered before our work concluded. Exhausted, we retired to the shady comfort of the luncheon table. Six days a week Grazia prepared a mountain of food for *pranzo*, the midday meal. I laid my sun-warmed belly to the cool grass, contemplating lunch.

La dolce vita. Italia. The best place for any dog.

The subject of food was never far from the lips of man or the ears of any canine. It moved life forward, gave life meaning. I once spent a good portion of a Roman morning sitting on the Pincio near a pair of sanitation workers as they cleaned out cans. They passed the time in heated debate over the preparation of *fettuccine Alfredo.* One claimed the necessity of Roman water as the only decent cooking liquid for the pasta. Mineral-laden liquid from the aqueducts imparted the perfect smooth yet sharp taste to the sauce. I certainly agreed. *Alfredo* was a favorite: cream and cheese and butter. Why not? My Contessa always brought large bottles of Roman tap water to the country with us. Grazia refused to make it without that ingredient.

I scratched an ant from my ear. It weaved through the grass, a grain of rice between its jaws. Soon, another ant passed by from the *terrazzo*, grain in tow. It would be but a short time before the remnants of a *risotto* dinner on the patio the night before were whisked away. An entire colony fattened.

Would they end up tasting like rice? Grazia's hens were well fed on chewy corn. Their eggs and flesh were as rich as the milky kernels they swallowed. The breasts of wild birds contained the tender, earthy flavor of rich soil and perfumed berries from the deep wood. Feral pigs that cleaned fallen acorns from the oak forest and robbed discarded grape skins from the compost below the winery yielded tender, lean roasts and sausage. I rolled over, waved my paws in the air and gave an arched stretch to my back. A scarab beetle crawled along the manicured grass. Its shiny cab flashed in the midday sun.

I mused at the flavor of a certain small Italian dog.

It depended, of course, entirely upon the season. Animals were what they ate. In Italy the menu revolved with the seasons. But as far as I was concerned, only one method of cooking was uniformly perfect.

Roasting.

Accompaniments varied. In summer, feathery wild fennel tops or branch rosemary. But no garlic. The whole cloves Grazia favored for roasting were too fierce for my digestion. Autumn begged Porcini and always complemented a plump duck bathed in red wine. Add a rabbit liver, pungent white truffle or hint of pear and *presto,* a masterpiece. Winter brought candied chestnuts and rich boar sausage. Saliva dripped from my tongue. It was nearly too much for my senses. I sniffed a tendril of errant thyme creeping through the edge of the lawn. Its clean scent stood out against the grass.

Simplicity. Not to be overlooked. A simple soak of anything in sweet wine, sprig of any herb for subtle interest did as well.

My chin was soaked when Grazia appeared, platter of *pasta al ragu* in her hands. The bells of Siena tolled once. The workers from the vineyard streamed to the table. Squisita followed Grazia, begging a first taste. The woman pulled a short piece of pasta from the plate and tossed it in Squisita's direction.

Penne. My least favorite. It always lodged in my throat. Though I could still catch my breath through the hollow of its tubular shape, it was a nuisance. Linguine was my pasta of choice. Sauces clung flawlessly to its long, flat surface. It had the perfect width. Not unmanageably wide like pappardelle, or of too little area like spaghettini. A whole length of it could be sucked into the mouth. Sauce deposited not so neatly around the snout was left to be enjoyed in the aftermath of the noodle itself.

Pure joy.

Squisita met me at the table. I licked a bit of sauce from her whiskers, savoring the lusty, sweet taste of ripe tomatoes. Fortunately, there was always variety from one meal to the next. Perhaps tomorrow *ragu* would dress linguine. In Italy, hope was always on the horizon.

The workers settled around the table amid a swarm of chatter. Soon more platters arrived laden with food. Wine was poured, voices raised and glasses emptied. There were several roasted chickens, speckled with pepper, cut into odd shapes, wedges of lemon strewn about them, long, flat loaves of soft, dense cornmeal bread, leafy wild greens, sliced ripe tomatoes, thin rounds of raw fennel with curls of shaved *parmigiano*. All were ready for a never-ending supply of delicate first-press olive oil.

Squisita and I occupied the savory underworld beneath the dining table. A delicious bounty of scraps fell from the frenzy above. I positioned myself directly under Umberto, a particularly messy eater. Soon there were bits of soft chicken and crisp fennel, bread soaked with oil and *ragu*, and *pecorino* cheese that followed the greens.

By the time *dolce* arrived, Squisita and I were in a state of dazed satiation. We decided against the indulgence of dessert. Instead, we wandered down the way of the flats by the creek. Summer leaves overtook the blossoms of spring. Only poppies remained. They swayed in a light breeze around the border of the vineyard. Bushes laden with huge roses marked the end of each row. We padded through the neat vines, arriving at the water's edge. Afternoon insects skimmed the surface of the creek.

Water. Salty cheese inspired thirst. I stood by the creek, now shrunken by summer to a trickle, lapping the cool stream and snapping at bugs. A spray of water covered my face as Squisita flew past me. Into the tangle of brush she went, disappearing like a bee into a bloom. I rushed into the thicket behind her.

Amazing, I thought. Nothing learned. I wondered at her fate come fall. No mercy for a dog of little brain. Hunters shot first, inquired last. I fretted through the brush. I did my best to catch up, until my nose reached the first low foliage.

Fox.

I stopped, pushing my snout deep into the soft dirt. Then I ran. I stumbled through the vines and brambles several lengths behind Squisita. Soon Squisita and I were scaling the side of the low hill that squatted beyond the stream, leaving the familiar wood behind. Prey out of sight, I surveyed the valley below from the smooth top of a rocky outcropping.

Being a dog of slight stature, my perspective was limited. But from the precipice, the hillside fell away before me. The view was immense. I scanned the valley below, noting the sun's position as it slipped toward the vineyard.

Grapes and gardens. My keen nose recognized the familiar scent of home: fermenting wine, blooming roses and herbs. Squisita sat next to me, panting. A wisp of drool hung in the air below her chin like a strand of spider's silk. The rise of a warm breeze from the valley floor carried it over the outcropping toward home. I nuzzled the velvet flap of her ear.

Andiamo. I would gather Squisita, turn back while I still had my bearings.

But she wanted the chase. Before I moved, the fox reappeared from behind the trunk of a beech to oblige. My plan was forfeit. We were all three off again, over the ridge of the hill, wooded and wild, down its slope into the next narrow scoop of valley.

I had to admit, the freedom was fun, the danger, exciting. My heart raced and the skin between my toes tingled. Squisita was well ahead of me. She had the benefit of stunning long legs and youthful vigor. Soon, she was out of sight. I followed her scent under the brush, stumbling through the briar and loose earth to the base of the hill. There I found Squisita. Stunned, she bled from the nose, trembling in shock and disbelief. She had arrived at the foot of the hill to find the fox weary of the chase, teeth bared and turned for battle. Her bluff was called. Surgical attack ended the pursuit, allowing the fox a speedy retreat.

Adventure seldom comes without payment. I sat down in front of her and licked the blood from her snout. I was certain she only meant to chase the creature, not to do it any real harm. Her pedigree did not include the company of dogs used for the hunt. I was as astonished as she at the malevolent behavior of the animal. After all, it was just a game.

Beast of little humor, I thought. Wild things were less predictable than those of noble root. All in all, they took themselves way too seriously. A fact owed, no doubt, to their upbringing. There was little idle time in daily forage. The comfort of domestication allowed for pure fun. And fun was integral to a happy life. I stood up trying to shake a collection of burrs from my coat.

Uncertain of how much ground we'd covered, I examined the surrounding area, sniffing the wind for direction. Long shadows hinted the afternoon was spent. The cover of darkness was near. I looked at Squisita. She was in no condition to make another crossing of the hill in darkness. I needed to secure shelter for the night. First, we needed water.

I dropped my nose to the spongy soil, divining a slightly metallic smell. I followed the scent, Squisita in tow, blood still oozing from her face. A hundred meters away, we dipped our noses into the cool thread of a creek and drank long and deep.

We followed the streambed for some distance, hoping to find aid. Most country people preferred to live in view of water. But the land on one side of the creek was vacant, rolling vineyard; the other, thick scrub and steep slope. Dusk forced us to move uphill into the safety of denser brush. The hollow of a dead turkey oak just big enough for two welcomed us. We curled together snugly for warmth and comfort. Squisita was soon in deep sleep. A gentle snore rose and fell to the measure of her breath. I listened to the cry of a hawk and the hoot of an owl. Cicadas punctuated the arid breeze with a shrill cry. The hair on my spine stood up and my haunches quivered. Creatures of the night began to stir in the cool exhale of a down-valley breeze. I gave a nervous yawn and batted my eyes hard, trying to blink light into the darkness. I had never before spent a whole night outside. It was frightening and lonely— and a taste of what could be.

Bitter, indeed.

What if the Contessa's strategy failed? What if, in anger and jealousy, Il Conte decided to let Umberto have the Contessa?

Destitution. Despair.

My head weighed heavy with the thought. Yet, my eyes snapped wide to every sound. Noises whirred and popped in the darkness. Mice scattered decaying leaves with the night breeze. Bullfrogs groaned along a gurgle of the stream below. Every crackle and call amplified by the absence of light raced my tired pulse. I rested my head atop Squisita's warm flank. My eyes closed and my heart slowed to match the gentle rhythm of her breath. Finally, the cadence of creatures wandering the darkness lulled me into the solace of sleep. With it came the comfort that dreams of home bring to those who have lost their way.

Chapter Twenty

I raised my head and cocked an ear.

Familiar sounds.

Digging, snorting, a grunt and soft squeal: wild pigs rooted close by in search of acorns and grubs. I wiggled from underneath Squisita's head to stand just outside the hollow.

Darkness enveloped the wood. Only one image came to mind: bristling, unpleasant boars with offensive breath and bad tempers. Perhaps they'd miss the scent of a certain small dog with a bad reputation among the company of pigs. The ripe scent of live pork on the damp night air confirmed my suspicions and provided some relief. The boars were close and I was downwind. But I was completely lost in the black of night. I let my nose fall and sniffed the ground, trying to divine whether or not the pigs had passed me as I slept. The proximity of pigs to the den of dogs was a danger.

No.

An odor of wild turnips surfaced instead. The scent heralded an invitation if it reached the group. I had seen the ugly boars finish carrion started by other predators. They even trolled shallow streams for fish. I had no intention of becoming a predawn meal. Yet, Squisita was a problem. I followed my scent back to the hollow. She slept sound as a puppy, breath deep and steady.

No common sense, I thought. If she had the wit to think twice, we wouldn't be stuck on the mountain. What she needed was a good tumble. I lent an ear to the noise beyond. If I didn't draw those pigs away, that's just what she'd get.

A bit of noise in the brush might work, moving them off site and down the hill into the bed of the creek. I started down the slope nose to ground and made a wide circle around the rooting. Once behind the noise, I rustled the underbrush with my nose and paws, trying to push the pigs away from the sound I made and out of range. But pig curiosity prevailed. Soon I stood whisker to whisker in the darkness with the bristles of an inquisitive sow.

Miseria.

She gave a lusty snort, filling my startled lungs with dank, disgusting breath. I raced away at top speed, headlong into the hardwood trunk of a tree. The sounder was upon me before I gathered my wits.

The commotion brought Squisita from the hollow. She commenced a charge from the other side of the group as dawn broke to offer a wide view of the enemy. The disgruntled pigs turned her way long enough to offer my escape. I skirted the sounder to join Squisita. Reunited, we touched noses then turned. The pigs were too close to permit escape. If we ran, we would be overtaken.

Only one thing to do.

Heads down, Squisita and I rushed the group together. We zigzagged a plait of paths, yapping and leaping through the group to confuse them. Soon the pigs appeared convinced. We had multiplied into a pack of irritation. When the largest of the boars peeled away from the others to find the solace of the creek, the rest of them followed.

Pure luck. Not hungry enough to put up with the foolishness of dogs. My heart pounded at the knowledge that few pigs ever gave up a meal as easily.

Squisita sat in the clearing, panting hard, ears askew, one side of her head caked in blood. Excitement over, I sat beside her. I brushed my tongue across the clean side of her face, grateful for the unexpected help. Her sudden insight into the solution of a dangerous situation made me proud. By summer's end she would be smart enough to know danger from delight.

Gratitude accepted, Squisita shook her fur. She fell in behind me as I made my way up the hill. I trotted in the opposite direction of the rising light, toward the hope of home. My ace in the hole was the set of the sun. If I played my cards right it would lead me to the vineyard. My empty stomach growled displeasure. I was starving. Thorns and burrs prickled my raw toes. My feet complained. Once again, I was feeling much and knowing nothing. I steeled myself against the discomfort and trudged on.

We traveled the undergrowth of the forest floor, stopping here and there to dig a bit when an interesting scent beckoned. Squisita paused to pull sweet berries from a thorny twist of vines that laced our course. But it was hardly a snack. Her stomach groaned, as well. I pushed her along. We could easily eat the vines clean if we spent more time, but the goal was to find the comfort of home before nightfall.

There was no need to tell Squisita the truth: I'd had a taste of the wild side of life and wanted none of it. Returning home to begin the hard work of getting all the people in my life into proper pairs was my only mission.

We dropped over the crest of the hill to walk through a dense forest of chestnut and beech. The scrub between the trees was thick. Closer to the ground, I found it easy to negotiate a path under the growth. Squisita had the greater challenge with long legs. She leapt over the brush instead, like a lithe deer over a garden fence. Soon the slope of the ground gave way to easy flat.

We found the narrow, twisting way of a country road. Its banks were lush with late poppies and lupine. Both directions looked identical. I lifted my nose into the warm midday air. I swiveled my head slowly and closed my eyes to concentrate on any hint of scent.

Nothing familiar but the white gravel road beneath me. And it was certainly not unique. One of a hundred strade bianche, they latticed much of Tuscany.

Squisita stared at me and whined.

Not wishing her to believe me incompetent, I made a quick decision. I started in one direction with the kind of determination that insinuates clarity of mind. We were off.

We followed the gravel road. Tiny wild strawberries graced the roadside in lonely patches, coaxed into late harvest by cool shade in the overgrowing summer brush. Famished, we pulled the ripest from their stems as we traveled.

Only two cars passed along the way. Unconcerned, neither driver slowed to inquire about the status of wandering, careworn dogs. Squisita was difficult to keep on track. Now and again she left the road to find the comfort of cool grass beneath a tree. Each time, just before I disappeared over the horizon, she ran to join me.

Another bend passed and a soft melody rose on the hot afternoon breeze. We both stopped. Panting ceased. Ears perked.

Song—from the vineyard.

Relieved, we ran until our chests were wet with perspiration falling from our tongues and our throats were dry with the dust of the road. There was no hesitation when a pool of clear water appeared in a flanking ditch. Bounding over the bank and into the stream, I stood belly deep in the cool water. It was heaven. Squisita followed suit.

We drank deep gulps of clear water. Thirsts quenched, we played in the refreshing pool. Squisita ducked and dodged as I splashed the water with my snout and legs. The mouth of a large, dry drainpipe lay just above our heads. We rolled together across the pond and back until Squisita leaped into the open pipe and disappeared. I stopped to listen. Her toenails clattered along the metal, then all was quiet. I raised one ear to the silence. Standing on my back legs I let my front paws fall against the opening of the drain.

Just as I thrust my nose into the opening, Squisita flew like a shot from end of the pipe into the water. I closed my eyes and ducked to avoid being hit as she passed me. A deep, steady growl, like no creature I'd heard before, echoed from the drain. I lifted my head in inquiry only to be greeted by an ample spray of concentrated skunk.

172

In one staggering leap, Squisita and I cleared the bank. We landed on the gravel at a full gallop, up the curving driveway guarded by soldier cypress, around the villa, through the open arms of the patio doors and into the safety of the kitchen.

Grazia's voice was a chime. "Ciao, bellisimi, benvenuto. It's about time."

I wiggled with pleasure.

Grazia was clearly relieved. Her exclamation gathered the entire household in short order to greet the returning adored. And I was immediately sick. For a moment I felt better. Then my belly lurched again. And again. Though there was little in my stomach, it would not be quelled. The skunk was having its revenge. The cheering crowd suddenly turned hostile.

Grazia swiped her broad twig broom across my fanny, pushing me ungraciously out onto the lawn. She closed the door. Umberto lifted Squisita onto the smooth stone counter that joined the wall of the apartment. He raised her torn ear and examined her bloody jowl. Then he pulled a shiny needle and a wisp of fishing line from a drawer.

The ensuing activity was a blur. I lost all track of Squisita. I continued to heave into a clump of burgeoning basil that was attempting to overtake a corner of the lawn. The peppery scent of its leaves was pleasant, but I knew that I would never again regard the herb in quite the same way.

Grazia busied on the patio, uncapping jars, pouring their dark liquid into a shallow washtub. Then she approached me with a large towel normally reserved for visits to the beach. Escape was impossible. She threw the terry cloth over me like a fisherman's net, hoisting me in the direction of the patio to plop me into the tub.

Conserva, I thought. Normally a delight. But the sea of tomato sauce held no appeal in the shadow of my churning stomach. I tried to scale the sides of the metal, but Umberto joined the abuse, adding firm hands to the assault. A good portion of my body was held under the sauce like a fat piece of penne. Grazia gave my fur a final ruffle with her fingers. The insult was complete.

She removed me to the large stone sink at the side of the terrace for a long rinse under especially cold water. I shivered at the chill until Grazia set me onto the flagstone with care. She seemed not to consider her previous act a violation in any way. I was deeply disturbed by the offensive behavior. It was not the return for which I'd hoped. The entire reception was demeaning.

A conquering hero, I had spent a treacherous night in the wild. I had managed to outwit a tribe of hazardous boar. And I had the manners to steward the instigator of the entire indecorous adventure all the way home. My only welcome: to be rebuffed by an impolite dip in a substance that frankly, to me, seemed a waste of perfect sauce.

A world gone mad. I yearned for the days when the people I knew behaved in a predictable fashion.

Yet, the last twenty-four hours, though difficult, were inspiring. It was time for change. A certain resolve took me now even though I had no idea where to start. I sneezed conserva from my nose. There would be a change, all right. I would make it. Shaking the water from my back several times, I glimpsed Squisita being shepherded into her apartment by Umberto. I tossed a muffled bark her way, but my throat and belly were sore from being sick. She didn't notice.

No matter. At this point, I didn't care. She deserved whatever fate Umberto delivered her way.

Little reward for deeds unnoticed, I thought. I crossed the hot terrazzo for the comfort of the cool tile in the cucina. The day sizzled under my sorry feet and, in every sense of the phrase, I could stand no more.

Chapter Twenty-One

I skipped the evening meal. Barred from the Contessa's bed because of my odor, I was confined to the kitchen. My eyes closed before dusk. I slept in the same position until daybreak.

The morning light was warm on my back as I lay stretched across my pillow, but it brought no comfort to my stomach. I opened one eye to my bowl across the *cucina*. Behind it drops of sunlight sprayed the wall as Grazia slid her polished crystal heart across the sill. I closed my eye to the dizzying display.

"Acquacotta, carino," Grazia said.

She set about preparing something bland to sooth my digestion. Hot water, conserva, sprig of mint, egg and parmigiano, the slurry was cooked quickly then set to cool. She tossed in generous scraps of crumbled bread to soak the liquid up like a sponge.

The aroma of the cooling brew was subtle, but pure invigoration to a dog with a restless belly. While I waited for the soup to cool I listened to the Contessa in the hallway. She was making arrangements for her summer intermezzo. My constitution brightened.

"Si," she said, "reserve a single."

Capri, I surmised. Summer was on its last legs. And the only place to be in the late summer was near the water.

"A single cabin, yes."

A beach cabana. Hours passed fetching toys floating on the clear, salty water; rows of stylish shops; a stop after lunch at the stand near the piazzetta for granita di melone, the sweet melon ice of summer. And the marvelous light of Capri. Far from the ire of Il Conte. Perhaps the Contessa's absence would make the Count's heart grow fonder. The first step to reconciliation.

It had been just the two of us for the last couple of years, dog and Contessa, roaming the lazy streets of the island. Long, languid lunches were taken near the sea. Feasts of tiny clams on fresh fettuccine, and grilled langostini, always punctuated the afternoons.

Glorious.

I gazed out the terrazzo doors. Squisita crossed the lawn beyond the patio in a careless series of leaps. I sneered.

A vacation from La Squisita. Perfect tonic for my constitution. The morning looked brighter. Soon I'd be headed south.

Squisita ended her path with a jump upon the low wall of the garden, knocking small pots of fine herbs from their stand to the ground.

Nothing but trouble, I thought.

Grazia delivered a perfect acquacotta with an affectionate embrace. The kind expression on her face spoke right to my heart. I forgave her the affront of the day before. I cleaned the bowl in gratitude, relieved by the happy turn to her mood. Soon my stomach followed suit. My Contessa entered the cucina, cooed in my direction and scooped me into her arms. The Count followed.

"I can go into Siena this morning before we start for Rome," he said. "Tell me the name of the jeweler. I will pick up your ring." The man took a glass from the cupboard, feigning interest in a small crack at the base. He kept one eye on the woman.

"I can't remember the exact name of the shop. I only know how to get there," said the Contessa. "Besides, I don't believe it's ready."

The Count's tone was irritated. "It's been months. I will call them, if you have a number. We can stop on our way. It's something very precious. You treat it as though it's a simple token."

The Contessa looked at me as she cradled me in her arms. "This is a something precious." She gave my nose a kiss and looked at the Count. "Do you remember why?"

The Count stood in the doorway, chewing his lip.

The Contessa shook her head, giving him an annoyed look over the top of my head. "They'll call when it's time."

"I will be here to answer," said Grazia.

"Call me," said the Count, scowling. "That ring is too valuable to sit in a shop." He put the empty glass on the counter and walked back down the hall.

The Contessa whispered in my ear, "Like trusting a rabbit to a wolf."

A quick kiss, a perfunctory sniff and I was passed, at arm's length, to Grazia. The Contessa addressed her too quickly for me to catch but one word. It was of little matter. A single word delivered a disparaging order.

"Bagno." The Contessa continued out the door and into the garden.

Santa Maria. Another bath. The day, once off to a good start, was turning bad. I wiggled from Grazia's arms and ran for the stairs when the phone rang. At the top of the steps, the ringing stopped.

The Count's voice was hushed. "Soon, cara. Even if I had the time, I can't just scour every jeweler in Siena. She's taking her summer trip; I come back to Rome tonight. We'll talk then."

That explained the bath. We were leaving for Capri today. One didn't grace the Hotel Quisisana in anything but immaculate condition. But I was green at the proposition of a long car ride. And I'd been given no time to prepare. My stomach turned as Grazia swooped me back into her arms. I went limp. Perhaps she'd think me too weak to withstand another turn about the tub. No chance. She had me at the outside basin before I had time to check the contents of my bowl as we passed through the kitchen. It was of little matter to her that I thought my odor perfect, like an aged piece of Tuscan beef.

The hegemony did not agree.

Just as Grazia lowered me into the sink, Squisita wandered by. She walked to the plastic sheet draping the great hole in the villa wall. Nose pushed into the corner of the sheet, she gave it a tug. The entire length broke free at the top. She ran with surprise. The plastic danced behind her, corner caught on a front tooth. It whipped in the air, slipping like a serpent behind her as she raced across the lawn. The activity brought Umberto from the cellar of the villa.

The man pulled himself from the hole in the wall. Covered with grit, he raced across the yard behind Squisita, a cloud of dust billowing in his wake. She ran in circles around him, making the man look a fool. It was all a game. At last, Umberto put a foot on the plastic as she ran by. The sheet came away from her tooth. She continued at full tilt back to the patio. He gathered the plastic and headed for the ladder that leaned against the house, just to one side of the gap.

The excavation was near complete. Soon it would be time to start the fireplace. There was no good excuse to put it off much longer. Except the absence of the ring.

"Needs better footing," Umberto had said first, then, "needs a whole new vent." The last time the Count questioned the postponement, Umberto replied, "Signora needs to choose a mantle before I can proceed." This seemed to buy the most time. Decision was never her strong suit. It was a slow process. Perspiration made Umberto a muddy mess under pressure to find the gem.

Tongue wagging, Squisita sat next to the basin that held me captive and watched. Pricking her ears, she gave a sneeze of enjoyment as she examined my indelicate situation. Her tail swept the terrace in delight through the whole indecorous affair. Her mouth curled into the ignorant smile of a naïve dog.

Completely unaware. Like a cuckoo. Her tongue hung too far below the mouth. Well beyond the limits defining the erudite culture of a sophisticated dog. I was embarrassed for her, for myself—for the whole world. I wished she'd disappear.

Squisita missed the hint. She took in every detail of the bath. I closed my eyes, partly to keep the suds from seeping in, but mostly to soothe my shrinking ego. At last, Grazia lifted me onto the patio and rubbed me all over with a plush towel. Squisita gave me a playful push with her nose, but I was in no mood for games.

The Count and Contessa appeared in the cucina doorway, luggage in hand, dressed for travel. The woman scooped me up and headed for the car. Umberto handled the baggage, giving the Contessa a sly wink as he helped her into the car. Right under the nose of Il Conte. The wink was not returned.

Arrogant, I thought. Immoral.

Next thing, I was in the shiny grey car, nose pressed up against the back window. Grazia drew a customary circle in the air with one finger, mouth forming the words, Santa Speranza.

Superstitious.

Guided by magic and saints, she covered all the bases. A peculiar blend of deity and demon guided her way. One circle and she considered us all safe in the care of a woman she called Our Lady of Perpetual Hope.

"Speranza," she once said, "means hope, and hope heals."

Squisita and Grazia grew smaller in the driveway as the car rolled down the hill. I never thought of magic as real. But I made a mental note never to wish anything disappear again.

*

My unsettled stomach and raw emotions made the trip to Rome hell. Even though we were bound for Capri, my mind stuck with Squisita. There had been no good-bye. Surely she realized it was beyond my control. My anger wasn't deep; I just needed a little break.

After all, I too had a social life. But what if she took it for desertion?

I spent the journey pouting in the backseat, disinterested in any offer of affection from the administration up front. The Count's attention was sure to be centered on La Donna Rosa once he reached the city, even if he intended to end it. I wished I could stay with the Count; somehow help him finish what the man had started. But the Contessa would never leave me behind.

By the time the car presented us at the termini, the main train station, I was a bundle of nerves, anxious over the Count's antics and excited by the promise of Capri.

Soon, the train to Napoli, a boat to Marina Grande, and the carefree oasis of an island wrapped in iridescent salt air. I breathed deep to welcome it and moved to the car door. The exhilaration reminded me that I hadn't touched grass for several hours. That had to be accounted for in the scheduling of time as we waited for the train.

The Contessa met me at the door and leaned close to my face. "Three weeks." The fine hair on the inside of my ear tickled at her breath.

"I think we all need a break, carino," she said. "Absence makes the heart grow fonder, no? You do what you can and take care of Il Conte. Perhaps there will be a change when I return."

A brief hug, token kiss, and once again I was nose pressed up against the inside of the car window. I was shocked. The Contessa had never before traveled without me. It was as though I'd been kicked. I couldn't breathe.

The Count and the Contessa met at the rear of the vehicle. I put my paws on the armrest of the car door, panting a fog of hot breath onto the window.

"I assume you'll go straight back to the villa," said the woman. "Grazia expects you."

The Count nodded. "Si, si."

The woman looked deep into his eyes. "Really?"

He didn't return her gaze, only looked down at a few pigeons underfoot. "Only a few days here, I promise. I have some business to attend to."

"No doubt," said the woman softly as she turned. She pursed her lips as though she knew exactly what appointments he planned to keep.

The Count pulled her bags from the trunk, kissed her on both cheeks, and she was on her way. She started for the termini doors then, with a grin and raised brow, turned and said, "If you never hear from me again, be sure to drag the harbor."

Brava, I thought. Tease him.

"That won't be expensive," the man said under his breath. But he snorted a smile and waved. "Ciao." He slipped into the car and it pulled away.

My Contessa melted into the crowd behind us. I couldn't believe my eyes. I never expected my wish to remain with the Count to be so quickly delivered. My heart sank. I had never missed a trip to Capri. I whined in protest.

"There's no room on a ship for a dog," said the Count.

A ship?

I'd been on a boat. Once. A small canoe: tippy and undependable. I saw no appeal in being on the sea. Beside it, yes. The beach was much safer, more fun. Harbor of hidden things in the sand.

Why would anyone go to sea?

"She wants to do something different. I know how she feels." The Count heaved a long sigh. "I wish it were all as easy as booking a trip."

Proven entertainment is the best entertainment, I thought. Better to stick with what you know.

"Solo ti e mi, Shimoni. Che pensi?" said the Count. "What do you think?"

You and me, indeed. Just charming.

We faced our apartment when the car came to a quiet halt. As soon as the bags arrived upstairs we set off in the direction of the Pincio: across Piazza del Popolo and up the stairs to the gardens.

The hot streets chattered with foreign speech and clicking cameras. Touristi arrived for summer. By the time we reached the park, I was parched.

With the park near empty, the Count released me and I was off to the nearest fountain for a drink. I lapped the crisp, clean water, careful to keep an eye alert to any familiar faces. The air was heavy and still in the clutches of high summer. It carried the smell of roses.

I squinted through the late afternoon haze until the Cleopatra came into focus. She took my breath. Lanky as ever and freshly coiffed, she was stunning even as the hot sun wilted all else around her. La Donna Rosa tagged along at the end of a long leash, fanning her face with a pale hand. I looked at the Count and whined.

"Lo capisco," said the man. "I know, I know. But I will keep her happy until I have that ring. Until it's on her finger, she'll stop at nothing, and she and the Contessa must never meet. Every occupation has both duty and hazard." He wiped the sweat from his neck and brow with a small kerchief and swallowed hard as he watched La Donna Rosa saunter our way.

"Ciao, bello. I've missed you." She pulled the linen from his hand and wiped the moisture from her face. "What are you doing up here?"

The Count met her with a short kiss.

"I'm lost." He hesitated. The man put a large hand on her hip and held her at bay, then pulled her into him, unable, as most males are, to eschew opportunity. His palm swept over the curve of her thigh. "Shall I follow you home?"

I sneezed at his weakness. Il Conte's duty did not seem entirely without pleasure.

The woman took his hand in hers and dropped the kerchief. I pushed it with my nose, then backed away. Sweat made it tempting but it was sticky with rose water as well. I sneezed again. The Cleopatra bowed her head and bared her teeth my way.

"There's no room for you in this equation," she growled.

"What makes you think I want to be added?" I kicked the grass up underneath my back feet in her direction.

"Go back to the farm, boy." The Cleopatra turned her back to me and sat down.

I bared my own teeth. "At least I have a farm," I said. I plopped under the shade of a broad umbrella pine. The grass was cool and damp from the humidity. What a bitch, I thought. A dog reflects the nature of its keeper. This was an ugly mirror to that soul. I yearned to let the man's secret slip, but I would bide my time, hoping the Count's scheme succeeded.

La Donna Rosa fawned over the Count. The man swooned. The revolting picture and the stifling air made me sick. If I could produce another ring I would. Right here under their noses. Then the man could walk away. I nibbled at the grass between my front feet. My belly improved, but the irritation remained. My tongue hung to one side of my snout, a vent to the heat and anger, until a familiar bark bridged the path. I answered and the Count turned. I retrieved the fallen kerchief from the ground. As quickly as they'd come together the couple parted.

Raoul appeared first, then his squire, just as the long light of the afternoon began its fade into streetlight. When they met, the Count embraced the slumped figure of the older man who held Raoul at the end of a leash. He lagged several feet behind, dripping tongue unfurled to within a cautious centimeter of the pavement.

I bounded to my friend, stopping short to greet him gently. Raoul sat unperturbed by the flagrant show of affection. His jowls leaked great trails of perspiration from the heat. Yet, the twinkle in his eye and gentle sweep of his tail across the grass exposed his pleasure at seeing me again. We touched noses. Important information was sniffed out. Then Raoul's person released the leash. We all walked across the Borghese Garden.

It soon became clear to me that something had changed. The elderly man reeked with heartache. From time to time he paused, drew a linen from his vest pocket to wipe it across his eyes, and blew his nose. The Count placed a hand on his shoulder.

I never saw a man cry before. I thought it a female trait. Yet, this man oozed despair. I looked around for Raoul's mistress. I liked to watch her throw corn for the pigeons from the bench by the lake. Sometimes Raoul and I would run through the flock, scattering them into the sky. The old woman always laughed, tossing the end of her blue headscarf their way in fun. Today, the bench was vacant.

"Gone," said Raoul.

"Intermezzo?"

"Disappeared." Raoul's eyes were vacant as though he were trying to forget.

I walked a short distance away. A homeless mutt slept soundly in a nest of taller grass reaching up underneath the trees. I skirted him with caution. I sat down on the other side of the tree. A large black ant scaled one of my paws. I picked it off, crunching it with my back molars. A lovely lemon flavor filled my mouth. The taste reminded me of Capri, the tart lemons hanging from overhead trellises, zest clinging to long pasta. The Contessa. Raoul joined me under the pines as an evening breeze whispered its way through the trees.

"My lady's gone, too," I said. "Where did yours go?" I pushed my nose through the grass, picking up more ants as I went.

"Il cimitero," said Raoul.

I stopped chewing. "How do you know?"

"She went to sleep one night and never awakened," said Raoul. "Strange men took her away to a place we visit now. A small photograph of her last Christmas marks the spot she lies beneath. I can still smell her through the fresh earth. I tried to dig but the cover is stone." Raoul smelled his paws and sighed. "The old man lights candles and mutters prayers, but she hasn't come back. There's only one reason."

"But you saw her go to sleep," I said. "She didn't fall under a car, or become very sick. She slept. Why doesn't she come back?"

"Morte." said Raoul. "Death has no return."

I looked at the slumbering cur nearby. He was still as wood, no rise and fall to his belly. Yet, I heard a gentle snore when I passed by. Sleep returned you. Death must be a gruesome keeper, I thought as I regarded Raoul. The old dog's eyes brimmed with tears. His pain broke my heart.

"Perhaps she still sleeps," I said, "in a dream too grand to leave. Haven't you ever had one of those?" I looked into the darkening sky. I wanted to give Raoul hope. A whole prosciutto, the deepest hole, great herds of small winged creatures within range: those were great dreams. "Who would want to come back?"

The old man and Il Conte walked across to the bench once used by the old woman and sat down. Raoul and I followed. We sprawled under the cover of the seat. Raoul dozed. I listened.

"Senza un bacio," the old man said to himself.

"Come?" asked the Count.

"That last night. I didn't kiss her." The man took a kerchief from his pocket. He wiped his nose. "I always did that," he said, then paused. "Well, almost always."

"I used to have that habit," said the Count, regret in his tone, "but the urge subsided."

"It is sometimes a challenge to remember the reason you began to kiss at all." The man smiled, mouth crooked, brows raised. "Illusions fall away under the weight of years, no? But that's the point."

"What point?"

The old man chuckled. "Much of what lies between a man and woman is false. Sometimes the truth must be buried in order to love one another." The man wiped his forehead again. He worried the linen between his hands. "Cling to the pleasant, discard the cross.

Memories are often better than anything that follows. In the end, that's all we're left."

"It's easy to give up," said the Count.

Raoul's old man looked at a lone starling swinging low in the dusk sky. "Do you love because you're loved? Or are you loved because you love?"

Il Conte turned his head toward the words and tipped it to one side. The bench creaked and Raoul snorted underneath.

"The answer you seek is in the difference," said the old man.

The Count frowned as he did when trying to make sense of the morning paper. The old man was quiet, content to let his words simmer. He rubbed his wrinkled chin.

"I gave up once."

"Gave up?"

The old man nodded. "She never knew. She was too busy trying to outwit me." He chuckled.

"I'm lost," said the Count.

"Una ganza," returned the man. "A mistress."

Il Conte blushed under the topic.

"Our children were grown, the house quiet. Perfect time for romanzo, no? But a woman sees with a different eye."

"No interest," said the Count flatly.

"Why should she? Women may lack reason, la biologia does not. Sex, after all, is a matter of reproduction. Her years for that are over. Why should her interest grow?"

"And that was that?"

"Only until I learned that if I wanted an invitation to the bedroom, I would have to earn it. God gives the young a free pass to go forth and multiply. As long as there is the possibility of procreation, everyone is interested in sex. That accomplished, the invitation becomes harder to obtain." The old man laughed. "You know what I mean."

It was not a question. I raised an ear.

"Si." Il Conte swept a hand over his hair and leaned back. A little grey in his hair shone silver under the sun.

"She's very beautiful," said the old man.

The Count looked up at the gathering clouds. "She's aged well."

"I mean the young woman in the park."

Il Conte blew a long breath out of his mouth. I sat up.

The Count scanned the Pincio for a long time before he answered, "I didn't have to work too hard in the beginning. Like magic, she gave me what I wanted."

"Does she give you what you need?"

Bravo, I thought.

The Count looked into the old man's eyes.

"Your wife or your mistress," said Raoul's master. "In the long run, who's the more expensive?"

I knew that answer.

Il Conte blew a loud breath from his lips as he rattled the loose change in his pocket. "I have just enough to buy us a drink."

The two men stood and ambled toward the path. I shook my fur from head to tail, roused Raoul, and we followed a few steps behind.

"The ground makes my bones ache." Raoul yawned. "At least there's extra space on the soft bed now." He smacked the drool from his snout. "And no mind given to illicit treats. I haven't had to have a bath since the woman left, either. Could be worse. Life's not so bad."

I cocked my head at his logic.

Raoul continued. "Ironic, isn't it? Life is really the only thing that causes death. I expect we all end up in il cimitero." He limped over the cobblestones at the end of the path.

"Not I. There's a little place by the stream below my vineyard I intend to claim. That is, if I still have a vineyard when the time comes." Then I recited the events that had shaped my life since we were last together. From the missing ring to the myriad indiscretions and the many games my people played with their lives—and mine. Finally, La Squisita.

Raoul saluted a hind leg to his ear as if to scratch. He swiped the air a time or two before settling back. "Females," said Raoul. "Part penalty, part reward."

This I understood.

"It may be simple to bring things right," said Raoul. "Look at me. One thing changed everything. Just find the right trigger."

At the end of the park, we all descended a narrow set of stone stairs to arrive in an intimate piazza lined by small cafés and bars and an assortment of round tables. The men chose a spot in the shadow of an old palazzo. The old man ordered aperitivi for himself and the Count, a thoughtful bowl of ice for us. Raoul settled into comfortable repose near me beneath the white tablecloth. He sucked an ice cube between his paws. A cough to clear his throat and I knew what was coming.

The old dog possessed an uncommon facility for dissertation whenever a quorum was present, and any number greater than a single dog constituted such. That determined, he began La Filosofia dei Cani Nobili: Philosophy of the Noble Dog. He had delivered the piece before. Credo of all canines, it was worthy of regular reflection. I knew it well.

Fundamental to canine logic were a few noble constants by which all dogs were guided. Raoul described them as inborn. Every dog shared them, be they domesticated, feral or ridiculous, as he liked to think of the curs on the Pincio.

First, dogs never let their past define them, and neither do they take life seriously. Every day is a new day for a dog; a new, exciting, anything-is-possible day. Any human can see that all dogs enjoy the charm of novelty.

Second, a dog's heart is easily won and difficult to break. And though pride may be the downfall of many creatures, understanding their own fallibility makes dogs loyal to even the worst sort of human being. As a result dogs have learned that it is a far braver thing to stay in a disagreeable situation, helping dispel the misery of man, than to leave it. That is the charge of man's companion. Dogs value bravery above all else; its degree, the measure of every dog. It is the noblest of canine virtues.

Third, dogs are philanthropists. They never pass up an opportunity to give. A pact was made in the early days of their ancestors. Hunting expertise for a share of man's kill. That reciprocity continues today, but now lies in the pleasure and benefits exchanged between human and dog. It's innate. An affectionate thresh, an endearing lick, a fond sniff about the crotch: these are all traded for room and board. One gets what one gives.

Finally, dogs never pass up the opportunity to have fun. It is the very heart of every living spirit; the essence of every dog. It encourages strong bonds and deep affection. If there is no pleasure, there is no life. This is the simple and abiding truth of existence. It all comes down to looking at life with a kind eye.

Raoul completed the treatise and the ice cube at the same time. He gave a raspy cough and pulled another cube from the bowl. I stood up.

"Bravery," I said. "How do humans judge it?"

"A high honor," said Raoul. "Particularly, as the measure of a man, in a woman's eye."

I thought the Count a coward to abandon the affection of the Contessa for that of another woman. "Can courage lure her back?"

Raoul coughed again, a deep straining cough that made the fine hair in my ears tremble. The old man lifted the tablecloth to place a reassuring hand on Raoul's flank.

"You only know by trying," Raoul said. "The right strategy will bring un soluzione felice."

A happy solution, I thought. If only.

And then, as abruptly as he started the discourse, Raoul said he was tired. "Home." He got up from beneath the table, giving a nudge against the old man's leg until the elder collected himself for the walk home.

The Count paid the bill and we all strolled along a street bathed in the light of sunset. The old man wheezed a cigarette between his teeth. An elderly woman crossed the street ahead, blue scarf trailing behind her head. The man stopped and watched her with furrowed brow. Then a gentle smile came. His chin quivered and his eyes overflowed with tears.

"I'm alone," he said in a soft, husky voice.

"With a lifetime of memories, my friend," said the Count. He embraced the man, kissed both cheeks and looked into his eyes. "May they keep you from your sorrow."

"Some say grief is proportionate to regret," said the old man. "I have but one." He looked into Il Conte's eyes. "No one need bear more."

"Riflettete," Raoul said when we parted at the corner.

The Count was pensive and silent as we strolled toward home, but my head echoed with Raoul's words.

"Reflect on the credo, follow a plan, and remember: one thing can change everything...."

Chapter Twenty-Two

August, true dog days of the Italian summer: lazy, humid hours of pitiless heat and generous fountains. Water was abundant and cool. If a small dog was discreet he could easily have a take or two in one of the lower-lipped vessels before anyone was the wiser.

Romans of any means thought it a scandal to be found in the city during August, for the heat is oppressive. Most of Rome was shuttered tight until September, but the Count found the solitude to his liking. Whether I liked it or not, with the Contessa still away, I was obliged to stay in town.

After a brief walk in the morning, disappointingly short of the Pincio, the Count left for his office. I spent several hours of every day in my own company. It was lackluster work. I guarded the quiet of my lonely apartment against all the neighbors who headed out of town. There was very little activity to worry over, few conversations to overhear, but it was work nonetheless. I took my task to heart, delivering a bark here and there, just in case anyone disreputable wandered by. The remainder of the morning was spent sifting ideas that might return my house to order. I suspected memory held the key in some way, but I had no idea into what door it fit.

By the time the Count returned each afternoon to collect me, I was well ready for a break from cerebral activity. Shops were closed for *siesta,* while most tourists sought shelter from the midday heat in the cool of museums. It was as though we relived antiquity; a time before the city lay swollen by the millions who now called it home.

We walked to the same *trattoria* every day except Sunday. The Count preferred a languid lunch inside the comfort of cooled air. We passed much of central Rome on our way. I loved the gleaming monuments and ornate churches, the delicate features of all the statues and, above all, the glorious bells.

Yet, as most dogs know, a place is most accurately defined by what lies in its streets. Rome was rich in definition, whether it was on its surface or twelve meters down. It was a layered city of art, architecture, religion and emotion, conquest and capitulation. Centuries of history lingered not in the grand museums or crumbling remains. All that was Rome, now and forever, lay between the cobblestones; dust whittled away by the steady grind of time. Now and then, I caught a whiff of an entirely different nature and composition: a disquieting scent of decay. It evoked excitement, yet eluded definition. Like a disappearing dream, the empire rested in its aromatic fragments.

I kept my nose to the gutter. The odors inspired hunger. By the time we reached the via del Seminario, my belly growled harmony as the Count sang under his breath.

"Dolci baci, o languide carezze," he crooned. Sweet kisses, tender caresses. Tosca. I assumed I would spend another lonely night in my apartment.

We reached the Piazza della Rotunda and paused in homage to the spectacular temple of the gods: Il Pantheon. It was my favorite building, standing like an ancient bookmark among younger palaces around the square. In a rare snow that once sprinkled Rome, my Contessa and I entered to watch the fascination of snowflakes drift, slow motion, in a singular perfect column through the aperture in its dome.

We continued through the crowd, leaving the hemispherical *duomo* of the Pantheon behind, until we arrived at one of the few eating establishments open during the vacant month of August.

The tiny Vecchia Locanda was a cramped, air-conditioned niche. Its tables spilled from the inside into the secluded arched street and the menu offered a *piatti del giorno*. Friday was sometimes herbed risotto with fresh fish. Monday, truffled rabbit, no matter the season. The food was fabulous. An effervescent owner never failed to ply me with scraps. A good thing, for the Count was somewhat absent-minded when it came to furnishing meals.

We were informed that the offering today was *fusilli con piseli e parma*. I thoroughly enjoyed the rough ends of salty meat and handful of shelled peas. The Count consumed the same atop a tidy heap of pasta. Meal concluded, the Count took some pleasure from a game of solitaire and a short *digestivo:* a glass of *Amaro* or the like. A bowl of water from the host for me and we were once again mapping the city streets.

Capital of ignored edicts and magniloquence, Roma teamed with enthusiasm for life. Important *piazze* filled with an eclectic mix of humans; immigrants not well off enough to leave the heat, tourists not smart enough to care. Supremely interesting to any dog, first impressions always came from ankle height.

Shoes. The initial stop for any dog. I was expert at assessing the essentials of a person on the basis of their footwear. As we entered an open market flanking the street, I put the experience to work. I sniffed a hundred soles. Shoes read like a diary to me, detailing activities — defining station.

Shoes make the man. And above the ankles, myriad dialects and dress. The abundance of diversity in the crowd was intoxicating in a way impossible for the countryside to match. There were dogs of every shape and fashion: females of groomed perfection and flawless manner; sensual, wild-hair bitches, unreserved and enticing. I closed my eyes to the dizzying stimuli.

None as beguiling as La Squisita. I examined the crowd. Soon every female began to look like her. My memory swirled with thoughts of early summer. Images turned over in my mind like pages in the Contessa's picture album. It left no room for indiscretion. With each female that passed, I knew my place was in the country. Home would always be the land that lay along the fat stream and the crook of a modest hill, between the broad tufa *villa* and the deep wood: the domain of La Squisita. Absence had worked its magic on my heart. If it could only do the same for Il Conte.

As we moved down the Corso toward home, clouds that spent the day hugging the horizon now loosened their embrace to fill the sky overhead. They quaked at each flashing bolt of lightning until thunder filled the air as though the empire itself were falling once again. By the time we reached the place where the smooth marble stairs ascended the Pincian Hill, a torrent of rain released upon the city. We raced up the staircase through the deluge, drenched before the final step, to the cover of an awning attached to a novelty stand. There we waited the passing storm.

I sat just out of the rain's reach, sniffing the moist air, enjoying the metallic smell of cool rain on hot pavement. In minutes the streets were flooded. Drains choked with another dose of history as the waters rolled down the slope of long streets and into the squares, a low tide of dirt and debris. I noticed a lone man in the *piazza* below raising his trousers over his knees, preparing to cross the flood. As he started, the water deepened. By the time he was midway, it reached well over his knees. Instead of showing dismay, the man began to sing.

He bellowed above the rain. *"O Sole Mio."* Feigning a meager paddle, he crossed the rest of the way to higher ground.

I stood to wag my tail in amusement. I once heard the same melody in Venice on a trip with my Contessa. The man mimicked a gondolier. I shook the rain from my fur, eyeing a glossy, chewy-looking oddity from the stand above me. I was certain it squeaked, and just as certain that I would never find out for sure. The Count thought me already in possession of too many toys. Resigned, I turned my attention back to the *piazza*. The gondolier now stood on a café table with a glass in his hand, toasting the crossing to no one in particular.

Italians. An approach to life that was truly canine. In Italy one learned to enjoy the time, not employ it. Every aspect of existence was lingered over. An entire people came to adopt an attitude fundamentally doggish: live and let live. No surprise the mother of Rome was so closely related to dog.

The Count was busy with a kerchief, wiping the rain from his dark glasses, a necessary accessory to Italian fashion in any weather. A wisp of pipe smoke curled above his head in the gentle breeze.

The pungent odor of *pignoli* filled the fresh air. I lifted my nose to the scent. The park was deserted. The rain washed it clean. Not even a dog was to be seen on the broad expanse of lawn and manicured garden.

Empty and silent, I thought. A wave of loneliness took me. I lay down at the Count's feet, crossed my front paws and rested my chin on the man's shoe.

*

Weeks passed without Raoul's company. It was the Count's habit to walk at noon, and Raoul generally held court in morning. And Greta had been aloof since the procurement of her new male. So, when in the distance I caught a glimpse of the shape I knew to be Raoul's old man, I jumped to my feet. I began to bend and wiggle.

The Count looked up, catching the old man's eye with a flamboyant wave. The old man returned the greeting with a feeble shout. But the closer he came, the less I threshed.

No sign of Raoul.

Chapter Twenty-Three

A few mornings later the phone rang. I awoke to the Count holding a receiver to my ear. My Contessa tried her hand at a proper bark. Though her inflection was wide of the mark, her accent was charming.

The Count talked into the phone. *"Si, si, si. Sicuro, cara."*

I listened as the woman requested a few of her winter things be brought to the country when we met her there. I suspected that she did not intend to return to Rome as long as La Donna Rosa remained in the picture. It would be a cold winter, indeed, I thought, for Chianti could produce wicked weather.

Il Conte returned bathed in the sickly scent of rose water less often these days. The man was clearly biding his time. Yet, the visits were still a force, as able to seduce as to repel. The Count returned each time in dull relief, senses muddled like syrupy *granita.*

The Count delivered a final word. *"Domani."*

I couldn't believe my ears: reunion with my Contessa in the country the very next afternoon. I ran through the apartment, top speed, sliding smooth turns around the dangerously polished floors. Straining toenails to grip the impenetrable surfaces of wood and ceramic, I dashed from room to room. Ears pinned for speed, rear end lowered for thrust, nose leading the charge, I was beside myself with delight.

Momentum spent, I slid to a stop on the thick carpet of the bedroom. The Count turned on the radio. Opera wafted from the large speaker in the corner of the room.

Rigoletto. Surely there must be a law forbidding opera at the start of the day.

"Questa o quella." This or that, came the words.

Credo of the philandering heart.

Non v'e amor se non v'e liberta. Love cannot thrive without freedom.

On the contrary, I thought. Nothing thrives without love.

The fall of a hanger onto the wooden floor of the closet led me to the Count. The man was rummaging through a line of the Contessa's silks and woolens. He held a list in one hand and several items on hangers in the other. I entered the long, windowless room. I stopped to sit just inside its door.

The Count parted the clothes on the rack, sliding them down the wooden pole to get a better view. He stopped. Straightening his shoulders, he cocked his head the way I often did when paused in contemplation. He folded the bundle of dressed hangers onto the floor, put the list between his teeth, and reached through the parted clothing with both hands. He retrieved a large book. It was bound by cobwebs and covered in dust. As he pulled it through the rack, something dropped to the floor. I entered the maze of garments for a quick search with my nose. The source of the clatter: a perfect, thumb-size seashell attached to a delicate tarnished silver chain. I mouthed it carefully, letting it stick to my tongue before securing it between the teeth. I re-emerged victorious, unnoticed by the Count.

We returned to the bedroom, the man to sit upon the bed with the thick book, I at his feet to nibble the prize. Despite the attempt at discretion, my mouth smacked as I sucked the salty shell. It brought the attention of the Count to its rescue.

With one rude finger the shell was extricated. "How did you find this?"

I followed his hand as it disappeared over the edge of the bed. I sat beside the Count. The fat book was split open in his lap. Its pages were dotted with yellowed photographs. Old feelings returned: the excitement of a first run at the beach; anxiety at learning to swim the clear, deep water. The best showed a youthful figure of a handsome young dog. My favorite. An aristocratic repose atop a dune of sand, cool Mediterranean beyond.

Memories of joyful days and a faithful couple. I yearned to feel that same security again: the pride imbued at the sight of one's family in good cheer. Loyalty could be a valiant struggle, but bravery was the noblest of virtues. If only the man realized it.

The Count turned another page and swept his palm across one of the pictures. "I'd forgotten." He fingered the small shell in his hand and turned it over, pointing to the inside of the shell. "You see?"

Tiny letters scribbled the trinket.

"'It's Now or Never.' The only song we heard that summer. This was the first gift I ever gave her, Shimoncello. There was a time she'd never be without it." He drew a long breath. "I might as well have given her my heart."

The Count sat still for some time before putting a warm hand on my head. He smoothed back the fur around my eyes and raised my chin with his palm.

"So, no Joker after all, but a little Jack of Hearts you are—lucky in love. Just like in a deck of cards." A gentle smile crossed the man's lips as he regarded the necklace. "*That* was magic."

Il Conte looked across the room to the mirror then turned away from his reflection. His face was childlike. A sad grace washed him, like a gypsy child at the Colosseo after a long day begging and little to show for it.

He walked to the radio, clicked off the opera and looked at me. "If it's going to be work in any case, I may as well do it at home, don't you think?"

Bravo. Finally, the voice of reason.

Returning to the album, the man paged to a large photograph of the couple. Standing knee deep in the sand, facing each other bent at the waist, hands behind their backs, a gentle kiss linked them. Like angels in a church fresco. The shell necklace graced the woman's neck.

I remembered the day. I helped dig the holes for us to stand in. Helped fill them, too. They were good, deep holes. But sand was always difficult. A good portion of it refused relocation. Soon, the people were stuck in the beach like umbrellas, surf washing up between them. I remembered it well.

"*Molte memorie,*" the Count said. "How many more?"

I rested my head on the Count's arm.

Then the Count slid the photograph from its jacket. "This is what I choose to remember. May it keep *me.*" He returned the big book to the safety of the closet, bending forward to replace it behind the rack of clothes. As he straightened, he pulled an armful of garments from their hangers. The man hesitated a minute, burying his face in one of the Contessa's favorite blouses.

Hems swept the floor at the Count's feet. I pushed my nose into the dresses. The woman may as well have been sitting beside me. I relaxed in her perfume, imagining the fabric, her delicate hand as it brushed my side. It was hard to breathe without my heart hurting. I missed the Contessa. My only wish was to be with her. I opened my eyes wide.

That was it, I thought. It was memory that kept the flame. The man stood riveted by a spell cast long ago, remembering. If the Contessa only met him, the Count was halfway there. His plan now had focus: tease the memory and tempt courage. My mind raced with possibilities.

Though I enjoyed the nostalgic look into the past, the present called. I had not yet enjoyed the benefits of a morning walk. Invigorated by the formation of a well-found plot, I was past famished, as well. I shifted my weight from one paw to the other while the Count finished gathering the Contessa's wardrobe.

The man packed it all into two large, square, leather cases. He dropped the shell necklace in his vest pocket and slipped the old photograph between the pages of a magazine. I edged nearer the front door of the apartment, hoping the Count would realize his neglect.

Upon seeing me anxious at the door, the man secured me to the leash. We moved without delay to the ground level of the building. Not a moment to spare. Out the main doors and into the street. I marked the first tire I greeted and the day began in the direction of the Pincio. Since the Contessa's call came early, there was the distinct possibility that Raoul might still be there. There was a chance for a proper good-bye before we left for the country.

Across the *piazza*, near the base of the stairs ascending the park, we stopped at a tiny bar overloaded with cigarette smoke and dirty boots. A dozen sanitation workers crowded at the counter taking coffee. The room rumbled with deep voices and laughter. Glasses clinked. Cups of coffee slid across the counter.

"*Cappuccino,*" the Count ordered. "*E due cornetti.*"

I propped my front feet on the rail bordering the base of the bar to position my mouth in closest proximity to the Count's hand. Soon I received my portion of a treat. I attempted to be clever in the catch of each bite. A good-humored crowd in any bar always added their own treats to the game. Soon the meal was augmented by bits of *prosciutto* and custard-filled pastry. It was all unnoticed by the Count, as he sipped his *cappuccino* and read the paper.

Breakfast complete, the Count led me a few blocks in the direction opposite the Pincio. Near Piazza d'Espagna, he stopped to press the buzzer outside a tiny shop.

The door opened to a young man in glasses. "*Buon giorno, Signore.*"

We entered a dim room filled with photographs and empty frames of all sizes. The Count presented the picture of himself and the Contessa. He handed it across the counter. The young man pulled an eyeglass from his pocket. He examined the photo with careful attention. Then he placed it between the covers of a folder. He dropped it into a box on the floor at the end of the counter.

The box was tattered around the top, one flap torn way. It looked like a box awaiting the sanitation company we left in the bar down the street. I was confused. The action didn't mirror the man's feeling. But there it was.

Trash, I thought. If it were up to me I would leave the Count in that box of waste as well. Use my hind legs to scratch a pile of Roman filth over the horrid man. Il Conte was beyond analysis. I pulled toward the door in protest. The Count chided me once for the rude behavior. I cast him a disgusted glance before succumbing to a tug of the leash and sat down in front of the exit.

The men exchanged a few more words before I led the Count back into the street. Time was wasting. My opportunity to see Raoul evaporated with the morning dew.

We forged the rushing traffic on the Corso, which was heavy under the burden of tourist buses. Finally, we climbed to the Pincio. I was released to the freedom of the great lawn beyond the gravel outlook. I wound a circuitous path in the inquisitive fashion of a small dog, tree trunk to bush and back again. Amid a confusion of cross currents, I tried to keep my own direction. There was plenty to think about. I looked around for Raoul. The old dog was good at fueling the spark of genius. I waited while the Count leaned up against a pay phone at the entrance to the park and dialed.

"*Ciao,*" he said. "*Si*—I know. I just can't come today. I am too busy."

Busy? It was the weekend.

La Donna Rosa's sharp voice abraded the air. Il Conte held the receiver away from his ear.

His voice rose. "Forget about the ring. No, no. Tomorrow won't work. I'm going back to the country."

The woman's voice grew louder still.

"*Allora.* I've been thinking about that and, the thing is"—the Count looked down at me—"I won't be coming again. *Finito.*"

The man's jaw was firm, but his eyes cheerless. Like contemplating a bitter pill, I thought. But the remedy was never so sweet. Who cared that the man threw away the photo of the

202

Contessa? My tail wagged. The exaggerated motion pushed me sideways into a nearby shrub. Elated, I raised a leg to a rigid stand of boxwood. I commemorated the spot; that hallowed ground on which the refusal of La Donna Rosa was given. A shrine, marked for generations to come: an altar of clear thought, monument to the power of dogs who do great things. My scheme was midway through. I had done what I could, and it was enough.

Jack of Hearts, how true. I jumped and wiggled as the Count finished his call.

The man regarded my antics as he would a ball bouncing on its own across the park.

"*Cos'e la sua problema?* Ants up your ass?"

I barked.

"Ring or no, *è finito*," said the Count. "I will call her bluff and pray she makes no trip to the country."

I danced around the park like a child until I saw Greta appear on the patch of lawn across the path. I lifted my nose in inquiry. Was she in the company of the male who introduced himself so rudely the spring before? Absent any boorish scent I raced across the path in her direction.

"It's done," I yapped.

Greta shied away from my advance. Not her usual greeting. But she was often reserved. Though fallen on hard times, she was still distinguished. Her heart was well within a jacket of svelte figure and elegant posture. Only a pause in her examination of a child's toy left behind sufficed to acknowledge me. I swung behind her to sniff a greeting.

A deep breath. So it was true. Greta no longer kept company with the blue-blooded brute of last season. Finished with him, she delivered a brood of puppies, sent them on their way and started fresh. She may as well have a memo hanging from her tail. I looked around. Tall, proudly aloof and clad in a shiny armor of jet-black fur, Greta's latest escort stood in the distance, tethered to her woman.

"Still in Rome?"

"The pups didn't bring the money we hoped," Greta said. "Two batches since winter. Not enough for a car. You can get to the country without one, but once you're there—" Her attention trailed off into the sky at a flock of passing swallows. "Cute, though, those pups," she said. The words caught in her throat and she coughed. "Now, we try again. With a better pedigree." She cast a glance to the male across the way.

She implied indifference at the variety of partners she'd had. But Greta's conviction was hollow. I sneezed disbelief and wondered if she really had a heart.

"Must be hard, seeing those puppies go," I said. "But it's a kind thing. Giving them to better homes."

"Show me the humanity in having your heart ripped away," she said. "Life is all loss and ever has been." She kicked her back feet out to tear against the thick lawn. "There's little hope." She sniffed the air. "You'd better get used to it. Your Count still strays. I can smell it from here."

Greta's tone made me uneasy. *"E finito,"* I said. "Il Conte told her today. Now things will change, you'll see."

"For you," she said. "Maybe. But some things never change. The curse of a broken heart: It still beats." She cocked an ear to the frenzied traffic in the square. Her eyes narrowed.

Before I had time to ask about Raoul, Greta headed in the direction of the lookout over the Piazza del Popolo. I struggled to catch up to her long stride, glancing back at Greta's woman. She had a book in her hand, oblivious to our wandering.

"Have you seen Raoul? Have you seen his old man walking alone on the Pincio?"

Greta stopped short of the marble rail at the *vista*. She looked deep into me eyes. She touched her nose gently to mine before looking away toward the lake and the empty bench where Raoul's old woman used to sit. "Gone," she said.

Certo, I thought. Females had a unique knack for stating the obvious. But where did he go? Surely Greta knew. It was her business to know everything happening in the park.

She sat down, gaze fixed on a nearby bush. "Raoul passed on," she said. "He's finished." She worried a sticky bit of tar on a paw.

"Dead?" My heart sank to my toes. "But how?"

"Old age," said Greta. She looked out over the *piazza* below. "Seventeen summers. Older than any dog I knew. His hips were always giving him pain. Must be a relief, don't you think? Like walking into the cool sea on a hot day." Her eyes glazed as though she were looking inward. Her chest rose and fell under the burden of a sigh.

My eyes welled. "Few live longer."

"And a few die younger," Greta said in a curt fashion. "Those of shorter leg, and flatter nose." She stood up, graceful legs tall and long snout pointed to the square below. "It's a blessing, really. Shorter lives see less pain."

I crossed my eyes to better gauge the length of my snout and its distance to the ground.

Greta walked in measured steps to the stairs and began descent. "Those—the lucky few," she sniffed.

Looking a last time to Greta's woman, I followed. I hoped she might see us slip away, and tag along. My stomach was queasy as though I were waiting for the vet in a room full of sick animals. At the base of the steps, just before the street, Greta stopped to sit at the curb. I sat beside her.

"There are good memories on the Pincio, Greta."

"Many years," was all she said. Touching her nose to mine once more, she let it linger there for moment. Traffic raced carelessly behind her.

I stepped back, away from the wind that followed the cars. The hackles on my back stood up at the threat. Something else disturbed the air. I raised my snout to Greta once again.

Desperation.

I turned my head away. Despair left me with an empty, hopeless feeling. Like tracing the smell of a freshly dead mouse only to find it poisoned: foul and forbidding. I blinked twice and looked up. There, as close as tomorrow, and just as elusive: the old gypsy woman. I couldn't look away.

A car screeched so close behind that I was sure I would be hit. I braced my toes against the cobblestones and closed my eyes.

But not soon enough to see Greta jump, eyes wide open, into the busy street.

Chapter Twenty-Four

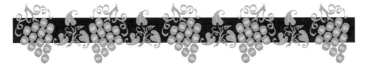

W hen the Count and I reached the *villa*, Chianti lay tangled in the large dark leaves of late summer. They clung to long limbs of gnarled grapevines and wisteria. Tall climbing roses and fragrant star jasmine held the stone house in a wilted embrace.

Squisita seemed thrilled to see me. We twirled and threshed a long greeting across the lawn and into the vineyard, drawing it out into a leisurely walk along the stream. She licked my snout and ears and my spirit bloomed with the attention. But it was the image of Greta leaping into the street, cars squealing, people shrieking, and the smell of death that stuck in my mind.

I'd never before seen the suicide of a dog.

Greta had reached her limit: death was a welcome release. She had a heart, indeed, and it had broken piece by piece, torn away with each puppy from her teat. The last thing I remembered was her cry and the blood spattered on the pavement, dripping from my whiskers as I sniffed her remains. I wanted to erase the memory.

Squisita and I walked back up the hill. I sniffed the air for my Contessa, suddenly anxious to discover her frame of mind. If she were near the end of her rope as well I would have to keep a watchful eye on her every move, but the woman had not yet returned to the *villa*. I relaxed for a moment before another snip of Greta's death flashed to my mind like a crack of lightning.

Horrible, indeed.

And the gypsy. Still following me about like a curse. Always appearing at a crossroad. Odd beyond reason. If only I could put it all together. I was bred to do better. So far I'd solved nothing, but I took solace in knowing I had a strategy. I would concentrate on pushing the Count to courage first, to bolster him in the eyes of the Contessa. After all, now entwined in Umberto's arms, she might need persuasion to change partners. I walked onto the patio to see who was around.

Umberto pulled spent stalks of corn in the garden below. The garden looked a mess. With a riotous harvest on the wane, everything from pruning to picking needed attention. I examined the side of the house. Winter was creeping forward, and the *villa* beckoned as well. Umberto divided his time between the soil and slurry. I had watched him sift through all the plaster twice, cursing softly, before starting the chimney. Still no ring.

It was there. It had to be. I'd seen it go down the vent with my own eyes.

The day after the Contessa's arrival, she stood sentry as Umberto put the last touches on the new mantle in the bedroom. Her mood was bright since her vacation, but now she played the stoic. There had been no bounce and thresh for the Count at their reunion. Just a simple kiss to each cheek.

Umberto gave a final dab of paint and shook his head. "Another will just have to be bought."

I raised my head from the window seat where I was sleeping and cocked an ear. The Contessa stood beside me.

"The Count will fume," she said.

"All smoke, no fire." Umberto leered, puffing his chest out like a male grouse. He pulled her to him, one arm about her waist.

I thought I might be sick. The man always wore the scent of a dozen women. He was a lecher.

The Contessa rolled her eyes under arched brows and raised a corner of her mouth to smile. "Not here."

"No fire without a spark," said Umberto. He slipped a hand to her breast and kissed her neck.

She pushed him away. "A pinch and tickle don't make a spark. Is there a man left whose idea of romance originates above his belt?"

I growled. The Contessa collected me in her arms. Umberto watched her examine a photograph of the Count on the dresser.

"Perhaps it made it all the way into the furnace. I could take the metal apart. The ring may be lodged in a joint somewhere."

"Cold weather's on the way. It won't do to be without heat." The Contessa put a hand to her cheek, looking down the reconfigured vent for a long time.

I licked her hand and nuzzled her ear. It still smelled of Umberto's cheap cologne.

Finally, she shook her head. "Forget it. It was meant for someone else. I never want to see it again."

"Who?" asked Umberto.

"It doesn't matter anymore. What matters is how to tell him it's lost." She covered her mouth and shuddered. "I suppose it can't be avoided."

I followed them back to the garden where they were soon up to their elbows, side by side. I was inspecting a row of late squash when I caught sight of the Count at the bedroom window. The happy couple in the garden made my belly turn, and I decided to join Il Conte instead. He was examining the plasterwork of the new hearth. Laughter brought the Count to the window where he stared at the couple below, listening to them chat and giggle.

"You think I'll be forgiven?" he asked as he scratched my head. "I suppose she doesn't think much of me anymore. It's quite a hole I've gotten myself into."

The Contessa walked down the hill and disappeared behind the winery. As soon as she'd rounded the building she came running back, an undersized boar behind her. She must have surprised the creature into a charge. Umberto leapt to her aid, waving his arms, shouting. He met the Contessa on the edge of the lawn. The pig turned at the threat of a large sickle in the man's hand.

Lucky. Just as I and Squisita had been. Most boars wouldn't turn at mere threat. Must have been a youngster, I thought.

Il Conte stood. He lifted me into his arms, glaring out the window. Umberto hugged the woman in comfort.

Bravery. It pushed the woman straight into the man's arms. Raoul was right. Women were partial to courage. But it wasn't supposed to happen this way around.

The Contessa gave the window a quick glance as though to be sure the Count was watching. Then she kissed Umberto on the cheek. I felt the Count's stomach twist. The man leaned back out of view. His grasp tightened. I squirmed. The Count's anger rose. There'd be little reconciliation under its influence.

"So, that's the game you play," said the Count, keeping his eyes on the woman. He sucked air through his teeth. "We'll see who has dug the bigger hole."

Holes were something I knew about. Small and large, broad as Grazia's fanny, and deep ones, too; I'd dug them all, guided by but a singular, simple rule: the danger of collapse was directly proportionate to its depth. The woman's aim to make the Count jealous struck pay dirt, yet the man was still digging. The walls of the hole were starting to crumble.

*

Autumn was spent in Chianti. The leaves paled on the trees. I had never seen that before. The tradition was to pass the fall in Rome. There, vegetation only faded to a crisp, then fell. Here, the shades were glorious. The Contessa's mood brightened as she believed she was successful in keeping the Count from his mistress. As far as she was concerned, we could abandon Rome altogether. The proclamation was issued: we would winter at the *villa*.

There was no way for her to know the man had given up La Donna Rosa.

The Count made periodic visits to Siena to play cards with friends. Grazia scoured the wood for early mushrooms. The Contessa and Umberto patronized the flats by the creek when the two were out of sight. I tried hard to come between them. I pulled the man's garments or barked at nonexistent creatures in the scrub every time the two embraced.

Umberto became more and more irritated at my antics. Often he kicked me away, but I didn't give up. I did my best to aid in the Contessa's design, thinking it might work the way she intended: to spur the Count to courageous action. Every time Umberto and the woman passed time together in the garden, I brought it to the attention of Il Conte. Yet, there was no action, no reaction, nothing. Only seething. I didn't understand it.

*

One morning as the Count and Contessa stood on the patio, near the newly finished wall, the woman came clean.

She pulled at the finger it had once adorned. "The ring is lost."

"The jeweler?" asked the Count.

"No." The woman took a deep breath. "Down the heating vent."

The Count's voice boomed. "Down the vent?"

I ran for the cover of a terra cotta pot and watched as Il Conte rubbed a hand across the stucco finish. A trail of dust fell in its wake.

The Count fumed. "Half a year's work, and an unholy mess, just to cover it up. Am I right?"

"Well," the Contessa said, gesturing toward the upper story window. "Now we have a nice fireplace instead."

"And now the ring, wherever it is, is worth twice as much." The Count stormed through the *villa* like a rabid dog. "You were right on one point. You'll need that *fireplace* to keep you warm." He stomped up the stairs to the spare bedroom and slammed the door.

I followed my Contessa into her bedroom. Spewing curses like water from a fountain, she disappeared behind the bathroom door. The sound of a bath being drawn washed her words away. I walked to the door of the guest room. Having recoiled from the slam, the door was ajar. The Count stood in the middle of the room.

He whispered a prayer like a dog too long at the pound. *"Grazie, Madra mia, molto grazie."*

I nudged the door.

The Count turned to look at me. "It's fate, no? To be rid of that curse. *Mamma mia.* I don't care the expense."

Then why the fuss?

The man walked to the window, looking down to the garden below. "But she made me suffer," he said. "Now it's her turn to pay, and my pleasure to charge her. We'll see just how far she'll go with that Lothario." Il Conte let the sheer curtain slip from his hand and stooped to pet me. "There is common ground to be found in equal sins, no? *There* is found absolution."

A peculiar sport, I thought. Ironic, as well, given that the Contessa ceased to make an effort when she sensed the Count didn't care. *Mamma mia* was right. The Count was showing bravery in the face of disaster: stiff upper lip and all, but it wasn't the kind to lure the Contessa back. The line was fine between stubbornness and courage.

I yearned to speak. I wished it until I was sure my gums were blue, to utter just three little words: never look back. The source of all problems was a refusal to forgive. Blame equaled heartache every time. There was a lesson for us both from *La Filosofia dei Cani Nobili*: dogs never let their past define them. I licked my snout, clenched my jaw and retreated to the comfort of the kitchen.

*

Days passed. The Contessa was more miserable than ever: quiet much of the time. Once in a while we rode to town with Umberto. For me, trips to Siena were nerve-wracking. Each time the despondent woman approached a busy street, I held my breath, worried she might accidentally follow Greta's path into the deadly traffic. I'd go straight to bed upon each return home, exhausted from the stress. Time crept like a lion behind sheep.

The winery stood in quiet repose, waiting for the crush. With Umberto often at market, Grazia disappeared beyond the edge of the winery loft with greater frequency. She never returned with anything more than a faint scent of the winemaker, and the satisfied look of a well-fed fox.

Annoyed at the time she wasted in the rafters, I sat at the base of the ladder, ear tuned to the odd sounds suggesting the breathless scuffle of a chase. I was ever hopeful of her success at a catch of *uccellini*, though I knew in my heart she'd long ago captured her prey.

Grazia was imbued with something I never sensed in her before: the rosy glow of love. It was not the same feeling the Count emanated in the wake of La Donna Rosa. Nor that trailing the Contessa, in the arms of another man. Grazia's whole spirit rejoiced, buoying every soul who came near. In her presence, there was always a soft word and gentle touch on offer. Life with the winemaker was full of hope, and she passed it on in kindness. She was doggish to her core.

My one true comfort came from La Squisita. She was a perfect companion except for those times when her inner she-wolf surfaced to pin me against a shrub or wall. I now understood the addled prattling of my old friend Raoul, though the learning curve had been steep. Volatility was a basic feature of female design. Over the summer I came to accept the pernicious with the pleasant.

Part of the charm, no?

Prolonged heat kept the hunters at bay. Game birds didn't pass to the north in such weather. We were allowed to roam freely as long as the hot spell continued. And continue it did, delivering an extra crop of blackberries that we eagerly pulled from the lower vines.

Bored one afternoon, with Grazia and the Contessa in the village, Squisita and I walked down through the vineyard. We crossed the brisk stream, pausing to turn the smooth stones under the water to reveal crunchy crayfish. When we found no more we

213

abandoned the activity to dig in the loamy soil that skirted the wood. Heavy rain soaked the ground the night before. The wet earth was cool between my toes. By the time we were finished we were covered in a fine coating of pale sand, as though we had rolled in breadcrumbs.

Afterward, we lay together baking in the heat of the sun on the bank of the stream. From time to time Squisita licked my face and ears in affection. I was lost in the pleasure of her silky tongue on my velvet ears, the slurping sound of her mouth, the sweet breath of streambed crustaceans wafting into my nostrils.

Nothing better, I thought. I closed my eyes to imagine us of greyer chin and failing eyesight, languishing beside the same stream, passing the days in the splendid company of each other and our people. I pictured Squisita becoming the wise dog I knew she could be, filling out and fluffing up, like a flower in full bloom.

A banging rose from the garden. Squisita and I stiffened at the activity. Umberto was back at work. A brief rain and steamy sun, and the last of the garden ripened. The warm, sweet scent of fruit hung in the air above every vineyard, inviting the exploit of an Indian summer. Harvest was near.

Afternoon ritual at this time of year was to cull overripe squash, fallen tomato and other such delicacies. We made our way to the garden, careful to forage beyond Umberto's watchful eye. His temper peaked with the heat. If we put a nose to something not rotten, the man delivered a swift kick. I no longer regarded him as a kind and clever man, but a sly predator. He took advantage of the two people I loved most: Grazia and the Contessa.

I cast a side glance Umberto's way and pulled the flesh of a sun-softened string squash from its rind. I was determined to stay alert.

The man skulked about the other side of the garden pretending to tend tumbling vines, alibi of a hoe in his hand. I was convinced that he was biding time for the perfect opportunity. A knock on the head with a garden tool and a small, rotund dog was indistinguishable from the bloated watermelons rotting in the back rows of the garden.

The *cucina* door banged and Il Conte crossed the *terrazzo* with an *espresso* in his hand. The man hummed *Rigoletto* over the rim of his cup. My belly churned at the memory of La Donna Rosa.

Umberto began to whistle. I turned an ear to the hedgerow where the man worked. Elvis. "Devil in Disguise" rose up above the dahlias at the base of the hedgerow.

Squisita moved from rotten squash to a forbidden ripe tomato and began to feast. In an instant, Umberto raised his foot. He caught her in the ribs and she gasped, shying away into the overgrowth of a rambling vine. I barked my deepest tone, bared my teeth and growled.

I was surprised Il Conte had not fired him given what he suspected—but I was relieved, as well. If Umberto left, Grazia was sure to follow. She was loyal if not true. Therein lies the rub, I thought. I snapped a fly from the air in front of my nose and gave a long swallow. If Umberto could only be eliminated as easily. My ear's pricked, hackles rising with an idea.

Umberto, the last divide. And Grazia remains. Finally: the answer. I regarded the Count through my eyelashes, snout full of warm, soft eggplant.

Grazia stood behind the patio doors watching as well, wooden spoon in her hand. The man tapped his pipe on the flagstone, pulled a tobacco pouch from his vest pocket and filled the pipe. Digging deeper into the same pocket for his lighter, he found instead the tiny shell necklace he placed there in Rome. I was shocked. After all, the man discarded the photograph.

Why keep this trinket? I made my way to the patio for a closer look.

Grazia narrowed her eyes as if straining to see the necklace. The man closed his hand around the shell. The silver chain looped through his fingers. He raised his fist to hold it against his lips and stared out over the vineyard, a faraway look in his eyes. Like that of

Squisita, left at the end of a long driveway. Grazia lifted her chin then disappeared into the *cucina.* I wagged my tail. There'd be no need for an incriminating handkerchief. The Count followed his heart, and it was clear his heart belonged to the Contessa. At once, the equation became easy.

A simple thing. Raoul was right, again. I bowed my head, revealing a single tooth to Umberto, who stood behind the cover of demolished eggplant. But I needed to convince the Contessa. Teasing the memory of happier days grew more difficult as long as Umberto was part of the picture.

Il Conte pulled the cards from their box. First to come was the Jack of Hearts. The man waved the card at me.

"More luck, you see?" He placed it on the table for a game of solitaire.

I met his hand as it reached down to pat me. You'll need more than luck, I thought.

"*Tra noi,* Shimoni," said the Count. "Between you and me—*non dici.*" He pointed a finger at me, putting it to his lips. "I have a plan."

I licked the palm of the man's hand.

So did I.

Chapter Twenty-Five

S quisita dug fast as she focused at the root of another tomato plant.

No lesson learned, I thought. Still, her enthusiasm was intriguing. I padded across the fresh dirt to investigate her motivation. Before I dropped my nose into the hole, a fat gopher emerged from a mound of earth several meters distant. Without hesitation, I set upon the toothy beast. I clipped a bit of fur from its hide before it managed to scramble into a nearby hole.

By the time Squisita joined me in the hunt, Umberto was alert to the task. He shooed us both out of the garden, angrily raising a shovel in my direction. I cast the wicked man a low growl and Squisita and I raced away, heading back over the vineyard to the stream below. We stopped at the lip of the bank. Several rough-looking dogs of uncertain ancestry drank at the creek.

Wild dogs.

I'd heard rumors in the village about packs of feral dogs, multiplying without limit in the countryside. Bold in taking spring lambs or plump chickens. And ferocious. I was territorial, but not enough that I would try to deny a group of larger, unscrupulous dogs the pleasure of a drink from my stream. Clearly, this rumor had teeth. I turned to Squisita. Before I could report, she was over the bank and into the stream.

Soon, the dogs were fighting each other for the privilege of fighting Squisita. As the entire pack of un-pedigreed mutts tangled, I ran to the top of the bank. I barked in all directions, hoping anyone and everyone would hear me.

Umberto was the first to reach the stream. He stood nearby, shouting to the group, trying to gain their attention. The Count followed close behind with Grazia's large, shiny-barreled rifle from the *cucina* in one hand, a small fire extinguisher in the other. He tossed the undersized tank to Umberto. The man pulled a short pin from its top and sprayed the rioting crowd with snowy foam.

Frankly, to me it looked like a lot of fun, less the gang of outraged dogs. The pack was dead serious. None turned but one: a large muddy creature with a flat snout and narrowed eyes. Mouth curled to reveal jagged fangs tipped with blood. It stared at me, but the gaze was not one of defiance.

A glance of recognition. I sniffed the air. The scent drifting up from the stream was unfamiliar. This dog was no acquaintance. The thought of it was ridiculous. No one with half a pedigree ran with wild dogs. Yet, its eyes searched me as though I stood above a hidden bone.

Umberto turned the tank to concentrate on the menace. Insolent, the dog took a few steps forward, undiscouraged by the foam. The Count shot the gun into the air several times. At the first blast, I raced for cover. I had never seen the Count use a gun before. As far as I was concerned, gunfire always begot lifeless creatures, usually the size of small dogs.

The noise scattered the renegades as well. When they were well away, Umberto moved in to fetch Squisita. Down in the mud, she peeked out through watery eyes, under a dirty brow. She'd managed to hold her own, with only a few bloody scrapes showing beneath a thick coat of grimy foam.

We all walked back to the *villa*. The Count rested the gun over his shoulder. Umberto, one hand on Squisita, pulled the empty extinguisher behind him. I slowed his pace. I would not embarrass Squisita by attending her bath.

I watched the two men ahead of me. They took long strides down the row of neat vines. The walk of courageous men. Their quick response to the danger of the wild dogs had been impressive. Umberto didn't think twice about entering the fray, and the Count displayed a brave sense for the handling of a weapon.

218

Courage, I thought, indicative of the Count's station. Bravery may very well have drawn the Contessa to him in the first place. As Raoul said, women revere courage. I wondered if Squisita found him plucky as well. I licked a small wound on my paw. Heroism could be dangerous though. I paused in the vineyard to pull a grasshopper from a vine post and crunch it between my teeth.

Danger. I lingered over the idea, stopped chewing and cocked my head. And misery, I thought, of the worst sort. I couldn't push the thought away. Over and over in my mind it turned, daring me to follow. And then it struck.

Wild boar.

For the first time that season the evening breeze brought a shift on the heels of deepening shadows. A bracing rush of cold air ruffled my ears. Even though the details were unclear, and winter a season away, my head danced with visions of frost and snow and feral pigs. Malicious, hungry boar driven out of the wood by winter's chill to punish a wicked man.

That was it. Now I had both motive and method for Umberto's ruin.

But the man was not stupid. He'd handled himself well amid the wild dogs. He would do the same in the face of pigs. If the idea were to be successful, Umberto must be caught off guard. That was the only way he would be out of their lives forever. Wild dogs barked in the distance. My thoughts turned to Raoul.

One thing changes everything.

For the better, I thought. Raoul would be proud. Up the slope of the hill toward the *villa*, I trotted. One of my back legs gave an optimistic hop every second step. I felt light, buoyed as the heavy burden of indecision lifted.

A simple plan, a happy ending.

Un soluzione felice.

*

219

By daybreak the next morning, the vineyard filled with bobbing heads and busy hands. Dense swarms of fruit flies and the odor of fermentation saluted the beginning of the harvest. Night had delivered no frost. I put an early paw onto the grass to test its firmness. Still wet. The rigor of a good freeze was weeks away. No boar would come ahead of it.

With the freeze at bay, the ripe grapes fell to the rescue of the winemaker. Workers, armed with hand clippers and *canastre*, bent and stretched around the vines. The oval twig baskets were filled, emptied and filled again in rapid succession, before the heat of the midday sun could raise the sugar content in the fruit. Fat clusters of *Sangiovese* grapes hung low and heavy in plump, sweet perfection waiting to become Chianti.

Squisita and I paced the vine rows one by one. We followed the progress of the pickers, rooting for grapes that escaped the baskets, or low fruit dodging the hand of harvest. Once in a while a worker tossed a bruised or broken grape our way. It was always a contest as to which one caught it first, but never an argument. There was plenty of battered fruit to go around.

As I popped each lagging grape between my teeth, I thought of the skins that would soon litter the compost. I imagined wild pigs following the scent of rotten fruit, plodding through fresh snow across the stream. I saw fat, mean pigs foraging in the icy cold for moldy grapes. Feeding on the ripe fruit gave superb flavor to their succulent flesh. Grazia was always eager to shoot her first pig of the season.

The winemaker cruised the narrow road that split the vineyard, sampling grapes from each repository. Dust in his wrinkles, he smacked his lips and rolled his eyes with pride. The harvest was met in perfect time. Voice raised in song, he stripped the unloaded vines with a saber-sharp secateur.

I sniffed the air. The autumn scent of burning leaves hung heavy in the valley. Threads of smoke twined in the air like confused vines above the stream. The coming hunt approached. As if on cue a flock of game birds crossed the sky overhead. Shots cracked in the distance. The Contessa arrived to secure me to a leash. The garden party of summer was over.

She led me to the truck that carried the grapes from field to winery. It languished under the shade of a row of cypress. Lifting me into the cab, I joined Squisita on the bench seat. We touched noses.

The first report, I thought. With guns in the wood, weeks would pass without the freedom to roam again across the slender valley. I put my paws upon the sill of the truck window. Open just enough to admit the cool breeze, it barred escape. Squisita and I heaved a sigh in unison, resigned to watching the activity in the vineyard from a distance.

Mountains of grapes, pale and dark alike, were separated by shade into tall wooden cases, stacked at the end of each row. The sun moved higher in the sky. The heavy scent of grape juice wicked into the warming air. Grazia searched the vines for the more abundant clusters to keep in the cool of the cellar. A thoughtful treat for Christmas Day.

No time to lose in delivering the fruit to the press, the midday meal was merely a snack during the crush. Grazia shared her sparse lunch with us: bread, cheese and a bit of delicious peppered sausage. She placed a bowl of water on the floor of the truck. Squisita and I each had a turn drinking before we were taken, one at a time, onto the relief of the long dry grass. She returned us to the truck. Umberto slid onto the seat beside us to deliver the fruit to the winery, then headed back into the crowd of workers for another load.

Squisita quivered as crows swirled past the truck windows. The proximity of small game without a chase was too much for her to bear. She leapt around the cab, paying little notice to me as I tried to avoid her paws on my head. Finally, she gave a jump toward the wheel, the gear shift popped and the truck began to roll. She froze in horror. I put my nose to the crack in the open window and howled.

Grazia was the first to see us. She wailed above the singing in the fields and everyone turned to view the crisis. Soon, they were all running behind the loose truck, yapping and carrying on like a pack of agitated dogs. Umberto was the first to reach us. He jumped onto the runner and opened the door. Squisita bolted through the opening and Umberto slid onto the seat. Brakes applied, the truck came to a comfortable stop just short of the wall bordering the vineyard.

Grazia opened the other door of the truck and coddled me. I quaked from the excitement and took to her arms with relief. She called Squisita to her side, gave her a half scold and an earnest pat, and ushered us both to the safety of the kitchen. Exhausted by the excitement, we curled together by the patio doors and tracked the frenzy of harvest through the windows.

By dusk, the modest vineyard stood naked against the cool evening. Workers gathered in the winery. The press continued as long as whole fruit remained. The winery was aglow with lights. Its cavernous rooms echoed constant clatter across the lawn. Squisita and I lay sleepless as the grapes bled under the creak and moan of the press.

All night the noise droned on. Frothy liquid ran from beneath the turn of a giant screw atop a barrel-shaped vat. Voices laughed and sang and shouted. Finally, sleep came to us both, but only in fits. We yearned to get out and run into the excitement surrounding the crush. I wakened before dawn. Light broke to reveal dark grape skins being tossed into oak barrels, ready to darken a portion of the wine for Chianti. The rest were saved to the compost that piled behind the winery. The skins were rich and sweet, and they thickened the air with their odor. I depended on it.

Grazia arrived as the morning sun peeked over the hill. I yawned and met her at the door. I threshed a greeting and then headed upstairs. Deeper sleep would come under the comfort of a feather cover. By noon I'd be as good as if I'd had a restful night. The Count passed me on his way down the steps in silence. I entered the bedroom and leapt upon the window seat. Water sounds emanated from the bathroom door. I surveyed the vineyard, barren and quiet after harvest. Changed by a single day.

The Contessa emerged from the bathroom wrapped in a thick towel, a gentle tune on her lips. I sat up straight at her change in mood.

She looked down at me. "What does sorrow do?"

I cocked my head and gave a quiet whine.

"*Certo*. It only makes more heartache," she said. "All the grief in the world never brought one smile. But smile? Soon enough, *someone* returns it." She scratched my chin and gave my tail a tug. "Things have taken a turn, no?"

Things had turned, indeed, I thought. It was high time she sensed it.

The Contessa entered the closet and dressed, emptying a hamper of dirty clothes onto the floor. The woman used her hands to fish through the mix of slacks and skirts, pulling loose change and papers to the safety of a small table. Then came the handkerchief, still reeking of La Donna Rosa. I wiggled my nose at the insult. The Contessa held it to her chin.

Her jaw set in anger, her eyes narrowed and mouth pursed. "*Bastardo.*"

I jumped to the floor. Reformed, I thought. This time, she was mistaken. I took an end of the kerchief between my teeth, tugged it from her hand and ran. No using this as evidence. The man had seen the light. I was too close to implementing my solution. I'd not let old news destroy the chance at returning my people to each other's arms.

The Contessa shrieked. Down the stairs I raced, through the hall and out the patio door. Il Conte sat at the *terrazzo* table, solitaire on his mind. I dashed across the lawn, past the winery, and splashed through the stream. At the edge of the wood, under a briar, I dug. I didn't stop until water puddled in the hole. Dropping the linen into the deep, it disappeared under the mud. I covered it with sand and sat down.

Buried. Along with the past. I watched the Count in the distance. The man rested his elbow on a neighboring chair back, concentrating on his game. I trotted though the creek and up the slope to the terrace. A window opened above.

The Contessa leaned over the sill. "Where did Shimoni go?"

"He's here," the Count said.

The woman eyed me, then scanned the yard with care. Staring at the Count for a moment, she retreated.

"Never been one for mornings, has she?" The Count sipped his coffee.

They knew each other's flaws. As Raoul's master had said, illusions fell away with time. Perhaps memory could overlook the truth. I put my paws upon the Count's leg and pushed my nose into the man's vest. The shell necklace rattled in his pocket.

Chapter Twenty-Six

After a few days, the wine fermented. At dusk, all gathered in the winery for a ritual sampling. Squisita and I attended on separate leash. I at my Contessa's side, Squisita with Umberto. Grazia, with a discreet wink and affectionate glance, helped the winemaker pour pale liquid into bulbous glasses. Not yet the rich black of Tuscan wine, this was the first rite of crush. I yearned for a taste.

The Count raised a hand in exuberance. All followed suit. Glasses were filled. Then bottles of older wine were opened and passed around. Laughter reverberated from tank to tank in the cavernous winery. One more fill, and the Count turned to the Contessa for a final toast. He saluted: the winemaker, the crew and the vintage, then clinked his glass to hers with such enthusiasm the glass fell.

As if by magic, a fortuitous pool of fragrant, fresh wine lay at my feet. I wasted no time in lapping up the puddle. It was bittersweet, but in its depth, a noble finish of fine Chianti.

I began to weave just as the group dispersed. I followed the Count and the Contessa in the direction of the *villa*. All track of La Squisita was lost. Fruit flies buzzed around my snout. Seeking drops of wine still wet on my mouth, they sounded as though they were propelled by loud, rickety engines. I intended to find rotting figs along the route home but the lawn and the shrubs and the trees blended hopelessly together. A hose hissed behind me as someone rinsed the winery floor. The grass was wet from the afternoon sprinkler. Soft mud squished between my toes like fresh manure. I sniffed my feet. Nothing but earth. When I looked up, the whole yard undulated like a reflection in a wavy pool of clear water. Head heavy, feet light, I prayed for a free ride to the kitchen, but the Contessa was nowhere to be seen.

A call in the distance. *"Vieni,* Shimoni."

The Contessa was hidden in a blur of inebriation. My tail was numb. I stopped once to lean forward, bending my neck around to catch a glimpse—assurance it was still where I'd left it. A crack of gunfire surprised me and I turned to see if hunters approached. Another shot rang from the deep wood. Pigs snorted in the distance. I turned my head one way, then another. The men lay hidden in the thick cover, flushing boar with their shouts. Somewhere Squisita howled at the temptation to follow. A flock of birds took to the air from beneath a shrub nearby. I shied at the threat of low-flying wings and shook myself twice. Nose down, eyes focused on the patio door, I trudged through a sea of cool grass toward the patio.

The Count and Contessa seemed miles ahead. They walked into the *villa.* I weaved through the open door, following a discreet distance behind, sniffing my way toward the couple. I slipped several times on the stairs, a back leg losing its balance over slippery edges. Light blazed from the bedroom. A fire in the new hearth. I teetered into the room. It was cozy and warm, a primal lair under fire's glow. Light danced across the walls in the shadow of the flames. I was dizzy from a wash of motion. My eyes closed tight to catch my balance. They opened to the Count holding my Contessa in his arms, one misguided hand upon her breast.

The mark of a lecherous man, I thought. I'd seen it before.

"Ubriaco," the Contessa said. The woman hesitated. Just as she had at Umberto's lascivious embrace.

"I don't have to be drunk to want you," said the Count.

"There's more to it than this."

"No simpler thing, in fact." The Count nibbled at the woman's neck.

"You can't have both," she said, and pushed him away.

Her tone invited the scent of roses to my memory.

The Count stopped. He turned his head and looked into her eyes. *"You* can?"

The couple stepped apart. The Contessa leaned on the window seat to look out the glass. *"Come?"*

"I've seen you in the garden," said the Count, "and on the lawn, and by the stream."

The Contessa tapped the toe of her shoe on the carpet. "You don't seem to mind."

The Count walked to the hearth and warmed his hands to the heat of the fire. "You still equate attention with affection. I stopped doing that long ago."

"Oh, yes," she said, "I forgot. *You* have what you want." She faced him, eyes flickering with firelight.

A thing of the past, I thought. I whined, hoping the woman might read my whirling mind.

"That's the way *you* want it," said the Count.

"A fire doesn't start by itself," said the woman. "You used to know. There is no such thing as token romance. A cursory touch doesn't pass for love."

"It used to be as good."

The Contessa brushed the man's arm as she passed. "It hasn't been good for a long time." She walked into the bathroom and slammed the door.

The man wavered a little at the impact. He rubbed the corner of his mouth, then gave his head a slight nod and sighed. I followed him down the stairs to the *cucina*, sprawling on my cushion beneath the table. I tried to avoid a circular configuration. Round things spun.

"So—wrong strategy," said the man, looking at me. "I guess memories aren't the only things we forget with time."

I blinked the man into focus before closing my eyes to the revolving room.

"The free pass expired," the Count said. "What now?"

Romanzo, I thought. The test begins.

Chapter Twenty-Seven

I had no memory of reaching my pillow, yet there I was. My eyes were sticky with sleep. As I struggled to see through the bright light of morning, vivid dreams still called:

Swirling wine and sticky mud, the rotten smell of compost thick with buzzing insects; flocking birds in cloudless skies, hissing snakes, boars grunting deep in the wood; growling dogs, ivory tusks, sharp teeth and bristly hair; a woman crying, the shout of a man, gunshot in the air. Squisita pronouncing a slow, mournful howl in the distance...

I looked around, half-expecting to see a sounder of pigs plow through the kitchen, but Grazia was my only company. I blinked her plump form into focus as she rubbed a white cloth around her heart-shaped crystal and set it in the window. My mouth puckered as though one of the Count's dirty socks had occupied it all night. I wobbled to my water bowl and drank it dry. Grazia stood above me, watching.

"*Povero carino,*" she said. "No more wine for you."

Water, I thought. No need to mention the grape ever again.

I gave a loud sneeze, returned to my pillow and set about the tedious job of grooming. My paws were tinged with purple. The under part of my belly was splattered with the liquid, as well. Fortunately for my stomach, it was tasteless. Only the color remained.

Just as I was finishing up between my toes, Umberto entered the *cucina* from the terrace. The door slammed behind me. I gave a jump. Umberto stumbled across the kitchen, bumping a chair on his way.

"*Attento,*" warned Grazia, brow crinkled into a frown.

Umberto weaved his way down the hall much the same as I had the day before.

Wine for breakfast, I thought. Crush marked the end of Umberto's sobriety. His stupor always peaked at Christmas with the ample flow of wine and celebration. The man was a seasonal drunk.

He grabbed the keys to the shiny grey car that hung on a peg at the front door.

Not the car, I thought. Umberto's tippling had been responsible for its swipe at the low wall of the driveway. He'd headed the car from the dirty road to the lawn for a wash. It went to the shop instead. And the Count went after Umberto. Now, only Grazia was allowed to drive Il Conte's car.

Grazia called behind him. "What are you doing?"

"Truck won't start," he said. "I have a game in town."

"I'll bet," she returned under her breath. "Let me drive you."

Brava.

Umberto acquiesced. Grazia pulled on a sweater and they drove away.

I lay back on my cushion. I didn't care they left me behind. Guns popped in the distance. The throbbing in my head was gone but sharp pain advanced at every shot fired in the wood. There was a definite price to be paid for the luck of the grape. My mind turned to Umberto.

I rewound the man's careless passage through the kitchen, his poor judgment at trying to commandeer the Count's car.

The carelessness of fools. A combination for disaster.

I slept the rest of the afternoon until Grazia returned. She entered the house without removing her coat and went straight to the stack of empty boxes in the corner of the kitchen. I followed her into the yard, and we proceeded to the garden.

While a brisk wind whipped her skirt, Grazia gathered a last push of bright tomatoes from the vine. The cupboards were already bursting with preserves, but she was not one to waste the opportunity of ripe *pomodori*. She pulled every last piece of plump red fruit from their gangly pale limbs. I followed her as she put several full boxes in the cool of the winery, just behind the fermentation tanks. The tomatoes would have to wait until she had the time to put them up.

"You stay here, Shimoni," Grazia said. She tied the end of my leash to a wooden rail on the wall next to the boxes. "I'm going to fetch a good bottle of wine for my *Bolognese*." Grazia disappeared down the stairs into the wine cellar.

I pushed my nose around the base of one tomato box. The scent was sharp and honeyed like the ambrosia of fine *balsamico*. I closed my eyes to the small flies around the fruit and took a deep breath. My mouth watered at the thought of fettucini steaming under the same foggy aroma—fresh tomato sauce. Reverie dissolved into a cough. Someone was in the office. I barked and the winemaker emerged.

"*Che succede?*" The man walked over to untie the leash. "Someone has forgotten you, eh?"

The winemaker looked around to an empty room then led me back into his office and sat down. He finished making a brief notation on a pad of paper beside him. A tiny fly emerged from my nose and I sneezed. The man turned, invited me into his lap and gave me a satisfying scratch under the collar.

"*Regalo?*" the winemaker asked. He opened a deep desk drawer, pulled out a small bag and took a piece of corn flour bread from inside.

I raised my head, laying my ears flat in a fashion that begs a question. It was not normal for the winemaker to invite me into the winery, let alone treat me.

There was a reassuring tone to the man's voice. "*Va bene.*"

I took the bread politely. It was soft and crumbled into every corner of my mouth. Small bits fell from my snout into the open drawer.

"Next time, you'll have a napkin," the man chuckled. He pulled several things from the drawer, and turned it over to empty it of the crumbs.

A car door slammed outside. I strained to see over the sill of the window. Umberto, returned from his game in town, had managed to start the truck. He and Squisita rolled down the driveway. I watched as they disappeared and gave a shallow whine.

"I know how you feel," said the winemaker. "Sometimes to wait for one you love is *difficile*."

Si. I rested my chin on the man's arm.

Replacing the contents of the drawer one by one, the man hesitated at the last. Raising his hand to the window, something blazed with bright afternoon light.

The breath caught in my throat. Sparkling in the man's grasp was a beautiful piece of crystal, perfect match to the other half of Grazia's glass heart.

"But one waits long for something precious," the winemaker said. The man winked at me. He took a photograph from the windowsill. Last year's Christmas picture: the whole vineyard crew, Umberto and Grazia. The winemaker exuded serene warmth as he regarded Grazia.

The fine wispy hair on my snout relaxed under its influence. The man smiled and set me on the floor. He put the photo in its place at the window and returned the crystal. Closing the drawer, he stood up. We walked into the winery. The man paused when he passed the tomatoes. He turned the top layer over one by one.

"It just might be time," he said. "What do you think?"

I put my nose to the fruit in the man's hand. It was glossy and firm, yet the skin yielded willingly to his touch. Ready, I thought.

"Like a woman, *no*?" The man gave the tomato a gentle squeeze until juice trickled down his wrist. "It's all in the timing," he said. "Let her sit too long and she'll rot. Handle her right, she'll give you everything you need."

I nudged the winemaker's hand. The man ate half the *pomodoro* in one bite and granted me the balance. I licked his hand clean.

Grazia emerged from the cellar with two bottles of wine.

"Let me," said the man. He took the wine from Grazia's hands and they walked as far as the *villa* together, then parted. The winemaker started his car and drove away.

I stood a long time on the *terrazzo*. The winemaker was yet another soul who would benefit from the loss of Umberto, I thought. A noble plot, indeed. Ample thanks for the kindness the winemaker showed me, and the love given Grazia.

I looked at the window of the man's office. Sunlight glinted off the back of the frame that held the holiday photograph. With any luck, the scheme would work. The group in the next year's photo would be smaller by one.

Chapter Twenty-Eight

Heavy rain cooled the days into October. The stifling weather melted away, but a new heat took over. Squisita was relegated to the apartment, only entering the yard while I stood behind closed doors. The separation denied us both the enjoyment of the change of season. I loved the crisp fall mornings in Chianti, even if they were experienced at the end of a leash. Paws were invigorated by brisk, frosty grasses. The *cucina* fire burned cozy scents into the cold air and defrosted toes frozen by the drop in temperature. But it was all enjoyed without Squisita's company.

Grazia finished the last tomato preserves. She completed the delicate daily polish of her precious crystal and set it on the sill to twinkle in the morning sun.

"The best gift I've ever gotten," she said as she closed the sink window to Umberto's whistling in the yard. She looked at me. "You know why?"

Her tone was that of a woman bearing treats. My mouth watered in anticipation.

"It came with kindness. And in kindness there is hope." Grazia jumped at the slam of a ladder against the *villa*. She shook her head and smiled. "Hope amid the ruins."

She followed the dancing light to a large shiny pot on a low shelf. Moving it to the sink, she filled it with water and placed it on the stove. Then, she made every surface in the kitchen thick with jars. The *cucina* jingled like the bells of Christmas each time she brushed against the table.

She prepared the tomatoes for several incarnations, beginning with whole tomatoes in liquid. I sat in the corner. *Pomodori pelati* left little chance an odd or end might reach the floor. I waited for the fortune of *conserva*. Chopped tomatoes often traveled. Soon, the house burst with pungent aromas. The *cucina* steeped for hours behind doors closed to the sudden cold. Grazia may as well have been bottling rare perfume.

Apex of the year, I thought. Insurance against the sacrifice of winter. I yawned and stretched, predicting the messier details of *conserva*. When the Contessa arrived from the hall, I got to my feet and licked her ankle in a greeting.

"Che succede?"

"Pomodori, Signora," Grazia responded, casting a look in my direction with a smile and wink. *"Attendere per un incidente."*

My tail wagged in return. Most of the food on the floor was no accident.

The Contessa walked to the radio on a shelf above the table and pushed a button. Music filled the kitchen.

I never understood the principle behind the radio box. It was mystery how something of such little size achieved such great volume. I supposed it to be the same principle guiding a diminutive dog endowed with a deafening bark.

My Contessa swayed to a slow rhythm as she helped Grazia with the *pomodori*. Then the song changed. The Contessa's eyes lit up like the fire under the pot on the stove. Hooking her arm through Grazia's, she swung her hips and swayed her knees. The two women slid around the kitchen to Elvis's "Blue Suede Shoes." I wiggled my own steps.

Excellent. An entire song devoted to shoes.

As the music faded, the Contessa rinsed her hands. She pulled on a sweater. "Last time I danced like that, I didn't need a sweater to keep me warm."

"La musica revives the past like romance promises a future, eh?"

The Contessa tipped her head at Grazia's words as though they were foreign.

"It's been a long time since I've heard a promise." She exited the *terrazzo* doors, beckoning me to follow.

I was content to remain in the steamy kitchen. Treasure was sure to fall my way. I had, after all, waited through the boredom of whole tomatoes. The reward for my patience was at hand. I was loath to miss it. Though the memory of a *pomodori* bath was never far from my mind, the scent of simmering tomatoes and herbs brought me to my feet, alert.

The Contessa closed the door. She walked across the lawn into the waning garden.

"How she must ache," said Grazia. "Il Conte, as well."

I was astonished. I wondered just how much she knew.

"I know what's in his heart," she said, "just as I know what's in his pockets." Grazia leaned down to scratch my ear in the very place that itched. "Your lady needs to start her own music."

The music started, I thought. The idea of the Contessa and Umberto skulking behind Grazia's back made my whiskers twitch.

Grazia watched Umberto root around the garden near the Contessa, his angry hands flying at the crows that sought the last of rotting fruit amid the vines. "She'll find no solace there," said the woman. "Music can't be found in someone with no song."

The Count appeared in the hallway to the *cucina*. He joined Grazia at the patio doors. I moved back a few steps. If the two people came to blows in defense of the situation, the only safe spot was under the kitchen table. But the man only growled under his breath, then retreated up the stairs.

"Who's using who?" asked Grazia. She nodded to the couple in the garden.

I joined her by the door. The Contessa edged closer to Umberto until he gave her a playful nudge with his hip. She laughed, then shot a quick look at the bedroom window. The shutters slammed above.

"Umberto uses the Contessa, she uses him; the Count uses them both to make her suffer." Grazia had it all figured out. She tossed her head in the direction of the room above. "So he takes his time trying to solve the problem."

She knew the plot. I knew the ending. My ears flapped as I shook my head. It ached under Grazia's stream of reason.

"If she waits for the Count to figure it out, she'll be an old woman, alone," said Grazia. "The first time man asked anyone for help, he got Eve. He's not about to ask again."

Soon. I gave Grazia's foot an encouraging lick.

She returned to the chopping block. The floor was wet with liquid dripping from the surface above. I licked most of it clean, and then sat ready to receive. To be poised, eyes forward, was the best offense in capturing any bit that might slip from her hands. Grazia leaned down to give me a pat. She took a clean towel and wiped my paws, sticky with tomato juice. I leaned into her leg, looking at my reflection in the shiny door of the refrigerator. My muzzle was tinged pale tomato pink.

"You're a mess," she said. The woman crouched down. Cupping her hands around my snout, she kissed my nose. "A lovely mess."

Si. I put my paws on Grazia's apron and licked her velvet face.

Umberto scaled the ladder at the side of the house. Shutters from above banged and latched shut as he closed up a sparsely used sun room for the coming winter. I walked to the *terrazzo* doors. Squisita raced around the yard at the ruckus overhead. Without hunting blood in her veins, she was not as prone to wandering the wood alone. As long as she had company in the garden, she would stay put, able to enjoy the freedom of the yard unrestrained by any leash. I heaved a sigh at her good fortune. I yearned to run at her side as she raced like her tail was on fire, down the slope, over the low wall and through the garden. At the top of the lawn, a row of winter pansies stood in small pots, ready to be planted in the tall ceramic jars around the yard. Squisita bolted through, sending them flying in all directions. I couldn't help but wag a return. I never knew another dog to make so much fun out of nothing. My loins ached for wanting her, but I knew there'd be no reunion until she was off her heat. Umberto shouted an epithet of curses in her direction.

Grazia shook her head at the noise. "One waits long who looks for the perfect mate," she said. "In the end, one is found whose faults are bearable."

Amen. I returned to the work of waiting for scraps, taking a half-dozen wedges in midair, missing only one. I misjudged the distance from my nose to the fruit. It bounced from my snout, skating underneath the stove to safety. There it would remain, in tempting decay, until spring cleaning.

Finally, Grazia moved on to the making of a thick paste: the pure concentrate of summer. She always let me lick residue of the rich, sweet reduction from the cooled saucepan.

The heat in the kitchen was stifling. Steam rose from the simmering glassware. Umberto entered through the haze and moved to the sink, holding a long wrench in one hand.

"The faucet still drips," noted Grazia. "Can't you fix it for good?"

"It just needs a little attention once in a while," said Umberto.

Grazia raised a jaded eyebrow. "Everything works better if tended to from time to time, no?" She reached over the sink to push the windows open, granting the heat escape.

"Some things require no maintenance," he said. "Others are full time." He stepped behind her, shooting a playful finger to the side of her ample waist.

She jumped, catching the beautiful glass heart with her sleeve. The sound of scattering glass against the hard porcelain of the sink declared only pieces of the crystal remained. The two people stared down into the deep basin for a few seconds. Then tears began to stream down Grazia's cheeks.

"*Sono molto addolorato, cara,*" Umberto murmured. "*Scusa me.*" His voice was low and contrite.

Sad and sorry, indeed. I walked to the distressed woman and issued a reassuring lick to her calf.

The man stooped over the sink to retrieve the shattered glass. He gathered the shards in his palm, examining the possibility of repair. "I've broken your heart."

Even a dog of poor eyesight knew the answer. Not this time.

Umberto turned to slip the mess into a bucket of trash at the end of the counter. Grazia whirled around to face him, her rosy cheeks wet.

"It can't be broken twice." She stopped crying and opened the capacious pocket of her apron.

The two looked at each other for a long minute until Umberto followed her silent order, sliding the handful of glass into its depths. She sniffed, then wiped the back of her tomato-sticky hand across her eyes and exited through the *terrazzo* doors. I pressed my nose to the glass. The man followed her across the lawn with his eyes.

"*È colpa mia,*" he said. "*Miseria.*"

Self-inflicted, I thought.

The man cradled his chin with one hand, placed the other over the doorknob. He hesitated, as if weighing the consequences of following the despairing woman. Then he shook his head. "No use to try," he said.

Let me, I thought. I raised a paw to the glass just as Squisita leapt in front of the patio doors. Something peeked from one side of her mouth. Its odor was subtle but unmistakable, even through the glass.

"*Funghi!*" Umberto cried.

The enchanted declaration of autumn.

He opened the door and I slipped outside. Freedom. As long as I showed interest in the mushroom, I would be trusted to stay close by. Finding *funghi* was one of my specialties.

I made several incomplete attempts at the prize before Squisita dropped it onto the flagstone and ran. I snapped half the mushroom up in one bite, and then turned to find Squisita. I closed my eyes to better focus on her scent, and was behind her in a flash, just within reach, all the way to the apartment. Her tail hair gave a fleeting tickle to my nose and I opened my eyes in time to see her squeeze through Grazia's legs and into safety. I stopped short. Grazia held a broom over my head, aimed in my direction. I knew she meant business. The fun was over.

"You can't have her," she said, then lowered the broom. "Porcini, Shimoni," she declared. "No one finds them like you."

The desperate, dry summer soil finally gave up its mysteries to that first hard rain of fall. *Funghi* could be found in every shape and size, shade and flavor. And I was a master at finding them. But time was of the essence. Wild pigs would be after them, too.

Umberto reached the door of the apartment with Grazia still guarding its entry. She cast him a wry expression, as if his redemption rested on bounty of *funghi* he found.

"The dogs will work well together, I think," he said. "She's already demonstrated the ability to find. Shimoni can teach her the rest. We'll diaper the bitch to keep him focused. They can *both* come with us."

"Like putting a blindfold on a bat," Grazia muttered. "Do what you like. We'll see how focused he can be."

Umberto's eyes sparkled. "With two dogs, we'll bring home twice as much."

Few things inspired the Italian more than the discussion of mushrooms. Even Italian dogs, particularly those with a bit of country sense, knew the power of the subject. It provoked argument on where to find them, contests on how to cook them, and exaggerated stories of size and number even from the most reserved enthusiast. And, in the market squares, they were gold.

What was left of a plump *porcino* dangled between the thumb and forefinger of Umberto's hand. Only a semicircle now, it was a lovely velveteen grey and thick as a Florentine steak. I made a failed leap at the rest of the trophy before Umberto carried it away, disappearing into his apartment.

I waited at the door, ear cocked to the general sound of rustling. Muffled conversation was cool and even. Anger vanished in the magic of the mushroom. Squisita was the first to emerge: neatly wrapped in an absurd-looking garment that protected her hindquarter from invasion. Even her tail was hidden. But the lovely scent remained. I sidled up to her shoulder and licked her face. It was heaven.

Grazia and Umberto arrived with a bundle of paper bags, a long stout stick and large twig baskets in hand. The woman's head was wrapped in a pale scarf, stout legs covered by three-quarter stockings braced at the knee with dark garters. They both wore thick leather boots laced to mid-shin and gloves to combat the threat of hidden snakes. Broad smiles reflected the therapeutic power a single change of thought can have on a broken heart. The focus was *funghi*.

The sun centered over the northern sky. There'd be no hunters at midday. Squisita and I were free to forage for mushrooms as we pleased until sunset. Grazia threw a knapsack over her shoulder and set a determined jaw.

Diana, I thought. The huntress. The man was only along to bear the spoils. If we were lucky, the find would be measured in dozens of kilos. Grazia would not suffer the weight of a broken back, too. I kept an eye on Umberto as we made our way into the wood.

The forest bordering the valley floor was crowded with mentoring pine and chestnut trees. Perfect encouragement to *funghi*. The four of us skulked through the wood sweeping for treasure, heads bowed, voices hushed in concentration.

Mushrooms were a miracle. A complete and perfect food: spongy texture, perfect balance between moist and dry, subtle flavor of raw earth. Stealthy prey as well. They offered a pleasant hunt, yet were an acquiescent captive: no chase to spoil the reward of discovery.

Squisita soon divined the nature of the quest. She pulled ahead of the group. I suspected a return to the vein of *porcini* that prompted the expedition. My pace quickened to keep up. If she located the same spot it would be a spectacular find, and take the pressure off of me. My brain was mush under her spell.

I reached her just as she disappeared into a thicket. It was dense and very dark. I was certain it yielded no *funghi*. But inside the air was cool and the light dim. I sniffed for evidence. A moment passed, my eyes adjusting to the shadow. Squisita had disappeared. I stood there, trying to clear my head. Then, the rustle of dry leaves under me, and a smooth, cool brush of my paw. I looked down between my front feet to catch the last portion of a fat snake as it slithered through the mulch in the opposite direction.

Without thinking I spun around, pinning the viper between my jaws just behind its head. It writhed objection. Wrapping its long body around my head, it allowed only one eye to peek through its scales. I tried to back my way out of the snake, but it had a firm grip on me. So, I ran forward in the direction I'd come, out of the thicket and down the path. I could hardly see. Grazia hummed somewhere in the distance. I bolted toward the sound. She shrieked as soon as she realized my cargo. Again, the snake slid, this time covering my vision completely. Umberto turned Grazia's way just as I ran in his direction.

The man beat the reptile about the body. He used the long stick brought precisely for dispatching vipers. He seemed neither to realize nor care that an undersized dog was the frame to which the snake clung. I winced under each blow. I wanted desperately to release the thing, but dared not. I clenched my jaw tight around it. The creature would no doubt bare bitter reprisal for the indelicate clasp of its endless neck. It slipped farther down my head, but my sight was still obstructed. I didn't see well enough to move again, so I sat down. The snake writhed around my head and neck. I was exhausted. Yet there'd be a stiff penalty if I spit it out. I'd seen snakes strike, teeth bared like a grappling hook.

Finally, Umberto peeled the serpent from my head. Grasping it by the tail, he uncoiled it like string around a bunch of long beans. Eyes revealed, I saw the body of the creature. It draped in the air, one end between resolute teeth, the other between Umberto's determined hands.

Umberto's voice was calm and quiet. *"Prego."* He gave a gentle pull to the snake.

I felt the creature stretch and shudder and returned the tug. The war was on.

Umberto's mild coaxing escalated into reproach. "Leave it," cried the man.

But I was no fool. Snakes were swift and exact. I held fast to my position. Digging in my paws, I shook my head for effect.

"Adesso." Umberto's eyes became slits. He lifted the tail of the viper over his head.

I rose along with it, high above the ground. Then the man twirled me in the air, a bizarre manifestation of a manic calliope, round and round, Squisita nipping at the creature every time it flew past.

Grazia shouted. "You'll break his neck."

"That's the point," said Umberto.

Lunatic. At the very least Umberto suffered under a severe limitation of character.

"I mean the dog," said the woman.

"Silenzio," Umberto said.

He took a few steps back to steady himself, a heavy foot landing square on top of Squisita's hind paw. She yelped a retreat.

I was quite sure the snake would split in two before its neck might snap. If anyone's neck was going to break, it was mine.

Grazia was right. All reasonable solutions offered only a short flight through the air to disaster.

But free of the viper, I thought. It just might work. If I released my grip at the proper time I might clear the fangs of the beast. A rough landing was a fair price to pay. I braced myself and watched the view whirl by. I was dizzy. Closing my eyes, I took a deep breath through my teeth. The meaty scent of the serpent filled my throat. I focused on the flesh between my jaws. I needed to be steady, able to run a straight line when I reached *terra firma*. Listening to the whoosh of the brush passing by, I tried to gauge the direction of a break in the trees. Whoosh, silent, whoosh, silent, whoosh. I opened my mouth and let it ride.

Grazia screamed. The wind whipped my ears as I hurled through the air like a football, then landed in a plush copse of mushrooms. I opened my eyes under a tall pine near Grazia. Squisita tumbled me back.

I snapped. I was in no mood to play.

Grazia scooped me up. She performed an immodest inspection for poisonous bites. Finding me free of danger she placed me on the ground next to her basket with an affectionate pat. She slipped me a tender *funghi* for my embarrassment. I shook the dust from my coat. Returning to the scene of the crime, I checked the status of my opponent. The snake lay dead on the ground. I scanned it with my nose. It was longer than I had imagined.

Stretched like a pair of silk stockings, I thought. Momentary pride came with the conquest.

Squisita sidled up beside me on three paws. The blow she'd suffered from Umberto was mean. A toenail bled, and she was reluctant to put any pressure on her hind leg at all. She offered a brief nuzzle as apology for the roll before turning her attention to the corpse. With a perfunctory shake to the middle of the lifeless reptile, she tossed it aside.

She seemed to notice no connection between my trials and the tribulation of the snake. Once again, unaware of her role as instigator, she vaulted like a hapless idiot around the clearing, despite her injury. I shook the pine needles from my paws and yawned.

Innocence, I thought. Acumen's obstacle.

I spent the remainder of the afternoon dedicated to Grazia's hind end looking for mushrooms, under the trees and out of trouble. Before the sun fell behind the ragged backbone of the western hill, we started for home. The bags and baskets were laden with several types of *funghi*. Delicate, sweet, dark conical caps; bitter, glistening pale flat-tops with white stalks; short, creamy, fat trumpets with frilled edges and a scent of dried fruit, and my favorite, the beloved broad flat of the meaty *porcini*.

My mind thus occupied, I didn't notice that the snake had vanished from the place I'd left it. I was well past the site before I realized I should have come upon the carcass. Dropping my nose to the ground, I followed my own scent back to the spot of execution. I stopped. The air was rank and sour. Like sweat.

Boar. Wild pigs never resisted fresh meat. They had taken the spoil. I worked my nose to range them. A biting wind fell from the shadows climbing the slope of the valley. With it came a whiff of *porchetta* on the hoof. A small group scoured the lower hillside.

Winter's turn. The snap in weather drove them down. Soon the cold would drive them to the easy forage of the compost. I regarded the pigs. Finally, my strategy was ready to be implemented. All I needed was the weather. Soon, I thought. Soon.

I watched as the sounder moved in unison up the slope. Umberto raided their visits to the warm, rotten feed after every new snow. Grazia was always close behind in hope of shooting a pig for roasts and chops. I'd seen the boar challenge the man at the compost before. Only the good sense of retreat kept him safe. Throw wine into the equation and the odds of a hazardous outcome multiplied.

I glanced down the gentle path to the stream below. Squisita limped into view from the thick brush. Then she bounced on three legs down the trail to the stream, trying to encourage me to follow. The old pig turned and listened. Mature boars seldom run from threat.

I could see it all play out: the black of night and the warm breath of boar lacing the icy air as I pretended to lose myself in the wood across the creek. Umberto would follow. It was the man's job. He was bound to come splashing across the frigid stream and head on into the brambles after me.

I flicked an ear toward the grunting on the hillside. The pigs were my ace. I closed my eyes and imagined them grunting their way through the man's flesh. The Count, brave nobility that he was, would surely attempt a rescue. Valor proved, worthiness restored, the Contessa's reward: her heart returned as well. But, with any luck, it would be too late for Umberto.

The air was electric with my plan. My pace quickened with excitement. All problems soon solved. I yearned to wag my tail but willed it motionless as I passed Umberto.

The first star broke in the east, just below a half moon, bright even as the dusk mounted. The windows of the *villa* glowed at the top of the hill. From a distant nub of a town beyond, the evening bells of Siena welcomed us home. I turned a final bend through the garden. Resolute, I marched toward the door and the solution to my problems.

Chapter Twenty-Nine

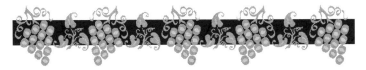

U mberto sat under the chestnut tree sorting mushrooms, counting kilos and calculating the windfall. Long ago, Grazia had disappeared in the truck for church. I circled the yard, weighing my options. The man tossed several disfigured *funghi* my way, but I didn't take any. Accepting food from the enemy only blurred the line between us. For my idea to work, I must purge all warm feeling for the man.

I regarded the apartment. Squisita was still sequestered, though weeks passed since she'd first come to heat.

Another opportunity lost. I stifled a yawn and lay down across the grass from Umberto. I now understood just how lonely a female can make a man.

A clatter rose from the driveway. A swirl of dust followed as Grazia pulled up in the truck. She walked to the apartment to fetch Squisita, who limped carefully across the lawn as she was led to the vehicle. Closing her safely inside, she proceeded to where Umberto sat sorting his gold.

"I think her paw may be broken," said Grazia. "The vet will know for sure."

Umberto pointed to a small pile of mushrooms. "I'll reserve these for his fee. He can eat them, or trade them just as well. Tell him."

"You tell him. I'll not barter with a doctor. The dog brought you to that find, now you can bring her to the vet," Grazia said.

Overhead, a band of crows passed close by. The two people watched as the brazen flock attempted to swoop through Umberto's harvest. The man shouted and waved his hand while Grazia ran to the kitchen for her gun. She emerged just in time to see them disperse, but she fired in their wake anyway. A crow was one bird that had no season, and the only one Grazia wished did.

I ran for the cover of the truck. Squisita yelped and tumbled about the cab. I stayed put beneath the vehicle, eyes closed, until the smell of sulfur cleared and the sun warmed my back.

Sun. I opened my eyes to the clear sky. Squisita had done it again. The truck was on its way backward, down the gentle slope of the lawn, straight for the winery. Umberto raced behind it and yanked the door open. In a split second, Squisita was free and headed, three paws running, to the flats along the stream.

Opportunity. It took me no time to switch gears from surprise to conquest. I dashed to meet her head on before Umberto had the truck fully stopped.

Squisita and I splashed across the creek and into the brush, where commenced a tumble of desire and affection, the likes of which I had never known. Twigs and leaves rumpled and snapped; the smell of damp, spongy moss in the cover of the overgrowth mingled with the flinty scent of love's longing; nips were feigned in jest. An all too brief pause of rapture, and it was finished.

Grazia's voice floated across the stream and into the brush. Squisita emerged first, limping less than she had. I imagined a certain anesthetic accompanied our union. My own paws felt a bit numb. There was sweat between my toes. I moved to the edge of the briar, careful to keep hidden. I knew I'd trumped Grazia's wishes. She'd take a broom to me for sure if she knew.

Worth the penalty, I thought as I watched Umberto escort Squisita to the truck and drive her away.

Grazia sat on the lawn. When she finished sorting the mushrooms into small bags, she set about marking each with a price.

Gold, indeed, I thought. For in them had come the true fortune of the day.

Chapter Thirty

A utumn's deep palette faded into winter. The days grew pale, brief and icy. Each morning, as the sun made its short climb above the pine-strewn hills, I jumped onto the bedroom window seat to welcome the first snow. And every day I greeted disappointment. Thick clouds gathered only to deliver rain. I sat most of the days, nose pushed up against a window, watching the sky, nothing but time on my paws.

Waiting. Like watching a dead man's hand.

Umberto studied the heavens as well. The man shared the desire for a snap of cold. Winter's hoar frost inspired the spring garden. As soon as it fell, he'd be rolling the soil, deepening the cold's beneficial effect on the careworn earth.

Ironic. Two creatures, poles apart, each anticipating the possibilities frost and snow would bring.

December's turn brought olives, late that year, delivered from green to red to a ripe dark purple. Umberto let the crop mature to a shine just off deep black. Not completely matured, but perfect for the most delicious oil. As soon as they dripped like wooden beads from the silver branches, he and Grazia gathered them in apron-like baskets belted against their waists. They picked them bare with both hands. Umberto used a long ladder to capture the fruit from the top of the old twisted trees. A fine mesh net spread around the base of each tree caught any fruit that fell. Squisita and I scoured the ground below for soft olives. From time to time, Umberto chased us away, but not before we pressed many olives between our teeth and crunched the pits as well.

"You're getting as fat as that runt you run with," Umberto chided Squisita.

I beg your pardon, I thought. I wasn't fat; I was stocky. It was a characteristic of my breed. And I was no runt. A younger brother fit that bill. So what if Squisita gained a little weight? It was all the man's fault. After all, she'd been off one foot for several weeks because of him. Now that she was healed, her usual romping was sure to burn away the extra. I gave Umberto a narrowed glance and led Squisita to the garden where we foraged in peace.

After the third day of picking, Umberto spent a morning loading the truck with large linen sacks of olives. Soon the truck would pull away in the direction of the *frantoia*, a community press. My mouth watered.

Olive oil.

Grazia always had a fresh loaf of dense corn flour bread waiting when Umberto returned from the press. Her ritual was to share the first taste of fresh oil with me. The dark, fruity extract enhanced everything it touched. And it touched most everything that reached the Tuscan mouth. To a small Italian dog, the special treat of cold, solidified olive oil spread across warm bread like butter was pleasure in its simplest form.

I bowed and stretched, pointing my nose skyward. A flock of late birds swept unfettered overhead. The valley was still except for the whirring sound of their wings as they flapped. No guns. Hunting season had passed. Freedom over my domain was restored.

I walked across the lawn to look through the windows of the *cucina*. Grazia was already kneading dough, readying bread for fresh oil. A dozen miniature *pan d'oro* sat on the dark wood of the kitchen table. At the oven before dawn, Grazia's rich Christmas cakes stood like golden stacks of hay across an autumn field. A heap of bright cloths lay over the back of a chair, poised for wrapping around each cake. The room sported an array of holiday gifts for friends around the valley. Beautiful bottles of every shape and size fenced the perimeter of the table. They stood prepared to receive the fresh-pressed oil when it arrived, another gift from her *cucina*. A bowl of new corks, adorned with bright ribbons, waited to seal each flask.

Christmas. The best holiday: crinkly wrappings, curly trimmings, festive treats. And to spend it in the country was my greatest pleasure. I was almost grateful La Donna Rosa had entered the picture. The Contessa had determined that the city be avoided for that reason alone. I rested my chin on the windowsill and closed my eyes.

Even though December visits in the past had been few, it was easy to distinguish the dichotomy of winter. The biting north wind of a *tramontana;* goose down on the bed and romps in the brief snows; a bowl of warm pheasant broth at night after sucking frozen water edging the creek by day. I would show Squisita how to bound through the banks of feathery ice that leaned up against the stone walls after a storm; teach her how to chew the snow balls away from between her toes.

Winter's passage led me to the instant I cherished most, the first sign of spring. With a fervent bulb pushing through the darkness of winter came spring and the anticipation of a new year. Days grew longer with each shoot; spring matured into summer, withered into fall, and a perfect circle was complete.

Each season, new adventure. The *terrazzo* door clicked above me. I looked up to greet my Contessa.

"*Ciao,*" she said. The woman reached a hand down to scratch my ear, then stopped short, attention on the table. "*I miei favoriti.*"

A bowl of pitted olives from last year's crop sat ready. The woman loved them. We often shared a few with a bit of *Parmigiano* in the evening before dinner. The woman picked a large olive from the bowl. A crack came from her mouth just as she closed her teeth around it. The Contessa winced.

She put a hand to her lips, retrieving the fruit and a small piece of white tooth. "*Miseria.*"

"*Dispiace, Signora,*" said Grazia. "I must have missed a pit."

"My fault for being so eager," said the Contessa. The woman held the tooth up to the light. Her mouth twisted as she felt the broken tooth with her tongue. She walked to the phone.

When she hung up the receiver, the Count arrived in the hall.

"*Che succede?*"

"You'll have to drive me to the dentist," said the Contessa.

"I'm not your chauffeur," the Count said. "I have my own plans."

The woman shot him a disbelieving look. "*Sicura.*"

"Perhaps it's time you learned to take yourself," said the Count.

The Contessa had never learned to drive. There was no need. The Count was always happy to take her wherever she wished. He used to wear a broad smile as he ferried her about Rome or into Siena. Now he seemed irritated with the duty.

It was the Count's own fault for making the Contessa dependent. Give a man a fish, so to speak. *Bastardo.*

The patio doors opened and in came Umberto. "I'm off to the *frantoia.*"

All eyes were on him.

The Count looked at the Contessa. "Why don't you have the man you're employing take you?" He crossed his arms and leaned against the wall, looking like a cat that's swallowed a pigeon.

The Contessa regarded the Count with a guarded air.

Grazia studied each face. "We'll all go," she proclaimed.

Minutes later Grazia, Umberto, the Contessa and I all occupied the front seat of the truck. A turn to the left and forty-some curves in a narrow road, the Torre del Mangia in Siena loomed ahead, taller than any *campanile* in Italy, save one. I settled into the cramped space between the two women for a short nap. There were many streets to cover upon arrival.

The truck finally rumbled to a stop at the entrance to the town. Umberto would go no further. Only a fool drove through the maze of one-way streets. *A piedi* was the best way to move around Siena. Grazia and the Contessa slid out of the vehicle. I stood to shake my rumpled fur into place. It was important to look one's best in sophisticated Siena. There might be a meeting of the noble women of Chianti over lunch. Appropriate fawning and a high possibility of treats always accompanied the meal.

Presentation was everything. It always increased the benefits. I licked my paws and smoothed the bristly hair on my snout with a forearm while my Contessa pulled me from the truck.

Umberto revved the engine to punctuate his impatience.

"Be back by three," Grazia said. "Church."

Good. Perhaps a turn with the Almighty would set the man straight.

"Va Bene," said Umberto.

The Contessa handed me to Grazia.

"I can't take him to the dentist," she said.

"He'll come with me," said Grazia.

Anything. Just as long as I didn't end up with Umberto.

"Ciao," called the man as he drove off in the direction of the olive press.

Grazia set me on the worn cobblestone street that wound through town toward the *piazza*. A short distance down the via dei Montanini I lifted my nose into the crisp air. Fresh wine. The winemaker stepped out from a niche in the wall of an ancient *palazzo*. He was dressed in fine wool pants and a fresh shirt. His face was clean shaven under dark eyebrows that tufted like feathers. Blue eyes twinkled the minute they caught Grazia.

They met with a kiss, once on each cheek, and then the lips. They did not bother to acknowledge the presence of a certain small dog. I raised a leg to the spot on the wall behind the man in recognition of the oversight.

"Sorpresa," said the man. "I spied you leaving and guessed you might have time to share an *aperitivo.* That load of olives will give us an hour, at least."

"An afternoon out?" asked Grazia as she smiled. *"Scandeloso."*

We crossed the busy street without recognition to enter a narrow door. Inside, we moved down the long, smoky room of a crowded bar to occupy a little table in the back. I tried to find a place beneath the table, but there was barely enough space to accommodate two pair of human feet. Patrons paced back and forth in dangerous proximity to fragile paws until I managed to slide between the legs of Grazia's chair. The two people whispered above me, hands clasped together beneath the table. The air was peppered with love and affection.

"Leave him," said the man. *"È basta."* He put a hand to her face and swept the hair from her brow. *"Prenda tre passi con mio."*

Three steps with me. An old Italian expression: let's do this part of our lives together. I wanted nothing more than for all of the people I loved to live out their lives in this way. Bound to each other, happy.

"I made a promise, *amore,"* Grazia replied. She took his hand and kissed it. "My faith does not permit me to break it."

The man pulled his hand away and scowled. "It is he who's broken the vow."

"His mistake doesn't give me permission."

"Often," said the winemaker, "it is easier to get forgiveness."

Grazia smiled. The man joined her, shaking his head in defeat.

Drinks arrived with a bit of food. Soon treats fell like raindrops around me. I scoured the floor like a low powered vacuum, quiet and continual.

Moments later, chairs pushed back across the floor. The couple headed for the door, with me in tow. Outside the two exchanged a slow, tender kiss. They nuzzled each other, and parted.

"A hundred Hail Marys," Grazia said with a crooked smile as she turned down the street.

We were heading for church. I wiggled with excitement. I'd never been to church before, but I loved the way Grazia smelled afterward. Incense and exotic odors spoke of strange places, like she'd come from a faraway land. I quickened my step. Soon I was leading Grazia down the via Bianchi di Sopra, two right turns, and a left into the Piazza del Duomo.

A huge gothic church spread before us like a painted castle. The patterns in the marble were exquisite: an intricate stone lace of color and design. We moved up the crowded steps. The entrance was packed with tourists and attendees, alike. At the top step, Grazia hesitated. As she slipped through the gigantic front door, I came to an abrupt halt.

I cast a look behind me to see what restricted the leash. The other end disappeared into the crowd. I turned around just as the group parted to reveal Umberto. The man peered down, handle of my leash in his hand, a crooked smile on his sour face.

Ditched for a deity. Grazia never intended I go to Mass. I watched her melt into the gloomy church. Unbelievable.

Umberto pulled me out into the middle of the square. With a wide yawn I sat down on the cold stones. Christmas lights hovered above us. Tiny bulbs glowed dim in the shadows of the tall marble buildings. The area teemed with people laden with packages and produce from the holiday market. Umberto walked back across the *piazza*. Obliged by the leash, I followed.

A few minutes later we were surrounded by a maze of narrow stalls, linked by strings of lights and shiny decorations. The air was heavy with the smell of roasting *marrone* and spiced wine. The pungent scent of pine from evergreen boughs mingled with wood smoke and a hundred aromas from rows of booths crammed with holiday wares. We were in the center of the Christmas market, surrounded by intoxicating scents and sounds of the season.

Umberto took his time winding up and down the lines of displays, stopping occasionally to sample or sip. He downed three cups of mulled wine and a slice of *pizza Bianca*. Hopeful that a scrap might fall my way, I walked the entire market before Umberto bought a paper cone full of warm chestnuts. It was nearly empty before I received my first taste.

Perfect. Roasted they were divine: warm, smooth on the tongue and gently sweet.

Chewing a soft *marrone*, Umberto leaned against the wooden back of a market booth and scanned the crowd. Then, his chewing slowed. His eyes widened. He cocked his head, lifting his chin to peer over a passer-by, as if to get a better view. Umberto disposed of the cone and we crossed the *piazza*. I dodged a horse-drawn carriage and children scampering behind a large ball. Umberto paid no attention to the danger they posed to a small dog.

Brute. The man had a steel heart. There was no safety in his care.

Old men sat on long benches, smoke curling about their heads, mouthing cigarettes as they talked. Water spilled from a spigot standing near a post and chain. I strained to reach it as we passed by. I managed to catch a few splashes with my tongue before Umberto pulled the leash taught and I was compelled to join him. The man paused at a window. I danced beside him. My feet were cold and I wanted a lift. Pulling at the leash to get Umberto's attention hastened the response. The man complied. He lifted me into his arms to see a window decorated with jewelry as I watched the man's eyes.

He had moved beyond the jewels. His eyes were riveted on something inside. At a long, low case in the cramped room beyond the window stood a slender woman in a soft pink coat. Cat-eyed and lanky. La Donna Rosa.

Umberto rang the bell several times before the door swung open. An old woman bent over a cane stood in tattered leather slippers, clumps of plaid lining peeking through the toes. She pressed a tobacco-stained finger to the bridge of her nose, readjusting her spectacles.

"*Buona sera,*" Umberto said.

The old woman lilted a reply. "*Buona sera. Viene, viene.* I'll be with you in a few minutes."

We followed her into the room. The light was dim. A threadbare runner on the floor smelled of cats.

No surprise. I scanned the area. A ragged, grey stuffed mouse with a bell for a tail rested in a corner. The ceiling was high and the walls, patterned.

"Follow me, *Signorina,*" beckoned the old woman. "There are more pieces in the next room."

We passed by. La Donna Rosa never even turned to greet us. As I looked down into the long case before us, all thoughts of cats dissolved: an array of guns, every shape, size and shade.

Miseria. I began to quiver.

There were long barrels with short handles, short barrels with stubby handles, handles shaped like ovals or squares, inlaid with wood or stones or jewels. Umberto fondled several of them as he would a ripe squash, squeezing it in his hand, contemplating its flavor. Then he pointed a gun in the direction of a large mirror on the opposite wall. He closed one eye and aimed at my reflection. I shut my eyes tight. With the cock of the gun, the man's calculated breath slowed.

Qui—adesso. Addio, mondo. A quick, painless death. I could hope for no more.

The hammer dropped with a loud click. I winced, opening an eye, expecting to peer through blood running out my ear and down my jowl. Instead, Umberto's face beamed in the reflection of a mirror across the room. I gulped twice, giving my snout a measured lick. Trying to calm my nerves, I averted my eyes to a large white cat crouched beneath the cupboard. My shivering was uncontrollable. I tried to squirm from the man's hands but Umberto had a stern grip. It was hopeless.

Voices sounded behind us. The two women appeared in the mirror. For an instant, the visage of the old, Roman gypsy passed like a veil across the jeweler's face. I blinked in disbelief and the image disappeared. I sniffed for a trace of her, but the air was too thick with the scent of cat to find anything else.

A trick of desperation. The mind: a capricious master.

I watched La Donna Rosa. She crossed the room like a wildcat, fluid and predatory. The old woman slipped behind the jewel case.

At least there was safety in numbers. Witnesses discouraged foul play.

"*Questo è tutto?*" La Donna Rosa asked. "And you've seen no ring as I described?"

"Such a jewel would be difficult to forget," said the old woman.

Her tone was harsh and relentless. "But I've spent weeks. I've looked in every shop. Is there anyone else who might have seen it?"

"*Una gemma* like that would have a reputation in this town, *Signorina.*" The jeweler closed the top of the case. It fell with a loud squeak, prompting the nervous cat to spit. When I made eye contact, the creature growled. I yelped a warning in return, feeling Umberto catch his breath as La Donna Rosa turned.

"*Poverino,*" the old woman said.

The tenor of her voice softened. "*Si,*" said La Donna Rosa. Her eyes widened at the sight of me. She tossed her hair once and met Umberto's eyes. She put a cool hand on my head. "*Come incantevole.*"

I raised a lip to bare a tooth, but the woman took no warning. She had found the connection she sought.

"*Si,* charming," said Umberto, leering her way.

Bait taken, I thought.

Slipping from behind the case, the old woman hobbled to the corner to coax the indignant feline from behind the furniture. She lifted the cat into her fragile arms and carried it to the next room. I gave a short bark at her exit.

Umberto's voice was low. "You've been looking for something special?"

"All my life," returned the woman. She looked at Umberto with round, dark eyes.

Devil. A demon, indeed.

"Why don't I buy you a drink and you can tell me about it?"

"*Grazie*," she said.

Umberto set me on the floor and we left the shop. Once in the *piazza*, I wasted no time in addressing a nearby post. It was not the most appealing target in the area, but I didn't care. I was just happy to be alive and out of the arms of the villainous Umberto.

We walked up a small *via* off the square until reaching a tiny bar. Inside it was warm and dry. I was exhausted from the strain of nerves. I curled into a ball at Umberto's feet and listened over the din of the crowd. My eyes were heavy under the noise and heat. Sleep came easily.

I awakened in time to hear only the last few lines of what I supposed was a lengthy conversation. The window to the street stood above me. The cobblestones fell in shadow outside. Daylight was nearly gone.

"Fate has a curious master," said Umberto. "If I hadn't followed you inside—"

"I'd never have found the ring," said La Donna Rosa.

"Well, I don't have it yet," chuckled the man. "Let's just say I know where it should be."

"And it should be with me."

Umberto reached for the woman's hand. "One spectacular gem for another."

"It could satisfy us both," the woman said. She tipped her chin and batted her eyes. Then she took a card from her purse. "My number in Rome. When you find the ring, call me. We'll celebrate together."

At that I raised my head. La Donna Rosa ran one finger down Umberto's jaw, punctuating her sentence with a tap on his chin. The sight sickened me. I sniffed the air beneath the table. Though sparks flew above, there were far too few to start a real fire, I thought. The two were trading on convenience alone. *Quid pro quo*: the ring for sex.

The man was a cad. He stopped at nothing to get what he wanted. He'd tossed the Contessa to one side to find his perfect match.

My eyes wandered up the street, through the crowd to the *piazza*. A familiar figure crossed the busy square in the dusky light. The Contessa was headed straight for us. She examined a small paper in her hand as she walked.

Shopping. A store with assorted toys and pet treats was just up the way. Visions of beautiful, brightly wrapped gifts nestling on my pillow Christmas morning swirled in my head: rubber balls, toy mice, perhaps the knucklebone of a dead pig. I loved to watch as she pulled special things from the shelves in the shop and always pretended great surprise on Christmas morning. The Contessa never guessed that all I did from the time she bought those gifts, to the time I opened them, was yearn.

The leash was limp and loose on the floor beside me. When the door opened to the café, I bolted outside. The Contessa met me in full view of Umberto and his most recent quarry. She stopped, looking as though she'd seen a ghost. The three people stared at each other for a moment. Then the Contessa took me into her arms and retreated the way she'd come.

I poked my nose over her shoulder to look for Umberto. I expected the man to follow, try to make amends. But he did not. He only stood outside the door of the bar, watching the Contessa walk away.

She made no sound until we were near a stand of taxis.

"*Idioto.*" She slid onto the back seat of a waiting cab, giving direction to the driver as she closed the door.

It was silent for a long time. I lay beside her, trembling. Anger and hurt shrouded us both in a mist of sour perfume.

"It seems now we're both being made the fool," the Contessa said. "And by the same pair." The Contessa looked at me. "I never intended it to go this far, anyway. But it was nice to think *someone* had time for me the way Il Conte used to. Remember?"

I remembered, all right. The same words came from the Count's lips. The timing was perfect. I sniffed the air from the cracked window. Let it snow, I thought.

"*Come?*" asked the driver.

"*Niente, non importa.*"

I could feel what little warmth the Contessa harbored for Umberto seep away. Outside, the landscape whirled in and out of the afternoon shadows.

"What I meant to say," she said, " —it was nothing."

Chapter Thirty-One

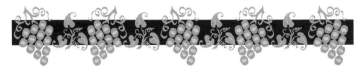

T he Contessa sang.

I turned an ear to the melody. Elvis. "I'll Never Let You Go" rang out from the shower, spilling from the bathroom tiles to the space below the door. I adjusted myself on the bed and listened. The water ceased with the singing.

The woman emerged, robe loose about her shoulders. Crossing to the bookshelves, she retrieved the large album of photographs and set it on the dresser. She paged through the book slowly, examining one particular picture as though it captured the outline of a ghost. Then she pulled it from the album and placed it on the dresser. The woman paused by the window, which was open a sliver. I heard Umberto ranting around the garden below.

The Contessa shook her head. "What a fool."

The house was full of fools. My eyes met hers.

"No more games," said the woman. "Pride only succeeds if two are willing to play. I give up." Back into the shelf went the book. She paused at the bed to give me a tousle, then walked back to the dresser. Tapping the photo she said, "This is my treaty. We'll see if he's willing to sign."

The Contessa disappeared into the closet and returned dressed. She pulled the picture from the dresser and headed down the stairs. I followed. When she reached the *cucina,* she put it on the table and poured a glass of water. Grazia sat nearby, mending a tear in one of the Count's shirts.

"You missed dinner last night," she said. "Are you well?"

"My tooth ached after seeing the dentist. A cab brought me home early. I feel much better today."

Grazia eyed the woman carefully, as if knowing what had really happened the afternoon before. Then her gaze fell on the photograph. "The shortest way to a long marriage, eh?"

I stood on my hind legs and tried to peek a view. Oh, for longer legs.

The Contessa looked up. *"Come?"*

"Fun," said Grazia.

The Count opened the patio door, crossed through the kitchen without a word and disappeared up the stairs.

The Contessa frowned. "And boredom, the longest way to a short one."

Grazia frowned and tapped the photo with her finger. "I've never seen you wear this."

"I lost it long ago."

Grazia looked at me and smiled. "But not the memory."

"No," said the woman. She stepped to the table and studied the photo. "Never that."

"Memories are like a good dog," said Grazia. She cast me a clever wink. "They retrieve many things. You may find it was never lost at all."

The Contessa regarded the woman in mid-wink. She raised her brow in question, but no query followed. Pulling a pale folder from a desk, she slipped the photograph inside. "Take me to town when you go to church."

*

An hour later we were all in Siena. Grazia headed to the Piazza del Duomo. I trotted a few paces in front of the Contessa, looking back from time to time, making sure she followed. The Contessa's fine wool suit peeked through the front of her ankle-length fur. Soft leather gloves warmed her hands from the chill of a December day. She was dressed to meet her friends at the usual spot.

Lunch.

We walked through the Christmas market and up a side street to a wall of windows.

Something different, I thought. I loved new places. Every restaurant had a specialty. I took the obligation of broadening my palette seriously.

When I reached the woman's side, she opened a narrow door and we slipped through. The room was small, shelves crowded with picture frames, walls covered with paintings and photographs. I raised my nose into the air.

Nothing edible. Chemicals and glue. This was no café.

A young woman appeared from behind a wide curtain. *"Buona sera, Signora."*

"Buona sera." The Contessa put the folder on the counter. "May I leave this?"

"Si," said the woman. She slipped the photo out and examined it.

"It's had some wear. Can you repair the edges?"

"A good mat about the photo will hide them." The woman motioned to the wall beside her. "Choose a frame."

The Contessa moved along the row of pictures. She touched the gilt edges of several frames, and then settled on a simple but elegant garnish for her photograph. "This one."

The young woman held the photograph up to the light but not high enough for me to see it over the counter. I was dying to know what it looked like.

"I'm not in town often," said the Contessa. "Is it possible to take it later today?"

The woman looked at the clock on the wall behind her. *"Si, credo.* If you don't see me when you return, ask for Chiara."

"Grazie," said the Contessa. *"A piu tarde."*

I followed her out of the shop. The minute we turned the next corner at Via del Porrione, the smell of food led the rest of the way. I focused on the creamy odor of *cannelloni*. It tugged me like a leash down the street to the entry of Osteria Le Logge. All dark wood and marble, it was my favorite restaurant. Waiters wearing white aprons and shiny shoes rattled dishes through the room. Two congenial men whisked the Contessa out of her fur coat, and me from her arms, in such a flurry it was as if by magic. Delivered back into her hands, I was granted a liver biscuit by the head waiter, who then ushered us across the room. A large round table surrounded by elegant women in perfect attire greeted us. As usual, they all took a turn fawning over me.

"Adorable," one said.

"Quale bravo ragazzo," said another.

I loved the attention, trying my best to be most charming. A gentle nuzzle or brief kiss was dealt every admirer. I sniffed the ears of each woman. Wood rose, lavender, verbena, hyacinth and castile soap. It was the same bouquet each month, no matter the season. The women fussed over the appealing shape of my nose and mouth, and the turn of my ears.

Lunching with the ladies, food was plentiful. Guinea fowl and duck, rabbit and beef; the scent of lemon and fennel filled the air. Samples were always bestowed on a dog of multiple charms. Aristocratic women always needed help cleaning their plates. I listened with intent when each woman spoke. I looked them in the eye and wagged my tail to punctuate interest. Chic behavior distinguished the noble dog.

One discerning lady leaned down to stroke my back and ruffle my ears. *"Un uomo piccolo, caro mio,"* she said, cupping my snout with hands smooth as doeskin.

I wiggled a thank-you. To be called 'a little man' by so fine a lady was high praise, indeed. I looked at my Contessa and she lifted me into her lap. She was having fun and her happiness was contagious.

True. I *was* sophisticated—and intuitive; much more sensitive than any other man in the Contessa's life. I nestled against her breast, contenting myself with the odd treat now and then from the table.

By the time *dolce* arrived, I was satiated. Meal complete, the conversation loitered over *espressi*. Soon everyone around the table was laughing and talking at once.

The lady to one side of me lowered her voice. "What do they say about sex?"

"Men need the luck," said another woman, "women need the lure."

"I need *romanzo*," said the lady in the next chair. "'Are you awake' doesn't translate."

"*L'iniziativa.* A woman better make her own romance. A man doesn't need it."

"Oh, believe me, I do," the lady replied. "Who said 'be the change you wish to see'? It takes initiative, all right. I'm black lace and *fantasia*."

Everyone laughed. The Contessa blushed. I raised both ears.

A white-haired woman at the other side of the table replied, "Gandhi."

"Are we sure it wasn't his wife?"

The whole table roared. Except the Contessa.

The woman by her side leaned closer. *"Va bene?"*

"*O, si,*" said the Contessa. "Christmas. I have a lot on my mind." She laid a tense hand on my side. "Spending the holidays here is much more involved than it is in the city. Grazia has taken over the *villa*. Baking and bottling."

"Well, it's nice to have you here. How long will you stay?"

The Contessa hesitated in her answer. "I really have no idea."

I suspected we'd all stay in the country until she learned La Donna Rosa was no longer a threat. I smelled her fingers. Happiness had given way to fret.

I granted her knuckle a long lick before I curled into her lap. Belly full, the din of chatter made me weary. The restaurant was steamy under a hundred voices and hot food. I closed my eyes, drifting off to sleep on the fragrant wings of chocolate nougat torte.

The nap ended when my Contessa rose to pull her fur from a waiter's hand. The women made their proper good-byes and departed. Each walked in a different direction when they reached the street. The Contessa and I retraced our steps to the little shop with the narrow door. My Contessa tapped a tiny bell at the counter.

Chiara appeared through a break in a wide curtain. She pulled a package from behind the counter. It was wrapped in plain paper, bound with simple twine. She untied the bow and opened the paper.

Raising the frame in her hands, she turned it to the Contessa. *"Bene?"*

Santa Maria. It was the same photograph the Count discarded in Rome. Astonishing.

The Contessa took the frame from the young woman and stepped to the light in the window. *"Stupendo. Grazie molto."* She dabbed the corner of one eye with a gloved hand.

The young woman rewrapped the photograph. She handed it to the Contessa.

"Ciao," she said, adding her best wishes for the coming holiday. *"Auguri."*

"Auguri," replied the Contessa.

We walked up the cobbled street. Lavish windows of elegant stores lined the way. I was grateful for the Contessa's slow pace. Window-shopping was the perfect antidote to a full belly. At the corner we stopped at a window draped with lacy things.

The Contessa narrowed her eyes. She regarded her reflection in the window and uttered one word. *"Romanzo."*

270

Inside, the carpet was warm and thick under my cold paws. The room smelled of gardenias. I found the source on a low table by the front counter. A single white blossom bobbed in a small bowl of water. I gave it a push with my nose. Its odor stuck to my whiskers like honey and I sneezed. The Contessa lifted me into her arms.

A woman with silver hair came from the back of the store. *"Signora?"*

"Questo," said the Contessa. She pointed to something in the window case.

The shopkeeper lifted it out of the display and spread it out on the table. It shimmered under the lights and the marble counter top shone through the gossamer fabric.

The woman nodded. "It's very fine. A gift?"

"How many years can it hide?" The Contessa smiled. She ran her hand over the edge of delicate lace around the hem.

"No man sees behind black lace." The shopkeeper winked. "Why not ask your husband to buy it for you? For Christmas. After all, it's really for him."

"Si, allora." The Contessa cleared her throat. "I think I'll take it now."

The woman folded the garment. Wrapping it in tissue, she finished with a curly ribbon around the middle, slipped it into a small bag and laughed. "I don't know why they like this kind of thing so much. It all comes off in the end, doesn't it?"

"Grazie." The Contessa blushed as she took the package and started toward the door. "I'm counting on it," she said under her breath.

Chapter Thirty-Two

T he *villa* shuddered at the noise of a falling hammer and clattering tin.

As soon as Grazia entered the kitchen, she opened the door to the cellar. *"Che succede?"*

The din ceased.

"The furnace stopped," Umberto shouted. "The whole thing has to come out."

Grazia put her glasses on and pushed her nose close to the thermostat next to the door. "It was working this morning."

I moved from my cushion to her side, sniffing the cool air coming from the stairway. Sweat and treachery, I thought. It was the ring the man was after.

Umberto emerged black with dust. "Best to get it done before Christmas. I can take it out—fix it."

"Il Conte won't like the mess," Grazia said.

"He won't have to see it," said Umberto. "I'll keep it to the cellar. No need for *anyone* to come down."

The pounding started again. Grazia closed the door.

The Contessa appeared in the hallway. "What's the racket?"

The Count followed her into the kitchen.

"The furnace is broken," Grazia said.

"It doesn't feel cold to me," said the Contessa.

The Count smiled. "Women your age don't feel cold."

"How would you know what a woman my age feels like?" The Contessa was not amused.

"He'll have it repaired before the snow arrives," Grazia said. She walked to the fireplace. "We'll keep the house closed. At least the kitchen will be warm."

"You see," said the Contessa. "Isn't it a good thing we can build a fire in the bedroom?"

"Favoloso," the Count said. "See to it the windows are tight or we'll be heating the outdoors. I'm bleeding money as it is." He pulled his heavy jacket from a peg by the door and pushed through to the *terrazzo.*

I followed. Even in the afternoon sun, the lawn stood rigid against the bitter cold. Every step prickled my paws. Il Conte walked across the grass to the edge of the vineyard. The vines were bare and twisted like the knuckles of an old man. I stood beside the Count as he sat on the low perimeter wall and pulled his pipe from his coat pocket.

"The last time I built a fire in the bedroom, what I got wasn't warm," said the Count.

Squisita looked up from the middle of the stream. Her legs dripped a slurry of mud from the creek bed, her round belly shivering against the icy water beneath her.

No sense, I thought. I wondered where it was, exactly, that her brain was disconnected. She appeared to make no correlation between her discomfort and the frigid stream.

The Count looked down at me. "What beats the female heart?"

I jumped upon the wall and sat with my back against the warmth of the man. Winding, I thought. Females had to be touched regularly to keep them running well.

Squisita bounded up the hill to meet us. She threshed a greeting then commenced a race around the yard. Two turns and she finished, ending back by the wall underneath me. She was slower these days. I owed it to the cold weather and the weight she'd taken on for winter. I leaned down to lick her head. She returned the affection with a thorough wash of my ears. The patio door slammed.

Grazia crossed the yard. "The Contessa has given me the rest of the day. I'm going into Siena. Do you need anything?"

The man looked up at the bedroom window. His tone was wry as he sucked on his pipe. "Not in town." Long wisps of smoke coiled around his head and disappeared into the freezing air.

I noted the man's bright red nose and ears before I closed my eyes to the attention of Squisita. A truck door clapped beyond. The vehicle rumbled away. I lay down on the wall, head hanging over the side to make Squisita's efforts easier. I was putty under the attention of her tongue.

The lonely splash of the stream in the distance was the only sound. No birds sang on winter's stage. Then, music from the *villa*.

The three of us turned in unison. Shutters to the bedroom were open and the window wide.

The Count shook his head. "That's no way to keep the house warm."

Elvis crooned in the distance. "It's Now or Never" filled the air. Umberto walked out the *terrazzo* door. The Contessa stood in the shadows behind the open window, peering into the yard. When the Count stood, she retreated.

"*La Signora* says the noise from my work has given her a headache," Umberto said as he passed by. He continued to his apartment.

The Count rested the bowl of the pipe in his hand, turned his head and furrowed his brow as though something odd had just occurred to him.

I felt the Count's temper rise.

"I'll bet I know what's coming." He glanced at Umberto. "But it will be cold day in hell when I'll compete with that." Il Conte looked at me. "Shall we let a woman know what it is to be spurned for a change?" He knocked his pipe against the wall to empty it, and started for the house.

I jumped to the ground and followed. Umberto rattled a dish of food from the apartment door and Squisita headed for the promise of an early meal. Winter made her hungry. The Count entered the kitchen, pausing at the music. He frowned. I walked down the hall ahead of him and up the stairs to the bedroom. A fire crackled to the music, but the door was closed. Il Conte put a hand on the knob and pressed his ear to the wood. I sniffed the crack beneath the door. Heat radiated, but not from the fire. My eyes widened. The man swung the door open. The Contessa peeked from underneath the covers.

A wicked smile crossed her lips. *"Ciao."*

The Count hesitated, as if he'd reached a T in the road and forgotten which way to turn. I sensed his knees quiver beneath his trousers. Then Il Conte set his jaw in decision.

"Santa Maria," he yelled, rushing past the woman to the open window. The shutters banged and the sill cracked as he pulled it closed. "Have you lost your mind?" The Count turned to face her, and paused again to draw a breath. "Are you sick?"

The Contessa was still for a moment, eyes big as walnuts. She tossed back the covers to reveal her scanty lace outfit, a bottle of *prosecco* and two fluted glasses. "Do I look unwell?"

"You will be with only that on," said the Count. "It's an icebox in here."

I winced. The Contessa's payment was apparently not complete.

The woman's eyes became slits. I felt her seething ire clear across the room.

"It certainly is," she cried. Off the bed she bounced, slamming the bathroom door behind her so hard the mirror over her dressing table slid to the floor.

The glasses fell together and broke. An open bottle of wine oozed onto the carpet. I ran beneath the bed.

The Count yelled through the door. "Now it's *you* who wants sex. How does it feel to be pushed away?"

I trembled at the tone of their voices, harsh and unkind.

The Contessa's voice rang like a cathedral bell. "*Sesso?* Not for me. I want to make *love*." Something shattered in the bathroom. "Or don't you remember how?"

The man growled. "I remember. That's the problem." He stormed out of the room and down the stairs.

Things continued to crash behind the bathroom door. I escaped to the safety of the *cucina*. Il Conte sat in a chair by the kitchen table. He bent over and put his head in his hands. The man's scent was hollow and tired.

"I give up," said the Count.

Those words again, I thought. My belly tightened.

The *terrazzo* door opened and in came Grazia. "It's freezing. I forgot my scarf," she said. The woman studied the Count as she pulled a piece of thick wool from a peg on the wall. "*Va bene?*"

"It's like spitting in the ocean." He looked up at Grazia. "Can we both be right?"

The woman put her hand on his shoulder. "No use in keeping score," she said. "In this game, the one with the most points never wins." Grazia walked to the door.

"You know so much?"

She turned. "Just enough to know that forgiveness is the only way home." Scarf in place around her neck, Grazia pushed back through the patio door. "If that's where you want to go." She crossed the terrace toward the truck at the bottom of the slope.

Couldn't have said it better, I thought.

The Count pulled me into his lap and scratched my ears. "You think La Contessa still wants to go there?" He stood up and walked to the door.

Obviously, I thought. It had taken bravery to do what she'd just done. The Count was too bent on revenge to see it. Yet, I knew he wanted the same thing: reunion. Perhaps it took more courage to stay together than to part, I thought. Love might be rediscovered on the common ground of valor. I watched Grazia.

At the middle of the yard she turned, motioning to the Count to open the door. "Does Shimoni want to join me?"

I wiggled a reply.

"Let me put him in his coat," said the Count.

He put me in my warmest wrap and all four paws were pushed though the sleeves. It was a shiny silver fabric, boxy in design, and in it I was cozy and warm, even though I knew I looked a bit like a four-slice toaster.

It was a small price to pay to get out of the *villa.*

Footsteps banged across the floor of the room above.

The man rolled his eyes. "I guess we'll see where it ends."

In the wood across the stream, I thought. Save a few missteps, we all headed in the right direction. Taking care of Umberto sealed the myriad leaks in the marriage vessel. There'd be no potential left for confusion or heartache. And Grazia would land with the love she deserved.

"We'll see." The Count put me on the floor and opened the door.

I trotted down the icy lawn to meet Grazia. The landscape glistened in the distance. Winter's approach was written in light snow on the hill tops.

Si, I thought. *Si.*

Chapter Thirty-Three

F irst stop was a flower stand. Grazia bought several bunches of winter pansies in small pots, which she put on the floor in the front of the truck. I peered into the foot well and sniffed the air. The scent was earthy and dense, but not floral.

Like La Donna Rosa. All show.

Grazia started the truck. It rolled along for some time before turning up a bumpy, narrow lane. The road was mottled with broad beams of low sunlight. Up the rough road we drove, passing through a gate in a high wall and coming to a stop.

Grazia attached my leash. We left the truck to pass through the opening of a tall stone wall that stretched around the perimeter of a large clearing. Inside, it was riddled with niches bearing portraits and candles and flowers. Smooth rocks dotted the grass. Some lay flat in the ground like stepping stones, others sat like chair backs against the wind. A man in a bulky jacket swept a broom as leaves twirled and danced around him. Here and there a bundle of chrysanthemums bobbed their heads in the wind as it whistled through somber iron gates guarding the end of the yard. Dusk settled.

I didn't mark the shrubs or grass. It didn't seem right. I looked up at Grazia. She concentrated on pulling a bit of moss from a crack in the wall above. The man sweeping in the corner stopped. He walked across the yard toward me and knelt to scratch behind my ear. It was welcome attention and I waved a hind paw in honor of the pleasure. I thought of Raoul and how his old woman always knew the best places to scratch.

I looked down the length of the wall. The niches looked like windows in a long house, each harboring photographs of people young and old, striking and plain. All looked out through glassy, hollow eyes. The house was full. Perhaps this was a place to post portraits of people who pass on. Those who have lost someone might come here to look. Others might recognize a face and aid in returning the missing.

The man stopped scratching me and moved on. I wondered if a picture of Raoul's old woman might be there in the yard somewhere. Maybe even old Raoul was on display.

But there were only humans.

My leash paid out behind me as I walked across the clearing. I reached the first few stones set into the grass. There were lights and flowers here as well. And more portraits of people.

No dogs.

As far as I was concerned, it was contrary to the canine law of combination: the principle whereby each human is permitted a dog and every dog allowed a human. The odds simply did not permit the entire place be absent a dog. I lifted my nose into the frigid breeze. With it came the renewed itch to dig.

Nearby was a place where soil had been removed. I pulled the leash far to reach it, peering at last over the edge into a deep hole. It was as large as any I had ever seen and perfectly executed. The sides were smooth and even, the bottom level. I couldn't imagine its purpose. It was much too large for a bone. And the season for planting had passed. A large mound of fresh dirt piled high behind the excavation. From behind came a low growl.

A cat. My hackles raised. A vivid image of the feline squall in the apartment vestibule returned to mind. Anger took me.

I bolted around the corner of the hole, tugging at the taut leash.

Grazia returned the tug, sliding me to the edge of the cavity. Under normal circumstances, I would have complied with her request, but the leash was spent. The cat now perched atop the dirt to watch. Instinct pulled me toward it. Yet, any move in its direction prompted Grazia to return the tug. I eyed the gap in the earth. Jumping across it required a certain length of runway for the launch to be successful. My paws were already partway over the edge of the hole. Dirt fell into the pit from beneath my toes in muffled bits. My collar was tight against my throat. A bark was out of the question.

I gave a soft whine instead. One glance and Grazia would understand my plight. She was too engrossed to notice. Instinct demanded I back away, though I knew what would come next. She did not tolerate crude behavior on the leash. I kept one eye on the cat as he moved away from the hole. As predicted, the woman responded with an abrupt tug. I went over the side with a yelp.

Grazia shrieked. Next I knew, she knelt by the side of the hole, arms outstretched, but her hands waved high above me. Her limited height did not permit a rescue. I barked. The bastard cat just sat, smug as a tick beneath a collar. I tried to climb the walls of the hole, but they were hard as rock. My hind claws found no grip at all.

Prisoner. My last overnight outside was no picnic. I had no intention of passing the dark in a yard of beady-eyed photographs. I barked in earnest until the man with the broom came to my aid.

I put my front paws against the side of the hole to meet the man halfway and was scooped out of the hole by the scruff of my neck. My skin pulled so tight over my jowl that I thought I'd wear a permanent smile like some of the people in the portraits around me. The man set me on the grass, gave me an apologetic pat on my rump and retired to his truck. Grazia, contrite in her neglect, smoothed my rumpled hair and brushed the dirt out of my ears and eyes. The cat disappeared over the mound into infinity.

"Not a nice thing to do," she chided. *"Poverino gatto."*

Poor cat, indeed.

Grazia was wholly occupied with my restoration when four men dressed in work clothes entered the yard, carrying a box as long as the seat beneath the window in my bedroom. The men strained under its weight as they walked toward the open pit, setting their cargo on the ground beside the hole. As any dog is always fond of discovery, I was very interested. The men turned to exit the yard and I approached the box. Sniffing the base and sides, I placed my paws on the rail skirting the rim to peek over the top. The tiniest odor of something bad met the tip of my nose: meat too long on the *cucina* counter in the middle of a hot summer.

Something dead.

I looked down at the flat stone beside me. The photograph of a man, stiff smile, black suit and a white kerchief in his pocket peered up at me between a bunch of pale mums.

These were portraits of the dead, not missing. And death apparently meant you retired to the ground. The cemetery.

I was an idiot. Unbelievable an intelligent dog such as myself had been so dense. Perhaps I was not as well-bred as I assumed. After all, I was yanked from my mother's teat long before I'd had a good look at her. Far too much time was spent pursuing life's pleasures to ever think of authenticating my parentage. And I'd never met another dog who looked exactly the same as I, yet I'd seen dozens of breeds on the Pincio that resembled each other.

A fraud. That would alter everything. What luxury came without title? I shook myself to rid such a ridiculous thought. Noblemen didn't keep mongrels.

I pawed at Grazia's skirt, scanning the photos gracing the rockery where she stood. Men, women, children: all resembling Grazia. Small candles glowed by each as well. A child with Grazia's eyes and nose peered out, stern faced. A man with her forehead and chin smiled the same broad smile I loved. One olive-faced woman stared out through onyx eyes from underneath a broad black hat. I leaned forward for a better look.

The gypsy.

"I miss her," said Grazia as she picked me up. She pulled a kerchief from her sleeve and dabbed her eyes. It was fine linen, with delicate lace around the edges and a slim satin ribbon pulled through the border. The odorless hanky I had come upon in the kitchen so many months ago.

I pushed my nose into the linen, again trying to divine an odor. Still, there was nothing there.

"This is all I have from her," said Grazia. "She kept it in her cuff. It was there when she left us." She pushed it back into her sleeve and gave it a pat. "It will be here when I leave you."

Leave me? I began to tremble.

The woman scratched my chin. *"Nervoso?"* asked Grazia. "It's only Aunt Speranza."

A dead woman dogged me. Impossible, I thought.

"No evil there, Shimoncello." Grazia gave me an assuring pat. *"Il contrario."* The woman rubbed her palm across the face of the photo to clean away the grime. "She sought only compassion in her life." Grazia looked over her shoulder to where the cat had been. "A lesson for us all." She smoothed the fur on my back and gave my head a kiss. "Spite will be your ruin."

I couldn't help but growl. The stern look on Speranza's face did not suggest goodwill. And the gypsy had never appeared with anything other than a sullen stare. Both seemed full of malice. Yet, it was I who was being chided for sin.

Grazia wiped a hand on her coat and chuckled. "The camera was no friend. It took her photo, but never her smile. She saved that for those she loved—and for little works of kindness along the way." The woman said in my ear, "A smile means you're doing your job. *Capito*, Shimoni?"

At the moment, I understood nothing. My memory retraced every sighting of the gypsy: the Pincian Hill, La Donna Rosa's apartment, Greta's suicide, the jeweler's shop. My head spun with details.

What was I missing?

We returned to the truck. Down the gravel path to the main road, I peered over the seatback at the blank face of the cemetery wall. Clouds covered the sun. The sky, the stone, the road were all a dull, lifeless grey. Dingy sheep stood on a barren hillside, gloomy backs against the wind, like clumps of dirty foam on a windy shore.

Grazia placed a steady hand on my back. She slowed the truck to a rumble at the main road and stopped. In the field across the road, a man carried the limp carcass of a goose. Two large dogs bounced at his heels, nipping at the feathers.

I glanced at Grazia, giving a hasty kiss to her hand as she lowered the window to adjust the mirror. The bells of Siena rang in the distance.

I considered the hours as it tolled. Darkness approached. My chin quivered as I rested my head on Grazia's lap. Cold air poured through the open window. Rain fell in cadenced drops onto the windshield. Two or three degrees less and: snow.

Four, and it would stick across the valley like cotton to a thistle.

Two couples. The perfect number.

Umberto, the odd man out.

Chapter Thirty-Four

C hristmas Eve. The gift of a hard freeze and heavy clouds lay outside the door. I stood, nose pressed up to the chilly glass. Umberto was early to the garden. He dug up the hard earth, letting the hoarfrost work its magic on the soil. Steam rose off the toiling man. It hung in miniature clouds above his head, twisted into the ether and disappeared.

Grazia was in the kitchen preparing holiday treats. Everything was polished until it sparkled the reflection of the cozy fire in the corner of the *cucina*. Dried figs sat on silver dishes; *ricciarelli,* chewy, almond-flavored, sugar-coated cookies beside them; fine candied Florentine fruit, half-dipped in the prohibition of dark chocolate were the final touch. Luxuriant grape clusters, hidden since harvest in the cool cellar, adorned a cut glass bowl in the center of the table. A string of dried *porcini* lay like mother of pearl across the counter near the sink.

At first light, Grazia set about making *antipasti* for the evening. Festivities opened with *crostini neri:* chicken livers in white wine, aromatic herbs, an oily press of fresh olives and tomato conserve.

Scent of heaven. The *cucina* was the center of the universe. I sat poised at the foot of the butcher block, bent on the capture of the tiniest bit of liver.

When Grazia completed the *crostini,* she swiped a fat finger through the paste and touched it to my nose. I balanced my whole being against her hand. It was like satin on my tongue. By afternoon the making of the *tortellini* was underway. The holiday was in full swing.

The best celebration of the year. If my plan worked, this Christmas would be the happiest.

The Count entered the kitchen with his cards. He whistled while he shuffled the deck, then made them into a fan. The man bent my way. "Choose one."

I touched my nose to a card at the end.

"Ha!" cried the Count. He pulled the card from the deck and showed Grazia a Jack of Hearts. "This card comes to him every time." The man rubbed my back and ears and smiled. "One day, you and I will to go to Monte Carlo."

The patio door opened and in stepped Umberto. "A package for you, *Signore*." He handed the Count a box wrapped in plain paper covered with black letters and stamps.

"*Finalmente*," said the Count. He set it on the table and tore at the wrapping.

Umberto returned outside to wrestle with a small pine on the *terrazzo*.

The Count motioned to Grazie. "*Vieni qui.*"

She abandoned her *tortellini* to stand beside Il Conte. He pulled a flat, rectangular box from the paper and cut the string, holding it closed with a small pocketknife. I thought it must be a book by the way the box was shaped. I loved books. The corners were just the right angle for chewing. And the glue used on the spine was the subtle flavor of sour cream. The Count opened the box. He lifted a beautiful carved frame from under a mound of scrunched tissue and set it on the table.

Grazia gasped. "*Che bella.*"

"*Si.* There's the luck of that Jack in here," the Count said. "You'll see."

Fortune, indeed. Not abandoned after all. Truly noble.

The photo in the frame was identical to the one the Contessa took from the young woman in Siena. I gazed at the Count, sorry that I had thought the man such a rogue. The picture had not been discarded after all, but honored. Il Conte beamed. He'd found his way home. My plan would close the door behind him.

The Count handed the frame to Grazia. She set about wrapping it in bright paper. Umberto entered *la cucina* with a tall, bushy tree dragging behind him. I took the opportunity of the open door for relief on the brittle grass, still frozen with frost the night before. The warmth of my breath punctuated the cold air as I moved from pot to pot around the lawn. I studied the wooded slope across the stream. Clouds were overtaking the hilltops.

The stuff of snow. The timing was perfect. This Christmas, I would give the best gift.

Noise from behind the winery led me down the slope and around the building. There stood Squisita, porcelain coat turned to a mottled grey, atop the steamy compost. She dropped to roll once more into the exquisitely putrid pile of garden cuttings and rotting food.

Near perfection. She was purple with grape stain.

One more shoulder to the mess and she would carry the stench of decay well into the New Year. I joined her on the mound as she took a final roll. When she got to her feet, I rubbed against her, ducking beneath her belly. I preferred to acquire the odor of the compost directly from her fur. The result was a heady blend of intoxicating scents.

By the time we finished, we were each a perfect mess. Proud and content, we headed in tandem for the *terrazzo*. Squisita and I sat by the doors, patiently waiting for admission. Now and then, I pulled a piece of garbage from Squisita's coat. A good deal of time was spent in mutual grooming until Umberto opened the kitchen door. We bounded inside. Grazia shrieked. Umberto bellowed displeasure.

The chase was on.

The kitchen was chaos. Squisita and I darted through the legs of the two people, weaving under the furniture as we ran. Chairs turned on end, dishes clattered. As far as I was concerned, we had been delivered in ideal form for a holiday dinner. Few times had I been so magnificent. So far, Christmas Eve was grand. The prospect of the day improved with each passing hour. Umberto closed every door to the *cucina*.

Trapped.

Definitions were subjective when measured between dog and man. One dog's ideal is another man's sin. I sat down underneath the kitchen table. Knowing the next step, I hunched my shoulders and dropped my head. Meanwhile, Squisita continued to bounce around the room, hapless victim of a man intent on inflicting a large dose of clean water to her cheery countenance. Umberto bent down to pull me from beneath the table. A small piece of tissue fell from his breast pocket to the floor. From it rolled a hallow sound against the tile floor. The ring. Umberto had finally found it.

The man grabbed up the gem. He folded it into the tissue and put it in the pocket of his jacket, which hung from a peg by the door. I growled.

"*Silenzio,*" said the man. "It's no business of yours." He pulled me up by my back legs and headed for the sink.

*

Baths concluded, I watched the short daylight fade above winter's muted palette. Clouds thickened and the wind began to blow a promise of snow across the vineyard. Squisita paced beside the fire, restless as she dried her fur. I sat by the glass doors, anticipating the first flurry. But anger welled inside.

If wishes were snowflakes, I mused, the fall would be deep. Over and over I remembered the ring falling from Umberto's pocket. The devil himself, I thought. I reviewed my plan.

The compost, the creek bed, boar on the move down the hillside, a dash across the stream, Umberto giving chase, pigs in the fray, Il Conte to the rescue—the brave and noble efforts of a certain small dog.

Adulation and reward, I wagered. I turned to the window and stared. The night was black through the glass. Empty.

Then, a flake. It drifted through the light spilling from the kitchen window. Another, and another. Snow swirled and spun in tight circles, scattering like dust across the landscape. It piled upon the stone wall and the broad terrace, the patio table and the vineyard wires. At the end of an hour, the pots edging the lawn wore fat white caps. They looked like elves standing guard above the winery. Everything looked different. Snow erased the rest of the world.

A fresh canvas. Ready for a new portrait of the family. Best to get the bearing of the new landscape, I thought. I put my paws on the glass doors and barked.

No one. I barked again, this time with more vigor. A sharp edge was useful in getting a point across.

Umberto came from the salon to the door. I barked once more for emphasis.

"*No*, Shimoni. *Resti qui,*" said Umberto. "No more trouble for you."

I couldn't believe my ears. Down the drain. All this time mastering a winning strategy and now, with a simple roll in the compost, months of work and worry ebbed like bathwater. I was tempted to take a bite out of the man right there and then. The low growl I uttered didn't help my case.

Umberto gave me a sharp look. "Don't you snarl at me, you swine."

I'll show you swine, I thought. Soon enough the man would be hip deep in the creatures. I eyed Squisita as she tried to burrow through a thick, soft pad by the fire. She was loathe to be still, but had no desire to go outside.

Umberto examined the snow. "*Va bene,*" he said. "I suppose if you're going to go you'd better do it now." He fixed a leash to my collar. "But I'm not going to have you running off to the compost again."

We pushed through the snow until Umberto guessed we were beyond the patio. I raised my leg to oblige the notion. Large flakes floated into my eyes and whiskers. It was impossible to see.

Perfect. I sniffed the air. Wet snow followed each breath into my nose. It masked all scent. I would have to rely on other means to find the far bank of the stream. Examining the yard, I was just able to see the glow of the winery light through the dense snowfall.

Direction. Good.

I gave a gentle pull to the leash, testing the man's grip. Umberto returned the tug.

"Abbastanza," he said. *"Andiamo."* Umberto did not wait for me to comply. He simply dragged me through the snow like a sled. The winery light disappeared into the falling snow.

Returned to the warmth of the kitchen, Umberto peeled off his coat, poured a glass of wine and headed into the salon. Christmas Eve everyone celebrated together with the pleasure of friends from around the valley. Baskets of *crostini,* plates of fine cheese and delicate biscuits were ferried from the *cucina* to the guests. Glasses were clinked and emptied and filled again. Umberto came and went from the kitchen with empty bottles one way; newly opened, the other. Soon the room beyond the hall buzzed with voices and laughter.

Squisita and I were barred from the salon. There were far too many friendly hands there for a dog whose figure was in question. Even though I benefited from a taste here and there at the foot of Santa Grazia, it did not compare to the spoils on hand at a holiday party. My Contessa knew the weaknesses of dogs and guests alike.

But I was not thinking about food. My attention lay behind the closed door. I turned the problem over in my mind. I couldn't allow this perfect chance at a long and happy life to slip away untested. There must be a way outside. I curled up beside Squisita in front of the fire and waited for an idea to come.

Soon Grazia was shuttling dinner courses to the dining room. A languid succession of exquisite aromas wafted across the *cucina.*

With each course, she paused to offer a small sample to me and Squisita. Grazia knew that even dogs celebrate the holidays. But Squisita took no interest in the food. I suspected she was sulking over her relegation to the kitchen, and was happy to eat her portion.

Dolce was the irony of a giant *Mont Blanc,* the pastry that had started the wheels in motion to the bizarre events of the past year. Crunchy meringue under a dome of whipped cream, swaddled in spaghetti-like strands of sweet chestnut paste and dressed up for the holiday by tiny rosettes of soft dark chocolate, it was as glorious as my plan. I never saw the Alp for which it was named, but I supposed it paradise if it smelled anything like the confection.

Following dessert, *grappa,* a bitter distillation of grape skins, was poured into delicate crystal glasses. Grazia rinsed a mountain of dishes. Umberto weaved a tray of glasses toward the salon.

The power of the grape, I thought. Perhaps, in his drunken fog, the man would open the door. When he returned to the kitchen for *biscotti,* I gave the outside door a scratch, and barked.

Umberto's voice snapped. *"No! Silenzio,* Shimoni!*"*

I tucked my tail.

Grazia and Umberto disappeared down the hall to join the others. A flurry of laughter and music rose up as the group sang in the other room. I sat beside the door, defeated, watching the big flakes turn to sleet, then rain. Hope flagged with the slumping banks of snow.

Cinghiale miseria. I'd been dealt a pig hand.

Just as I wondered how much worse it could get, as if by magic, the *terrazzo* door opened to reveal the winemaker. The short man was wrapped in a bulky coat, thick scarf tucked around his neck. A dark beret pulled down over his ears.

"Ciao, cani," he said. *"Auguri. Buon Natale."* The man's cheeks were flushed; his nose glowed in the firelight. He handed Squisita and me each a biscuit and granted us a jovial pat.

291

Better than nothing, I thought. The man was not the answer to my problems, but at least Christmas wouldn't be passed without any gifts at all.

The winemaker pulled another object from his pocket. He cradled it in his hand and kissed it so gently I was sure it must be something small and furry. Then he walked to the sink and placed it on the sill. I blinked the object to focus in the flickering light. The other half of Grazia's crystal heart.

The man returned to us, pulled a bottle from inside his coat and set it on the kitchen table. Topped with a bright bow, it was wrapped in broad label.

The new wine. His gift to the Count and Contessa.

A sharp breeze caught my nose. I sat up. The *terrazzo* door was carelessly ajar. Without a second thought, I raced outside.

Chapter Thirty-Five

T he winemaker shouted behind me, but I was already well away
from the *villa*. Snow had turned to rain and melted into wide
pools of murky water. The lawn was thick slush. Like *granita*. My
paws burned with cold. I trudged on, down the slope, in the
direction of the compost. A cover of mushy ice sealed its ripe scent
from the air. I dug through the heavy slop into the warmth of the
rot. I let all four feet sink into the decay. Steam escaped in long
plumes, lifting the pungent odor. Another bath would follow, but
never again at the hand of an evil man. I sat awhile on the top of the
warm mound, an island of relief in the cold. Soon the wild pigs
would come.

I listened to the rain fall. The woods across the stream rustled in
the wind.

But there were no leaves on a winter tree. I raised an ear.

Pigs.

The animals descended along the hillside. A crack of brush here,
a distant snort there, they moved toward the strong scent below.
When they broke through the brush across the stream the noise
ceased. With heavy clouds cosseting the moon, the black night hid
the sounder. Only their long breaths in and out, sniffing the air for
direction, gave them away.

At the approach of human footsteps from around the winery, I
was poised for the next phase of the operation. Umberto was well
under the influence of simple gifts and good wine. It was time to
put the plan to action.

I jumped from the compost and ran straight across Umberto's
path on my way to the creek bed. The man uttered a few obscenities
and followed, slipping twice before reaching the creek as well. A
short way down the stream I sniffed. No scent. We were both
downwind. I scanned the banks. Under the spell of the grape,

Umberto wavered and swayed, unsteady and blind in the all-consuming dark.

"Shimoni," Umberto called. *"Vieni, piacere."*

I listened to his voice. Cold and hard, like all the times the man had kicked me; as hollow as every lie he'd ever told. My hackles rose under the falling rain. I held my breath, pointed my snout toward the other side of the stream, and ran. I had crossed the Rubicon. There was no turning back.

Umberto followed, his face screwed up in the pouring rain. He crossed the stream and fumbled into the dark wood, passing just to one side of me. His hands groped at twisted remnants of failing vines blocking the way. A rustling came through the brush. Umberto panted, catching his breath, running toward the hidden sounds like a feral dog in pursuit of wild prey.

His voice was sharp. "Shimoni. Shimoni, *vieni qui.*"

Come, indeed. Come deeper into the wood, you scoundrel, you *ignobile.*

"Shimoni. Shimoni." Umberto added a piercing whistle to his plea.

A familiar noise came from the thicket, rumbling through the brush like a strong wind in bare branches. I stopped. The weeping night flooded with the bark and growl of a dozen wild dogs.

Umberto's speech wavered. "Shimoni, *adesso, per favore.*"

For the first time I sensed panic in the man's voice. It was something for which I was not prepared. My belly tightened. I hated fear in any voice. Dread and sorrow, I thought. Any dog not wild was wired to soothe those feelings. Even at the bidding of a wicked man. I struggled hard against the call to aid.

Umberto cursed again. *"Cretino."*

My belly softened. Cretin was correct, I thought. Umberto was no good and never would be. I turned an ear to the barking beyond. The pack of dogs was a surprise, but just as useful. They could do as much damage as the boar.

I shook my head to clear the thought of rescue once and for all. The silver tag gracing my collar jingled a double warning. Everything went silent. I froze. The sound was familiar to the pack. Such announcements originated from small dogs.

Position betrayed, I began to pant. Taking a step forward, I strained to hear the direction and distance of the dogs. Instead, there were footsteps. Deep growls rose with the approach. Umberto crashed through low branches, frantic to reach me first.

Stepping in the other direction, I craned my neck, widening my eyes to the hollow darkness. With another thud, the man tripped across a fallen limb in the rutted path. Plunging headlong into the brush and mire, the angry dogs were upon Umberto before he got to his knees: an angry mix of mud, melting snow and gnashing teeth. I turned toward the house, baying the slow mournful whine reserved for injury or desertion. My deed was done.

Snow clouds parted. A full moon flooded hazy light onto the shoulders of the creek. At the top of the bank stood Squisita, body wracked by a fervent, silent bark. If she could have been heard, every neighbor in the valley would have come. Umberto would have a chance.

Ironic. The man had silenced his only savior. Yet, I was overtaken by a sense of deep melancholy. Something about it was all wrong.

Umberto's plea in the distance encouraged my gloom. It blurred the black-and-white portrait of an evil man I so easily painted in my mind's eye. All that remained was a muddled, impressionistic grey. Memories bubbled up like water from a spring, from a time before infidelity took root in the family tree. Long ago simple pleasures came from the kinder hand of this man: a particularly ripe tomato or string squash; the close attention to a chronic itch with a vigorous scratch. Long ago, but memory still. I shivered. Grief began to well inside me. My chest was hollow, my breath short. I was no better than the man I judged. This was murder.

Umberto's voice echoed in the darkness. *"Aiut—aiutame."*

I heard the man kicking at the dogs, trying to fend them off as best he could.

The Count rounded the corner of the winery. He and Grazia rushed to the bench above the stream. I couldn't see her face in the darkness, but I knew the outline of her body, smooth and round against the glow of the winery. I didn't see the shotgun in her hands, but I heard it. The click of the hammer as she cocked the gun reached me clear across the creek. I shuddered at the frantic tone of her voice as she called to Umberto. Even though she'd finished with him long ago, her voice brimmed with panic. I could no longer deny my nature. With shoulders set and eyes closed, I ran to the man as the gun fired behind me.

Umberto lay in the slop of mud and melting snow, groaning. The feral dogs had backed away at the gunfire, but instinct pushed me into the thick of the pack. I dodged the largest dog, managing to lead him away from Umberto. Easily distracted, the rest of the dogs followed suit. They continued pursuit into the prickly brush, so close behind I felt their hot, stinky breath as I gasped to catch my own along the way. The pack would soon be on me. Only great skill and a good deal of luck would extract me from the chase.

I hoped for another shot to startle the dogs back into the wood. With the largest dog snapping at my tail, it was time to employ an evasive maneuver. I closed my eyes and abruptly stopped.

Propelled by blind speed, the entire group passed straight over the top of me. As I stood to shake the frigid mud from my dripping fur, the gun cracked across the flats. The dogs scattered. Except for the leader of the pack, who turned to face me, backing me into the creek.

"I know you," growled the dog. His flat snout and narrow eyes, one blue, one brown, were ghostly in an eerie light thrown off by the moon as it peeked through the clouds.

I focused on his muzzle. "That day last summer," I said. "You and your friends attacked my bitch. Right here in the stream."

"No," said the intruder. "That's not it—entirely. Everyone knows you. The dog who thinks he's so grand."

"I have papers, if that's what you mean," I said. "Something you wouldn't know about."

The wild dog sneered. "Really? What are you, anyway? Whatever it is, you don't look a thing like your pedigree."

"And you would know? When's the last time you saw anything purebred?"

The cur lowered his head. He opened his mouth to show a regiment of gleaming teeth. "I know plenty," he said. "Your father was a Chihuahua."

Insults. My legs shook. "You can do no better?"

The feral dog snickered. "Have you ever met him?"

I blinked. My chest tightened. I'd barely met my mother.

"I have," growled the dog. "*Un amico.* A friend of mine." The intruder paused, pulling a lip back to jeer. "And I knew your mother too—right here in the stream."

My heart sank with my paws into the sticky mud of the creek. I closed my eyes to focus on what remained of my mother's image. Attempt failed, my eyes opened to the ugly face of the wild dog in midair, fangs bared and whiskers twitching, as he made a final leap in my direction. Another crack. Then another. My ears popped as gunfire flashed in the night. Only a brief twinge at my back complained as the mongrel and I dropped together into the mud. Grazia once again proved her ability as an able shot. The hideous mutt lay dead.

I struggled to push my snout from beneath the bony mass of fur. The rest of the pack growled a retreat into the cover of the cold night. I was in shock. Not from the attack, nor the gun, nor the weight of the corpse on my small body. What I'd heard had stunned me.

I pushed out from under the carcass, shaking an initial layer of sludge from my back and turning to sniff the dead animal. Its wet body steamed in the frigid moonlight like the vapors from the compost. The odor made the hair on my neck stand straight up. I staggered toward Umberto.

The Count helped the injured man up and across the stream. Grazia stood guard, gun at her side, whimpering in the moonlight. I trotted beside them as we returned to the house, but they ignored me. Falling in a short distance behind, I tucked my tail and was silent. I had caused the misery this time. Only a wild creature tries to take the life of a man. I was ashamed.

Common, after all.

When I reached the *cucina,* I retired to my bed under the table. My limbs barely moved from the cold and exhaustion. My neck hurt just under one ear, and for the first time I noticed blood dripping from my shoulder. No doubt the wild dog had taken a piece of me. Grazia entered the kitchen to rinse a cloth intended for Umberto's wounds.

"I think the hospital is best," said the Count as he entered the kitchen.

Umberto followed, leaning against the wall of the hallway. *"Non dottore."*

"You need stitches," said the Contessa as she slipped between the two men.

"I'll take him," said Grazia. She tossed the cloth over her shoulder, walked to Umberto's jacket hanging on the peg and rifled through the pockets for the keys to the truck.

"I'll drive myself," Umberto snapped, starting for his jacket.

It was too late. Grazia pulled his keys, and the ring, from his pocket. Wide, disbelieving eyes stared at the gem. Then they all focused on Umberto.

Grazia held the ring between her fingers. "I think we all know this is not for me."

Umberto snorted, looking at the Contessa. "You said yourself you never wanted to see it again. It's as simple as that. Just doing you a favor."

Grazia's eyes were cold as she stared at Umberto. "The favor is for me." She handed Umberto the cloth and nodded as though she'd made a decision. "Clean yourself up."

Umberto headed for the bathroom in the hallway.

The Contessa pulled the ring from Grazia's fingers. "It all started with favors, didn't it?" She looked at the Count.

"It all started with me." The Count stepped to the Contessa's side and took her hand. "But I ended it months ago. I played a foolish game not telling you, but you hurt me, too. Now, I'm afraid I've lost your good opinion."

The Contessa took her time in pronouncement.

She put a hand to the Count's cheek. "But never my love. There has been more than one fool playing the game. Can we somehow go back?"

The Count took the ring from her hands. "Is this a thing you can choose to forget?"

The Contessa smiled. She pulled a package with bright paper from the kitchen table beside her and handed it to Il Conte. "This is what I choose to remember."

The Count ripped the paper open. He looked so surprised, I thought he might faint. He raised the photograph and held it to the light, his smile breaking into a chuckle. Reaching for the box Grazia had wrapped for him earlier, he handed it to the Contessa. "Merry Christmas."

The Contessa opened the gift. "*Lo stesso*! Exactly the same."

The twin photos finally met. Laughter filled the kitchen. It was the first time I'd heard them both laugh in a very long time and it made me feel warm all over.

The Count placed the photo on the table and looked at the Contessa. "We both lost our way somewhere and the magic, too. Being right became more important than being loved. How do we take ourselves so seriously?"

"We forget to laugh," said the Contessa.

"That's the magic." He shook his head, holding the ring before him. "This is what I choose to *forget*."

Grazia crossed the room to Il Conte and opened her palm. They stared at each other, their thoughts passing between them in silence.

The Count nodded, dropping the gem into her hand. Umberto walked back into the kitchen and Grazia walked straight to him. There was little expression on her face, as though she'd imagined the scene before. No surprise, no sorrow, her voice was laced with relief. "You may want this, but you'll not need it in hell. Go, so I can be rid of you."

The words hung in the air, then followed Umberto out the door.

The Count touched the frame of one of the photographs. "A memory I want to keep." He rustled through his vest pocket, placing something in the Contessa's palm. "And you—keep this. *Romanza non casuale.*"

"No token romance." The Contessa's face beamed. *"Prendi tre passi con mia."*

"More than just three," said the Count. He put his hand to the Contessa's cheek and leaned close to kiss her.

The Contessa smiled Grazia's way. "Memories *do* retrieve the strangest things."

Grazia began to cry, but there was no pain in it, only release. I wanted to run to her, comfort her, but my eyes were closed fast. I was numb and couldn't move.

The Contessa knelt by my side as though she'd just taken notice of me. Her voice sounded as hurt as if she'd just found a favorite piece of silk I'd chewed. "Shimoni." She wept.

Disappointed in the manner of a small dog, no doubt. I felt the gentle warmth of the Contessa's hand on my neck, but the pleasant face of reunion had soured. Through my gruesome plot, I had proven to be far less than noble.

Morning. I focused on Christmas Day. It always arrived with warm hearts. And, as all dogs knew, affection was the great healer of an injured soul. I relaxed into the safety of sleep, thinking of Raoul.

Chapter Thirty-Six

I awakened in the loft of the winery. I got to my feet and blinked twice to make sure I was not dreaming. Stretching, I yawned. There was neither ache nor pain to confirm the horror of the night before. But I remembered it all. Truth was the only thing that stung me now.

I had no memory of the journey that brought me to the loft. Never mind. It was all I had imagined. *Prosciutti* hung from under the protection of long, wide shelves. Dried *porcini* clung to cotton strands anchored by tidy bows beside the hams. Measured rows of moldy cheese stood atop the shelves shielded beneath long strips of linen. Dozens of black starlings, the ones I'd always yearned to chase, sat quietly on the beams above. I barked.

Taking flight, they swooped and whooshed around the rafters. A sudden rush of air lifted my ears. For a moment I felt as though I, too, were swooping with the birds as they dodged and weaved in dizzying patterns. My stomach fluttered just the way it did when my Contessa launched me into the air over the soft bed. Indeed, I never felt so peaceful and happy. Even after hearing the words of the feral dog. It didn't seem to matter anymore. I lifted a wiggled nose, trying to catch a whiff of the flock as they darted by.

No hint. The air was devoid of scent. I owed it to the chill of winter. Voices in the distance invited me to the loft door. It lay open to the garden view. The snow had melted and a vivid world stretched before me. A thousand hues of green and gold edged the dark brown vineyard soil. Leafless amber vines etched every spectral wire between posts of the vineyard rows. Red winter berries danced. A gentle breeze rippled over the orange clay pots on the lawn, bobbing their clumps of purple pansies. The stream sparkled the deep azure blue of a morning sky laced with bright, billowing clouds.

Santa Maria. Exquisite. My eyes watered as though I were too close to the heat of a fire. Tears melted down my nose and whiskers. I was warm all over and feather light. Just as I'd been the first time I'd seen Squisita and knew my life would never be the same. My gaze settled on people in the yard.

Grazia, the Count and Contessa stood under the outstretched arms of the barren chestnut tree below. The winemaker leaned on a shovel close by. Grazia held a bunch of tangled mistletoe and holly in one hand and a beautiful, big soup bone in the other. The bone must surely be a gift for me. After all, it was Christmas Day.

Absolution, I thought.

The Count held my Contessa's arm. She cradled a small bundle in a paisley shawl of marvelous color, bound by golden sash. She stepped back to reveal an excavation of decent size and proportion in front of her, under the great tree.

A perfect hole. I tried to remember when I might have dug it. The fissure was quite substantial, as large a hole as I ever accomplished. Empirically speaking, it was a triumph. Yet something wasn't right. It was too perfect. The sides were smooth, the bottom flat.

Squisita bounded from the *cucina* to the crowd surrounding the hollow. She looked fit and svelte, her coat lustrous in the sunshine, as though spring arrived and the weight of winter had been shed. Bursting between the winemaker and the Count, nose to the ground, she dug with admirable vigor. When the winemaker restrained her with a gentle pull of the collar, I barked.

I wanted to join her, to join them all. I wanted to quit the loft that I had so often yearned to explore; to dig and to run—to go home. I would sneak up behind Grazia, free the enormous bone from her grip and run to the flats to share it with Squisita. I barked and barked but no one turned. Not even Squisita with her fine ears always tuned just for me. I leaned a bit farther out of the upper door for a better view.

The Contessa laid her bundle gently into the hollow. She knelt by the gap and placed her hands over her eyes. Grazia placed the twist of mistletoe and holly, and the gorgeous porcelain bone, in the same careful way. Then the winemaker began to fill the hole with dirt.

Never before had the Contessa been so touched by my work. Though in my opinion, some of the more splendid cavities warranted exactly that emotion. And Grazia was never one to use them as a safe deposit for things of tremendous value, like a bone. Yet, the facts lay before me. I'd created an opus of such splendor that the two people I held most dear finally appreciated my effort. With a sudden rush of pride, I watched Grazia waddle to the *villa*. Squisita stayed behind, dancing about the yard with the vigor of a bitch who'd lost track of her brood.

"Va via," the winemaker shouted. He waved his arms twice to shoo the dog away, but she turned to dig more earth up around the hole as quickly as he filled it.

Sniffing the dirt as she worked, she punctuated her effort with a sharp cry from time to time. Finally, she gave up. As the man finished the repair, she sat down by the new landscaping and howled.

The moan of a deeply disturbed creature, I thought. Indeed, all were of dark mood and little humor as they went about their business.

Grazia emerged from the *villa* with a large basket. She ambled across the lawn and stopped. Squisita thrust her snout into the basket and pushed the contents around with her nose, emerging at last with a tiny black-and-white toy. She set it on the ground and repeated the task, until four small fluffy objects lay on the lawn.

New toys, and a partner ready to play. I tried with all my might to will myself to the ground, but somehow, I was frozen in place.

Then the toys began to travel. Each wiggled a short way through the grass until they were rounded up by Squisita.

Puppies. Memory took me back to the brambles by the autumn stream. A wave of warmth rose from my paws to my ears. My puppies.

The winemaker laid a soiled hand on Grazia's shoulder as she bent low to the mound. She placed my collar on the fresh earth. The happy breath of fatherhood caught in my throat. Now, I understood.

More than one dog had fallen to the gun last night.

Grazia pulled a white kerchief from her apron to wipe across her eyes and nose. With one finger, she drew an imaginary circle in the air around the grave. The winemaker pulled her to him and they embraced. The Count knelt beside my Contessa and placed his arms around her shoulders, brushing the hair from her temples with the back of his hand in a very affectionate way. I was deeply touched by the man's gesture. At the base of the woman's neck, a tiny golden light glimmered in the bright sun. I squinted my eyes to bring the object into focus. The shape of a small shell sharpened.

The necklace. I sat down at the edge of the loft door.

The Count's face was clear in the morning light. He wiped moisture from his cheek and stared off into the distance toward the flats along the stream. The look of a contented man, one who found his way home. I knew that feeling well. And Grazia was held by the one she loved. Her eyes danced even through her sadness, the same way Squisita's eyes sparkled when I licked her face and ears.

A look of great affection. My eyes pooled. The pups might never know their father, but they would all know love.

Il Conte pulled a single card from his pocket and pushed it into the loose dirt at one end of the grave. The red and black colors stood sharp and vibrant against the umber soil. The Jack of Hearts.

Noble, after all, I thought. A title earned not by outshining another, but in simply outshining oneself. A warm breeze tickled the fine hairs beneath my belly. Death was not so gruesome a keeper. Afloat in a sea of calm, I closed my eyes to rest.

Suddenly, I saw Raoul in a broad meadow of tall grass beneath a cerulean sky. When our eyes met, Raoul began to run away, daring me to chase. Clouds parted at the edge of the clearing, revealing vacant heavens beyond. Raoul bayed: *Change your mind, the rest will follow.*

The howl trailed into a song rising from the mouth of the Roman gypsy. But when I looked up, the face I saw was that of Grazia's great-aunt Speranza. For the first time I caught her scent. Warm bread, fresh *basilico* and first-press oil: the hope of finer things to come.

Heaven.

Finally, the woman smiled. "Kindness," she said. The word rang across the meadow, and in its echo returned the sound of a bell.

I raised an ear in homage to the ringing. Somewhere far beyond, a solitary bell of slightly minor note tolled from the tall tower of Siena. Welcoming Christmas Day, it beckoned me to follow. I lifted a front paw beyond the edge of the field, drifted into a whisper on the wind and disappeared.

.

Acknowledgments

M any have contributed to this book. First, Don McQuinn: author, mentor, and steadfast friend. Champions, as well, were friends and authors John Saul, Mike Sack, Terry Brooks, Dorothy Allison, Susan Wiggs and Kathleen Antrim. Garth Stein, Veronica Randall, Jonothon Mischkot, Adam Marsh and Leigh Layman also deserve credit for their much-appreciated wisdom.

My agent, Elizabeth Evans, at Jean V. Naggar Literary Agency, gave this book the finest tuned editing I could have asked for and never gave up in seeking a fine home for my work. Elizabeth, you are absolutely the best.

To the reader: Thank you for giving your time to *Jack of Hearts*.

My husband and daughters furnished support around the clock. Jerry, Erin and Sara, without your help this book would yet be in the works. I love you all beyond words.

My eternal gratitude goes to Shimoni. Kenyan born, he passed the majority of his days in *Roma* and knew it well. Epitome of an urban dog, life in the Italian countryside was something about which he only dreamed. Now, that's where he is; beside a broad tree outside a small garden, but forever in my heart. Ann, Francesco, Chiara and Julian: *Grazie* for allowing me to share this extraordinary wee creature.

Most of all, this book belongs to my mother, Ruth. She knew what it was to spend most of her waking hours at a keyboard. Though she enjoyed only a fraction of the notoriety from writing she deserved, she had every success in encouraging me to accomplish my dreams. Mother, whenever I understand my own children less, I love you more. You were truly *nobile.*

About the Author

R obin F. Gainey grew up in a household full of pencils, erasers, Underwood and Royal typewriters (one of each) and cases of liquid paper. Raised by her author-grandmother and an extended family of eleven women and two men, there was always something to write about. Throw in a secret side of the family recently revealed and we now have a multi-volume saga. It wasn't until mid-life that she began to air any of the "legacy-linens" in public, mostly embroidered and dyed to embellish the truth. "Write what you know" is mostly what she does. And what she doesn't know, she makes up. It's fiction, after all.

Not fiction: Robin partnered in the creation and opening of The Gainey Vineyard in Santa Barbara County, California. She presided over various culinary programs offered at the winery and, with Julia Child and others, helped found the Santa Barbara chapter of the American Institute of Wine and Food. She also oversaw the continued breeding and showing of champion Arabian Horses that was begun by the Gainey Family in 1939 in Arizona and Minnesota. Later, she returned to Seattle to find her heart in writing. She won a Rupert Hughes Award for Fiction for the short story upon which the novel *Jack of Hearts* is based. She has completed two literary novels and is working on a third. She divides her time between her two favorite cities: Seattle and Rome, Italy. When not writing she enjoys reading, cooking, horseback riding, skiing the mountains of Colorado and traveling the Inside Passage of Western Canada aboard a boat, with one husband, two daughters, two Jack Russells and a cat.

Please visit Robin's websites at www.robinfgainey.com.

73500362R00195

Made in the USA
San Bernardino, CA
06 April 2018